JOSH PERRY

BURDEN OF THE MONARCH

BLADE OF RAILS

BURDEN OF THE MONARCH
BLADE OF RAILS

JOSH PERRY

Cover Illustration by www.books-design.com
Published by JoshReadsBooks
2021

This book is the first in the **Burden of the Monarch** series

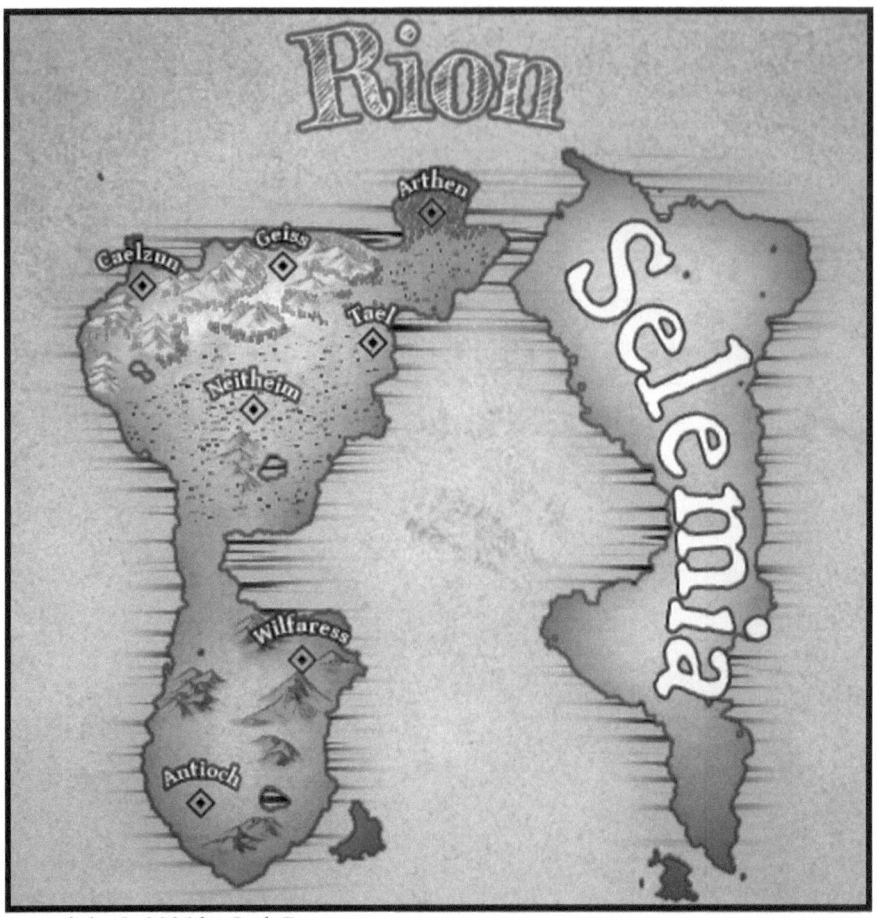

First Printing: *2018*
Second Printing: *2021*

ISBN: 978-1-7770324-2-5

JoshReadsBooks

www.https://joshreadsbooksdotcom.wordpress.com

TABLE OF CONTENTS

INTRODUCTION

A five hundred year war has concluded through the absolute end of a civilization. The Selemian people have been wiped from Rion without exclusion by the military forces of The Citizenry: the remaining society in power across the planet. This extinction, however, did not come without prompt. The primary conflict between the Selemian people and The Citizenry can be glimpsed in the following passage of a war journal drafted by Julius Leefve: a Selemian General.

'They have blacksmiths in their settlements. They toil in their shops. Pouring passion into labour. Yet they give them nothing as payment, no coin, no land. The blacksmith must then take from the farmer his harvest, because he has nothing to pay him with. He takes from the baker her bread for the same reason. He has but a blood splattered piece of gold in his possession which gives him the authority to rob. The entire country of them are but thieves, taking from one another endlessly. Never rising above and creating for themselves a paradise away from servitude.'

The Citizenry has long since the early times had a focus on community. In that, every member, so long as they are providing the community with something as a result of their lives; are entitled to the full benefits of the community in return. Every person born upon Rion which takes on a profession, academic pursuit or other deserving role within The Citizenry is given a gold token with royal red details. This token provides the citizen with proof that they are contributing to The Citizenry and may take for themselves what they wish in leau of payment with coin. These beliefs are beloved by The Citizenry and form much of their civil culture; discouraging gluttonous or selfish behaviour. Even the very monarch of the people pursues their position as their fair contribution.

The Selemian people detested them for this. They believed that such behaviour was the sign of weakness. As both civilizations grew throughout the ages eventually their borders touched and war erupted. Generations of fear followed as the Selemian people adopted atrocious tactics to demoralize their opponents. They encouraged random and public assaults on civilians. Those who would carry out these attacks would don masks reminiscent of elephant skulls moments before their slaughters began.

With generations of war came generations of innovation. The greatest of these innovations was the *Astaria Essence Engine*. A device that is capable of generating electrical energy utilizing a magically enchanted gemstone as its core. While magick is rare and indecipherable to most across Rion; ruins and abandoned places hold remnants and tools that can be salvaged so that their remaining magical energy may be transferred into precious stones. The Astaria Essence Engine allowed the invention of hovering vehicles, firearms and a plethora of simple electronic and industrial devices. It was with these tools and the dedication of incredibly skilled warriors that the war was ended and the militant Selemians were no more. Their settlements spread across the eastern continent of Rion now lay barren of any population and have been thoroughly destroyed; their remnants dismantled so that they may return to nature.

The war ended five weeks ago.

CHAPTER ONE

THE FURTHEST THING AWAY IS TIME

A steady chug of black pours out of the smoke stack of *The Tristram*; a three car length black, red and gold war-train which hovers half a metre above various yellow shades of prairie grass. The Tristram moves at twice the speed of a galloping horse parallel a river towards the small town of Gelghen. There is a single large armoured panel door on either side of each train car; each of them are closed shut with the exception of one on the right side of the back car. The middle car has a large steel cannon with a rifled barrel installed on top of it.

Sitting on the edge of the opened panel door is Bell. Bell is tall, well built, quiet and at a glance very solemn looking. His clothing consists of intricate black leather boots, metal greaves and a dull breastplate mostly concealed underneath a dark brown leather long-coat. Bell wears half a form fitting detail-less white mask over the lower portion of his face; unstyled short brown hair covers his head. At his side in an immaculate and translucent sheath is his blade Ehre; a thin and very sharp sabre. Bell stares out across the prairie landscape as its details skip and sprint into blurs.

"How close are we Howarth?" Bell speaks in a calm voice towards a speaker module installed alongside the inner train wall.

The speaker module crackles as it comes alive. "Not too far off now." Gunnery SGT Howarth replies. "I'm still not sure if this is an...appropriate response Bell. I mean the threat of what they've reported. Ten or twelve bandits? I'm imagining just the consideration of something like *The Tristram* coming to their door would break up their operation."

Bell blinks with impatience. "And maybe that is the reason their operation exists in the first place. They have been given the benefit of an under-reaction in every other instance." Bell swiftly jumps to his feet and steadies himself with his right hand against the edge of the panel opening; he leans slightly off the edge of the train.

The speaker module crackles a few times as it prepares to do something. "Alright. *I trust you*." Howarth notes simply; the crackling speaker punctuating his speech. "We'll be circling Gelghen. Signal when you want your pick up."

"Of course." Bell confirms before casually stepping off the train and landing without difficulty. The Tristram quickly trails away from Bell and soon becomes something in the distance. Bell begins walking towards Gelghen which is now only a hundred or so meters away. The town consists of maybe fifty wooden buildings built next to the small lake at the end of the river. There are five people standing in the centre of the town; all of which are armed with simple swords or axes. These people are staring out at The Tristram as it runs in circles around the border of the settlement.

"What is it doing?" One of the people asks out loud.

"Maybe it is just watching?" Another of them replies.

Bell emerges from the shadows of one of the town's buildings. "Actually." He speaks clearly; immediately catching the attention of all the individuals standing outside. "It is waiting for me."

One of the people points their sword at Bell. "An' who the hell are you?" She asks with what certainly isn't grace.

"I am someone who is tired." Bell responds and then quickly draws Ehre to slash behind him; deflecting an arrow fired at him from the roof of one of the buildings. As Bell turns his back the woman and the four others rush towards him. The archer draws another arrow and fires at Bell. Bell steps to the side and drops his posture slightly; allowing him to catch the arrow with his left hand before it pierces the dirt ground. Bell lunges forwards towards the charging woman and with the caught arrow in his hand quickly unleashes a flurry of stabs into her knees. As the woman falls forward Bell pushes the arrow through her neck and boot kicks her towards one of others; both fall. Another arrow flies towards Bell and is cut in half with Ehre. One of the bandits throws his axe at Bell as another closes the distance and attempts to slash at him. Bell moves towards the slashing bandit, grapples his arm, breaks it at the elbow and forces him in the way of the thrown axe. In a fluid motion Bell ducks under another arrow fired at him, pulls the axe out of the bandit's chest and then throws it at the archer. The axe sticks into the forehead of the archer and quickly causes him to flop backwards dead. Two bandits stand a short distance away from Bell wavering their weapons towards him with an amateur's threat; one has his face and body covered in blood and dirt.

"We'll just leave." The bloodied one says; his eyes pacing between Bell and his companion.

"You won't." Bell replies; walking towards them.

The bandits back away slowly. "We will." The other one replies. "This was all too much anyways. We got caught up. Just stopped thinking. Too many things happened, but that wasn't what-." Bell jolts forwards at incredible speed and pushes Ehre through the bandit's heart; Ehre's hilt bashes into the chest of the bandit and aggressively thrusts him towards the ground as Bell pulls back on the blade.

The other bandit stops, falls backwards and begins crying. He pulls a knife from his boot and shakily moves it towards his own neck. *"I'll...I'll just....do..do...do it myself. That's. "* He breaks down and starts panicking more.

Bell walks behind him and speaks in a calm voice. "It wouldn't be easier. Doing it yourself. You'd miss. Cut too shallow. Draw a curvy line." He easily takes the knife from the bandit's hand and tosses it into the dirt away from them. "The last thing you want is to be sitting there *maybe* bleeding to death, pissed off because you screwed *this* up too."

The bandit laughs in a macabre way and in that exact moment Bell presses the tip of Ehre swiftly into the back of the bandit's spine; killing him suddenly and painlessly. Bell looks away as an instant reaction to the corpses and peers out towards the rest of the town.

The voice of an older woman rages from inside of one of the buildings. "Why would you do such a thing!" She shouts at Bell from an open window on the second floor. She is a larger well muscled woman with short red hair. "That boy was surrendering. He wasn't your enemy any longer. You just *murdered* him."

Bell shakes his head. "All things have consequences. It is only our egos which trick us into living otherwise. I do not believe we should live in a world where that is a common consideration to forget."

"You do not get to decide what the world does or does not do!" The woman argues; becoming increasingly distressed by the corpses in the centre of her town. She disappears from her window in a huff.

Bell looks away from the woman's window and searches through his pockets; producing a small device which looks similar to a torch if it were made from bronze. He holds it up towards the sky and it shoots out a bright green orb of light that hovers above the town. The woman from the window rushes out of her front door and kneels next to the corpse of the female bandit.

"I know who this was. Her mother lived here. She had family that loved her." She laments through her growing tears and upset.

"We can either be fearless when we make decisions and make them for ourselves. Or do nothing and have them be made for us." Bell speaks while staring at the female's corpse. "Both are permanent. Both are real. We can only hope that in *some way*, this is what she truly wanted."

The woman scoffs in anger and spits violently. "*You think she would want this?!* To be slain like cannon fodder by some genocidal soldier?"

The Tristram appears at the entrance of the town and parks its self as close to the middle of the square as it can. Bell shrugs as he looks inwards towards the town. "If someone can be anywhere else, and this is still where they have decided to be." He shrugs again. "The logical answer is that they're just getting what they asked for."

A loud pneumatic hiss emanates from The Tristram as one of the doors positioned on its back car opens up. From within emerges a tall and densely muscled man in green canvas overalls, matching leather gloves and boots with a stout braided beard of blond hair. He carries across his hips various sizes of technical tools and gauges. He is Gunnery SGT Howarth. He stares at the corpses in the centre of the town and raises his eyebrow poignantly. "I count five."

"*Six*" Bell says under his breath; raised cheek bones tease a soft smirk underneath his mask.

Howarth looks around and pokes his head into an alley or two. "I thought the report said there were more."

"You want to take more of our children?" The woman screams at Howarth.

Howarth reacts with a confused expression and looks absurdly at the woman. "We get reports that your town's mines have been commandeered by bandits, your supply routes have been raided and that your central leadership has been imprisoned. So you decide your primary concern is going to be that you know the people who are doing bad things to you?" Howarth imposes his question with stringent intimidation. The woman attempts to reply but isn't given permission by Howarth's gravitas. "*Abandon your bullshit*. More often then not it is the people we love the dearest who are able to hurt us the most."

The woman looks up at Howarth, looks down at the corpses, looks at their weapons, closes her eyes for a moment then walks away. "That doesn't make it easier."

"It isn't supposed too. All it does is let you actually get to the place where things are." Howarth notes confidently before turning his attention to Bell.

"I imagine the rest are in the mines. Holed up. Finding homes in the shadows." Bell notes.

"Mhmm." Howarth agrees. "I'll let Mel set up once you give the all clear."

Bell nods. "I would wait. I trust our reports. *But...*"

"Something feels off?" Howarth questions.

Bell lets out a huff of air and looks around the town. "They have all these resources. An entire refinery available to them. Yet I can't see anything around here that looks like a fortification."

Howarth kicks one of the bandit's weapons laying about on the ground and examines it briefly. "Their weapons are shit too. This one here just looks like some bush knife you give kids when they go out to take a piss in the night. Not any sort of fighting weapon."

"Keep The Tristram locked up until I return." Bell instructs Howarth.

Howarth rolls his eyes. "Because I need your order to do my duty." He stares at The Tristram. "You know precisely how precious this vessel is to me."

Bell nods then walks towards the largest of the buildings in Gelghen. As he sheaths Ehre the blood and disrepair brought upon the blade by the skirmish is cleaned and repaired; made to look brand new again. He presses open the large wooden doors of the building and peers into a barely lit room. The floor is made of shale, the walls of cobblestone; these walls have various hooks with mining equipment and clothing hung up upon them. There is a large cargo elevator in the centre of the room. He enters the elevator and presses the descend button; one of only three options. The elevator shivers slightly and the sound of rattling heavy chain shoots down the entire column of nothingness which it is suspended above; it descends with a surprising smoothness which is only disrupted every other moment with turbulence.

The elevator lands awkwardly; a few of its chains collect in slack and smack onto the top of the cage. The mines are completely dark. Echoes and fabricated bits of noise can be heard from deeper within. Bell looks up indiscriminately at nothing, chuckles slightly to himself and then presses forwards into the darkness of the mine. He wields the small brass machine from before and places it into a front facing pocket on his jacket; as he does it provides a brief ten feet of green light in front of him.

Darkness has an inherent ability to make things terrifying and it does so in a constant cycle. At first something terrifying manifests before you, you have no idea what it is and you thus presume it is something awful. Then it becomes more and more rock-like as you become closer and closer. You relax, enjoy a breath and quickly lose it as another lump of darkness appears upon your path. While it looks very similar to the rock you just encountered, you find yourself asking; how many rocks can there really be?

Every step Bell takes shows him nothing. The mine is long, it has been worked for generations and its depths span the length of some memories. Wooden support beams placed every few meters hold the ceiling up about nine feet high. The tunnel trails on at a slight decline. Without segue a pitch black figure briefly appears in Bell's cone of light; they both stop moving instantly. Bell stares at the black figure and it does not move. Bell steps backwards and the figure disperses. Bell steps forwards again and it is no longer standing where it had been. Bell spins around swiftly and can see no figures anywhere around him. Ehre quickly finds its self in Bell's hand; held with an apprehensive grip. He continues walking slowly into the mine. The walls begin to widen and soon Bell is within a chamber illuminated by wide stone braziers. A deep mined pit carved with stairs of stone leads down to an impressive and sprawling ore refinery. Suspended above a vat of boiling metal is half the body of a man hung by his wrists on chains; his form severed from the hips down; the wound has been cauterized by the rising heat. Bell sprints down towards the suspended individual.

The individual's eyes open and he begins screaming incoherently; throttling about awfully on his chains. His screams cause the metal below him to boil with greater veracity; other pieces of refining equipment erupt to life and begin functioning. The suspended individual's eyes focus intensely and he stares at Bell with demented attention. "They wanted more and now they have more!" He shouts at Bell.

"What do you mean?" Bell questions; honestly not expecting a coherent answer.

"Oh ho ho! More and more! We're all here to be together. *To the ground with us all*!" The suspended individual cheers; now completely forgetful of his pain and suffering.

Bell slashes one of the chains suspending the individual with Ehre and breaks through the brittle material with ease. The suspended individual swings into the vat of metal and begins sinking into a puddle of himself. *"Oh joy! To be chosen."* He cheers as he descends into the molten metal. The refinery equipment stops, the braziers of flame blow out. The mine fills with smoke, darkness and whispers from a hundred different corners.

CHAPTER TWO

FEAR IS A DIMINISHING RETURN

The smoke surrounding Bell obscures even further his already challenged view of the mine around him. He can feel in his feet the vibrations of entities moving about in the area. Shadows walk through the smoke and into the small cone of light provided by the brass device. Bell slashes at the shadows but his blade tastes nothing but air; cutting through the wispy shadows as if they were not even there. The shadows collapse onto their knees and begin pounding their fists against the floor where Bell's own shadow is shortly cast. Bell feels no pain but his shadow appears bludgeoned and broken; it is dragged away by the shades. As his shadow leaves him Bell feels heavier.

Utilizing the most hopeful of steps Bell retraces his path to the tunnel which he had entered into the mine initially. Blocking the entirety of the tunnel exiting the mine is now a wall of corpses; flayed and sewn together with thick staples of iron. Bell cuts an exploratory slash open in the flesh wall and reveals behind it dense concentrations of rock and rubble. "There isn't really anywhere to go Bell." The many mouths of the many corpses upon the flesh wall speak in unison. Bell takes a few startled steps backwards and with lightning speed raises Ehre; pointing it towards each of the various faces upon the flesh wall. "Here is where you want to be. *With us*." They taunt.

Bell stares further at the flesh wall and decides to disregard it. As he turns around the stone braziers placed across the mine ignite with white flame. The flash of light dramatically illuminates the entire mine. Equally across from where Bell is standing at the mouth of a different tunnel is an atrocious looking humanoid. The humanoid is over ten feet tall with lanky extremities. Its body is entirely dark grey with three long gnarly toes and four long gnarly fingers. Its head is simply that of a fowl if it had been smacked centrally with a recently sharpened hatchet. The braziers flicker intensely for a few moments longer as the humanoid stares directly and obviously at Bell. It begins to move towards him in a slow four legged meandering motion as the braziers empty of flame and the mine is again pitch black. In the darkness Bell can hear the pace of the creature pick up. Bell quickly decides upon one of the many tunnels to run towards and bolts. He rushes as quickly as he can; tumbling a bit in his haste and using his hands to continue running and push him back up to his feet. The humanoid is close behind; its deep and *excited* breath growing louder as the chase goes on. Bell nearly matches the pace of a deer at full sprint and quickly finds himself taking turns which lead him deeper and deeper into the mine. The humanoid is persistent and without falter as it chases after Bell. The flight gains him no ground; Bell runs into a well lit cavern with hundreds of melting candles dripping down the walls. The humanoid enters the cavern and places its hands at length against either side of the tunnel; blocking the passage.

As Bell studies the walls he realizes that under the candle wax is flesh. The walls *beat* organically like a heart and the floor shakes slightly in tandem. "It will be good to have you come home." The humanoid teases with a high pitched and distressing voice.

"This is not my home." Bell affirms confidently.

The humanoid falls down onto its knees, balls its self up and suddenly morphs its form. Emerging from the ball of terrifying monster is a picture perfect image of Bell's wife; Temple. Temple has shoulder length blond hair tied into a tight bun. She wears a long dress adorned thoroughly in thin plates of steel with a massive white great-sword sheathed on her back. Her face is fair, mildly scarred with some sun damage and primarily highlighted by her delightful brown eyes. She shares her height of six foot one with Bell; though she is slightly more slender. "But this is." Temple flirts; motioning her hands down towards and across her body.

Less then a second passes after seeing this Bell launches forwards with his fist and attempts to strike Temple. Temple disperses in a wisp of shadow causing Bell to smash his fist into the wall of wax, flesh and stone; displacing each in a loud *SQUISH*. Bell pulls his hand from the wall and draws Ehre. "You have made a mistake, *monster*. Showing me my deceased wife."

Temple reappears at the other end of the cavern and makes a pained expression begging for attention. "Oh but Bell, *my love*. You don't truly mean that. *I'm right here*. You could lay everything down and just come to me. *We're all here, I promise.*"

A steady stream of tears begins pouring from Bell's right eye before his left; neither challenge his resolve or focus. "You were scary before. When I was caught up in what was before my eyes." Bell takes a few courageous steps forward. "But you have chosen an impersonation of my worst nightmare." Bell shakes his head. "Which just reminds me." He wipes the tears from his face with his sleeve. "That if my reality has already shown me the worst of my fears." An abrupt breath clears his throat and deepens his voice slightly. "Then you are nothing more then some *evil asshole in a dark room*."

"What a flatterer you are." Temple compliments. "There are more ways to join us." She melts into a few different ball sized aspects of shadow which crawl into the walls. From the walls emerge dark creatures with roughly humanoid shapes; their only features are human mouths across their arms, legs, face, stomach and neck. "You can become a small part of each of us!" The mouths all speak together.

Bell violently kicks the first of the creatures which approach him and he is pleased as its head rips from its body and bashes against one of the walls. The other creatures rush towards Bell and he begins slashing towards them. Using the tip of his blade in tight swipes to insure he can accurately hit the shorter quickly moving targets. As one of the creatures dies it melts into the ground and another emerges from the wax wall. Bell kills droves and their numbers do not dissipate. The creatures keep coming, doing their best to bite a chunk out of any piece of Bell they can get to.

Realizing that a straight forward melee is fruitless; Bell shifts strategy. He wields his blade in a defensive style that quickly strikes any approaching targets but does not advance or take offensive action. After defeating a wave of the creatures and buying himself a bit of time. Bell takes the bronze light creating device from his front jacket pocket and twists it in half; causing a loud cracking noise. With a snap-like action Bell pushes the device into the wax wall and begins running blindly into the dark tunnels to escape the cavern. The creatures chase him for a few moments but as Bell gains a bit of cover within one of the tunnels the bronze device erupts into a pillar of flame that rapidly spreads; igniting the closest wooden support beams.

The mines begin to collapse as the supports burn up and drag each other down. Bell rushes away from the devouring failure of rock and debris behind him. Natural flames re-ignite within the braziers across the mine. As Bell reaches the exit he sprints quickly through a *puddle* of what used to be the blocking wall of flesh and rubble. Upon reaching the elevator he leaps on top of it and begins climbing up the chains; throwing himself up a meter or more at a time. Bell rushes out of the mine and out of the building which houses access to it just in time for all of it to collapse into its self; creating a deep wide absence in the terrain where the building and mine used to be. Bell stands just a short distance from the collapsed terrain half panting with exhaustion and laughing out of nervous amusement.

One of the pressurized doors on the back car of The Tristram quickly opens and from within emerges Howarth and Mel. Mel is a middle aged woman trained as a medical alchemist. She has her red hair cut short and wears a padded white robe with three red stripes on either of her shoulders; indicating her status as a non-combatant. She is plump without appearing unhealthy and seems kind at a glance even from a distance.

"What in all of the hells just happened?" Howarth shouts out towards Bell.

"Ghoul breeding grounds." Bell replies bluntly. "Looks like they used the bodies of the bandits and their captives to do it." He shrugs. "Who knows how long one of them was waiting down there for company."

Mel's face drops slightly into disappointment. "So there are no survivors?"

Bell walks towards The Tristram and pulls himself up towards the train; lingering in the doorway "Just me."

"Mhmmpfhh." Mel protests. She addresses Bell very seriously. "You couldn't do anything?"

Bell shakes his head no. "Breeding ghouls are like house fires. Anything that isn't saved within the first few moments just gets lost." He continues into the train-car.

Mel nods. "Thank you for trying. I'm sure I'll find something to do to help the people who remain here."

"At least the ghouls are dealt with." Howarth seems pleased to state. They follow Bell back inside.

Bell takes off Ehre's sheath and then sits down on a couch surrounding a square four person table. The last train car on The Tristram is primarily an operations room. Whatever supplies someone could need in the field or for battle are stored here alongside ammunition for the train's primary cannon. The walls are a thick metal that has been painted a pleasant soft green. "I'm glad we have been able to help here, and that the monsters are dead. But a collection of monster corpses doesn't give anyone a utopia. The people that live here cannot rebuild their livelihoods on the foundation of a ruined mine and a lack of mortal threats. No matter the infrastructure we could mend."

"I'll be able to help. Our aid *can* change lives." Mel asserts.

Howarth smiles positively towards his wife; unwavering in his support.

"Our aid helps for a few days Mel. We both know the only *real* way we can take care of these people is if they move nearer Neitheim. But there is a non-existent chance of that happening considering how *townies* feel about moving." Bell responds factually.

"By helping now we make it easier for them to help themselves later." Mel begins to argue.

"And I've never said it doesn't." Bell admits as he closes his eyes to relax; leaning his head back slightly. "Just we know how they're going to react. They'd rather die out traditionally trying to build log cabins in a deforested field then live a decent life any other way."

"Yes *yes*." Howarth quips. "We could gift the townies paradise and they'd instead demand their routine and a bad cup of regular coffee. We've heard the jokes."

Bell removes the form fitting mask from his face and stretches a few of his facial muscles. The mask has a series of extending and retracting panels on either side of its width which adjust to fit upon Bell's face perfectly; these panels tuck into themselves neatly when the mask is removed. "I just wish blades solved more problems."

Mel tuts. "Trying to solve all our problems with blades is the very reason we can't seem to stop running out of them." She begins unpacking tables, trunks of preserved food and carpentry manuals.

"And trying to solve problems with words that are better solved with blades always ends up putting more weapons in more hands." Bell responds with friendly argumentation; smirking at Mel in their debate.

Howarth rolls his eyes. "So you're sure it is safe for us to deploy here for a bit?"

Bell nods confidently. "I burned them out with fire. Collapsed the mine from pretty deep within. I'd probably go so far as to fill the whole thing up with concrete and tar and call the spot permanently abandoned. But we should be safe."

Howarth lets out a sigh of relief. "*Good.*"

"Agreed." Mel giggles. "The girls are bored beyond belief. I know this because they've told me ten billion times."

"They have radio don't they?" Bell jests.

"Of course they have radio, toys, books and board games." Mel informs Bell with sincere dignity. "They are thirteen and sixteen year old girls on a war-train that travels Rion seeking out crime and evil. What do you think is more exciting to them?"

Bell smirks and rolls his shoulders in understanding. "There is only ever so much to see on the wrong side of a window. *I get it.*"

The speaker module in the train wall crackles as Howarth picks up its receiver. He presses a five digit password into a small series of buttons under the speaker and it connects into the main speaker line. "Greetings to all passengers of The Tristram. The lock-down is now ending and all exits will be available. That is all." Howarth speaks into the receiver then hangs it up promptly. "I'll help you set up your stuff Mel." He offers. Mel nods in thanks. Bell drifts off into an unintentional nap.

⌐⏜⌐

Ehre is removed the slightest bit from its sheath and Bell jolts awake instantly. He stands up and grabs Ehre then secures it into its sheath. A young girl screams at the commotion and falls backwards onto the ground. She has red hair, a tiny frame and very determined eyes. She's

22

wearing a light blue denim dress which trails down to her knees; it has sewn patterns of flowers and vines detailed across it. "Sorry!" She screams loudly and awkwardly at Bell.

Bell stares at the girl for a moment, takes a second to let himself wake up and then half smiles at her. He ruffles his hair and sits back down. "Me too." He looks around the room. "Why are you in here alone Ylinia?"

She shrugs. "Mom is busy working with the people of the town. Dad is with Alim working on the train."

"What about Courtney?" Bell questions. "She's not that much older, and I know Lance's daughter is...focused. But you two seem like you get along."

"Court is great." Ylinia affirms with a smile then pushes her lips into a small pout. "She's getting busier and busier too." She waves her head side to side then smiles. "But I admire her. She says some day she is going to pilot a submerging machine that mines metal from deep in the ocean."

Bell nods. He pats the spot on the couch next to him kindly. "And what is it you think you will do?"

Ylinia sits on the sofa and shrugs. "I dunno. There are lots of things *to do*."

"Too many sometimes." Bell admits.

Ylinia smiles. "What do you do?"

"Me?" Bell laughs. "I hit things with a sword and try not to trip over my words."

"Mom said you were a soldier." Ylinia remarks as if she is displeased with his answer.

Bell becomes solemn. "I was...am..." He pauses and huffs. "*Yes.*"

"And you fought in *the war?*" She questions with a bit of excitement. Bell nods in response. "Was it as bad as they say it was?" She asks naively.

Bell smirks and swallows down a bit of offence. "I do not believe there has ever been a point in time where war is not worse then they say it is. The things done by both sides were horrendous."

"Were you there until the end?" She inquires.

"I was." He answers.

Ylinia stares at Bell for a moment before abruptly asking another question. "Do you think the Selemian people deserved to be made extinct?"

There is a brief silence brought on simply by asking the question. "No I do not." Bell responds simply. "But what is and what should be are not always the same things. They did not deserve to be wiped from this planet." Bell sighs slightly. "They did not, *however*, provide an invitation for things to be any other way."

Ylinia angles her eyebrows with confusion. "I can't say I entirely understand what you mean."

Bell nods. "Have you ever had vermin in your home? Or in a cabin room?"

Ylinia nods back. "I have."

"And if you encounter vermin. What is it you are to do?" He asks as if leading up to something.

"Ensure a trap master is notified so that the vermin may be quickly addressed." Ylinia answers in a way that suggests the information has been drilled into her.

"Mhmm". Bell vocalizes. "Do you believe the trap master, his tools or his poisons would be necessary. If we could simply ask the vermin to leave or find its dinner elsewhere?"

Ylinia sits on this consideration for a moment before softly saying "*Ah.*"

Mel walks into the train car briefly and spots her daughter talking to Bell. "You better not be telling her war stories!" She light heartily threatens. Mel places down a box full of forms and papers and starts to sort through the storage cabinets.

"All war stories sound the same. *Clink, scream and repeat until you can't.* There you go kiddo, you've heard em all." Bell explains with a smile then leans forwards a bit on his knees. "It is before and after a war where there are the *real* stories. But we tell those all the time."

Mel rolls her eyes. "No violent stories! No good can come of her hearing about severed heads and dying men."

"Unless I happen upon them." Ylinia interjects then stares at her mother. "I thought we talked about this mom. There are no censors in my books, there should be no censors in my ears. I want to live in the real world."

Instead of treading over an argument long since laid to rest; Mel recites its highlights in her head and brings herself to a calm. "Sorry love. You know I just worry." She drags out a long wooden box from the storage cabinet and lays it on the ground; removing a few farming tools from within before putting it back into storage.

Ylinia smiles at her mother. "I know. Thank you. I love you."

"Love you too." Mel replies then leaves the train with the tools tucked under her arm.

Bell stands up and attaches Ehre's sheath to his hip again. He cracks his back with a drawn out stretch and makes a mildly pained noise while doing so. "Are you hungry Ylinia?" He asks her casually.

Ylinia nods passionately. *"Generally."*

"Let us see what we can find in this little prairie town then. Mhmm? I'm sure there is something tasty to find here." Bell offers. Ylinia smiles with excitement and runs up ahead of him out of the train. Bell follows a few steps behind; placing his mask back on before the sun hits his face.

CHAPTER THREE

THE PLACES WE LIVE

The day is bright and notably windless. Set up outside of The Tristram are a series of tables and tents which are manned by Mel. Within each of the tents are four cots; most of them have someone laid upon them receiving or waiting for medical assistance. Mel is in the midst of stitching a wound for one of the townspeople as she spots Bell and Ylinia. "Where are you two going?" She questions without breaking focus on her suturing.

"Food." They answer in unison.

Mel laughs slightly to herself; much to the horror of her patient. "Bring me back something sweet if you find it then! This heat is bringing out my cravings." She jokes.

"We'll see what we can find Mom." Ylinia pleasantly responds. She has to take many steps to walk at the same pace that Bell does; however she follows with steadfast determination and a lack of complaints. They look around at a few of the stores in the town square. There is a small grocer: mainly stocked with cans and preserves, a furniture and utility store that seems to do mostly commission work as there aren't many items available on the floor, a postal office with a postal box that is two generations old out front, a closed flower shop and a few small residential homes that were likely owned by the abducted leaders of the town.

Bell sighs slightly. "It seems that we're at a slight lack for choices."

"Well we're not going to buy preserves when we have the exact same things back home. That is stupid." Ylinia declares while sneering at the grocer.

"I see your point." Bell chuckles. He stares out past the limits of the town and into the lengthy prairies surrounding it; it is almost comically void of anything other then grass or bush. His attention turns to the river which collects beside the town into a small lake. "Can you fish?"

Ylinia scowls slightly. "Well *yes*. You know there is just that really nice pond on the train which I frequent." She stares silently at Bell.

Bell smirks then shrugs his shoulders. "Me neither." He points at the utility store. "Want to learn?"

"Please!" Ylinia cheers and then takes off towards the utility store. She is inside the building before Bell has walked half way towards it.

As Bell enters the store he nods towards the shop-keeper who is whittling something delicately in his hands at the counter. The shop-keeper is an older man, bald and well toned for his age. He wears simple tan clothes under a beautiful green carpenter's apron signifying his membership in a guild. The shop-keeper nods back towards Bell then continues whittling. The store is simple with three rows in the middle divided by ceiling to floor shelves; all the details are wooden and traditionally designed to be timeless. Bell follows the store to the back and peers down the last of the aisles. Standing there is Ylinia with three different fishing poles in her hands.

"Which do you like the most? This one has a really cool stick thingy, and I like the handle on this one, though the string is a weird colour, and-." She goes on until Bell takes one of the poles from her hands and examines it.

"This one looks fine." Bell admits.

Ylinia raises her eyebrow then her voice. "That is the first one you looked at! How do you know it is good?"

Bell shrugs then looks at the other two fishing poles which Ylinia is holding. "Those look good too." He notes casually then moves the fishing pole in his hand around slightly while staring at it.

"But this one is already right here. So if it looks good too." He shrugs again. "I think it is the one I'll get."

Ylinia places both her fishing poles down on the ground and stares at them. She judges between the two. They are, in function, identical. One is a slightly lighter shade of wood then the other and is set up with a translucent green fishing line. It appears *to her* that they are entirely different entities with vastly different qualities. "I'll take this one." She takes the plainer rod with a darker shade of wood and delightfully hugs it; placing the other one back without even making eye contact.

"Alright." Bell accepts at face value. "What made the decision for you?"

"This one is honest." She states plainly.

"*Is it now*?" Bell inquires further.

Ylinia nods decidedly as they begin to walk towards the inventory counter. "A plain tool isn't trying to lie to you. If it says it does what it does and looks like it does what it does. It is honest, trust worthy. If something needs to be flashy for me to believe it will work? It is likely that something is lying to me or its self." She shakes her head. "And I will have none of that *shit*."

Bell breaks out laughing as they approach the inventory counter. "You're pretty *intense* there Ylinia." He laughs again. "Rock on though."

"Just the two rods?" The shop-keeper asks.

"Just these." Bell replies and quickly flashes his possession of a red and gold coin about the size of a compass.

The shop-keeper smiles and nods. "I hope you enjoy them. I made those two just this summer past; had a good time doing it too. I think they'll serve you quite well."

"I'm sure they will too. Thank you for your skills and dedication." Bell compliments politely then shakes the shop-keeper's hand.

"You're very welcome young man." The shop-keeper replies.

Bell smiles at Ylinia and they then leave. They start walking towards the lake. "It is about more then just fishing rods." Ylinia picks right back up.

"I'd imagine so." Bell replies. "What is it that you mean?"

"I take what I believe seriously." Ylinia states absolutely. "If I'm saying something, or doing something, and I don't have a reason for doing it. That is the stupidest thing ever. But *so many people* do just that! It is very very annoying. They don't take what they think or believe seriously. *I do*. So I have to act like it for it to be true." She explains quite capably. Bell smiles and looks towards the river, he attempts to open his mouth to say something but is cut off by Ylinia. "Don't say that I'm smart for my age. I hate that. You shouldn't expect me to be stupid."

Bell smiles with pride. "Tons of young people are stupid." He admits with a respectful tone.

"And that is their fault. Or their parents. Or...*somebodies*. But I'm a person. Don't presume another person is stupid for any reason other then them proving they are. *Okay?*" She requests with what actually seems like tapered frustration.

"Absolutely Ylinia." Bell looks her in the eyes as he speaks. "I will never treat your youth like a handicap. From here on forwards until forever." He promises with prominent intensity.

Ylinia smiles. "*Good.*" She confirms with an up-lifted perk of excitement. "Now let us *feeeeed*." She over extends her pronunciation with a deep tone in her voice. "I possess the sort of hunger which will mandate looser clothing after it is satisfied." She jokes with a giggle that sounds exactly like her mother's.

"I don't believe this will go that quickly." Bell notes as he takes the sheath off the fishing hook on the end of his line. "I've heard rumours that ninety five percent of fishing is sitting." The lake isn't far; and they follow along its edge up towards the river.

"Is the other five percent catching fish?" She asks.

They find a small spot in the shade of a few trees. Bell smirks. "*Hoping to catch a fish*. Is the technical answer." He flicks the fishing rod towards the river and the hook is caught by the current drawn directly down the centre. The line picks a spot a bit of a distance down from them.

"That looked pretty good." Ylinia notes hopefully. "I think?" She raises her eyebrow and stares at Bell apprehensively as she speaks. "*Right?*"

Bell shrugs whilst focusing on the translucent fishing line. "Fish are in water. The hook is in water." He tightens the creases in his forehead slightly while he considers the equation. "That should be it right?"

Ylinia smiles and laughs. "It should be. I wish we had a fishing grate though. It would be much easier."

"Have you read about fishing grates in your books?" Bell asks casually.

"No." Ylinia responds softly then casts her own line into the river; a bit of a distance up from Bell. "We had one under the river bridge in *Tael* where I was born. Maybe once a week we'd close it and all the fish would smack right into it, dead, ready to eat. We'd pull them up in a big net then start salting them for everyone to get their families portion."

Bell smiles. "Salt fish is a special sort of delicious isn't it?" He admits with a romantic inflection.

"It is." Ylinia agrees with disappointment.

"Do you miss home a lot?" Bell asks while his posture begins to relax.

Ylinia nods in short bursts a few times. "I didn't want to leave at first. I refused. Yelled." Her physical energy depresses as she reminds herself of the loss. "I understood *why* after my parents explained how much they feared losing me. How they didn't want me to be the victim of some random attack at home while they were giving aid to the war just to keep me safe." She huffs slightly. "Even when something makes sense, it still sucks sometimes." There is a brief silence; during which Ylinia stares at Bell almost unintentionally. "Do you miss your home?"

Bell shrugs while unintentionally scrunching his forehead up. "*I,* never found my home in a building. There were a few places that I liked living in growing up. But most never lasted long. Before the war ended, I don't believe home was as safe of a word. It was a fragile term."

"Home wasn't a building?" Ylinia questions.

"*Mhmm hmm.*" Bell vocalizes while swaying his head. "Home was...*a place*. It was my head against my wife's chest. Her hand on my back. A few hours of sleep ahead of us before we had to do anything." He smiles pleasantly. "That was home."

Ylinia's eyes water slightly. "*Was?*"

Bell nods. "My wife Temple died during the war."

Ylinia gasps. "*Oh no!* Was she caught in one of the random attacks?"

Bell smirks; honestly suppressing a bit of a laugh. "No, *no*. Temple was a soldier like me. *Better then me* if I'm being honest. We grew up as *witnesses* to a generation at war poised to exclusively be preceded by generations at war. I think from the first moment she ever saw the aftermath of one of the attacks. She was determined to be a part of whatever it was that could stop the fighting." He explains with a smile.

"So what happened to her?" Ylinia inquires as respectfully as her curiosity allows her to be.

Bell shrugs. "What happens to most soldiers. *Other soldiers.*" He looks up into his head for a moment as he recalls certain details. "We had just had our defensive perimeter breached on the north-eastern front. The Selemian military had retreated from a whole leau of smaller battles giving us the impression we were on the verge of finishing them off. But the retreat let them stock soldiers and over run our defences. Temple had been installed as the commander of the north-eastern front." Bell takes a deep slow breath. "They brought over ten thousand soldiers to break our defences. They had thousands of swords and rifles levelled against us. Temple charged against them, with...*what*, near *a hundred people*? Despite reports from witnesses stating it sounded like the entire front would be shaken apart by the footsteps of our enemies." He lets out a heavy sigh with an odd expression of admiration. "When they were finally able to stop her, she brought their numbers down to nearly two thousand and bought us enough time for me and reinforcements to reach the front and push the remainders back."

Ylinia's eyes widen immensely. She attempts to do the calculations in her head but becomes frustrated by the arithmetic and stops. "*How is that even possible...*"

Bell smiles. "She had a unique sword. She made it herself from the shin bone of a mighty beast. It could cleave seven men in half with a single swing and she was *fast* with it. Faster then something that size should even be able to move."

"Wow." Ylinia replies with a starstruck glaze over her eyes. "Can you tell me how you fell in love with her?"

"*Uh.*" Bell mumbles as he attempts to contain the sudden deep beat in his chest. "I fell in love with Temple when we were very young. I, *uh*, remember we used to run out into the woods and collect herbs from the meadow. *Now*, my sister told us both that we should never do so, because of the monsters that lived throughout the woods. I can remember it clearly, the dumbfounded, *what type of nonsense did you just try to feed me* look Temple had on her face when we heard that." Bell smiles warmly. "She told her that monsters don't get a pass no matter what. They don't get to take just because they're scary, they don't get to kill just because they're strong." Bell places his hand over Ehre as he reminiscences. "The next day we started training with practice weapons her brother made for us in his spare time in his armoury. *Every morning, every afternoon, every evening.* It was a year before we ever went foraging in the woods again. When we returned from that first trip, alongside the herbs we collected, we brought back the pelt of a grimrar and our first few scars. But I mean, after falling in love with her that very first moment. I just, *kept doing it*. Every smile she had, every thing that excited her. When I saw her pushing herself to be strong or felt her supporting me. Even now, just telling you this, I haven't stopped falling for her."

Ylinia whimpers slightly. "That is very sweet." She wipes a tear from her eye then stares at the river. "She sounds pretty cool."

Bell smiles and nods firmly. "The coolest. She would of liked you. She'd be happy that you have questions to ask about the past. As opposed to living blissfully like today is the first to occur."

A stomach gurgles loudly. "I think we're fishing wrong." Ylinia critics with a pained inflection.

"Alright." Bell becomes decidedly more serious. "Reel in your line. I'm going to try something."

Ylinia raises her eyebrow then cautiously reels in her line. "*Alright?*"

As the fishing lines are pulled from the water Bell focuses on the river. It is wide, strong and mostly clear. The depth is maybe seven meters or more in some spots. Bell retrieves five daggers from within his jacket and starts tying fishing line to the ends of each of them; making sure to leave a large amount of slack before tying the ends of the lines to his belt. Bell stretches his back slightly, relaxes his chest and then swiftly throws each of the five daggers into the river. After the daggers pierce the river Bell wraps his hand up in the lines and jolts each of them back towards him. Upon four of the daggers are speared trout averaging a foot or more in length. Bell insures that the fish have been killed by the blades and then strings them up on some additional fishing line. "Food now exists."

"We have a fish processor in the kitchen?" Ylinia notes.

"Home cooking it is then." Bell agrees.

⌐Ⴑ

The Tristram consists of three thirty meter length cars. The last car is the operations room. The centre car is the most heavily fortified and features the living quarters as well as the kitchen; access to the rifled cannon is provided from within this car if one has the appropriate security clearance. The front car stores emergency weapons and ammunition but is primarily devoted to housing the engineering centre; which contains the astaria essence engine that powers the entire vessel. Inside the engineering centre are various mechanical devices, stores of replacement parts and the small cabin where the train is commanded.

Bell and Ylinia are in the kitchen. The kitchen is mostly white, well maintained and filled with storage. Each of the storage cabinets have circular handles on them which lock whenever closed; preventing things from flying about while the train is moving. A steel

35

box with a tube on the top and a tube on the side is on the counter; it is vibrating and humming quietly. Both Bell and Ylinia are staring at the machine diligently.

"How long is it supposed to take?" Ylinia asks impatiently.

Bell stares longer at the machine before answering. "I do not-" The machine dings and out of the side tube slides out two perfect fillets of trout. "*Know*." Bell finishes sarcastically. Ylinia cheers and drops a whole fish into the top tube. Bell takes the fillets of fish and tosses them into a frying pan with a few dollops of butter from a can.

A door down the hallway opens up and out comes Courtney. Her hair is long, brown and held in a tight bun. She is fit for her age and tall; making her appear as if she is a young adult. She is dressed in official civilian clothing which is perfectly tailored to her shoulders. Her pants are a dark green, her collared shirt a dark tan. Her boots are made of a strong leather that is sewn together with thick cord. She wears clear round glasses with thin lens; designed to reduce the amount of stress focusing causes her.

"Whatever you guys are cooking smells delicious." Courtney remarks as she enters the room and smiles at both Bell and Ylinia.

"You're more then welcome to have some." Ylinia offers.

Bell nods as he manages the cooking fish. "We'll have some for everyone luckily enough."

Courtney takes a seat at the kitchen table and watches as Ylinia takes a few fillets of fish and lays them out on a plate for Bell. "I heard that you encountered ghouls in the mine Bell?"

"I did." Bell affirms.

"How could you tell?" Courtney inquires.

The frying fish sizzles loudly and fills the room with a wonderfully warm smell. "Ghouls are fed by fear. I mean they eat us up to give birth to more ghouls, but it doesn't sustain them. They just need matter to make matter. Fear fills their stomachs, makes their hearts happy. When ghouls establish somewhere as their breeding grounds they get a certain degree of control over that area." Bell waves his hand in the air a bit. "*You know*, something like making the lights go on and off. When there are enough ghouls in the area they can appear as awful monsters and chase you, or take the form of loved ones that attempt to talk you into sacrificing yourself." Bell chuckles a bit. "Honestly ghouls are kinda just *tactless assholes*. It is their biggest indicator. They get a quick glimpse into your fears and they just try to hit the biggest sore spot as brutally as they can."

Courtney laughs. "Well I'm glad you dealt with them. Though it does make me curious why they were here in the first place."

"I can't say for sure honestly. They had set up their *shrine* pretty deep down in the mine. It's possible that a ghoul existed there long before the mine did and the bandits simply had the unfortunate luck of finding it." Bell guesses then shrugs. He flips the fish in his pan to check both sides for done-ness then places them onto a warming plate with a glass lid. The other fillets of fish are added to the pan alongside more canned butter."

"Monsters like being monsters right?" Ylinia considers the notion.

"I *imagine* so." Bell replies casually.

"Then maybe they follow people that act like monsters. If the bandits took over that mine. Hurt and stole from people. Maybe that's like, a mating call for ghouls." Ylinia develops her query.

Courtney chuckles. "I believe it." She yawns widely; holding her jaw at its most open for a few moments longer then most would whilst making a loud deep noise. "Do we know when we're going to be moving out again? I'm hoping we'll do a stop off at Neitheim soon enough. It's been almost a few months since I've been able to collect the latest issues of *Submerging Advances* or any of the other academic journals. I don't want to be behind." She notes with honest concern.

"We should be soon enough. Maybe after this if enough of the townies decide to come to the city, we'll get to swing by." Bell shrugs. "Though it is far beyond me to command Howarth to take this train anywhere he doesn't want it to go."

Courtney raises her eyebrow. "You think so? Me and Ylinia often joke that you're the only person other then Mel who can get him to do anything he doesn't want to do."

The oven clicks as it continues to heat the stove top burners. Bell turns the stove off and places the last few bits of cooked fish onto the warming plate. "Me and Howarth just know how to communicate. He'd never ask something of me he knows I am unable to do or entirely unwilling to do and I pay him the same respect. It is the least I can do to repay him letting me join this vessel."

Ylinia brings a smaller plate up to the fish and takes one of the largest fillets for herself. To fill in the rest of the plate is rice and canned roasted potato. She starts eating by herself without wasting any time. Courtney opens up the side door of the train car and shouts out towards Mel. "There is dinner if you want some. Tell the dads too please."

"Alright Court. Thanks for letting me know." Mel shouts back.

Courtney; satisfied with her job as a notary makes herself a plate of food. She takes a large serving of the rice and slathers it and the potatoes in a salty red sauce. She sits next to Ylinia at the table; pressing her forehead against her shoulder as a subtle greeting. Ylinia scratches Courtney's head in return and the both of them smile sweetly. Bell makes up his own plate and sits across from Ylinia and Courtney. Not much time passes before Mel comes into the train alongside Alim, Alim's husband Lance and Howarth. Alim is a tall and rather slim man with a sophisticated face, dull green eyes and black hair; he dresses much like a professor would in heavy red satin with black and brown stitching across it paired with thick circular glasses. Lance is average height with blond hair down to his shoulders and incredibly attractive. He is wearing what is in function a less flow-y purple and green gown. Each make a plate of food and sit around the table.

"Thank you for getting this food guys." Alim states towards Bell and Ylinia. "It makes the difference to have a bit of fresh protein in the diet."

Bell nods in response. Ylinia smiles widely. "Of course! We had fun doing it. Bell threw knives at the fish."

"Like...for fun?" Mel questions with concern.

"Not like that." Ylinia insures with embarrassment. "To catch them. We were having no luck with our rods. So he tied some string on his knives and just caught them out of the river."

"Well it is delicious." Howarth declares loudly before anyone can raise a fuss about shanked fish. "And the timing is pretty good too. We're just finishing up the maintenance on most of the systems now. We should be set to go in a few hours if need be."

Mel sighs. "I don't know how much longer I'll need. The bandits had been siphoning so many of the resources from this town. Some of these people are in pretty bad shape. I've isolated a few that I don't even think I could clear for travel to Neitheim if they wanted it."

"These people seem strong. But it is hard not to be scared when your health and safety are not consistently positive things. They may consider a voyage to the Great City if they feel as if it is a choice they want to be making. Instead of it being one that is pressured upon them." Alim attempts to advise.

"They're stronger then most I think. But they heal and hurt like anyone. They've been telling me that since so many of their youth have gone to Neitheim to seek *grander* lives; the mines which initially allowed Gelghen to even be founded have gone without work for nearly ten years. This place is being exsanguinated by Neitheim's growth." Mel remarks with mild upset.

Lance awkwardly drops his fork onto his plate and causes a small clink in his rush to speak. "Don't forget that they don't know why it is Neitheim has to grow. They have monsters here, they watch the fields for them. But they have never had bombs in their bakeries. They never lived with the fear that the crowd of strangers ahead of them will pull out elephant skull masks and start hacking everyone around them to pieces with machetes. They just got to hear about it happening on the radio."

"It doesn't explain to them why we make our homes in towers of steel. Or why our walls have defences pointed at both sides. We see access to consistent food, water and resources. We see a grid of safety. The city gives you everything only at the cost of the reminder that you are living there." Alim attempts to explain. "To some. That is as much of a dead end as a bear trap or life in an empty field."

"They're just scared of what they don't know." Howarth adds. "To come to Neitheim, to be a part of something that has been moving so fast for so long. It isn't easy to just sprint up to that pace of life. We're used to it. But the daily reminders of threats." He shakes his head a bit. "*Hell,* during the war you couldn't go a day without hearing or seeing some memorial. It was impossible not to read the reports in the city. *Here*. You know there are monsters living in the outskirts, you know what they look like. *There*, you had to check to make sure they weren't creeping behind you. Because *you knew* they liked watching."

Lance places his hand over Alim's. "It is such a grace that the war is over then, is it not *Howarth*? The only monsters left are the beasts."

"They should of been the only ones." Howarth denotes.

"Now they are." Bell reminds him solemnly. "We have the incredulous attention to detail of Izelle Bei to thank for that."

"Do you really trust her? Her claims are so...*absolute*. It could almost seem like overconfidence." Howarth considers.

"*Trust me*." Bell assures. "She crafts strategy like reality is simply a plot and she is a masterwork playwright. There is nothing left up to chance. No presumption trusted. She's the type of person who could tell you the status of every pen she has ever authored a letter with. She is the type of person who made one mistake, many many years ago and formed her entire personality around making sure something like that would never happen again."

"You knew Izelle?" Courtney asks curiously.

"She facilitated his transfer to The Tristram." Howarth interjects.

Bell smiles and nods. "We worked together. She was the head of special operations. Myself, Temple, Dii and Saranias Nicholl were her limbs. She always said we were her tools to win the war." Bell looks up at the ceiling slightly then exhales. "We were, if nothing else, certainly the ones capable of ending it."

"She did succeed. I read the essays she wrote during her campaign. What she wrote in '*I'm Tired of Blood*' was phenomenally insightful. I only wish that the Selemians would of had a chance to read it. So maybe that they would be able to understand. To see themselves." Courtney explains with a defeated inflection.

"Why are you a tool Bell?" Ylinia asks him directly.

Bell considers the question for a moment. "How should I answer that question? Should I give the official reasons or the ones I believe?"

Ylinia's eyes widen. "*Both*." She states as if it should be obvious.

Bell chuckles. "*Officially*. I am professional, well versed in military tactics due to my time spent as a ranger. As well I am recognized as a blade-master in each of the Great Cities of Rion." He smiles again then rolls his eyes. "Though I have always believed it is because Izelle was present when Temple was captured."

"*Oh*! I've heard this story. *Bell*, are you sure Ylinia is old enough to hear this? I just mean...erm." Mel sputters with concern.

Bell smiles at Mel and then at her daughter. "She's a wise woman Mel. She'll be able to decide what she takes from this story."

"She's tougher to shake then the both of us." Howarth agrees.

"So? What was this thing Izelle saw that made her believe in you?" Ylinia continues to question.

"Temple had been captured by a mobile armour unit; some fifty soldiers with cannons. They had set up an ambush at an inn and poisoned her, she was then locked in a cage, covered in some sack, her hair cut forcibly, bruises made across her face." Bell becomes very serious as he considers the memory. "I didn't even remember to draw my sword as I ran up to them all. Izelle tells me I just grabbed the first stone that was under my feet and used that to bludgeon the brains of every single *prick* that caged up my wife. Rifles could not hit me. Blades were not able to strike me down."

"So she was impressed you killed a bunch of dudes with a rock?" Ylinia asks; slightly disappointed.

Bell shakes his head. "*No*." He smiles. "She was impressed because she saw how fiercely I would protect what was important to me. She saw no hesitation. Only *problem solving*. That has always been a passion of hers."

"I guess I see her point then." Ylinia concurs.

The table goes silent. Everyone finishes up their meals. They smile at each other through the silence; convincing one another that it is alright to just eat and not maintain a seamlessly engaging dialogue.

Courtney takes all the plates from the table and places them in the sink.

Alim opens a bottle of wine and pours out half full glasses for everyone.

Lance kisses Alim dearly and holds onto his arm as they all move from the kitchen table to a living room and sit around on a few couches surrounding a low wooden coffee table. Courtney sits between Alim and Lance. Ylinia sits next to Mel and Howarth. The families settle into comfortable conversation and relaxation.

Bell leaves the train to sit outside, lean against a tree, close his eyes and try to see his family too.

CHAPTER FOUR

A HERD ON THE HORIZON

The morning light timidly fills the plains across Gelghen; making the surrounding area glow a solid gold. The soft blue sky is almost entirely cloudless. Outside of many of the homes across Gelghen are boxes of the townspeople's possessions and other such luggage.

Bell awakens under a tree curled up slightly in a ball. Over top of him is a thick quilted blanket; he is unaware how it came to his possession throughout the night. Bell folds the quilt and with sleepy eyes watches the various villagers pack and prepare as he saunters towards the middle car of The Tristram. The side door is locked and is opened with a complicated looking translucent blue key about the size of a paring knife. Sitting in the kitchen of the car is Alim and Lance. The strong aroma of freshly ground coffee permeates the entire train-car.

"Morning Bell." Alim greets with a polite wave.

Bell nods sleepily and begins preparing his cup of coffee. "Mhmm". He barely manages to reply.

Lance laughs slightly. "Not a fan of the morning are you Bell?"

Bell sips his cup of coffee and swallows the boiling hot liquid impatiently; demanding its effects despite the sloshing magma in his throat and stomach. "Mornings are fine." Bell remarks then sneers as he looks around the room. He lets out a deep breath of severe anxiety and his posture becomes cloistered. "I'm just...*getting used to being awake again*." He swirls his wrist around slightly. "It takes a bit."

Alim nods and takes a punctuating drink from his coffee. "Take your time then friend. It appears that today will be busy. Mel has been informed that many of the families here wish to move to Neitheim."

44

"Oh?" Bell responds with honest surprise. He blinks slowly then smirks. "I guess the world can change after all."

"Howarth confirmed with central earlier this morning. We're facilitating their transfer." Lance adds.

"When?" Bell asks then polishes off the last of his coffee; quickly preparing a second cup afterwards.

"Early afternoon. Mel is putting together a caravan with them right now." Lance answers. "Though it's a shame they've been out of the loop for so long here. If they had a proper hitch or trailer we could pull their caravan right behind us."

Alim chuckles. "Yes. But our understanding of normal has been morphed by the lives we live. We travel the country in an artificial metal snake. Neither me or you are military personnel and yet we have trained with rifles. We have been in homes illuminated by electric light and made warm through heated floors. We have more passive knowledge regarding the factual nature of reality then they do from folklore or wives tales combined." He nods fastidiously as if agreeing with something. "All considered. If they had a compatible hitch just laying around. I might be more likely to worry then cheer."

"What would possibly worry you about that?" Lance questions.

"Imagine you were to be exploring a cave, mhmm? And you come across within it an entire town of mountain people." Alim goes on.

"Don't tell me you believe in mountain people Alim?" Bell pokes fun.

Alim shrugs his shoulders as formally as possible. "I will not state yay or nay on the actuality of anything until I can personally affirm it. These mountain people are hypothetical, if it makes you feel any better." Alim smirks then continues. "So as you come across these mountain people. Their settlement is poor, badly planned and dimly lit. Yet you notice as you stare longer and longer that each of the mountain people is wielding an astaria firearm; a weapon which can only be created through the masterful collaboration of an arcane academic and a grand-master watchmaker. Knowing this; what would you believe about their possession of such weapons? That they were divined into their hands? Birthed alongside them?" Alim shakes his head. "No, just as if the people of this town had a compatible hitch. You cannot find in your hands something which has not been created by yourself or taken from others."

"So you fear thieves?" Lance asks.

Alim shakes his head. "No more then the average man would." He pauses for a moment to consider how he should phrase what he wants to say. "I fear deceit. Those that hide away their lies forge them into weapons that hang on thin strings, teetering away on invisible timers before falling on some unsuspecting fool."

"Lies certainly can become that." Lance agrees.

Bell finishes another cup of coffee, instantly remakes it then begins cracking his various joints in a frequently rehearsed routine; an apparently rather pleasant one to proceed through. "Do you figure my help will be needed to prepare the caravan?"

"Honestly?" Lance pretends to offer. "I think everything is taken care of." He shrugs. "Hell *I* don't even have something to do."

"When we return to Neitheim you must replenish your stock of paints however. I would love for you to work on the walls in our cabin." Alim states proudly then sways his head side to side. "It's such a shame to have someone of your skill with us here and yet give you nothing to work *with*."

"You paint?" Bell asks Lance as kindly as he can.

Lance laughs then nods. "I guess you haven't been around long enough to have seen me do that yet eh?" He smirks then looks away with some sort of attempt at modesty. "I'm sure I've looked positively useless then." He laughs a bit to himself. "I actually went to Fellenfurth to study art. My guild rewarded me with a seal of mastery and during my term as an explorer my mastery was recognized by four of the nine Great Cities." He rolls his eyes slightly. "I'd of got them all, had there been more time before our home became this train."

Bell's eyes light up with admiration. "I believe it. To seek recognition from each of the Great Cities is a terribly challenging task. Just to be granted the recognition of one is substantial enough to establish a successful career. Four is very impressive."

Lance nods. "Thank you. I hope that in time I will be able to gain the audience of each of the Great City guild masters and prove my mastery to them."

"Good. *And then what?*" Bell asks as if by some verbal reflex.

"*Erm.*" Lance pauses for a moment.

Bell shakes his head. "*Sorry.*" He closes his eyes and takes a deep breath. "Temple used to reply to every definitive statement like that. She said if you don't know where you're going you're a special brand of dimwit for trying to get there anyways."

Lance deflates slightly, waves his arm towards Bell and sighs. "I understand." He smiles. "It doesn't bug me. But I don't know if I believe that there is always *somewhere to be*." He focuses his eyes for a moment. "Sometimes, what must be done takes you nowhere."

Howarth charges into the room with a solemn look on his face. He wears the annoyed expression in such a way that it is impossible to misinterpret. Howarth turns his attention to Bell. "*Bell*, if you wouldn't mind coming with me please." He asks, pauses, then finishes abruptly. "I require your consult on our preferred path to Neitheim."

"Of course." Bell agrees with a nod, chugs his cup of coffee, makes another then goes along with Howarth into the front car of the train.

—⊥—

The front car of the train is in a state somewhere between recently cleaned and in the midst of frantic use. The floor is a dark grey tile and the walls a darker shade of brown. Workbenches placed across the area are scattered with various mechanical bits and bobs. Schematics, notes and tool hooks are placed on every available bit of wall. There are re-enforced black metal doors separating the navigational controls of The Tristram and its power core from the main floor of the first car. A small window views into the power core where a large astaria essence engine is installed; a nearly invisible purple energy vibrates outwards from the circular gold contraption; watching the device function brings on a mild sense of calm and sleepiness.

Howarth opens up the door leading into the navigational room and motions with his hand for Bell to enter with him. Inside are two small chairs facing a wide window and a slanted desk which has installed upon it a plethora of devices displaying basic geographical information, maintenance levels of the systems throughout The Tristram and all available steering controls. Howarth sits in one of the chairs and taps one of the digital screens within the slanted desk; the screen flickers a dull green before activating. The screen is only capable of producing low quality images and text; all rendered in a dull barely visible shade of green against a bright grey background. "I have been informed by Central Command that they have been detecting incredibly odd seismic activity in the area of the Kiminolp Mountains."

Bell raises his eyebrow. "Seismic activity? I'm pretty sure this vessel hovers above the ground. So I hope we'd be safe."

Howarth raises his head. "It is not tremors they said to be worried about." He sighs. "It's what's causing them."

Bell's eyes focus intensely and his heart starts to pound within his chest more aggressively. *"Were there bombs?"*

"No, no no." Howarth almost apologizes. "It isn't that type of thing." He grimaces slightly. "They don't know what is causing it. It's inconsistent. But whatever it is. *It is moving fast.*"

"Mhmm." Bell barely remarks. "I'll partake in the transport on the edge of an open train door then. Watching out for whatever I can. If it'll make you feel better."

Howarth smirks. "It does." He laughs slightly. "Though I admit. I find it amusing that I do."

Bell raises his eyebrow in response.

"You know, before you were transferred to this vessel we had a larger crew. During the war when we were running supplies and evacuating those made homeless by the destruction. We had two extra cars on this train. One that held many beds and living supplies. It was for the refugees. However the war has ended and an offer was made on that car by a travelling tour company." He huffs as if slightly upset by the outcome of things. "We traded it for a few months of preserves and ammunition in good faith." He pauses for just a moment to take an extra long breath. "The *other* car, *however*, carried military personnel. Twenty five soldiers had been assigned to us to assure our safety. We didn't go anywhere without them." He chuckles. "And now one guy, *you*, has replaced them all."

Bell nods. "I guess I have."

"So I gotta ask. What the hell? I mean, you could probably cut a hundred men in two easier then I could pick up a few boxes of parts from the floor." Howarth declares. "So how the hell is that possible?"

"Honestly?" Bell asks.

Howarth nods firmly. "Exclusively."

"*Life in the mountains toughens you up.*" Bell says while shrugging his shoulders. "I've trained my entire life alongside Temple. The two of us became as accomplished as we could with technical skill. We studied all there was to study." He pauses for a moment to consider how to say what he wants to say. "Our momentum has always seemed enhanced. We were capable of gaining strength far faster then any other whom we trained alongside. For all intents and purposes, it appeared for a long time that we lacked *the ceiling* which so commonly restrains others. Standing between us and our intentions was not the blockade of reality, but a trial of endurance and dedication."

"Has it always been that way?" Howarth asks while examining the seismic reports displayed on the dull green screen.

Bell nods. "We sensed it after our first battle. We searched in the forest for something to prove our skills against. A grimrar found us, tracked us for a few clicks before it decided to set its trap. It crawled down from the trees, each of its six furry legs spasm-ed with excitement as it pounced towards us." Bell laughs. "Do you know what I did?"

Howarth sways his head. "I'd hope you got out of the way in time."

Bell laughs again. "I punched it in the face."

Howarth laughs a bit. "You punched a pouncing grimrar in the face?"

"Instantly." Bell chuckles. "Didn't even realize I'd done it till the thing crashed into the ground." He wags his head slightly. "But who does that? Who sees a six legged spider puma and just punches it in the face?" Bell shrugs. "It was an indicator of something. And our success in that battle made me fairly confident that that *something* wasn't *entirely just a death wish*. It was..." He perches his lips together slightly. "The proof of my potential. *Our potential.* It was as if you were holding out your hand towards a biscuit on a distant table, attempting to will it into the air and towards you; *then suddenly it does exactly that.* Since that fight. I've been living in a world where I can make that biscuit float." He smiles mildly. "But as to why?" He shrugs. "It must simply be a benefit of birth."

Howarth smirks. "Then you're lucky this isn't an arithmetic examination where showing your work is just as important as getting the right answer."

Bell nods. "Were that the case; that more life events would be replaced by arithmetic exams. I'd of failed long before I encountered the grimrar." He attempts to examine the seismic charts which Howarth is scanning over but can only make sense of the most basic information; namely that *something* is happening *somewhere*. "Do you have a preference for our path to Neitheim? Does The Tristram have an ideal way to go?"

"More or less." Howarth notes. "The mountains are too dense, the forests might work, and the plains are quick." His eyes flicker into the back of his head for a moment. "We could take the primary roadways if we are willing to backtrack slightly."

Bell waves his hand to dismiss the idea. "You've been wise to avoid the primary roadways so far. They can be safe like anywhere but the urgency of their recovery pales in comparison to the repair of the Great Cities. The further you stray from Neitheim, the more common bandits are on the roadway, some of which use salvaged equipment from the war." Bell takes a few short series of breaths. "We could deal with them. Maybe even mitigate the risk. But with a caravan of civvies. Just one arrow, one bullet or one blade has to go the wrong direction and we've ruined the life of someone who simply wanted to find a better one." He shakes his head. "The plains give us the best overview. Whatever approaches us wouldn't be able to do it without us knowing."

"Alright." Howarth agrees. "We'll cross the plains until we reach the Kiminolp Mountains. From there, I hope that the Shaded Highway directly towards Neitheim will be safe?"

Bell nods with most of his confidence. "They've been expanding the perimeter of safety around the city week by week. Last I was there, some repairs on the Shaded Highway had began. There was definitely traffic on it. Army, merchants, relic acquistioners." Bell rolls his hand in the air. "Etcetera etcetera."

"Good. I'll update central on our route. We should be set to go shortly." Howarth explains kindly.

"I'll be ready when you are." Bell replies then stands to leave.

Howarth nods in response. "Before you go."

"Mhmm?" Bell murmurs.

"I have a request for you." Howarth asks. "Something that must be kept between the two of us."

Bell's eyes widen and he turns his head slightly to the side; he retakes his seat and forges simple but dedicated eye contact with Howarth. "Yes?"

"Ylinia." Howarth says with a smile. "She is my treasure in this world. My motivation, my perseverance. I have done everything to give her a better world to live in. But you know as well as I do that the world is not always responsive to a desired peace; it does not always obey."

"You want me to protect her?" Bell interrupts.

"Well of course. But I expect that of you for each of us." Howarth pauses for a second. "*However,* the best soldier in the world can only be effective if they are present and no person has ever fully realized their potential within the cage of constant surveillance. *No,* Bell. I want you to teach Ylinia how to protect herself."

Bell becomes solemn. "She is rather young."

"Many are." Howarth replies. "Youth, however, does not repel shrapnel, blades or evil doers."

"*Alright.*" Bell simply states. "I'll do what I can."

"Thank you Bell. I hope you know how much I appreciate *everything* you've done." Howarth adds the slightest touch of emotionality to his delivery.

"Of course Howarth." Bell smiles. "Help, is, *what I do.*"

The people of Gelghen have packed away their livelihoods into a large caravan with a steel frame and a dull red canvas cover. The caravan is pulled by a set of twelve horses; each of which seems uniquely strong and well bred. Young children and their care-takers sit inside the caravan while all others who are capable march alongside it. Ahead of the caravan is The Tristram which its self has fully packed up. Mel stands near the caravan speaking with the people of the town before they begin their voyage. Bell sits on the edge of the opened door of the back train car with Ylinia; both of whom appear notably impatient.

"She talks so much sometimes." Ylinia complains. "I don't get what there even is to talk about. *We're going here. You follow us. Don't not follow us. Continue to do the same thing until we are done doing it.* What else is there to convey?" She asks while glaring at her mother continuing her conversation with the townspeople.

Bell shrugs. "I think some people talk because it is the only time they hear a voice in their head. It's the only time both them and their thoughts are within each others company." He attempts to explain.

"You're skilled at putting things delicately." Ylinia notes. "Tis just as easy to say some folks are weird or stupid."

Bell chuckles. "Simple explanations aren't always the best. Sometimes there is just a fraction of stupid, a fraction of weird; not enough to wholly define something."

"You don't like it either." Ylinia notes. "How long all of this is taking."

"How do you know that?" Bell questions.

Ylinia points down at Bell's legs which have been casually bobbing up and down for the past couple of minutes. "You're practically oozing impatience."

"I'm adjusting to things moving along at a different pace. It has been a long time since *just* sitting and waiting was an option." Bell explains.

"Dad said that was the worst part of the army. The sitting and waiting." Ylinia notes.

Bell smirks. "For some, *yes*. I never got that luxury. If I was finished one place I was expected to already be half way towards the next. Izelle wasn't the sort to let us forget about the precise urgency of our operations."

"Did you enjoy it? Always having somewhere to go?" Ylinia questions.

"Erm." Bell flares his nostrils with uncertainty; jostling the portion of the mask which covers his nose. "It depended. If I was going somewhere with Temple. I would of been happy on a ten thousand kilometre long trail that leads nowhere. On my own, I just felt a rush to get back to her."

Ylinia stares at Bell knowingly. "It sounds like you fought the war for her."

Bell nods. "You wouldn't be wrong." He points out at Mel who has began walking back towards The Tristram; barren of any shame for the wasted time she chatted away. She walks over towards Bell and Ylinia sitting on the edge of the opened train car door.

"That isn't where you're going to be for the whole ride is it sweetie?" Mel questions her daughter with obvious concern.

Ylinia nods. "It is." She informs her with a smile. "The breeze is *wonderful*."

Mel stares sternly at Bell. Bell rolls his eyes sarcastically and smiles. "I know, *I know*. I'll watch out."

Mel lets out a diluted breath of relief. "*Alright*." She makes a half turn then looks out towards the plains. "It should be a boring commute." She attempts to convince herself. "Signal up front if you need anything, *alright?*"

Both Bell and Ylinia nod firmly in response.

The eyes of the villagers are glued to their town as they leave it behind in the caravan. They wave goodbye to the few who have elected to stay in the town; many of whom are older. The townies walk with a great weight in their steps. It takes just about half an hour for Gelghen to entirely dissipate into the background and be forgotten by the horizon.

The trail across the plains is hot; the sun beams down upon all with uninterrupted intensity. While the view of tall golden grass, small divots of pond and bright blue sky is beautiful; it quickly becomes monotonous as it repeats in a convincingly never ending cycle. Bell and Ylinia have retreated a bit within the train car to hide in the shade. They both are sitting on the ground with their backs against the wall.

"How much longer do you suppose it will be for us to get there?" Ylinia asks.

Bell shrugs. "I never count."

"Why not?" Ylinia asks with a confused inflection.

Bell shrugs. "Why would I want to know exactly how much time I lost waiting to get somewhere?"

"Mhmm." Ylinia ponders. "*I guess*? I think it is easier to know how patient you need to be if you know how long you're going to be waiting."

Bell laughs. "Is that patience or endurance?"

Ylinia rolls her eyes. "Whatever you want to call it."

"Patience can save your life Ylinia. It has saved mine." Bell advises.

"Patience has saved your life? I thought that was the job of Ehre." She retorts.

Bell sways his head side to side. "Ehre is a tool. A magnificent one, one I do very much owe the consistency of my breathing to. But regardless of my skill, or the quality of my blade. Patience is the key to victory in battle because the blow which ends your opponent only occurs in the perfect moment. It does not always seem that way, with blades slashing so quickly and shields blocking as they can. But the true blow which takes a life; the one which seals the deal. That strike takes place only in a precise moment, a moment which you must be willing to wait for if you indeed intend to take advantage of it."

"What does this moment look like?" Ylinia asks.

"It depends. Sometimes it is on the seventh swing of your opponent's blade when their fatigue finally causes them to alter their form. Sometimes it is as simple as waiting for your opponent to make a mistake and at others it is when they fall for your misdirection. Patience isn't what *makes* the moment, it is what lets you see that it is there."

"Alright." Ylinia acknowledges with a firm nod. "You say that as if it is something I'm going to use tomorrow."

Bell sways his head. "Not tomorrow." He admits in a soft voice. "But what if it was? Would you be able to hold a blade?"

Ylinia's eyes widen. "If it was tomorrow?" She stares out at the passing plains. "It would likely be my last tomorrow."

Bell stands up with sudden energy and offers his hand to Ylinia. "Then I think you are ready to learn a few things."

Ylinia takes his hand and stands alongside him. "I admit that I suck with a sword and you think that qualifies me to learn?"

"Yes." Bell states simply. "The worst blade users in the world are those who automatically believe they are better then any other. But if you admit to knowing nothing, then you won't get in your own way when it comes to learning *everything*."

Ylinia giggles with mild excitement. "So do you mean to say you're going to train me to use a blade?"

Bell nods. "I am going to teach you how to protect your life, and if need be, the lives of others. A blade is one of the ways to do so, yes." He walks over towards a locked wooden chest, opens it and from within produces two straight lengths of polished wood roughly the shape of short-swords. Bell places both of the wooden swords under his arm and turns to face Ylinia. "Do you know what one of the largest challenges for someone new to a blade is?"

Ylinia sways her head. "I can't say."

Bell hands Ylinia one of the swords. He takes the other in his hand and holds it straight outwards from himself. "Most believe it is something related to their swing." Bell swings the blade around his wrist in a few distracting circles then quickly brings it back up to the straightened position. "Few believe the largest challenge of a blade is simply being able to bear its weight." Bell swings the wooden sword around and places it again under his arm. "You try. Just hold the blade out straight as long as you can."

Ylinia raises the sword straight up and as it comes close to being perfectly level; the blade wavers. Ylinia endures the weight of the sword for a few seconds before she lowers it again and places her free arm on her right bicep. She lets out a bit of an exhausted breath. "I never would of guessed."

Bell waves his hand towards her to dismiss the concern. "Nobody does. But not everybody takes it so well." He chuckles to himself slightly. "I would like to train you Ylinia. *I will* so long as you work with me. But to gain these skills. You must decide on your own terms that it is something you want to achieve. Because I can give you the best instruction possible, every tip and every secret. But I cannot bequeath you the motivation which fuels those discoveries."

Ylinia nods stoically. "This is something *I* want to learn."

"Good." Bell quickly declares. "Then this *bokken* is yours. Keep it safe, treat it the same as you would a steel razor. Practice holding it straight out like I showed you until you can do so without even the slightest tremble. When that time comes, your lessons will start."

Ylinia forgets to respond as she stares with joy at the wooden sword in her hands. Her smile grows wide and she looks up at Bell. "I will practice every day."

The intercom in the wall crackles and Howarth's voice can be heard softly through it. "Bell?"

Bell walks over towards the speaker and presses a button. "Yes Howarth?"

"Look at what we're approaching?" Howarth asks.

Bell raises his eyebrows. "Give me a second." He says then walks over to lean out of the open door and peer ahead. The Tristram is heading towards what appears to have been a town; it is now only the barren frames of a few buildings. Bell returns to the speaker. "Have there been any alerts from central about what happened here?"

The speaker crackles. "None." A moment of nothing but static passes. "It looks like on the map this town was called Relun. Other then a sizable granary, there wasn't anything notable here. It couldn't of been a targeted attack."

As The Tristram draws closer the destruction of the town tells a more complicated story. The buildings haven't suffered fire damage but appear, instead, to have been destroyed with a force equal that of an explosion. The destructive force passed through the town on the southern side and spread through every building and person violently across towards the north end. Bell speaks softly into the intercom. "I'll check it out. Get on the cannon just in case." He orders.

"Done." Howarth replies quickly; the static disperses and the speaker turns off.

Bell looks over at Ylinia. "Do you want to come check it out with me?"

Ylinia is consumed by surprise. "*Uh*...are you sure?"

"I am." He replies confidently. "Do you expect to survive in a dangerous world knowing nothing about what makes it so deadly?"

"I guess not." She agrees; sheathing her wooden blade in a loop tied around the centre of her denim dress.

The pair step off the train and walk towards the ruins of the town. They can hear the activation of the cannon upon the train behind them as each of its mechanical systems are supplied power; it moves upon its swivel base with a deep *whirring* noise. Bell steps through the wall of one of the devastated buildings and stares at the damage.

"These buildings offered no resistance to whatever came through here." He notes.

"What do you think it was?" Ylinia asks.

Bell perches his lips slightly in the corner of his mouth. "I don't think it was just one thing." He admits as if displeased by his own guess. "None of the damage is consistent."

"So what does that mean." Ylinia questions.

Bell shrugs. "I don't know yet." He answers as they step over the destroyed front wall of a building farther into the town. Each of the buildings past this one have suffered the same trampled over and through fate.

The town has been built around its granary. The building likely once stood tall but has been entirely destroyed; only what seems to be half of the grain can be found throughout the rubble. Few scraps can be found of those who lived in the town; as it appears only the odd splattering of blood or ripped piece of flesh can be discovered.

"These people. Were they eaten?" Ylinia questions while starring at a few broken pieces of human rib-cage that have settled atop a pile of broken wall.

Bell shakes his head. "*Some of them.*" He looks around briefly then decides to stop. "The others were just crushed. As if they were in the way."

A few of the townies from the caravan rush into the town and are shocked as they behold the destruction. "What has happened here!?" One of them shouts out loud.

"Monsters, most likely." Bell answers dryly.

"Relun destroyed by monsters. That is craziness." The townie declares.

Bell shakes his head. "This isn't craziness." He begins walking back towards The Tristram. "It is exactly what happens in the real world." He sighs. "There is nothing we can do here now anyways. Lets not hold up any longer then we need to." He states in a rather commanding tone.

Ylinia looks up with concern as she follows Bell back towards the train. "Are you worried about this?" She asks him.

Bell nods with confirmation.

"Do you think whatever happened here is going to happen to us?" Ylinia continues to question.

"It isn't likely." He replies.

"Then what has you worried?" She asks again.

Bell raises his hand and points in the direction which the trail of destruction seems to lead. "We're going the exact same way."

CHAPTER FIVE

REAL THREATS

"What could cause such destruction?" Ylinia questions curiously. Both herself and Bell have returned to the last car of The Tristram as it continues along its trail.

"Many things." Bell answers stoically.

"But, the way it looked, were they hungry? Is that what did it?" She continues.

Bell shrugs the slightest bit. "*I don't know Ylinia.*"

Ylinia stops and stares up at Bell. "Well why not?"

"Because there were too many conflicting signs. Some of the townspeople were eaten, some not. Some of the grain was eaten, some of it was left like invaluable dirt. Monsters have proven themselves to be unfortunately vile things, a plague upon this world, but they are consistent within their species. A goblin will always prefer the raw flesh off a human rib, they will never suddenly decide to supplement their diet with a spinach salad. So to have had all this varied destruction, it must of been many different monsters of many different species. Few of which are known to even communicate between themselves, none the less feed and rampage together."

"What does that mean?" Ylinia asks with concern.

Bell huffs loudly. "It means we're in the midst of something that so far refuses to make sense." He looks around the train car for a moment and then looks down at the ground. "This many creatures, if they're indeed what is causing the seismic readings. I fear they could accomplish more then destroying some defenceless prairie town."

The intercom in the train wall crackles awfully. "Bell, if you wouldn't mind coming up front for a bit. We're having a bit of an issue." Howarth's voice requests.

Bell looks over at Ylinia. "Come on then."

Ylinia flicks her head to a kilter. "You sure? They *just* asked for you."

Bell shrugs. "And here I was thinking you accepted my offer to train you."

"I did." Ylinia states almost defiantly.

"Then come on. You can't see the problems of the world from a distant room. You need to look straight at them, feel the fear of not knowing what the absolutely correct thing to do is, then be made to make that decision regardless." Bell instructs her.

Ylinia rushes up to Bell's side. "How does looking at problems make me better with a blade?"

"It lets you know if you need one, for starters." Bell jests. "In reality. The ideal manner to wield a blade is with the same mindset that you would a surgical scalpel. Its edge is sharp, its back strong, and it is used to cut out exactly what is causing the concern. Only some problems however, can actually be fixed by this precise removal, others will only trick you into thinking they can be. It is very useful for a blade-master to know the true effectiveness of their tool."

Ylinia nods. "So then what use would a blade-master be in a world without problems that can be solved with blades?

Bell chuckles. "I've always attributed my health to the various practice routines I endure with Ehre. If there was no need for blades to taste flesh in the world. I'd test the waters of success as a duelling instructor; for sport."

"Do you think people would practice with swords if they were only to be used in such a fashion?" Ylinia questions curiously.

"I'd hope." Bell responds. "People still train with bows in a world with rifles. We still learn to run despite our creation of vehicles." Bell smiles and shrugs. "I think we like the inventions of our world as much as we like the traditions. I believe there is a place in peace for them both."

Bell and Ylinia make their way through the moving train via connecting doors. They arrive in the front car where Howarth, Mel and Alim are standing around a work bench.

"Bell, good." Howarth remarks as he arrives; he glances at Ylinia shortly with a smile. "Some of the townies are requesting we return to Gelghen to insure that it will not suffer the same fate as Relun."

Bell shakes his head. "How does that make sense? Whatever destroyed Relun is going the exact opposite direction."

Alim raises his hand with frustration and points it towards Bell. "Exactly my friend. That is the sort of stubborn we are dealing with right now."

Mel adopts an understanding expression to glance over towards Alim with; she smiles softly. "They are just scared. They have never seen such destruction."

"And it is our fault that they have never opened their eyes? It is in their backyard that this has occurred. Not ours. Relun is not the first town to be destroyed by monsters. They can't possibly think it is a unique circumstance. *This is why we created the Great Cities in the first place.* So that we could stop hoping an idyllic surrounding will magically protect us from the evils of the globe."

Howarth crosses his arms tightly. "They can't possibly believe how much safer the Great Cities are. They've only heard stories. Who is stupid enough to have their anxiety quelled by the existence of a mythical safe place they have never been?" He pauses for a few seconds. "I vote we carry on."

"They'll feel like prisoners." Mel protests.

"They'll get over it." Alim notes.

"Do you agree with this Bell? Simply pressing on?" Mel attempts to gain someone on her side.

"I-" Bell begins but is interrupted as the entirety of the train shakes violently.

Howarth jolts around and walks into the control room. "*Fuck.*" He says under his breath as he quickly jumps into the primary driving seat; disengaging the auto-pilot which has been maintaining their speed. Outside the window is a massive horde of creatures that spreads nearly a kilometre wide and half as long; all the monsters march in tandem in the same direction. The train car shakes again and a pounding is heard from the outside. "Bell! Get out there. I'll get on the cannon."

Bell nods and sprints off. He opens up the side door of the front car and peers outside. On top of the train car is an earthen imp; a species of goblin with rock-like skin and short wretched wings which are capable of propelling the creature a few meters at a time. Bell grasps a handle on the outside of the train and pulls the entirety of his weight onto it; with his free hand he smashes a button and closes the train door. Bell climbs up the side of the train using a few foot holds and handles. The earthen imp stares at Bell and makes a deep guttural roar. Bell lowers his stance and opens his arms. "Come ere big guy." He teases. The earthen imp lunges towards Bell with incredible speed. Bell dodges the lunging monster and grabs its leg as it passes by; he spins around on his heels quickly and throws the imp harshly into the ground below. Bell taps the side of the cannon twice loudly enough for a slight *CLANK* to be heard within the train. The cannon whirrs to life and begins aiming towards the herd of monsters ahead of them.

Bell looks behind the train. The caravan behind them is being chased by goblins riding dyruen: monstrous deer which suffer uncontrollable and excessive muscle growth; causing them to appear quite disfigured. Bell sprints towards the edge of the train as the cannon fires off a shot into the herd ahead; blowing a chunk of dirt out of the ground and devastating each of the creatures around the impact. The herd breaks into three different packs of varying sizes; rushing away from the cannon's assault. Air whips through his jacket as Bell jumps from the edge of the train and directs the tip of his boot into the chest of one of the goblins. The goblin nearly falls off the dyruen but is able to grasp the edge of its impromptu leather saddle and hold on. Ehre is drawn with a seconds notice and slashes the goblin's arm clean off from the elbow; it falls into the dirt and is trampled by its own momentum. Another cannon fire bellows and destroys one of the escaping portions of the horde; causing the survivors to stray even more. Bell grasps the reigns of the dyruen's impromptu saddle and guides it towards the other goblins. Bell rides up beside one of the other goblins and with a single slash cuts into the spine of the dyruen which it is riding; causing them both to tumble over and break their bones in the fall. The remaining goblin peers behind its self and starts panicking. Bell closes distance as the goblin searches through a satchel tied to its chest and produces a circular object wrapped in some sort of tanned flesh with a fuse sticking out of the top. The goblin quickly rubs the fuse against a rough plate of metal built onto its armour and ignites it; throwing the grenade backwards towards Bell. With little time to react Bell intentionally slips around his positioning on the dyruen and holds himself underneath the creature as it continues to race forwards; the grenade explodes above both of them and its heat and shrapnel cover the dyruen. After the explosion settles Bell twists himself around to be on top of the dyruen again; the beast is only mildly harmed by the destruction. Taunted into a rage Bell's dyruen rushes forward as its muscle explodes with energy and fervour. Bell jumps from his beast onto the back of the goblin's and quickly stabs the monster through the heart; tossing him off the dyruen.

The townies with the Caravan breath a sigh of relief as they watch Bell dispatch the chasing goblins. Bell mercifully executes the dyruen which he is riding upon and jogs to catch up with the caravan. "How long ago did they appear?" Bell asks.

"Just a few moments ago. They circled around from the middle of the herd it looks like." One of the townies answers.

Bell nods. "Did it look like they were leading it?"

The Townie laughs. "It looks like they were getting kicked out. Came to chase us so they'd feel better."

"*Alright*. Keep close to each other. We'll endure this." Bell simply states before sprinting to catch up with The Tristram. He rushes up to the last car's side door and pulls himself up to stand on one of the foot rests. He uses his key to open the side door and quickly tumbles in; rushing to the front car of the train as quickly as he can.

"Are you alright?" Ylinia questions with worry.

"Mhmm." Bell vocalizes. "What is our condition here?"

"Howarth is doing his best to repel them from here. Their numbers are immense. It is too difficult to hit them all at once." Mel informs him.

"Alright." Bell acknowledges then moves to join Howarth. Howarth looks over, says nothing and continues operating the train and cannon simultaneously; utilizing a set of aiming controls built into the primary steering wheel. "We should call this in." Bell states plainly.

"Already did." Howarth replies shortly. "They're sending *The Royal Mounted Cavalry* out of Neitheim to intercept the herd."

Bell nods softly. "Understood." He stares out at the dispersing herd ahead of them as Howarth lines up another cannon shot and destroys a few of the monsters. "This feels a bit gross." Bell admits.

"Agreed." Howarth says without taking any pleasure in the words. "I feel like I'm executing fish in a barrel." He grits his teeth slightly. "And not even the sort you can fry up later to mitigate a bit of the guilt."

Bell chuckles as the cannon fires off again. "I know what you mean." He tightens his jaw. "*This-*" He holds his hand out towards the window and the herd of monsters. "It's like if your home was infested by rats that look like kittens. I mean, you know they're gonna do harm, shit in your cupboards, chew the wires, the whole annoying pest shtick. But when it comes to getting rid of them, it's hard not to be the one who feels like a monster."

"Woulda figured you'd be more at peace with such a circumstance." Howarth notes.

"Me too." Bell agrees, rolls his shoulders then sighs. "I got lucky I think. I got to fight the sort of asshole who planted bombs in schools to make a point." Bell flattens his palms and motions them in the air as if they were plates of a scale. "It is easier to feel like the good guy when those are the sort you're calling the bad." He sighs again. "And monsters suck. They do. But there is always that part of me that knows they are just animals, trying to survive with the tools they have been given to do so."

Howarth nods in a short burst. "Beasts are just beasts. They may kill, they may destroy, but they are not aware of the consequences of these choices, at least, few are. Monsters are the ones who can choose prosperity for all, but do not desire it." He lines up another shot with the cannon and destroys a few more of the rampaging creatures. A device within the control desk starts ringing. Howarth presses a button next to the device and adopts a formal version of his own voice. "Gunnery Sergeant Howarth reporting."

"Greetings Sergeant. This is Cavalry Master Nuinez. We're just a click off your location. Will be coming in hot with a set of sixteen steeds. What can you report?" The device speaks with a female voice.

"We've been engaged with a large herd of beasts. Multiple species. Little to no organization. They're stampeding, barely paying attention to us. Doing a hell of a job dodging cannon fire though, I can't get more then a handful at a time."

"Understood Sergeant. If you wouldn't mind disengaging your cannon fire. We'll take it from here." Nuinez states confidently.

"Ceasing cannon fire. See you in a moment." Howarth responds. He presses a few of the buttons on his steering wheel and the cannon whirs loudly as it sets its self back into rest mode. He lets out a deep breath of relief.

A few moments pass then ahead of the herd in the far distance can be seen a long line consisting of sixteen heavily armoured knights riding along on top of large blue steel horses; each of the knights wields a gun metal grey lance that is about fifteen feet in length. The Royal Mounted Cavalry disperse in their ranks and begin spreading outwards to encompass the entirety of the herd within the perimeter of their half circle; as they continue to charge towards them. The cavalry point their lances at one another and activate them; summoning thick constant arcs of wild yellow and blue electricity that resist the swaying of their mighty galloping. The crackling of the electricity only grows louder and wilder as it begins making contact with the herd; bifurcating any who come in contact with it. The steel steeds march through and trample over the beasts without hesitation; not stopping until they have passed through the whole herd; leaving behind them only the scattered corpses of the various beasts. Nuinez: the most central amongst the line of cavalry; raises her right hand high in the air and the arc of electricity dissipates.

Howarth smirks like a little boy. "That is never *not* cool." He jokes.

Bell chuckles and nods to agree. "This Nuinez. Have you heard of her?"

"*Not really*. I got the memo regarding her promotion. She was one of the youngest cadets to ever be promoted to the *RMC*. She rode with her first outfit when she was sixteen and pretty quickly proved herself worthy of even more then that." Howarth notes then pauses to think. "That was nearly three years ago now. It doesn't surprise me to see she has taken such command."

The Royal Mounted Cavalry convene between themselves then form a trail. Nuinez is in the lead followed by her cavalry organized behind her in two neat rows. The Tristram slows then stops completely. Howarth, Mel, Ylinia and Bell leave the train to greet the cavalry. Nuinez gracefully dismounts her steed and offers her hand out towards Howarth. Nuinez shakes hands firmly with each of the members of The Tristram then removes her angular steel helmet.

"Thanks for replying to the call." Howarth opens up.

Nuinez nods very formally with a youthful smirk. "Of course sir. It was my pleasure." She motions her shoulders out to crack her back. "That was the most work I've had to do in the past week. I'm glad to see I haven't gotten rusty." She jokes. Nuinez appears younger then her years with bright eyes and short brown hair. Her smile is persistent yet professional.

"I doubt very much that would happen." Bell states rather seriously. "You all seem well practised."

Nuinez smirks. "Prerequisite for joining my company. You gotta practice hard every day. If you can't do something in your sleep, I don't trust you to do it beside me in battle." She says without a single hint of sarcasm.

Ylinia approaches Nuinez's steel steed and stares at it. Its metal skin moves over various plates that have been expertly designed to appear like the musculature of a biological creature. The steeds large blue eyes contain constantly jolting crackles of electricity.

"Would your horse feel it if I pet it?" Ylinia asks without looking towards Nuinez.

"Juniper likes a good neck scratch." Nuinez replies. "You wouldn't think it. But the Steel Steeds are as sensitive as they are resistant."

"Is Juniper a normal horse inside this metal?" Ylinia questions again.

"*Oh god no.*" Nuinez replies with sudden horror. "Juniper has an essence engine for a *heart*. Her metal skin was produced by our master steed-smith and given life through *magic*."

Ylinia softly scratches under Juniper's neck; to her notable pleasure. "Dad says essence engines are only *kinda* magic."

Nuinez smiles and pats the side of Juniper's neck. The Steel Steed moves so that it can press its forehead against Nuinez's then return to its resting position. "I believe it is slightly more." She admits with a wide smile.

"So how far out of Neitheim were you when you got our call?" Mel inquires.

Nuinez shrugs. "Nothing too far. We were probably an hour and a half into a routine patrol when we heard you needed a hand. Bolted on over the second we got the call." Something tied off onto Juniper's saddle starts vibrating aggressively. "Well would you look at that, it must of heard us." She jokes then retrieves a large handheld radio from her saddle pocket; pressing the button which accepts the transmission.

"Nuinez. This is Central. Seismic readings are off the charts. Have you addressed the concerns noted by The Tristram?" A deep male voice asks from within the radio.

"I have sir. A large inter-species herd of beasts was stampeding towards Neitheim. We deployed our arc and successfully stopped the stampede." Nuinez reports.

The radio is silent for a few moments then the same voice returns. "Seismic reports are still coming in now from the Kiminolp Mountain Range." There is a pause of silence. "Does The Tristram still have a civilian convoy?"

"They do Sir." Nuinez replies.

"New orders then Nuinez. You will complete the escort of these civilians to Neitheim and assist in their processing. The Tristram will be assigned the investigation related to the seismic activity within the Kiminolp Mountains." The radio sputters slightly. "*Is that understood?*"

"Yes Sir. I will escort the civilian population towards Neitheim while The Tristram redirects towards the Kiminolp Mountains."

"Good work Nuinez. Central out. We hope to see you all home soon." The radio turns its self off.

Nuinez looks over towards Howarth. "Any issues with that?"

Howarth sways his head. "None at all. Though I'm curious now."

"*Agreed.*" Bell considers firmly. "We should go *now.*"

Howarth looks at Bell and notes the instantly growing lack of patience on his face. "It was nice to meet you Nuinez. Best of luck to you and your company. Thank you for the assistance."

"Not an issue. Best of luck with your investigation." Nuinez responds rather formally. "And thank you for giving Juniper some love. Not everyone does." She compliments much more jovially towards Ylinia with a smile.

"She's a very beautiful creature." Ylinia replies whilst staring kindly at the Steel Steed.

With a simple motion Nuinez throws herself on top of Juniper and grabs the reigns. "Do you plan on heading back to Neitheim any time soon?"

"*Hopefully.*" Howarth replies.

"Then if you do, we should all dine together." Nuinez offers politely. "Until then, ado." She motions with her hand for the other cavalry to follow her; they all go to speak with the caravan of townies.

Mel rushes over towards Howarth. "We're going to go charging towards the seismic activity?"

"We are." Howarth replies simply; not indulging Mel's more dramatic approach to the circumstance.

"What could possibly be doing something like this? Obviously it isn't going to be something *safe*." Mel notes.

Howarth stops in his steps and very firmly looks at Mel. "Mel. My darling. *I love you*. But I fear that we have passed the point in our lives where *the fear of our safety* is a valid concern. There is no reprise. Maybe there will be the sort of peace and safety you crave in the years to come. I would love to live in that world. But right now, the place that we live still has a need for walls and still has a need for weapons. I love you so dearly, and you need to accept that. Because what we're doing here is the most we can be doing to bring us towards that safer place." He pauses for a moment, looks at Ylinia, then back to his wife. "I will not stand by, on account of fear, so that everyone that comes after me can do the same thing. **I just won't.** *Do you understand?*"

Mel is taken back by the absolute seriousness of Howarth. She is silent for a bit, looks at her feet, reaffirms herself then smiles at her husband. "I understand love." She stares up at the sky. "I want to live in that world too."

Howarth pulls Mel tightly against his chest and kisses the top of her head. "*We will get there*. I promise you." Ylinia joins in the hug behind her mother and holds her arms around the knees of both her parents tightly.

Bell turns away and holds his breath until he feels nothing behind his eyes; discouraging a sudden sadness. "I'll be in operations. Keep me posted for when we get there." He mumbles while walking away.

━━⌐L━━

The Tristram rattles slightly at full speed; no longer inhibited by the trailing speed of a caravan behind them. Bell sits alone on the couch in the operations car of the train. His legs are up, his head rested against the arm of the couch and a large cup of coffee on the coffee table within reach. He has his mask and Ehre placed on the table beside his cup of coffee in a straightened row of organization. Without opening his eyes he reaches out to take a sip from his coffee and places it back onto the table in precisely the same spot it was before; matching the previous circle of condensation exactly.

Courtney walks into the room with a large book in her hand and a mug of coffee in the other. She sits down on the other side of the couch that Bell is resting on. As she sits she looks up from her book and peers at Bell. "Do you mind if I read here?"

Bell sways his head. "*Nope.*" He replies. "Do you mind if I nap here?"

"Not at all." Courtney replies sweetly then points a single of her thin fingers into the air. "So long as you don't snore."

Bell chuckles softly. "The habit has been trained out of me." He turns to his side and wraps his forearm under his head like a pillow. "Don't you worry." He quickly dozes off.

━━⌐L━━

"Sorry to wake you. But Howarth needs you on the intercom."
Courtney speaks softly while poking Bell in the shoulder to wake him
up.

Bell looks around the room and shakes his head. He has inside
of him at that precise moment zero desire to do anything. "*Alright.*"
He replies with a distant murmur. He quickly puts on his mask and
attaches Ehre back to his hip; then saunters over to the intercom on
the wall. "*What?*" He asks the box.

"We're nearing the mountain range now. If you wouldn't mind
coming up front." Howarth requests.

Bell stares at the intercom for a full thirty seconds before
manifesting within himself the ability to reply. "*Alright. Just let me
get a coffee.*"

"I just made a fresh pot a little bit ago. Should be in the
kitchen." Courtney speaks up without looking away from her book.

"You're my favourite person that exists right now Court." Bell
manages to reply before rushing towards the kitchen and pouring
himself a large cup of coffee. He drinks the coffee as he heads
towards the front of the train; moving aside his mask for each sip in a
rush. As he enters the room Howarth waves towards him.

"You wouldn't believe what is happening." Howarth says to
Bell.

Bell sips from his coffee. "*Mhmm?*" He vocalizes
inquisitively.

"There has been an earthquake under us for the past half an
hour." Howarth states.

"Uh huh." Bell acknowledges then drinks his coffee.

"We've been hovering above it so it hasn't effected us. But the
closer we get to the mountains the more it is obvious that there is
some serious stress in the region." Howarth is obviously worried by

the circumstance as he explains it. "Whatever is doing this, *whoever is doing this*. I can't say I've ever seen something like it before."

Bell shrugs. "I'm ready to see whatever it is." He takes a sip of his coffee. "I can't do much to help with enigma or unforeseen *nonsense*. But I can stop a problem when I come across one." He waves his hand around in the air in front of him with a mild frustration. "All these webs leading to possibilities. I just wanna know where I gotta go, *you know*?"

"We're rushing as much as we can." Howarth assures Bell. "I admit I had hoped that the Royal Mounted Cavalry would be riding alongside us."

Bell sits on a stool and rests his elbow on a workbench. "Can their steeds match our speed?"

"*Easily.*" Howarth replies confidently. "Those things get to the sort of speeds that have a guaranteed death rate upon collision."

"Huh." Bell notes with the mildest of intrigues.

"I trust that we'll be able to address any concern that pops up however. We are well equipped." Howarth explains confidently.

Bell sighs knowingly. "Izelle sent us here. She wouldn't do so if she didn't think we would succeed."

Howarth raises his eyebrow. "How can you possibly know that?"

Bell shrugs. "I just do. She does this type of thing." He spins around his coffee spoon in his hand slightly. "She knows that I don't do well if I get bored."

"So she sends you...*us* on a mystery goose chase the size of an earthquake?" Howarth questions with wide eyes.

Bell nods. "That is most likely the case. *Yes.*"

Howarth laughs. "It would be within her scope of power to have Central assign us to this."

Bell stares very seriously at Howarth. "I am only going to say this once. Because it is a penultimate statement that should be above any and all questioning. *Do not presume Izelle is incapable of anything.* If she says she has your literal heart in her hand then I wouldn't for a second think it wise to call her bluff. Even if you could feel a beat in your chest."

"*Alright.*" Howarth blinks a few times. He stands and walks over to the command desk. "We're almost here."

Bell follows after Howarth with his nearing empty mug of coffee. "*Joy.*"

"Are you gonna be alright once we get there?" Howarth questions with concern.

Bell rolls his eyes. "I'm dragging my feet not my ass. *I'll be fine.*" He rests his left hand on the handle of Ehre.

"Even better." Howarth says with a smirk. "Because we're going to let you off here. Ideal range for the cannon." He begins to slow the train down and turn it to become parallel to the mountain range.

Bell places his empty cup of coffee down on the table and cracks his back. "I do admit. I'm curious what Izelle *thinks* this could be. She wouldn't put me on its path if it wasn't worth my while." Bell smashes the button to open the train side door. "*Hopefully,* I'll be right back."

Howarth nods. "See you soon Bell. Be safe."

Bell begins walking towards the mountain range. The ground beneath him shakes like the bed of newly weds: with extreme motivation and only a conceptual idea of what it should be doing. As the mountain range becomes closer there is a visibly large opening leading into a cave. The ground surrounding the cave's exit is pattered with hundreds of different monster tracks. Bell is roughly two hundred metres away from the entrance to the cave when a long stalactite begins speeding towards him like a bullet. Bell barely manages to react in time and slashes the projectile in half with Ehre; the sheer force throwing him violently into the dirt. Bell chuckles with amusement as he gets up off the ground. Two more of the stalactites speed towards him and he manages to dodge them both. From within the cave emerges a humanoid figure made entirely of boulders that is ten times the height of the average man. Despite having no notable head on its shoulders it *cries* out loudly in a deep distorted voice as it sprints towards Bell; the ground trembles beneath its feet in repercussion.

Bell sprints towards the Golem with Ehre drawn.

The Golem tears off portions of its own back and throws the flurry of stones at Bell.

With an instant reaction Bell slashes through each of the stones which would collide into him; causing a poof of dust to appear behind him as he bursts through the eviscerated rock. The Golem violently pounds its fist into the ground and Bell is thrown by the sheer displacement of terrain.

Quickly regaining his foothold Bell rushes towards the Golem and jumps onto its arm; raising himself as the Golem raises its arm. Bell jumps from the highest point he can onto the place where the Golem's head should be. Bell stares down between his feet and stabs down a few times; to no effect. He sighs loudly and jumps to the ground from the top of the Golem as it attempts to swat at him with both of its hands. He lands with ease and sheaths Ehre.

The Golem attempts to smack Bell with his open palm but is stopped as Bell grabs its wrist and pulls it down into the ground. Bell twists the Golem's wrist around and further contorts the creature into submission. Swiftly Bell climbs on top of the Golem's chest and with his hands held together he begins bashing it; each blow creates a deepening impact site within the Golem's chest.

After ten of the aggressive bashes the Golem ceases all movement and dissipates into hundreds of separate rocks.

Bell's hands bleed profusely; parts of his wrist have been broken. Without paying it much attention Bell forces his bones back into proper alignment and waits; allowing a few peaceful moments to pass before the bones fuse themselves into place and the bleeding stops entirely.

The ground below Bell still shakes; even more violently now then it did before. The shaking stops, Bell smiles, then the side of the mountain explodes away.

Massive chunks of earth covered in trees and life fly from the mountain and crash into the surrounding area; leaving craters of destruction. From within the mountain emerges a creature larger in size. It stands on four thick legs at a height just under the clouds. It is covered in scales, moss, precious gems, ore and has large spiralling asymmetrical horns made entirely of intertwined tree roots. Its face appears similar to that of a moose but features two additional eyes in the centre of its forehead with another one under its neck.

"Goddammit nature will you just fuck off?" Bell finds himself incapable of internalizing his frustration.

The massive creature takes a few steps out of the mountain and further destroys the terrain; each of its steps rattles the ground as if the earth itself were a plank of wood battered by waves upon the ocean. The creature makes a deep bleating noise which is so loud and unusual that it places an absolute terror into the chest of any who hear it. The eye underneath its neck vibrates around with paranoia until it locks onto Bell and fixates as if held in his direction by a strong magnet. Bell quickly starts sprinting away from the creature towards The Tristram. A cannon is fired in the distance; striking the side of the creature fruitlessly. The creature takes slow steps towards The Tristram.

The side door of The Tristram's middle car opens up; Bell jumps directly in and nearly slips onto his ass as he attempts to land. The train door slams behind him and Mel is quickly on the intercom. "He's in. *Go, go, go!*" She screams. "What the hell is that thing?"

Bell shakes his head and begins rushing towards the front of the train. "No clue." He huffs. "Nothing good."

"What are we going to do about it?" Mel asks with half present panic.

"Something that works. *Hopefully.*" Bell replies. The train starts to speed up. Howarth is sitting at the drivers seat and focusing intensely on each of the various bits of information being presented to him. Bell sits in the seat beside him. "Where are we going?"

Howarth sways his head side to side. "Nowhere. I'm not gonna lead this thing towards anywhere *people* are."

Bell nods. "So we're stalling it out. Hoping it'll wanna chase us."

The cannon fires off loudly. "We'll keep it distracted. Even if it just makes us a pest."

The creature bleets loudly; shaking the organs inside of everyone in the train.

"Do you still have a siege tool? The hook and chain?" Bell questions.

Howarth nods. "We do. *Why?*"

"Get ready to fire it." Bell sighs. "I think I have an idea about how to deal with this creature. Once the tool hits; keep the line tight." Bell leaves the room and walks to the train door. He opens the door, exits the train and stands on top of it. Bracing himself on a few foot grips and handles while the cannon adjust its aim.

A loud clunking noise sounds from within the cannon and then it fires with excessive force; propelling a heavy set of barbed hooks connected to a thick steel chain towards the creature. The hooks sink into the creature's skin and it doesn't even acknowledge it.

Bell climbs onto the chain, takes a moment to assure his balance and then begins running on top of the chain towards the creature.

Howarth pilots the train in a way that keeps the chain taunt enough to be run on without it becoming slack and swinging. Bell produces Ehre from its sheath and as he gets close enough he uses its piercing tip to assist him in climbing the side of the creature. Bell shoves Ehre into the side of the creature's rib cage and pulls down with all of his weight to create a large incision.

Utilizing the breadth of his acrobatic capabilities Bell pulls himself into the incision with Ehre close to his chest. The creature moans loudly and stomps into the ground; creating a deep fissure which portions of the Kiminolp Mountains descend into.

From within the creature Bell travels deeper and deeper; whacking his way through the insides of the creature like one would with overgrowth in a jungle while trailblazing. Bell follows the heavy beating of the creature's heart and once he finds himself as close to the powerful contractions as he can; he slashes Ehre through it entirely.

The creature dies abruptly.

Bell begins rushing out the way he came as gravity quickly takes over the mass of the creature. Bell jumps out of the incision a great distance above the ground; he lands and breaks one of his ankles as he does. Without the time to stop and linger on the pain Bell runs forward just in time for the creature to fall violently into the earth and send out large seismic tremors; which hit Bell easily and toss him forwards nearly fifty meters. His wrist breaks again as he lands; Bell rolls over onto his back and breaths deeply a few times.

With obvious disdain Bell painfully forces his broken joints into their correct alignments as they quickly begin to heal. Bell lays back entirely, glances at the dead creature, huffs with saddened disappointment and closes his eyes.

The Tristram quickly rides up besides Bell and from within Mel rushes out. "Bell! Bell are you alright?" Mel drops to her knees besides Bell and starts checking his vitals; covering her own hands in the viscera which thickly coats Bell.

Bell presses Mel away with his hand. "I'm fine." He half sits up and lets out a deep exhale. "I think I just want to go now."

Mel offers Bell her hand; helping him stand up straight. "You're covered in blood. How much of it is yours?"

Bell shrugs. "Some of it." He rolls his neck around on his shoulders. "I'm not bleeding anymore though. I think I just need a shower." He looks away from the downed creature and gets onto The Tristram.

Few words are spoken. But aboard The Tristram there is a unanimous decision: they will travel to Neitheim.

CHAPTER SIX

HABITS OF DEMAND

The Tristram has travelled without break from the edge of the Kiminolp Mountains north towards Neitheim. The Great City can be seen from a vast distance away. The walls surrounding the city are tall, black and made of anodized steel. There are small slits in the wall which are filled with tall tinted panes of glass; providing a brief glance into a city filled with well built singular buildings. Installed around the entirety of the city's walls are cannons equal in craftsmanship to The Tristram's own mounted cannon. There are four gates entering the city installed around the circular walls at the north, western, south western and eastern most points. At each of the gates entering the city are two two storey high guard towers each of which have two present soldiers guarding the gate with scoped rifles. On the ground between the guard towers are a platoon of soldiers whom wield large metallic shields and long thin spears made wholly of a light black metal. The Tristram is addressed via radio long before they reach the gates.

"This is Neitheim Border Services. Please declare your vessel and its purpose in arriving here." A female voice on the radio asks Howarth at his command desk. Ylinia sits in the seat next to him anxiously looking out towards the Great City.

"Greetings. This is Gunnery Sergeant Howarth piloting The Tristram. We're a class one nomadic operations vehicle seeking a refuel for our supplies and morale." He formally explains.

"Welcome home Sergeant. We'll prepare a private loading bay for you at the south western gate." The voice affirms.

Howarth smirks. "Thank you very much."

Ylinia vibrates with excitement in her seat. "It has been so long since I've been here." She stares at the city as they approach the south western gate and its massive door descends into the earth automatically to let them pass. "I wonder if it is still the same place."

The south western gate opens up to a paved privately walled off lot with a few paths leading to separate apartment like buildings constructed of grey brick. Individuals wearing grey canvas military uniforms wave beacons of light to direct The Tristram into its loading bay. Each of the apartment buildings feature tall loading bay doors; the closest of the apartments to the city wall has its bay door open. The Tristram is led into the bay and as soon as it is parked; the individuals in the military clothing begin assessing the train.

Everyone from within The Tristram leaves in a rush. They are greeted by Cavalry Master Nuinez; dressed now in a formal officer's suit which is entirely black silk adorned with silver bands across the biceps and shoulders. "It is good to see you all here!" Nuinez declares.

Howarth steps forwards to shake Nuinez's hand. "You as well." He stares back for a second at Mel and Ylinia. "Myself and my wife were originally from Neitheim. Before we began travelling."

"This should be good for you then. To return home to Neitheim and for the first time have nothing change. No districts have been left abandoned after attacks. No businesses closed due to threats on their safety. You can truly begin to feel the honesty of the city's recovery." Nuinez gleefully informs them.

Courtney steps forwards and smiles. "Will we be staying here?" She asks while pointing her finger around the building.

Nuinez nods. "Treat this home as you would your own. It will be yours as long as you are here."

"These were not here the last time I came to Neitheim. How long have they been here?" Alim asks; his hand firmly clenching Lance's.

"Just finished them up over the past three weeks. Good thing too. We have one a bit more central and it has made a huge difference." Nuinez gleefully explains. "And as pretty as they are. They have been designed to comfort those who lived in Neitheim during the war. *So* the windows are bulletproof glass, the building materials are highly resistant to explosions, there's access to a bomb shelter from the wine cellar." She rolls her hand in front of herself a few times. "*So on and so forth.*"

"Good to hear it." Howarth affirms. "So, *dinner*. Tonight would be wonderful. If that works for you?"

Nuinez nods formally. "Of course. I hope to see each of you tonight at *Fecchun's*. We have a seven thirty reservation."

Lance makes a nostalgic noise of glee. "Fecchun's? I don't think I've had anything in my wardrobe over the past few months that could even be worn on the same block as that place." He turns to dramatically face Courtney. "*Love*, we're going to have to pick a few things out before tonight."

Courtney dramatically turns to face her father. "*Well of course.*" She sarcastically replies. "It could not stand that we go out to our first dinner back in the city without wearing something fresh." She giggles. "It has to be pulled from the rack no less then three hours before it is on my shoulders or I just don't think I'll be able to enjoy myself." She smirks then sticks her tongue out at Lance.

Nuinez smiles widely. "I look forwards to seeing *both of your dresses*." She winks with jest. "Please feel free to call me if you need anything." She hands over a ring of keys to Howarth. "Here are a few sets of keys for the doors." She smiles again. "I'll see you all later."

Howarth begins sliding off individual keys for the apartment and handing them to the crew. The bay only has one door which leads into the apartment. On the apartment's main floor is a sizable living room with a few couches, a large set of windows, many board games, books and puzzles as well as a radio. On the coffee table there is a wide slab of wood with a hole in each of its corners where incense sticks may be placed; a pristine clean white feather rests in the middle on top of the slab of wood.

A wide staircase leads from the living room upwards to a hallway. From the living room the kitchen is accessible as well as a short hallway that has three doors within it. The kitchen features a metal oven with three coiled filaments on top of it, a single sink made of copper, an '*L*' shaped wooden counter-top and a wide refrigerating cabinet made of wood, metal and sealing plastics. Of the doors on the main floor; two lead to bedrooms with double beds and the other to a washroom with a copper sink, bath and toilet. Upstairs there are three more bedrooms, another bathroom and access to a patio which has a table and four chairs upon it.

"Does anyone have any preference for their room?" Bell asks out loud whilst the entire crew stands within the living room.

"Well if everyone is okay with it. We could give both Ylinia and Courtney their own rooms down here. Then we'll all take one respectively upstairs?" Alim suggests.

Mel smirks with what is an attempt at *innocence*. "We're going to have a proper bedroom to ourselves?" She chuckles unintentionally. "What a concept."

Howarth smiles to himself. "It will be nice to take a break from dodging each other around furniture."

"Or waiting for the one washroom to empty out in the morning." Courtney complains.

Ylinia opens up the refrigerating cabinet and peers across its contents as if it is a treasure chest. "What time is it?" She asks no one in particular.

Bell scans the walls and finds a clock hanging over the archway that leads to the kitchen. "Just a bit before one. Why?"

Ylinia produces from within the refrigerating unit a few items wrapped in parchment paper which have written on top of them the words '*Turkey Pot Pie*'. "Because there is pie for lunch!"

Mel begins to assist Ylinia in unwrapping the single serving pies.

"Is it cool with you guys if I take the room closest to the patio? I think I'm going to spend some time out there tonight. I don't wanna wake anyone if I come in late." Bell asks as he turns himself to face Howarth, Alim and Lance. Courtney has stealthily already gone to check out her bedroom and unpack a few things from the train.

Lance smiles and waves his hand permissively towards Bell. "Take whichever one you want Bell. I'm surprised that you're not rushing off to crash into the nearest bed. That *thing* the other day. That creature. I didn't know things could be that huge. To have taken it down on your own, you must be exhausted beyond belief."

Bell shrugs. "I feel more regret if I am honest. To have it be my responsibility to slay such a rare being. Despite it obviously being a walking disaster. I wish that there had been more options."

"When it comes to considerations of safety. The lives of people, good people, will always outweigh the consequences of guilt. While I admit, even though I only glanced at the creature from the window, and despite the fact it is without doubt a rare breed of monster. Its death will spur on a thousand lives." Alim attempts to console Bell.

"I promise my skill with justification is exuberant." Bell jokes with a stoic look on his face. "I did it. I know why I did. Looking at the degree of damage it was capable of inflicting on the mountains. The fact that its mere presence sent hundreds of monsters running in fear from their caves. I do not believe it should of been permitted to go anywhere. The risk to safety was immense." He closes his eyes for a few moments then takes conscious breaths in through his nose and out through his mouth. "It's like even if you were to discover a *beautiful* volcano, it's still gonna burn down your house and bury everything you love under half a meter of rock and soot when it erupts; if you build your village in the valley underneath it." He sighs. "Doesn't matter how good at them I am though. Justifications are exhausting."

"Then you should focus on other things." Lance attempts to perk up the tone of the conversation. "What is it that you want to do here in Neitheim Bell?"

Bell stares at Lance for a moment as he considers. "I can't say I've thought about it tremendously. I was just focused on getting here." He mumbles a bit then hums to himself as he considers longer. "Nuinez said that the districts are the same as last time. So if it still stands, I should visit the basilica."

"Is there more that you can possibly train with your blade Bell?" Alim questions.

Bell wags his head. "Training is not like furniture Alim. In that once you possess it you may always possess it, or find yourself comfortably seated upon it. It is closer to a currency, to be gained, saved, spent. If you do not maintain your training, you will eventually run out."

"Always on the verge of a lecture, aren't you?" Alim teases.

"So critiques the civic engineer!" Bell teases. "It is ideal for the health and cohesion of the mind and body that they both strive for the same thing. I cannot attempt excellence with my blade if my tongue is a blunted useless tool; if my thoughts cannot be as clear as I intend Ehre to be." Bell explains then turns to face the front door of the apartment.

Alim nods, collects himself for a second then smiles. "I apologize Bell. You live your philosophies. I scribe mine."

"Enjoy the basilica!" Lance adds. "A master never forgets their pupils. I imagine you'll be well received."

"Mhmm." Bell notes. He peers over towards Ylinia as she finishes pushing the unwrapped turkey pot pies into the oven. "*Howarth*." Bell says just quietly enough for him to hear.

Howarth nods and walks over to Bell. "Yes?"

"Would you mind if I took Ylinia with me to the basilica?" Bell asks with a calm inflection.

Howarth smiles slightly. "It seems she is enjoying being here." He glances at his daughter and then back to Bell. "But she should go with you. She shouldn't pass up the opportunity to walk the halls of such a place with one of its masters."

"Then you will have to come to terms with something." Bell states sternly.

Howarth raises his eyebrow in curiosity and vocalizes a "Hmm?"

"The masters of Neitheim's basilica are talented with blades to a near impossible degree of excellence. They know these weapons down to the slightest element of their construction. They are academics of steel and combat." Bell lets out a heavy breath. "They will take great interest in Ylinia. Her spirit, the fact that she will be arriving alongside me. *She will* return with a blade and the immense responsibility which wielding one requires."

"She'll be training at first, won't she? It isn't like they'll make her fight in some arena for her life?" Howarth questions.

"I have promised to train her and I will." Bell assures him. "Part of training is learning how to handle the weapon at your hip. How to care for it, carry it. But there is also the consideration of what it means to carry steel. Blades are designed to kill. It is their purpose. In training to use one, you adopt this purpose. Once you accept a blade you are cursed with the reminder of its implications. She *must* bare that weight or all the training in Rion will be fruitless."

Howarth stares at Ylinia for a moment then exhales peacefully. "I believe she will do well with such a responsibility." He glances at the door which Bell is eager to leap through. "But if you wouldn't mind waiting to finish lunch. I don't think it would hurt anything."

Bell steps back from the door and tidies his clothing. He smirks, patters his feet and then seems to relax slightly; quelling his raising impatience. "We can wait for lunch."

"Thanks." Howarth replies as he crosses his arms. He peers over towards the door and smirks. "Step outside with me for a moment?" Bell nods in response and the two step out the front door of the apartment. There are a few benches outside the main door which both the men neglect to sit on. "You know what the weirdest part of being here for me is Bell?"

"The peace?" Bell speaks quietly while staring out at the edge of the city's wall; a mild paranoia in his eyes.

Howarth shakes his head firmly. "I don't smell cigarettes." He laughs a bit. "That was always the best part about coming back to Neitheim. Drop off, pick up, munitions transfer, whatever it was. Every soldier on board knew that coming to Neitheim meant we got a decent chance to load up on smokes again. Some of the guys would get giddy, start twitching their knees, playing with their lighters." He chuckles a bit. "Then when we got here? You'd be hard pressed to find a single one of us without their mouth drooping smoke like a bush fire." He shrugs his shoulders mildly. "Of course we all knew it was a shit habit. Even the guys who smoked their first pack twenty minutes after getting it."

"You just figured bullets and blades kill you quicker. So if you're taking your chances with them as well. Where is the real risk. *Eh?*" Bell questions.

Howarth touches the tip of his finger to his nose a few times. "I don't think anyone wanted to die tomorrow knowing they didn't have their smoke today because they were hoping they'd be healthy twenty years down the line." He looks up at the sky a bit. "I'll tell you what. A funeral in a war ain't much. But it hurt a bit less if we could say we saw our buddy just the day before smiling with his smoke." Howarth huffs. "As stupid as that is."

Bell shakes his head dismissively. "It isn't stupid." He smirks. "Do you want a smoke now?" He asks in jest.

Howarth shakes his head. "*Nah*. I want those twenty years now. Or fifty, or seventy. If I can get em."

"Good." Bell replies.

"Do you?" Howarth asks.

Bell doesn't react well to the question. His palms become clammy. He stares indecisively between different groupings of things he isn't paying attention to in the distance. "*Uh*."

"Sorry." Howarth apologizes and reaches out with his hand to place it on Bell's shoulder.

Bell steps back quickly and shirks the hand on his shoulder. His head twitches a little bit and he pulls his hands together over his chest. He breaths, ineffectively, as deep as he can before speaking. "*It's*." He pauses. "*Alright*." He focuses on breathing for a moment. "It's just, *you know*." He rotates his shoulders as he moves his hands around in an unorthodox loop. "Minutes used to share their value with blocks of gold. When Temple was here, I cherished every second. With her gone, all I feel is the weight. Every minute passes and another block of gold is laid on my back." Bell sighs loudly. "I had hoped eventually there would just be enough weight to make me sink. To finally buckle my knees and let me suffocate under it all in peace. But it is never enough, it is just so close that you think it might be."

His breath is ruffled as he attempts to reign it in despite the trepidation within his chest.

"I'm sorry." Howarth repeats. He stares away for a moment and then back at Bell. "If you need me to carry some of the weight. *I am here.*" He sternly states.

Bell nods a few times with a soft bounce. "I'm sorry as well. I shouldn't detract from your joy. I think I'm a bit jealous." He laugh cries slightly; sniffling loudly under his mask as he does. "Or at least some petty part of me is." He wipes his face clean with his forearm in a swift motion.

Howarth chuckles. "You let me keep my family Bell. Your actions, the use of whatever power it is that you have. It gave us every moment we're going to have from here on out, every smile." He huffs. "But despite feeling like I have everything. I cannot give you a single thing. What I can do is promise you, no matter what, you'll have a family with us."

Bell smiles as strongly as he can; summoning a slightly crooked straight line across his face; completely obscured underneath his mask. "Thank you Howarth." He motions his head towards the apartment and lets out a deep exhale. "Should we check on lunch?"

The streets of Neitheim appear barren with even the slightest bit of decoration standing out immensely. The buildings are constructed with a combination of steel, brick and wood; these buildings typically stand two floors high. The doors of these buildings are all steel; some show signs of swords having slashed against them; many of the walls have bits of shrapnel still lodged within. Windows are typically barred and it is never more then a few minutes before a patrol of well armed guards passes you in the street. Bell, Courtney, Lance and Ylinia all walk side by side down one of these streets; a few other residents of the city are their company though none make eye contact with one another. Ylinia has left without the wooden blade; upon Bell's request.

"Are we sure that there *is* a fashion district left?" Courtney asks between the members of her group.

"The pretty stuff is inside." Bell notes.

Lance nods to agree. "Neitheim architecture is all about being tough on the outside and beautiful on the inside."

Ylinia smiles as she stares at the various signs installed across the buildings; many of them simply state the singular item type which they sell on the inside. "I think that will start to change."

"I hope so." Courtney replies with a disappointed look on her face. "It almost feels like we're walking through a military camp that is trying to impersonate an industrial apartment complex."

Bell chuckles. "That is closer to truth then you probably intend." He motions around with the tip of his finger. "These stores were often the fronts for anti-terror operations." He points to the second floor windows located throughout the buildings along the street. "There would be snipers in those windows just waiting on the signals of agents posing as cashiers or store clerks below. The first sign of someone reaching for a mask or pulling a weapon. They'd have rifles levelled at them."

The group traverses onto a light purple stretch of cobblestone which features various clothing stores on either side; each distinguished by the name of their in-house designer.

"Let us hope that *snipers in the attic* is not the motif they forever decide to embrace then." Courtney remarks.

Lance smiles. "Darling. I believe we have arrived." He motions to the various stores surrounding them.

"Will you two be okay from here?" Bell questions whilst staring through the mostly tinted windows of the various stores.

"I think we most certainly will be." Lance admits shamelessly. "Do you agree love?"

Courtney smiles then nods fastidiously. "I know none of these designers." She shakes her head then crosses her arms. "That will not do." She laughs slightly. "We'll see you two later at dinner?"

Ylinia wraps her arms around Courtney; hugging her tightly. "*Absolutely* Court."

Bell waves goodbye to Courtney and Lance then begins walking quickly down the street; Ylinia sprints slightly to catch up and must maintain a very brisk pace to follow Bell accurately.

Quickly ahead of Bell and Ylinia is the Basilica of Neitheim: one of the prestigious blade-master universities. Each of the Great Cities hosts a basilica. The basilica is unlike most buildings in Neitheim in that it is distinctly regal and roughly the size of a market square. The building is built with white steel beams and various shades of re-enforced transparent stained glass; in varying shades of black and white. The basilica is tall; reaching nearly six floors high with a sharp towering point. Out front of the basilica is a courtyard with bright white grass and a black cobblestone trail that forks into two paths as it traces the outline of a unique standing water fountain. The fountain pours with water of often changing colours and glows vibrantly as if filled with magical electricity.

The instant which Bell takes his first step on the white cobblestone of the basilica courtyard its two large front doors open and from within march out five individuals. Each of the individuals wears a fitted full face white mask, a black cloak with a fur collar, steel pauldrons and a white set of leather armour with steel plates installed over top various vulnerable locations on the body. Each of these individuals wields a blade of some style at their waist.

"Bell!" One of the individuals shouts loudly. "You have returned to Neitheim!"

Bell nods towards the individuals. "I sought the camaraderie of old teachers."

"There is no such thing as an old teacher." One of the individuals speaks.

"Only more experienced learners." Another of the individuals answers.

"Who is it you have brought with you?" One of the individuals asks.

"My name is Ylinia." She responds cheerfully.

The individuals surround Ylinia at a short distance and stare down at her in a semi-circle. "That it is." One of them replies.

"She is here to create a blade." One of the individuals says.

Another of the individuals laughs. "Bell is too kind to just ask us right away. He doesn't want to make us feel unappreciated."

Bell blushes slightly; a reaction which is mostly obscured by his mask. "You are always appreciated masters."

One of the individuals laughs and waves their hand at Bell. "We are not offended. To give knowledge skill-fully, to truly pass something on. You must accept that the execution, the application of what you teach will never be performed in front of you. The only real proof of your lectures or lessons is in them changing something when you are not around to repeat them." This individual points towards Bell and then towards Ehre. "Bell has only become more of the master that he was when we gave him our approval."

"And what do we believe will become of this one?" An individual states whilst staring down at Ylinia.

"A blade-master." Ylinia answers for herself.

Few of the individuals chuckle to themselves. "A truthful statement."

"She has none of the blockades that others have. The skilled warrior who brings only death with our lessons. The duellist who only ever competes." One of the individuals adds.

One of the individuals kneels down to look at Ylinia on her level. "There is none of the disillusionment of expectation within her. Her muscles have not prepared to begin as experts."

"Ahhh." One of the individuals notes. "But she is not without fault." He points at her chest, elbow and neck. "She is wise...and forgiving. Capable of great foresight and harsh judgment."

The first of the individuals which spoke shakes its head and each of the others return to a formal line next to one another. "She shall have her blade."

"Just because you stared at me?" Ylinia questions loudly.

"Some stare, some study, some see." The first individual responds. "Can you tell which it is that we can do?"

"Well, I mean, not-" Ylinia is cut off before she can continue.

"It does not matter which we do. We can stare, we can study, we can see. What is more important then either of these things is that we *know*." One of the individuals replies. "Or is it that you believe we are wrong, and we should ask that you turn around and leave?"

"*That isn't what-*" Ylinia is cut off again.

"Do not play stupid games if you do not seek stupid prizes. Do you understand girl?" The same individual questions.

Ylinia chews on her thoughts for a few seconds then nods. "I understand."

The individuals each bow to Ylinia; an act which strikes Bell as odd. "Then please follow us. You must meet our blade-smith Titus." One of them speaks then they each turn around on their heels and begin walking into the basilica. Bell and Ylinia follow behind.

The halls of the basilica are beautiful. The floors are made entirely of glass and feature bevelled depictions of tile. The design philosophy of the basilica becomes more obvious as one walks into it; as the stained glass walls of the building become darker and darker in shade as they become closer to the centre of the structure. The individuals lead Bell and Ylinia to a near centre room on the third floor of the building. This room is a moderately dark grey and has a few electrical lights installed within its ceiling.

Smithing tools are organized across the room in a luxurious collection. A clear glass wall separates a third of the room from a patio that overlooks one of the oldest districts of Neitheim.

On of the patio leaning over the balcony's edge and staring out at leisure is a very tall, very fit bald man wearing a leather apron, an oil stained loosely hanging white shirt and dark black pants further worn by oil, soot and fire. Peeking out of the edges of the man's silhouette are two long curling whiskers; shooting like sprouts from either side of a well maintained moustache. The man peers behind himself as the individuals, Bell and Ylinia enter the room. The man abruptly adjusts himself to appear slightly more formal and enters the room with his chest proudly puffed out.

"Hello to all ye." The man states with a powerful voice. "What have ya brought to me?"

Each of the individuals acknowledges the man with a polite nod. "We have a request of you master blade-smith Titus. The girl is to meet her sword." One of them answers.

"Is she now?" Titus questions. He kneels down deeply and stares right into her eyes from a slight distance. "She looks young."

"I am young." Ylinia replies.

Titus notes this and nods. "Self aware. This is good."

Ylinia tightens her forehead; gaining a few crinkles in her brow. "I'm not a cat."

Titus nods respectfully as if recording the information in an official archive. "Not presenting as any sort of feline-hybrid humanoid. This is in its self *valuable information*." He smiles widely as if enjoying a game only he is playing. "Are there other species to cross off the list?"

Ylinia's eyes widen. She visibly fights off the requirement to shake her head. "*No.*"

"*Equally interesting.*" Titus replies. He rushes off to one of his desks and retrieves from within a blade with a deep groove carved down its centre. The blade features a unique tip with an enclosed path leading to the deep groove. He returns to the others with this blade and presents it with both of his hands to Ylinia.

"Is this my blade?" Ylinia asks.

Titus laughs deeply, loudly and awkwardly; none of these things matter to him. "*No.* This knife collects blood. Keeps it where it needs to be. Lets me take it where I want it to be." He motions cutting the side of his forearm with the blade then leaving it there at an angle. "All I ask is if you would rather I cut you, or you cut yourself?"

Ylinia raises her eyebrow then stares up at Bell with a slight panic. "What does he mean?"

Bell lets out a deep exhale. "Blades are more then just pieces of metal Ylinia." He shrugs then rolls his eyes. "*At least ours are*. The blood, your blood; is used to alter the steel. It speaks to the blade-smith. Tells them what language the steel in your veins speaks." He sighs slightly. "It is an important part of the process."

"If that is the case." Ylinia admits with a huff of acceptance. "I would rather you do it Titus. I don't want to get too much or too little."

"Few choose themselves." Titus explains. "Those that do often require me to forge blades as tall as they are." He snatches Ylinia's wrist in his hand and turns it so that he can clearly manipulate her forearm. "Though you can never tell what sort of edge a heart craves." With a simple slash Titus cuts open a portion of Ylinia's arm and begins collecting blood along the groove of the knife; she yelps mildly in pain. Titus sniffs the blood as it collects upon the steel and revels in the energy of it as if there is an aura of extravagance emanating from it. He extends the tip of his tongue and tastes the slightest bit of the blood before he is instantly possessed by an overwhelming need to create. He rushes towards his smithing tools and fires up his forge; tossing the blood soaked blade into a trough of clean oil.

One of the individuals produces a wrap of cotton and tightly bandages Ylinia's wound. "All has changed now girl. There is only the matter of patience left."

"I don't struggle with that." Ylinia informs them.

"None do until they do not. Much like a dam breaking. There is not much time in between transition." An individual replies.

"So then where do we wait?" Ylinia asks.

"Ahh." An individual vocalizes. "That is up to your steward." The individual moves to face Bell. "Is there anywhere particular within the basilica that you wish to reconnect?"

Bell's eyes widen and he hums to himself for a moment. "Part of me misses the classrooms the most. But only in the way they were before. With all the subjects left to learn, deadlines to meet, forms to master." He chuckles to himself. "I believe now, I would just like to see the chapel."

"A room that possesses benefits you have rarely required." One of the individuals remarks.

"Yet still one that has done favours for both himself and others." Another of the individuals adds on.

Bell cracks each of his knuckles individually. "The chapel taught me that the best way to avoid being stabbed in the chest, is to experience being stabbed in the chest every which way that it is possible, then learn to avoid such things ever happening *again*." He chuckles. "This has served me well."

"Then you wish to make a prayer?" An individual asks.

Bell nods. His right hand rests on Ehre's handle. "I believe I would enjoy that, *yes*."

Each of the individuals nod. They begin leading Bell and Ylinia towards the central most location in the basilica: the chapel. The chapel is however not a place of traditional prayer. It is instead the location of one of the few permanent magical enchantments left across Rion; as only the other Great City basilicas feature this room.

While within the chapel it is impossible to come to *lethal harm*. Blades with the sharpest of edges will bash against your skin as if you were born from rock, hammers will throw you to the ground but never smash your skull. To pray in the chapel is to duel with the intensity of a real fight; to use every technique and skill you are capable of without the risk of fatal consequences.

The chapel is a beautiful room. Long white silk curtains trail down from the ceiling against the walls. There is a railing surrounding a large square in the centre of the room. The floor of the chapel glows lightly with a shade of blue. There is an unavoidable vibration throughout the chapel; one that can never truly be ignored as it sources from every object and piece of architecture present.

"Your prayer Bell." An individual speaks softly. "Do you have a request regarding who will pray with you?"

Bell nods respectfully. "I would ask that the five of you each join me."

The individuals all stare at Bell for a moment then bow respectfully. "If that is what you request." They each step into the centre square of the chapel; finding a spot in line with one another across from where Bell will be.

"What is it that you are doing Bell?" Ylinia questions with deep intrigue.

Bell smirks; raising his cheek bones noticeably. "I believe we are going to fight." He relaxes his smirk. "And our blades are going to converse." He cracks his neck slightly and looks over towards the individuals with a short glance. "I believe I am going to enjoy both."

"Will you be okay?" Ylinia questions.

Bell places his hand on Ylinia's shoulder and nods slowly; doing his best to assure her confidence. "None can die in the chapel. So we will all be fine. But do your best to watch how each of us fights. It is not often you get to study the technique of six different blade-masters."

Ylinia nods steadily. "I will pay the best sort of attention that I can. Good luck Bell."

"Of course." He remarks then turns his back to Ylinia and walks into the square. The individuals across from him unsheathe their blades then bow deeply. Bell takes a deep breath, pulls Ehre from its sheath, swings the blade around with a swift rotation of his wrist then exhales. He looks out towards each of the individuals. "*Let us pray.*"

CHAPTER SEVEN

TRANSPLANTED CONSEQUENCES

One of the individuals rushes towards Bell at immense speed while unsheathing a simple short-sword with a decorative silver handle. The short-sword stabs in bursts of seven, fifteen and seven again within a matter of a couple of seconds.

Bell deflects the stabs with Ehre and dodges those he cannot block.

Another of the individuals appears from behind Bell slashing down towards him with a six foot long great-sword that features a sharpened round tip. Bell pushes off the ground towards the great-sword and bashes with his free hand the blunt edge of the sword; forcing it into the ground below. Bell attempts to kick the great-sword wielder but is dodged.

A short-sword stabs towards him and hits him in the thigh. Bell pushes his thigh into the wound, grabs the short-sword wielder and violently slams him towards the ground; smacking him against the great-sword stuck there.

The other individuals unsheathe their blades and approach Bell; among them is a sabre, a long-sword and a scimitar.

With a violent tug Bell rips the short-sword from his thigh and tosses it at the great-sword wielder approaching from behind; striking him in the chest and sending him to the floor. The three remaining individuals each charge Bell and engage him from every angle.

Bell deflects, parries and strikes as best he can. The scimitar slashes near his face and forces him to jump back, he smacks away a stabbing long-sword and responds with a stab of his own only to have his wrist slashed by an interrupting sabre. Ehre is smacked from his hand and his knees are kicked out from under him; Bell falls to the ground and signals his defeat.

The individuals quickly sheath their blades and help Bell up. They each join hands momentarily in a circle, nod their heads then share a collection of warm smiles.

"That was insane." Ylinia notes with wide eyes. "The way some of you moved. The speed, the strength of your forms." She takes a moment to consider her words. "It seems unreal."

The individuals do not react to the compliment. "It is the distinguishable difference between an apprentice and a master."

"You are definitively masters." Bell humbly admits.

"Masters who are greatly benefited by the unique nature of this room." One of the individuals notes whilst holding his hand upwards towards the ceiling. "In the throes of real war. You would kill each of us if we were not able to quickly land a decisive blow."

Ylinia raises her eyebrow. "But you guys won?"

"The *five* of us won." An individual corrects. "We have prayed together before. We know the extent of our capabilities; as vast as they are. They cannot compete against that of a Varyian."

Ylinia raises her eyebrow and her intrigue becomes piqued. "Varyian?"

"He hasn't told you girl?" One of the individuals speaks. "Of course not."

Bell rolls his eyes. "It undercuts how much I have trained and studied."

"It undercuts your ego." Another of the individuals quips.

"What are you?" Ylinia asks Bell.

"I come from Varyia; as did Temple. Varyia is a...*hidden community* within the mountains; impossible to discover by outsiders." Bell explains; he stares mostly at the ceiling as he does. "Our roots there began ages earlier then the first fire of your people. However there has rarely been reason for us to leave. In our home, we reside in more *authentic* forms; adorned with scales and wings. It is as our souls transfer here, upon whichever whim, that we adopt a more *human* appearance. The nature of our energy, *however*, is forever changed by Varyia."

"His flesh mends on its own, his strength is multiples that of a pristine human. It is why our weapons can stab him in the chapel without being considered lethal harm." One of the individuals adds on. "His speed and silence excel many practitioners of the same skills just as well."

Ylinia nods. "And what are your disadvantages?"

Bell shrugs. "All those of any man. The chaos of emotion. The fragility of a sentient mind in a physical body." He looks around then shrugs again.

"And from Varyia?" Ylinia continues her curiosity.

"Every Varyian has a treasure, something which is so close to their heart that they will die without consideration to protect it. Something that is at the very core of their existence." Bell answers. "As some may covet hordes of gold, so do each of us have a *treasure* of our own."

"What is yours?" Ylinia asks naively.

One of the individuals nearly gasps; completely out of character. "You already know girl."

Bell's face furrows and he closes his eyes; allowing himself a single breath of incredible depth. Ylinia watches him, considers things for a moment then looks down to her feet. "*Oh.*" She suffers a realization. "Bell, I'm..."

Bell waves his hand towards Ylinia. "It isn't your fault."

"What was hers?" Ylinia asks.

"It sounds funny, but, uh, she had this...*bakery?* She put together a few sorts of bread there. Traded it for very little; enough to keep her going. The thing is she had this modified kiln she used to bake the bread. It gave each of her loaves a perfect golden crust. That kiln was something she constructed from a very young age. She was always tinkering with it, tooling around with the settings. She was obsessed honestly. But it was her treasure, so I never raised any complaints." Bell explains with a smirk. "While the bread she made was delicious, her real passion was the ever-lasting flame which baked it." He chuckles slightly.

A bell rings loudly with a clean chime. Bell smiles and the individuals nod between themselves. Ylinia mostly looks confused.

"Your blade has been born." One of the individuals notes.

"I can't say I like how that sounds." Ylinia replies.

Bell chuckles. "The birth of a blade is important beyond belief. But it is likely that it will share the same disinterest in tradition as you do."

"Tradition is the propaganda of intelligence." Ylinia replies, looks down at her feet then wavers her head slightly. "I heard Alim say that once when he was head first in a book."

One of the individuals chuckles. "Let us go see Titus."

A stone pedestal has been moved into the middle of Titus's workshop. Resting over top of it is a silk table cloth; veiling beneath it the sheathed form of a short-sword. Titus stands next to the pedestal with a proud look upon his face. "Blood tainted this blade in a way I have never seen before." He declares.

Ylinia approaches the pedestal and stares at the veiled blade. "May I?" She questions with tapered excitement.

Titus nods. "It is yours. Like any other organ inside you. I have not the right to with-hold it."

Without hesitation Ylinia rips off the silk table cloth and stares at the black sheath of the silver handled blade. "It looks so *fancy*."

She declares as she picks it up off the table. As she unsheathes the blade it glows with a fluorescent yellow; as if the steel is the shade of the sun. Ylinia's eye glaze over for a few seconds and then she suddenly appears out of place in her body; as if she has *just* been somewhere else entirely. "This blade is known as *Bumble*." She states with absolution.

"Welcome to the world *Bumble*." Titus greets the sword.

"Thank you for this Titus, and all of you." Ylinia stares around at everyone in the room. "Do we begin training now?" She questions.

Bell shakes his head. "In the morning. We have a dinner to attend this evening." He smiles. "It will be wise to eat your weight tonight. Because the first day of training will take your energy away like nothing you have experienced before."

"*Leonardo*." One of the individuals speaks to another. "Take the girl to the lobby of the basilica. Bell will be along in just a moment."

The individual whom wielded the great-sword nods. "Of course." He replies. Pointing with his hand the direction which he intends Ylinia to walk. Ylinia looks at Leonardo then to Bell before closing her eyes and nodding. She straps Bumble to her hip with a thick leather belt and follows Leonardo to the basilica's lobby. Bell turns to face the remaining individuals.

"*Masters*." Bell states blankly; staring at a wall as he speaks.

"You know the war ended." One of the individuals questions.

"I do." Bell replies.

"You know there is no way to bring Temple back to your side." Another adds on.

Bell trembles slightly then nods. "I know this, *yes*."

One of the individuals steps forward. "Why train the girl?"

Bell shrugs his shoulders. "She should learn. Look at her. The people she knows. There aren't many ways her life can head that this training won't benefit her."

"So you're doing it for her?" An individual questions.

Bell nods. "She isn't replacing anything." He shuffles his posture. "I'm trying something *new*. Temple said I would be an amazing father-" Bell pauses for a moment to linger on the statement. "-and that is something which I am at peace with never getting to realize. But it is possible, maybe, that I can excel as a mentor. If what I know. The lessons of my life can be turned into the tools of a better person. That is an acceptable reason for me to live." He briefly makes eye contact with each of the individuals. "And that is, *definitely something I need.*"

"Most help the world for selfish reasons." An individual replies.

"There is not less value in goodness simply because it is motivated by the gain of the self. Recognition, treasure, skill. All things we may want to see in ourselves; *and* if one seeks to gain one of these in surplus. They are not made evil for gaining them through truly virtuous acts." Another individual adds on.

"So you approve?" Bell asks.

"We trust." One of the individuals replies.

"Your mastery would mean nothing if it did not earn you that." Another continues. "But we must always be sure." The individual motions its palm. "There are many ways to walk along the same pathway. Many have found themselves burning away a portion of their path; only to discover too late it is what brings their very journey to an end."

Bell shakes his head. "I became a soldier. My skills garnered me great success. But war is not what I want her training to guide her towards."

"Good." One of the individuals states.

Bell turns to Titus. "Anything that I should know about her blade?"

Titus nods. "Bumble has not yet decided what it wants to be. But it is a powerful tool. All I can say is that upon the last strike of its creation it radiated with electrical energy; exactly like that created by an astaria engine."

"It will serve her well. Thank you for your work Titus." Bell notes.

Titus nods firmly and extends his hand to shake Bell's. "Always." He motions the tip of his nose towards Ehre. "Has that one served well?"

Bell smiles. "Beyond any expectations. Even with your reputation. Ehre has been a companion with few equals."

"Then we wish you well in your future." The individuals speak in unison.

⎯⏚⎯

The crew of The Tristram approaches *Fecchun's;* a high end eatery offering private dining rooms for some of its guests, immaculately waited service and live musical entertainment.

The restaurant is infamous for its membership in the *Orrery;* an organization which facilitates a collective of skilled travelling chefs.

During the war *Fecchun's* took a harsh stance against terror and violent crime in the city by establishing a friendship with the *Blue Blood Birds;* once a local mercenary group and now a dedicated service of those who protect the safety of the streets. This friendship allowed *Fecchun's* to stay in business during the war as the skilled members of the Blue Blood Birds were able to run effective counterterrorism operations in the neighbourhood surrounding the restaurant; bequeathing the district its most luxurious and thus famous descriptor; *safe*.

"I have no idea what it is I'm going to eat." Courtney notes in pure culture shock. "What if I get the wrong thing?"

"Do you think that is an option?" Alim replies.

"What do you mean?" Courtney questions in her panic.

"*I mean.*" Alim begins. "What do you think constitutes *wrong?* Do you think they might put things on their menu that suck just to shame you for accidentally ordering them?"

Courtney stares back at Alim for a moment, down at her shoes then back at Alim. "I'm not confident enough to write it off completely." She admits.

Each member of the crew is well dressed. Courtney and Lance have each selected fine clothing with very similar shades of dark purple; her in a long gown and him in a matching suit. The rest of the crew are dressed more strictly; with military greys and dark browns constructing the majority of their stiffly fitting formal wear. The men are dressed in suits each denoting in a small manner their status or rank on The Tristram. Alim is wearing a simple brown suit with a few official insignia on the chest. Howarth is wearing a grey suit with a few fabric designs in a darker grey adorning his wrists; his chest has a few stitches of silver and gold cord. Bell is dressed in a grey suit similar to Howarth's with more notable silver and gold stitching around the chest. A long white design which appears similar to that of a blade stretches down the length of the back of Bell's jacket. Each of the men have a pair of leather shoes which have seen years of intensely intermittent use. Ylinia is wearing a simply cut light brown dress with a regal geometric pattern across the back of her shoulders. Mel is dressed similarly to her daughter with the addition of silver and gold stitching across her chest and two white strips across either of her biceps. Their hair is tightly wound into a bun and their shoes are very slight heels with two thin leather straps crossing over one another on each foot. As they approach the restaurant Bell removes his mask and places it into the inner pocket of his jacket.

Outside the restaurant is a small courtyard where there are a few stone benches surrounding a simple fountain with a large agate centre piece. The restaurant its self is an older building that has been well maintained. Made of a clear white stone; the building has light blue stained glass windows behind thick bars of black steel. A well dressed female with luxuriously stitched kevlar armour greets the crew in the courtyard with a bow.

"You are the guests of Cavalry Master Nuinez yes?" The well dressed female asks.

Howarth nods. "We are." He affirms.

"Lovely." The greeter replies. "Please follow me to your dining suite. It has a most wonderful view of our performer tonight." She informs them in a very professional manner then turns on her heels; beckoning them to follow her with her slow leading steps. She takes them into the restaurant and immediately up a set of stairs to the right where they follow along a long hallway of white tile and brick to a large private dining suite. The suite has a long table where all of the chairs are on one side so that the diners may view the restaurant's stage through a long one way window. On the other side of the room and behind the chairs is a glass door which leads out to a small balcony. Seated at the table is Nuinez, dressed now in a form fitted lavender dress; she stands as the crew enters the room.

"It is good to see you all again."

"And you." Mel replies; seeking a spot next to Nuinez quickly.

"Has the city treated you well during your return?" Nuinez questions.

Mel nods and looks back at her husband and daughter. "It feels new being here." She smiles. "After all the suffering this place has seen. It is good to have it feel *new*."

Everyone in the crew finds a spot at the table. Bell sits at the very edge of the right side. "I'd love to see where it will be in five years time." Howarth adds.

"You'll have the chance." Alim replies. "I spoke to a few of the civic engineers here after getting a chance to catch up on their latest essays. They say more and more space is going to be designated as residential. With the Selemians gone, they are much less afraid of accidentally making the safe-house of a terrorist."

Nuinez smiles. "As much as I love to talk shop." She points out through the window down to the stage where a tall, obviously shy woman in a heavy long dress takes the stage. She has with her an eight stringed mandolin. "We should watch the performance. There will be time to be social afterwords." The performer strums a few of her strings whilst vocalizing. She cannot look at the audience which has filled out the public first floor of the restaurant. She strums a few strings again, adjusts herself so her back is properly straight then breaths in slowly.

♫

There just isn't much, that, doesn't hurt now.
I don't even know how, I got so turned around.
All I can see, is the sort of place that I have let myself walk into.
Pain and suffering, are the thieves of the time we were once spending.

And it hurts.
Mhmm hmm.
It hurts to know I'm losing.
It hurts not to know.

Where its all heading.

There isn't anything, that is left in the way.
Its the barren emptiness that I hate the most.
I've tried to scream and make it better.
But I don't think I can be loud enough.

And it hurts.
Mhmm hmm.
It hurts to know I'm losing.
It hurts not to know.
Where its all heading.

Why do you disperse?
I want to see a face I know.
There are strangers here that I don't want to introduce myself to.
You used to make them go away.

♫

    Bell stares deep in the eyes of the singer, looks down at his table and writhes in awkward pain as the hair across his forearms and back whip to shape and cut the air in half as they do. Bell stands as politely and stealthily as he can and leaves the dining suite; poking out onto the balcony which overlooks the calm Neitheim evening before he can hear the third chorus. He is however; *followed.*
    "Not a fan?" Alim questions.
    Bell smirks. "I guess not."
    "Not many folks *guess* music." Alim replies.
    Bell shrugs. "I think I do." He stares back into the other room where the young singer is giving everything she has to the energy of her performance. "I just can't do it."

Alim raises his eyebrow.

Bell sighs. "Pretend that she means more then she does." He sighs loudly. "I mean it's impressive that she can do that, and that she sounds good doing it. But to have that talent and spend it singing about worthless nothings. How an emotion feels, the ways you can linger on it." He waves his hands around in front of him. "I don't need a field journal on the subject to understand feeling shitty feels shitty. You know? It seems so useless to me. To throw all this emotion in the air then provide no advice on catching it. *Whats the fucking point?*" He questions with directionless frustration.

Alim smiles then chuckles; looking back at the room slightly himself. "I don't think that is what they feel when they hear this music."

"I know." Bell admits then chuckles in a sarcastic way to himself. "Kinda pisses me off honestly." He chuckles again. "They're not really thinking about it. And if they were? They wouldn't want to hear it in the first place. Because it doesn't give them what they think it does. It's the illusion of depth. The comparison of your pain and the idea of pain making it feel like there is more then there is. But substance is created, not referenced; and it pisses me off when someone calls a puddle deep because they gave it the nickname *ennui*."

Alim stares at Bell without saying anything.

Bell looks away and down at the city streets. "*I know*." He admits. "I sound like an asshole."

"I wasn't going to point it out." Alim admits. "*But yes*. A pretentious one at that."

Bell smiles. "Temple used to do that for me." He smirks widely. "She'd pinch my elbow in this...*weird fucking way*." He laughs. "It was like a shock through my whole arm. Especially after she perfected her technique. *Just.*" Bell poses his thumb and pointer finger together while snapping out and making a sort of hissing sound. "*Like that* and I'd get the message."

Alim smiles. "All your stories have told me that Temple was very well prepared for you." A statement which makes Bell smile. "Though I must ask, what is it about the singer that really bothers you?"

Bell shakes in place, lets out a few heavy sighs then shrugs with all his might. "I don't *really* know." He rolls his hand in front of his face. "I guess it just seems so. *Simple.*"

"Singing? Playing an instrument?" Alim suggests.

"Singing a sad song about being sad. Getting something out of that. I hear something like that and I'm left with a hundred unanswered questions and considerations. But the people who like those songs, they listen to them *because* they want a simple sad song. It does something for them that just...stupifys me." Bell admits with a sort of anxious impatience in his breath. "I'm upset that it doesn't do more for me. That I can't understand the aid it provides. That I don't enjoy it? I mean, *shit.*" He admits with a blatant expression. "I've had some tragedies. *I have.* But the absolute last thing I want to do is dissect them over and over again. That's such a waste of time. And if the very purpose of that dissection is just to start actually dealing with that sadness? Then I'll just skip to the part where I'm dealing with it."

Alim smiles. "You know what I have come to learn about you Bell?"

"Mhmm?" Bell questions.

"Your impatience is very ingrained." He jests. "Deep *deep deep* down in you. There is something counting out every fraction of every second." He waves his hand towards Bell as one would when suggesting mercy. "*Now*, don't get me wrong. I believe entirely that it must *gnaw* at you when you waste even one of those fractions. I mean. It's a possession most of us never bother with the accounting for, and here you are, with a triple checked stock."

"So?" Bell asks with a tilted head.

"So you need to realize that's not what everybody else does. You might have a bird's eye view of your life, with a focus on all the things progressing and moving around you. But everybody else is just looking straight ahead. I know how it feels to you, how it must feel. The average person, you couldn't imagine how *goddamn real* this all feels to them. So when something hurts, when they lose something. They don't see that pain with the perspective you do. It feels much more overwhelming." Alim explains.

Bell sighs. "*I know.*" He lets out a deep breath and shrinks his posture. "But I can't just sit there. The frustration overflows whether I debate it or not. I don't know how I should make myself react."

Alim motions his hand around the setting. "You excuse yourself, look at something pretty and talk to a friend." He suggests. "That isn't that awful is it, no?"

"No." Bell agrees while resting his forearms over the railing of the balcony.

"Why did you come out?"

"Oh this pandering shrew possesses the lyrical creativity of a wooden brick." Alim admits dryly. "I almost feel compelled to give her a lesson on the *stagnation of a theme*." He jests with his own veiled frustrations. "But it isn't for me. So I just leave."

Bell smiles, looks out at the city and sighs. "If only more were capable of that transition."

Alim spins his head swiftly as he catches the server entering their private dining room. "We should go take our seats. I don't want to miss hearing their menu."

The pair return to the dining room where the performance has settled into a full band playing instrumental classical music. The server speaks just loud enough that she can be heard in all portions of the private dining room. "Your chef tonight is known as *Jasaa*. She has been with The Orrery for three years and hails from Tael. She has prepared a menu highlighting the varied catch of her city's fishing community." The server bows slightly then hands out wooden planks where each menu entry has been burned into the plank in very fine detail. "I'll give you a few moments to consider." She then leaves the room again.

Each debate their meals together for awhile before ordering and pairing their food with various artisanal juices and wines. The fish comes prepared first raw, then fried, then steamed and then piped into the shell of a beautiful pasta. The meal concludes to a multitude of pleased faces and exhausted body language.

"Did you all enjoy?" Nuinez asks the sort of pandering question we all ask once in a while when we too have enjoyed the festivities.

"Beyond delicious." Courtney replies.

"Truly divine." Lance adds.

The others all agree similarly.

Nuinez takes a sip from her glass of wine. "So that beast you encountered. Within the Kiminolp Mountain Range?"

"What of it?" Howarth asks curiously.

"Do you know what it was?" Nuinez replies.

"I'd be lying if I said I did." Howarth admits.

Nuinez reaches down next to her chair where in a leather satchel she has stored a scroll case. She clears a bit of room on the table then places the scroll case in the centre of it; opening it from the right side to display a bright white canvas just about a metre in length. Upon the canvas is a detailed press printed depiction of the creature which emerged from the mountains. "Known as *Erkdwu.* These creatures have only been encountered twice before. It appears, from what we can determine, that they are *grown* near the centre of the earth. They create earthquakes as they crawl through the earth and towards the surface. Some crawl to the surface at a speed of a centimetre every year. Others, likely like the one you encountered. Get impatient."

"Grown?" Courtney asks with a high pitched curiosity.

Nuinez nods assertively. "Upon dissection. It appears these creatures are closer to trees then they are beasts." Her eyes widen. "Myth states their seeds are created by the core of our planet and that they will grow as large as the space they occupy allows."

"Terrifying." Ylinia adds.

Howarth adjusts himself and focuses his eyes. "So, do you mention the Erkdwu for any specific reason?" He investigates.

"Of course." Nuinez admits freely. "Are any of you aware of *Statute: 55c* of the Resource Code?" No one in the room pipes up. "It is a specific ruling. Discussing the rightful ownership of the precious materials to be gained from a felled *Great Beast* such as the Erkdwu." Nuinez waves her head slightly. "Though I admit some of it is *less then concise*. The core statement of this specific statute is that the one whom brought upon the end of the creature is the one with legal right to the materials. *Killers Keepers* so to speak."

"So I own a massive lump of tree monster?" Bell asks.

Nuinez nods. "For now. We've received formal communication from the Maxicilius Orthodox Casino. They have had a long standing requisition for the supplies of such a beast and are willing to provide immense compensation in trade for the rights to its remains."

"*No.*" Bell sternly replies.

Nuinez seems caught off caught. "Uh, no?"

"Why no?" Lance asks out loud. "Do you *want* it?"

"What would you even do with it?" Mel adds.

Bell crosses his arms and sighs. "I don't *want* it. I want nothing to do with Maxicilius."

"Not a gambler?" Howarth asks casually.

"Never by preference." Bell answers before turning his attention back to Nuinez. "What could the orthodox possibly want with the remains of an Erkdwu?"

Nuinez shrugs. "Requisitions do not require one to input their motivation."

"Maxicilius is one of the saddest goddamn places on this planet." Bell notes with deep discomfort. "They must have some purpose for it. There would have to be a reason."

"It's a casino Bell. People go there to relax and enjoy themselves." Lance argues. "Maybe people will go there to see the beast preserved."

Bell rolls his eyes. "People go there to become slaves to Fuergl Caps."

"That does not mean that *you* must if you are simply visiting." Nuinez attempts to get things back on track.

Ylinia stands straight up, accidentally disturbing the balance of her chair and sending it backwards loudly. Everyone becomes silent in the room and stares at Ylinia; whom blushes, steps around a few times then lets out a cutesy huff. "I don't like not knowing what we're talking about. What is Maxicilius?"

Howarth smiles at his daughter. "Maxicilius is an Orthodox Casino. So, its a place that has many different sorts of gambling games, card games and skill games. Each of these games has a chance to give you a pay out reward in the form of the slightly psychoactive fungus known as a Fuergl Cap. Now, some people, come, play, spend or eat their fuergl caps, enjoy themselves in a restaurant and leave." Howarth takes a short breath. "*Others*." He admits shamefully. "Forget there is a world outside. See, there are many many homes located in the Maxcilius Orthodox Casino. There are restaurants and buffets throughout the game floors. People can live their whole lives there; and if they decide too? Maxcilius is happy to host. There are floors you can only gain admittance into with a certain amount of stored Fuergl Caps. There are high win percentage only floors, exclusive apartments throughout the casino, different levels of pride up for grabs if one has a large enough collection of prizes." Howarth glares over at Bell to note his obvious disagreement with his assessment. "It is a competitive and at times very hostile place, *however*. The people who take it seriously, the ones who live there. They value every prestige the place offers with a sacred honour. There have been many across Rion whom have simply abandoned their stance in life to chase the prizes of the orthodox."

Ylinia nods her head. "Thank you." She leans down to pick up her chair. "*Sorry*."

"What are they offering him?" Mel asks.

Nuinez coughs a few times to clear her throat then smiles. "*I have no idea*." She confidently answers. "Though they have assured me the multitude of possessions and resources they will offer will be more then you could consider."

Mel looks over at Bell. "You're staying on board The Tristram, right Bell?"

Bell nods. "*That was the plan*." He answers; unsure of how deep he'll dig his own grave.

"Well then in a way. That means it is for us as well. And as much as our military supplies have kept us going. Even if we get something from them we don't need. We can just trade it for something we do if it is in fact worth something like they say it is." Mel argues.

Bell stares. Ylinia, Lance, Nuinez, Howarth, Courtney, Mel and Alim all stare back at him. Bell closes his eyes and lets out a deep sigh of acceptance. "*Fine.*" He snarls while reaching across the table and snagging a lone roll of bright red salmon sushi.

"Then we'll leave in the morning." Howarth announces. He nods towards Nuinez. "The transport of the beast. Is that our responsibility?"

Nuinez wags her head. "Maxicilius has offered to take care of all of that. As soon as we confirm with them that you will be proceeding with the trade."

Bell stands and nods towards Nuinez. "Confirm it then." He takes a few steps towards the door exiting the room. "And I'll see you all in the morning." He leaves abruptly without waiting to see how the others respond. As he nears his last few steps in the restaurant he places his mask back on and steadily walks the city streets.

Neitheim is quiet now. Though, ultimately; it always has been. The quiet before consistently felt poised *just* before the introduction of a cataclysmic symphony; blaring at the loudest possible volume. So while you heard nothing, the buzzing in your ears and pounding in your heart never made it really feel *quiet*. *Now*, it is much more like you are simply in a place where not much is happening and the little that is consists mostly of sleep. It makes one paranoid until the paranoia too grows bored and then all that is left are the considerations of pathing. '*I should step there, quickly take this corner, avoid the dip in the road where there is a bit of mud still*' and the like.

Bell swiftly makes his way to his room in the military apartment. His room is simple with well crafted furniture filling it. The bed is large, the cabinet tall and regal while the small desk and chair which look out the window seem almost invisible in the wide space. The ceiling is rather tall for a bedroom and has many dangling strands of feathers, beads, shells, gems and bones in a sparse collection.

With a careless flop Bell collapses onto his bed and stares up at the ceiling.

In the centre of his ceiling sitting upside down with her legs crossed is Izelle. Izelle is an incredibly muscular woman with thin, short black hair and richly detailed tattoos of maps across her hands, arms, neck, chest and legs. She is wearing a well trimmed dark green dress that is bound with thick canvas ribbon around her wrists, elbows, knees and ankles; securing the clothing without impeding her flexibility or comfort; a black veil covers her mild bust.

Bell stares at Izelle who stares back at him. They compete in this way for a couple of minutes before Bell turns his head back, exhales and closes his eyes.

"No hello?" Izelle questions; her voice is assured but keen and sharp in tone like a child's.

Bell rolls around in his bed. "I *just* left people Izelle. *I'm tired.*"

Izelle drops from the ceiling and lands on her feet without any concern. She stares up and down at Bell then sits on the opposite side of the bed at the very edge. "I'm sorry. My visitation availability has been...*lessened* as of late. It was either this or three weeks from now."

"What could possibly restrict *your* availability? You wouldn't let anyone else make your schedule; they might miss a second." Bell teases with a shared sense of suffering.

"Too many eyes." Izelle admits. "Even if you can avoid one hundred. They have sent a thousand. And I will not believe myself above failure in a thousand attempts at something."

"How logical." Bell compliments. He sits up and glances over at Izelle. "So, *go on*, tell me why you're here."

Izelle dismisses her desire to roll her eyes, then nods. "What do you know of the name *Caesar Aungveius*?"

Bell shrugs. "That it isn't mine."

Izelle sighs. "He is the operative responsible for splitting the Agents of the Cauldron. A fighter, a leader, a brilliant mind and a traitor. He sold our weapons to the Selemians during the war. Giving lethal aid to the attackers whom randomly massacred our streets in the name of their *values*."

"I thought we were finished with loose ends *Izelle*." Bell critiques.

"On that particular length of string." Izelle amends. "There is a never ending ball which we must untangle."

Bell waves his hand in front of himself; as if to usher Izelle forwards. "Go on then."

"Caesar refuses to put himself in any situation one could describe as precarious. His current rendition of safety is within the Maxicilius Orthodox Casino on an exclusive high roller residential floor." Izelle pauses for a second, breaths, blinks a few times then shrugs. "And yes, I already considered the concern. You *cannot* imagine the amount of effort required to know where he is and be able to gain that information without it being a large enough leak in his security that it would cause him to move and invalidate the intel anyways." She lets out a quick huff of air before continuing. "*Ultimately*, we need him to die." She states plainly.

"And a flat out assault would give him far too much time to escape wouldn't it?" Bell questions.

Izelle nods. "As would a covert attack. It would require impossible feats of stealth, *even for you*."

"I don't know if that is true." Bell attempts to defend himself.

"You say to the woman who sat silently on the ceiling?" She argues.

Bell smirks. "I see your point."

"I know you've never even glanced at the exclusive floors of the orthodox. But they are like vaults. Never mind that the entire casino is a thousand kilometre hole in the ground with the most advanced anti-tunneling defences Citizenry minds can muster. Each of the exclusive floors *link* through the other. If you can't expertly get past the well trained guards, mechanically locked doors and repeating ballista installations. *Good goddamn luck* getting past the next couple hundred before you reach the actual floor that Caesar prefers to spend his time on." She speaks faster and faster as she remembers more and more about what it is that she is talking about.

Bell chuckles. "This leads me to believe that the Erkdwu was not agitated by natural means."

Izelle smirks; almost with pride. "One could say that." She rolls her eyes. "Requisitions are public domain. *Anyone* can see what you want if you're asking the world for it."

"*How useful.*" Bell notes with a teasing inflection. "So we go to accept this trade. Who receives us?"

"No one of note. A deacon who manages within the first ten floors. A relative new hire. He'll be instructed to lead you to one of seven different suites on the 500th floor; depending on availability. There you will be met by a cardinal and twenty some of his personal bishops. They will flaunt a contract, entice you with food and offer you the very room they host the meeting within; all without cost."

"How does meeting with a bunch of religious ranks help me out?" Bell questions sternly.

Izelle sighs. "Of a thousand floors, I get you through five hundred. Is that not worth being in a room full of crazy people?"

Bell stares, can't think of something to say fast enough and just grumbles instead. "So is Caesar attempting to become a cardinal? Is that it?"

"He couldn't care less about the cardinals, the papacy or really anything to do with the structure of the casino. He is there because it has stood as a protected solitary entity insurmountable by either political giant in a five hundred year long war. I believe it is a place he *respects* for its solidarity. However, the protection it grants his defected agents is likely just as much of an advantage."

Bell nods, sits back down and then lays flat on his back. He yawns; intentionally making it as loud as he possibly can to overstate his growing dis-interest in consciousness. "Where does he stumble upon his stab wounds Izelle?" He asks with growing impatience respectably tucked away somewhere in his deep breathing.

"*Later.*" She states slowly. "I admit, in a straight fight. You'll rip the throat out of Caesar faster then he'll remember he has one. That isn't the problem here. He is a man who threatens more then just what he can personally grasp. He has contingencies collected in pages. If you kill him there and then, we'll never learn what he has hidden behind the curtain."

"He has something planned, doesn't he?" Bell inquires.

Izelle nods then looks away. "*Something.*" She admits shamefully. "And if he dies. It will happen, without a single other person knowing entirely what it is."

"Bombs under any number of benches, in any amount of bags, targeting any number of things." Bell considers. "Without the master plan, or some sort of blue-print." He pauses, thinks on it again, closes his eyes in pain then lets out a deep resolving breath. "We would all be made voyeurs of our own suffering."

"He's creative. Which is a terrifying thing." Izelle adds.

"I understand your intent." Bell agrees steadily. "What is my mission?"

With a wide smile Izelle explains. "We need him on the edge of desperation, but with enough perseverance to forgo a half-measure. He needs to believe that *only* if he gives it his all will he be victorious." Izelle explains like it is simple science.

Bell raises his eyebrow in response.

"So we kill his agents. Force the use of his back up plans."

"And you think that will work?"

Izelle nods firmly. "He is a powerful man, but a man. Without the agents he turned to his side and the unique prowess which they possess. He would have no foothold on true power."

"Good." Bell accepts the plan with a relaxed pleasantness. "But one thing Izelle."

"Mhmm?" She questions with a curious inflection.

"You're lying to me when you say you don't know what he is planning. Aren't you?" Bell blatantly asks her while maintaining an absolute eye-contact. Izelle freezes up. "You don't have to tell me. I've served under you before. Compartmentalization saves lives; *I get it*. I just want you to fess up to the bullshit."

Izelle smirks and rolls her eyes with immense sarcasm. "I don't know *exactly* what he's planning." She rolls her eyes in the reverse and stares at Bell. "*Better?*"

"Much." Are the last words Bell speaks before falling asleep unintentionally; an act he finds the opposite of selfish.

CHAPTER EIGHT

THE REALITY OF ALL THIS

It is a crisp morning with freezing wind as The Tristram leaves Neitheim; its destination the Maxicilius Orthodox Casino. Bell is sitting in the open door of the third train-car; staring out at the distance without really paying attention to it. Mel enters in a formal grey military uniform; free of any adornment other then a white strip running down either side of her profile. "We're apparently going to be getting quite the reception." She remarks with a bit of glee in her voice. "This might be a better time then you think it will."

Bell resists the desire to say something negative. "*Maybe.*"

"I know it must be hard to try and enjoy yourself. But this could be a chance to learn *how* again." Mel offers.

"I'd like the chance." He accepts. "If it happens to come along."

Mel nods. "Well, good." She seems unsure. "You're not mad at me, right?"

Bell smirks slightly; the only indication of this while he is wearing his mask are his raised cheeks and the flush across the bridge of his nose. "Not at all Mel. You made a good point. It isn't wise of me to be both inconsiderate and immature."

"Well. *Good.*" She finishes, stares out the open train door a bit herself then leaves.

Bell continues to sit.

⊐⌐

One could be forgiven for over-looking the Maxicilius Orthodox Casino as it resides *below* the lake-town of Celinn; which is its self fifty some kilometres north west of the Great-City Tael. Celinn is surrounded by a dense pine forest. The lake which it is built around is a deep dark blue traced with a constant flicker of a silver shimmer; regardless of the time of day. The buildings of this town are short, dense and constructed almost entirely of cleaned pine logs brushed with a natural staining resin; bestowing upon them a molasses like colour. A single cabin in the town bares the red and gold seal of The Citizenry: the embassy; which is its self a mostly abandoned building staffed liberally for tradition and appearances sake. This is because Celinn is a functional ghost town that exists almost wholly as a passage between the world above and the descending floors of the Maxicilius Orthodox Casino below.

"Bagel?" A vendor on the street offers Bell as he stares out at the town from the edge of the open train door.

Celinn also produces an unreasonably large amount of bagels for a town of its relative small size. The cause for this is indeterminate.

Bell nods and reaches out to accept the bagel. The vendor smiles warmly as Bell quickly takes a deep bite into it. The bagel is warmed with a texture of rustic grains and is filled with a light garlic butter.

The Tristram stops and parks its self near a large set of stone stairs descending in a spiral down a depth to a well guarded door constructed of thick steel; stained onto the door is a square sigil depicting a geometric fungus upon it.

Bell hops off the train and begins walking down the stairs; as the rest of the crew pack up and follow behind him.

As Bell approaches, the guards at the door stand as astutely as they can while adopting kind posture. They are each dressed in homogeneous grey armour with full face masks and sharply angled plate armour. "Hello sir." They both greet. "Do you require any directions or assistance?"

Bell wags his head. "I'll be fine."

"Then please proceed into admissions sir." They reply and wave him inside.

It takes mild effort to cause the doors to open and behind them lays a lobby with an outrageously tall ceiling and more columns of marble then could ever be structurally required. The room is divided in half with the centre being cut by a collection of glass booths where well dressed casino personnel manage entry into the casino's sovereign borders.

"You there." One of the guards points out at Bell. "You and your people have been selected for a random check." He explains.

Bell looks back at the others and they each shrug while maintaining eye-contact. The guard leads the group to what appears to be a wall; the guard knocks on the wall three times and it opens; revealing a room without windows and walls of polished steel. The room is a hall which has an iron cage in the centre of it bridging passage between either side. The guard unlocks one side of the iron cage and motions with his hand for *The Crew* to enter. Inside the cage are two wooden chairs, a kitchen table with multiple scuffs on its legs and a thick roll of leather hanging over each side as a cover on top.

"Weapons on the table." The guard informs as he locks the cage from the inside.

"Should we be worried?" Mel whispers to Howarth.

Howarth barely moves but seems confident in his eyes. "We *should* be fine." He reassures her as he retrieves a long dagger with an aged leather sheath from behind his belt and places it on the table. Each of the members from the crew produce at least a single weapon. Ylinia finds it difficult to part with *Bumble* while Bell doesn't allow Ehre to leave his sight; forcing himself even to go without blinking as the blade sits still on the table.

The guard rolls the leather from the table over each of the weapons and then carries the bundle of steel to the locked door on the other side of the cage. The door on the other side of the hall opens and a large group of individuals enter; each dressed in an identical black leather armour and mask. Four of the individuals dressed in black leather wield heavy crossbows which they have pointed at the crew in the cage. The guard is let out of the cage and the door is quickly locked behind him. He places the bundle of wrapped weapons against the wall, nods at one of the people in black leather and leaves without looking back.

"Bell." One of the people dressed in black speaks accusingly.

Bell stands and walks over to the very edge of the cage. "What?"

"Are you aware that debts can never be destroyed?" The same person asks; his voice is gravelly and young.

Bells nods. "Sure am."

"And as debts are passed on to the next of kin. So are the wrong-doings." The man pauses for a moment and stares at Bell. "Your wife, Temple. She murdered our heir and left the canon of our leadership to become corrupted by new faces."

"Was your heir a dick?" Bell asks casually.

"How *dare you?!*" The man objects.

Bell shrugs. "I just mean. She never had the patience for that sort. *And.*" Bell motions his hands around the room to put focus on the circumstance. "If you're pulling stunts like this? I could see where she was coming from."

The man looks back at his comrades and the small portion of visible brow behind his mask furrows. "Finish them off. I want this room clean in case we have another entry get flagged."

The crossbows each fire loudly at Bell. He shields himself with his arm and ends up with three thick crossbow bolts pierced halfway through his forearm; while another glances across his ribs and smashes to splinters on the floor. With a quick burst of strength Bell places his hands within the iron bars of the cage and bends them away from each other; creating a wide gap. Bell casually steps out of the cage as the identically dressed people each draw a short black blade; throwing their crossbows to the ground if they are holding them. The swords are poised at Bell but only wag in his general direction. With a swift swing of his fist Bell smacks off the heads of the bolts stuck in his forearm and pulls out the remaining portions from behind; a few clots of viscera fall to the ground as new flesh is spun from within the wounds.

"What the hell?" One of the sword-wielders states fearfully; he stares back at the one who was speaking to Bell at first. "I thought he was just some dude?"

"He is your *objective* you whelp. Don't question me during an operation." The leader scoffs back at him.

Bell cracks each of his knuckles and flails his arm a bit; adjusting to it again. "So I'm gonna go ahead and guess you're not precisely a *governing* agency are you?"

"We're from the Narvellien Recollections Guild." The leader answers then reaffirms the grip on his blade. "And we're going to complete our duty." He charges forth and stabs forwards with both of his hands on his blade. Bell side-steps the blade, grabs the man's wrist and then quickly punts the face of the sword with his palm; projecting it out of the leader's grasp and half of its length into the floor. Bell maintains his grasp on the man's wrist, twists his arm then snaps it cleanly at the elbow and shoulder; allowing him to fall to the ground in shambling pain. Bell firmly places his foot on top of the man's back.

"Where is this *guild* you hail from?" Bell asks the crowd of Narvelliens; each of whom are frozen in place staring down at their dismantled leader.

"Floor three oh five." One of the Narvelliens answers. "SE quadrant. We own the *Narvellien Hanging Gardens.*"

Bell lets out a huff of mild frustration. "*Thank you.*" He takes his foot off the leader. "How legal is your operation?"

One of the Narvelliens shrugs. "Depends on how many people hear about it."

"I mean is it sanctioned? If one of the cardinals was to catch wind of this. Would you have a whole herd of inquisitors down your neck?" Bell further explains his inquiry.

"Not *that* legal." The Narvellien replies. "We have a right to pursue any debt owed to us. Using a weighed amount of force dependant on the size of the debt."

"Dude, shut up." Another of the Narvelliens shouts.

"Should I?" The other argues back. "Or do you just like working *in the black?*"

Bell steps towards the cage and forces the door open. He points at the bundle of weapons against the wall and nods at Howarth; who quickly makes his way over and retrieves the weapons; distributing them appropriately. "So here is what we're going to do. You're each going to lay on the ground, chin to the floor and wait for the inquisitors to come take you to prison. *Then* we'll all walk away from this relatively alright." Bell stares at each of the Narvelliens with an unblinking glance. "But know this. You exclusively owe your life right now to the sovereign status of the casino. If I catch wind of any of you, or even some unlucky bastard wearing your cute team uniform on my side of the border. *I'll be coming.* Understood?"

Each of the Narvelliens relieve themselves of their weapons and drop to the ground prone. None speak; but it is easy enough to imagine a shared chorus of the acknowledgement "*Understood.*"

Within moments a squad of inquisitors arrive: the official guard of the Maxicilius Orthodox Casino. They wear rimmed hats, blue scarfs and armoured jackets similar in design to a naval officers. The commander of the squad introduces himself diligently to Bell. "We apologize profusely for this transgression, *erm*." The leader looks up and down across Bell's armour but is unable to discern any obvious rank from it. "*Sir?*"

"Sir is fine." Bell allows.

"Sir it is. I am Commander Yung. These *insects* have been the bane of my organization for the past few months." Commander Yung waves his hand with fury in no specific direction.

Bell watches as the inquisitors attach multiple different cuffs and restraints to each of the guild members whom are then stacked onto carts like barrels and taken away as prisoners. "Criminals of that sort. They're like mice. In the walls. Scavenging around on the opposite side of the room simply because that is where you aren't. I understand the sort."

Commander Yung chuckles a bit to himself. "They do scurry much the same. They must be fucking like em too because there seem to be more every time I poke my head back in to check." He huffs.

"Well, I do wish you the best in your upheaval. But I must admit. None of this was the business I had expected to attend too. We have arrived to attend to the trade of our Erkdwu." Bell explains; attempting as best he can not to sound rude.

"Of course." Commander Yung states apologetically. He points his hand in the air and spins it in a tight circle. Instantly three of the members of his squad rush over towards him eager to take an order. "This group. Fast track their entry. Upscale their accommodations to the five hundred and twentieth floor. *The Piazza*."

Each of the three inquisitors nod in comprehension. "Yes sir." They break and lead the crew from The Tristram directly into the casino. There they are quickly logged into the border admissions and brought alongside all their luggage down through the many floors of the casino. While walking the streets Courtney and Ylinia stare with wonder at the various lights, fires and displays of entertainment and skill which litter the casino floor. There are many street performers with musical or magical skills; each silently begging for the same thing.

Each set of ten floors within the casino have their walls coded with a specific colour or pattern which is continued throughout the set in a shifting saturation of colour. The first floor of the casino features solid golden walls which progressively become darker as one proceeds to the tenth. The eleventh floor features dark golden walls with white strips that progressively become lighter as they descend towards twenty. These designs vary and become quite detailed in some of the deeper levels.

While there is a depth of design variation; there are only ever a maximum of three individual colours used on any set of floors. Within a set of floors there is little variation in the sort of business or games which have flourished there. However the set immediately following a rather conservative or humble one may be incredibly hedonistic or shameless.

Many of the floors favour the style of thick marble columns, tall ceilings and wide streets; intricate carvings are common among the buildings with many featuring needlessly complex details alongside other additions all in the pursuit of *gilding the lily*. While the floors change slightly in size they are all relatively half a kilometre long by half a kilometre wide; with ceilings of the same relative height.

The five hundred and twentieth floor is long past the point of exclusivity. The three hundredth floor is the first floor which restricts access to general tourists or citizens. To progress past the three hundredth floor one is required to have stored in a bank at least three thousand fuergl caps. It is also past the three hundredth floor where there are passages that skip through many sets to lead directly to deeper or unique floors which can only be entered by specific individuals.

The walls of floor five hundred and twenty are a deep dark blue with a pattern of waves and jewels.

The crew are led to a luxurious property known as *The Piazza*. The Piazza has a tall white metal fence surrounding it. The property features an introductory courtyard with a few small fountains, statues of various historical figures and a flourishing botanical garden spreading about between the various columns leading up to the main entrance of the building; its self covered in vines and flowers. Within the building is the strong smell of vanilla and sandalwood. The furniture and decorations all match the same white and pale green colour scheme.

The three inquisitors which led the group here nod in unison towards Bell. "You should be safe here." One of them reassures. "And Cardinal Smythe will be joining you shortly. We apologize for the traumatic start to your trip here and we extend with our deepest apologies the benefits of this room, and floor, free of any debt for an entire week." They nod again. "We hope it will begin to make amends for the transgression you have suffered."

"It helps. *Thank you.*" Bell replies before staring at them silently while they leave.

"You two made friends everywhere you went eh?" Howarth jokes.

Bell nods affirmatively. "Naturally." His eyes search the top of his head for a moment. "Temple was given authorization to take lethal action whenever and *wherever* she saw it as required. She could have discovered something about their leader and deemed him too much of a risk to the general population."

"If she were given such an authority. Wouldn't she be absolved of any earned debts incurred as a result of performing her duty?" Howarth questions.

"If the debt was assumed through normal means?" Bell shrugs while speaking. "*Sure.*" He chuckles. "*But.* This debt is really just some idiots coming up with a justification to *get even.*"

Courtney raises her hand. Everyone stops, looks over and then Bell nods at her. "*Okay.*" Courtney attempts to gather her strength. "Not that I mind talking about what happened but *I'm really excited to actually go check things out do you think that would be okay?*" She states in a break-less flurry.

"Go on Court." Bell speaks permissively. "Just don't leave the floor without company, alright? I know it feels like a theme-park. But it is just as much a city. Be on the look out."

"Of course. Ylinia will come with me, right?" Courtney asks while staring at Ylinia.

"Sorry. But for now. I actually need her." Bell counters.

"Oh?" Courtney, Howarth and Ylinia all respond simultaneously.

Bell nods. "The Narvellians. I want to pay them a visit. I think it would provide a unique lesson." He explains himself.

"And what is this lesson?" Ylinia questions.

"Let us say, *conflict resolution.*" Bell answers.

"I'll come along with you dear." Mel offers to Courtney. "Alim, Lance. Would either of you like to join?"

Alim looks over at Lance and the pair nod collectively. *"Sure."* They each answer.

"Will you be alright to manage the trade Bell?" Mel asks.

Bell smiles and plops himself down onto a long sofa. "I think I'll manage."

A portion of the crew leaves. Now only Bell, Howarth and Ylinia remain within The Piazza. They stare between themselves for a few moments before Ylinia rushes off to walk around the property.

"Don't stray for too long." Howarth asks of her as she leaves.

"Of course." She replies with whimsical charm.

Bell stares over at Howarth. "Have you ever met a cardinal before?"

"Nope." Howarth replies. "You?"

Bell shakes his head. "Nope."

Howarth looks surprised. "No shit?" He chuckles slightly. "I totally had you pegged as the sort who'd met every kinda person there is to meet."

Bell groans with slight pain. "Oh no. I'm, uh...an apprentice when it comes to meeting folks. Amongst my instincts, *that*, isn't really one of them. That feeling that jumps up inside of you and forces you to rush across a room and say hello. I don't have it."

"So your wife *met you* then eh?" Howarth jests.

"We were aligned. Both path and presence." Bell corrects; doing his earnest not to sound rude.

"I should of figured." Howarth remarks with a smile.

A herd of thumping steps can be heard manoeuvring towards the room where Bell and Howarth are sitting. Soon there are twenty some men entering the room each dressed in variations of the same base white, blue and gold robes.

Leading them is the one presumed to be *Cardinal Smythe;* a tall unpleasant looking man who seems unaware of his intimidating disproportions. His robes have obviously been tailored to accommodate his bulging gut in a somewhat flattering manner; using a few lines of gold to make him appear a tiny bit slimmer. He is wearing the hood of his robe down around his wide shoulders. He has a beard which is fuzzy, short and white just the same as the hair on his head. In his right hand he walks with a cane that has a large decoratively carved chunk of ruby on the very top of it; the cane attacks the ground with a high pitched scrap after each of his steps. He coughs, loudly and shamelessly; audibly dislodging phlegm. Cardinal Smythe looks behind himself and motions with his head at one of the men behind him. He clears his throat again. The man looks embarrassed then rushes ahead of the crowd.

"Presenting the 9th of his name; Cardinal Smythe." The embarrassed man speaks loudly.

"Oh, *I get it now*." Howarth instantly comprehends something; sharing an immediate and knowing glance with Bell.

"Yepp." Bell agrees quietly with a smirk. He waves towards the cardinal. "*Hey*." He greets.

Cardinal Smythe doesn't immediately know how to react, pauses in his thoughts for a few moments, smiles, *politely,* then ruffles his robe slightly. "Greetings to you both. I apologize. I'm dreadfully behind on my lessons regarding *surface trade*. I haven't a clue what to expect."

Bell smiles, stands and walks over to shake his hand. "It is alright. We, *uh*. Abandon our titles during trades. So that we can do so as equals. It is a rather...nonchalant tradition we hold." He pauses for a moment and stares at each of the orthodox members whom have come to attend the trade. "If you'll abide it."

"You would have me dismiss my flock?" Cardinal Smythe questions with a voice naturally distorted by age.

"The scale is rather unbalanced with so many on your side." Howarth adds. "It feels like you don't trust us."

"Yet you carry weapons and I have upon me only the counter connected to my fuergl bank. Who is truly the one who should be intimidated?" Cardinal Smythe asks in return.

Bell shrugs. "Then let us be quick. You have what you want, yes? The recovery went well?"

"It did. The specimen has been recovered in a wonderful condition. Despite pressing challenges by wildlife. Our designers will be well equipped for this year's exotic exhibit." Cardinal Smythe answers rather pleasantly.

"Wonderful." Bell agrees with an exhale. "So what have you deemed worthy trade of such a great beast?"

"Something we have been tinkering with. Do you remember anything of the *Gailing Blade?*" Cardinal Smythe asks poignantly.

Bell nods in response.

"We never met her. But when the scraps of the war were collected and what remained was given *value*. We came across the treacherous weapon she wielded. An atrocious device. Like a staff with a fan of blades on either side." He sucks on his teeth. "The weapon was immaterial. The design horrendous and likely only viable in combat because the Gailing Blade practised exclusively with the stupid thing. But the metal. It was lighter then anything we had seen before. It moved within a mechanism at lightning speed. With the weapon blade as our initial subject. We created a blend of metal we now call *spark steel*. With this spark steel we have created a defence system for your train. I believe its features will astound you." He smiles widely. "Exclusively yours, of course."

Howarth looks over at Bell. "*Your train, eh?*" He quietly jokes.

Bell rolls his eyes. "That sounds exciting. *Train Armour?*"

Cardinal Smythe wags his finger towards Bell. "Not train armour. That is a primitive way to understand it. A defence system is *more*. It can summon a blade five times the length of a spear faster then you can blink. It can create a plate of shielding instantly to protect from incoming assaults or cover the entire train in the event of a catastrophic crash."

"That is *more* then armour." Bell agrees while trying not to seem impressed. "Then we agree."

"Just like that?" Cardinal Smythe seems shocked.

Bell looks over at Howarth with a stupefied look then shrugs towards the cardinal. "*Yes?*"

Cardinal Smythe laughs deeply. "I see. Well, the surface does not *barter* as we do. You're much more absolute."

"My thing for your thing. *That's the deal*. Trying to argue more for my side or less for yours is just *kinda shitty*. Don't you think?" Bell questions.

The cardinal seems offended but is capable of reigning in his shocked response. "I observe your opinion." He speaks politely then reaches out with his withered hand. "Do you shake in conclusion?"

Bell extends his hand and firmly shakes his with the cardinal's. "We do. Thank you for sharing such fascinating technology."

"Mhmm. Good. We'll install the system onto your train during your stay. I wish you both well." Cardinal Smythe replies then quickly turns to leave. He can be heard speaking in a gallant fashion to his flock as he returns to them.

Howarth looks over at Bell and smiles in a wicked way. "What an ego on that one."

Bell smiles. "They have an aura of personality for sure."

"Do you think we should fear them?" Howarth questions.

"They probably think we should." Bell admits with a shrug. "And we're fine with them thinking that."

Howarth smiles, turns around then looks down a long hallway. "Ylinia!?" He shouts then waits. A few moments pass.

"Dad!?" Ylinia shouts back.

"I think you're heading out soon!" He shouts in return.

"Kay!" She replies.

"So, *conflict resolution,* eh?" Howarth questions Bell.

Bell smirks slightly then looks away with his eyes. "It's the most, *professional* way to make that statement."

"She is going to see what it is you do with that sword, isn't she?" Howarth asks with a knowing inflection.

"She will see which decisions are made simply by virtue of having a blade at your hip." He answers. "The presence of a blade turns the free will of those who notice it into something very divided. It is good for her to see as many renditions of that division as possible." He stands as straight as he can then tidies his jacket. "Eventually she'll start memorizing them, then she can react to them as quickly as she encounters em."

Ylinia appears in a rush and then smiles at both her father and Bell. "Alright, *lets do it*." She enthusiastically declares.

Howarth kneels down to his daughter and gives her a deep hug. "Be safe my love."

Ylinia smiles and hugs her father back; wrapping both her arms tightly around him. "As much as is possible."

Bell and Ylinia wish Howarth a short goodbye then leave. Ylinia has become decently accustomed to walking speedily alongside the inpatient Bell. They have many floors to ascend to reach their destination. Each section of stairs leading between a floor has a wide central staircase and on either side automatic stairs which traverse both up and down. The automatic stairs have exits which one must quickly side-step into to get off at their floor as the automatic stairs typically connect multiple floors. In some passages there are additional sets of automatic stairs which can only be accessed by those who have hoarded enough fuergl caps to be known as a *high roller;* the most revered and holy of civilian statuses within the Orthodox Casino.

Finally they reach floor three hundred and five. Each floor is divided roughly into four quadrants: North-East, South East, North-West, and South-West. The three hundred and fifth floor is a business floor. There are various construction companies located here. Carpet producers, rug weavers, house builders, plumbers and the like. Each of the businesses is relatively small and seems to feature a family sized apartment unit on top. In some of the alleys are clam-shell looking garbage units which lock with large industrial twisting bars of steel. The walls are a blue and green wavey pattern while the light descending from the ceiling is similar to a silver sunlight.

Only a few moments pass as they venture through the South-East quadrant of the three hundred and fifth floor before they find the *Narvellian Hanging Gardens*; a tall building with a stone fence around it. A large bronze sign affixed on the front of the stone wall just next to a steel bar gate reads 'Official Headquarters of the Narvellian Recollection Guild'.

"This seems to be the place." Bell notes obviously.

Ylinia nods. "Pretty spot."

Just inside the fence is a small grass courtyard where there are a few wooden benches. The building its self is a brown-ish purple with dark mahogany wood features. "I guess so, yea."

"Feels kinda weird though. Like, I see the grass. I know this is just a house. But the smell, the feeling in the air. It isn't what you'd expect." Ylinia notes.

Bell nods. "Being this far underground throws your senses off." He sniffs deeply. "Everything is a bit subdued down here until you get accustomed to it."

The pair open the gate leading towards the building and enter the Narvellian Hanging Gardens. Inside is a small lobby which features a few landscape paintings, a nice carpet and a long desk where it appears someone normally would be sitting; the spot is currently empty. Behind the desk is a wide door that presumably leads into the gardens. Bell sniffs deeply and is caught off guard. "It smells, sweet. Do you notice that?"

Ylinia shakes her head. "Just smells like flowers to me."

Bell sniffs again then shrugs. "Must be that." He moves past the desk and pushes open the doors leading into the gardens. The hanging gardens are contained in a large two storey room kept almost entirely open; with only a few crystal columns of support holding up the roof. The room is very humid and features a dense collection of bright flowers and thick vines. Bell holds his hand back towards Ylinia with caution. "Let me just check ahead quickly." He says as quietly as he can before sneaking further into the gardens.

As Bell reaches a circular platform he notices in the depth of the vines are the ensnared corpses of individuals wearing the Narvellian uniform. As he stares longer and harder Bell comes to realize that there are at least sixty corpses hidden entangled within the hanging gardens. Bell snaps back to look at Ylinia where she is held fiercely with a palm over her mouth by a well defined man with dark hair and sunken cheeks. The man is wearing a long red leather jacket with thick black lines patterned across it like fractures in glass. Under the jacket is a dark brown collared shirt with a silk-like texture and

142

leather trousers with studded and re-enforced joints. The room becomes absolutely still as the man maintains eye-contact with Bell.

"I have lost something Bell." The man speaks with a solemn voice. "That essential connection between me and all of *this*. Man, I've just stopped believing." The man chuckles to himself, places his free palm flat against his face and closes his eyes; his grip against Ylinia tightens as he does. "I admit, I...don't really know what else to do with myself. *I feel like a leash less dog*. And oh boy! There is just so much to chase. What will I do if I catch it?" He cackles slightly. "Just chase something new you know!"

"Look, I don't know what you want, But if you just-" Bell attempts to speak but is cut off.

"*Oh no*, that isn't what we're doing here." The man responds. A flash of light fills the room and suddenly an image of the man can clearly be seen within each of the crystal columns around the room; each rendition of the man in the columns is wielding a long and fiercely serrated knife. "You people think you're *gods* because you manufactured an extinction. You're just the wind bashing dust against a barren field taking credit for the creation of an ocean." The man tightens his grip again around Ylinia then stares down at her. "There is always more to lose Bell. Do not think *you* are empty. You will find there is no lack to the pain you can feel. There is no point where the pit stops becoming deeper." The man's voice reverberates from within each of the crystal columns. The man swiftly draws the knife each of his other depictions wields and as Bell breaks into a sprint towards him the man places the blade under Ylinia's right armpit and slashes up. Ylinia's severed arm flops to the ground, she collapses to her knees and each of the crystal columns violently explodes all within the same burst of seconds.

Bell is thrown by the explosion into a wall with intense force; his shoulder breaks the wall and he hits the floor harshly. A loud series of cracks echo through the whole building as the ceiling begins to fail. Without allowing himself to process the pain Bell pushes himself off the ground and sprints towards Ylinia where she is laying on her side shaking consistently; her eyes are distant and her mouth slightly agape.

The man is nowhere to be seen.

Bell picks up Ylinia, grabs her arm and begins rushing out of the building as it concludes collapsing inwards. They rush into the streets with a fierce amount of blood streaming across Ylinia and down Bell's chest. Realizing the degree of the blood-flow Bell stops in his tracks and carefully puts Ylinia on the ground. Without hesitation Bell takes off his jacket and rips out the lining to fashion a wide tourniquet then tightens it around the remaining stump. Her arm has been severed in line with the body and it takes a few forceful attempts for Bell to pinch enough loose skin so that the tourniquet may functionally be tightened. Bell knots a well hidden dagger from his boot into the tourniquet and twists until no length remains. Bell doesn't stop to check how successful his attempt is after tightening the tourniquet before he again has her against his chest in a rush towards help.

A barricade of guards attempt to stop Bell in his sprint and are each scattered across the hallway as he charges through. Bell reaches the five hundredth and twentieth floor in less then three minutes; a series of broken tiles, stairs and walls trail behind him as evidence of his extreme rush. He shoulder bashes the front door of *The Piazza* and immediately enters the kitchen where Mel, Courtney, Lance and Alim are all settling in from their shopping trip. *Chaos instantly fucks the room.*

"What has happened?!" Mel shouts in panic as her daughter is placed onto the kitchen table *beside* her arm.

Bell shakes his head. *"Knife."*

As if a switch has been flicked behind her eyes Mel becomes a being of pure focus. Her speech is monotone, quick and concise. She begins preparing supplies from her bag left on the floor. Bell falls back from the kitchen table; his vision blurring.

Mel quickly produces a large ceramic bowl, a bag of grey powder, a flask of what appears to be a viscous puke green liquid, a few tree roots all of different ages, the skin of some sort of ursine and the sticky fat of an aquatic being. Mel processes and combines each of these ingredients into the bowl then places the bowl on a burner; turning the stove-top on as high as it can go. She quickly examines the severed arm upon the table; discovering that it has been shattered to a point that would hinder even basic function.

Bell slides down against the wall, crooks his head into his shoulder and starts breathing only every other second.

With expert care Mel removes the tourniquet and slathers Ylinia's open wound with the warmed concoction. Ylinia whimpers and screams as the potion soaks into her wound; it dries like instant cement; her bleeding stops entirely.

Bell fully loses consciousness with his last fading memory being Mel covering him in a thick blanket.

CHAPTER NINE

THE FAILURE AT YOUR FEET

Bell awakens in his room on *The Tristram*. The room has been cleaned. Its walls are barren; mind a few production logos printed onto the steel. Other then the twin sized bed there is a wobbly looking night-stand.

The train is currently still.

Sitting across from Bell on a stool is Izelle. Izelle has her back leaned flush against the wall; her eyes sorrowfully locked onto Bell. Bell glances over at Izelle and she instinctively looks away. "I'm sorry." She admits without making eye-contact; her gaze turns to the floor. "There were many variables at play. I thought I had accounted for them all. Obviously I hadn't."

"Who *was* that?" Bell asks.

"That you don't know him by name does not already explain it"? She questions then quickly follows herself up. "I checked up on the Narvellian Hanging Gardens. A few moments after you returned here with your bundle of chaos." She jerks her head as if smacked with something. "*I should of seen it. I should have been able to tell that he was getting too close.*"

Bell rolls over. "Is Ylinia alive?"

Izelle nods firmly. "Almost in better shape then you. She woke up half an hour ago."

"How long was I out?" Bell questions with an absurd and confused inflection.

"A couple of hours. Just short of six I think?" Izelle answers then shrugs slightly. "I only arrived a few moments ago."

Bell struggles to sit up then decides not too. He exhales deeply; a static pinching soreness spreads its self across his chest. "What was his intent?"

"If he has one?" Izelle questions. "I believe he is seeking *us* out."

Bell raises his eyebrow. "Like me and you?"

"Those of us who ended the war." She answers.

"Then he should be chasing down those who searched every cave to slaughter the refugees. He should go against those who invented the poisons we put in their wells. We fought the battles, but the end of the war was chased down by exterminators." Bell aggressively spews his words.

"He doesn't care." Izelle states with a wave of her hand. "Those *exterminators* were no different then farmers preparing their harvest or a rancher slaughtering its cattle. They were just people playing a part in the process; gears moving things along. He doesn't care who cleaned up after the war, he cares about the people who stole victory from his betrayal."

"Me, You. Dii, Saranias. We're going to be hunted now aren't we?" Bell asks solemnly.

"I believe so." Izelle confirms. "We have only one advantage."

"And what is that?" Bell asks.

"I've poisoned *The King*." Izelle states blankly.

Bell stands to his feet, rushes towards Izelle, places his hands firmly against her shoulders and pushes her *into* the wall directly behind her. "*You did what!?*" He does his best to muffle his rage.

"Richard is old! Befallen by a terminal illness. He has no chance of recovery. No doctor, no device. Nothing can extend his life. At least this way, his end will benefit us a chance to fix things. To end the life of this madman." She explains hastily.

Bell lightens up his grip and takes a step back, he looks at the floor and huffs deeply. "I know nothing of such an illness."

"Almost no one does. It must of been one of the few secrets that has properly been kept across the entire Citizenry." Izelle admits.

"Don't you see? Caesar seeks us all alone. To bring us misery, to distract us from our abilities. So that he can take us from this world at our lowest moment. If we are all brought together for an unavoidable circumstance. Something, *sudden*. He will be forced to make a move."

"Mhmm." Bell vocalizes then moves back to the bed to sit at its edge. "When *The Monarch* falls. The greatest of the age will arrive at the footsteps of the Palacia Tranquil; seeking service for their skills. *The Clash of the Crown* begins." He speaks as if quoting something. "Do you think Dii will even listen to your summons? She never has before."

Izelle reaches behind her back and produces a crisply folded letter; she passes it to Bell. The letter is addressed to Bell with a thick golden ink and a royal seal over top. "It is not *my* summon she must listen too."

Inside the letter is a hand-written paragraph personally inviting Bell to attend the clash of the crown as a potential heir. It is signed by '*The King: Richard Nio*'. Bell looks up at Izelle with a somewhat hysteric look in his eyes. "This isn't even the ceiling of how far you're willing to go, is it?"

"There is no *ceiling*. It is an ever ascending height matching whatever I must conquer. That is why I am here in the first place. That is my *real* skill." Izelle admits shamelessly. "It was consensual. If that makes you feel any better."

Bell stares at Izelle for a few moments before deciding that it doesn't much matter if she's lying. "Are you amongst those selected by The King?"

Izelle nods. "I was within his initial batch of *obvious* choices. As were you."

"Of course." Bell responds. He looks around the room and then places his elbows on his knees. "Is anyone out there mad at me?"

"It comes and goes." She explains. "I'll go speak with them next. I'll explain about Caesar."

"Now the secrecy is gone?" Bell questions sarcastically.

"They are to be the escorts of a royal heir. They get to know a few more things now." Izelle explains simply.

"What will you tell them?" He asks.

Izelle stands astutely then stares out the window at the sun for a moment. "That approximately twelve hours ago. Our King passed away. You have been selected as a potential heir and have been summoned to Caelzun on the authority of The King's dying wish to compete for the role of monarch. As they are family, and members of a military transport. They are to be provided a ceremonial promotion to royal escort as they accompany your arrival." She lets out a long breath. "Does that work for you?"

"Mhmm." Bell confirms then closes his eyes and takes a deep breath. "Then just remember to go to the front door. They'll be a bit concerned if you just suddenly appear from my room."

Izelle smirks then rolls her eyes. "*I didn't forget.*" She lies then moves towards the window.

"Oh, and Izelle?" Bell questions and as Izelle turns around to face him he quickly stands and smashes a vial hidden away in his jacket; spraying its contents in the face of Izelle. A light blue substance drips down Izelle's right cheek.

Izelle shrugs in an understanding fashion. "Fair enough." She responds. "I'm surprised you remember how to ruin an agent's mask."

"I never trusted them honestly." Bell admits with a shiver. "Wearing old witch skin as a mask? I understand that there is some pretty serious residual magic in that stuff. But anyone willing to wear *old person flesh* is capable of a bunch of things that freak me right out."

"Honestly the only part about their organization that frustrates me is that it was an intentional decision to never record *how many of them there were*. I have no idea how many agents have remained loyal, how many defected, how many are in the shadows or aren't. You just have to start accounting for everyone and no one being one of them."

Bell sighs loudly. "That sounds super annoying and like it would be a frustrating waste of time."

"You cannot imagine how much that is the case. Don't worry though. I plan on testing everyone in the crew regularly. If anyone is replaced. I'll catch it." Izelle assures.

⊥

Another hour or so passes before Bell finds the will to get out of bed; startled awake by the train beginning its voyage. As he dresses properly and prepares to leave. Mel enters the room the same moment he reaches for the door. She stares at him as he stands there not knowing what to do.

"It isn't your fault." Mel opens up with the statement. "Ylinia and Izelle have explained thoroughly. Without knowing he was coming, there was nothing you could of done."

Bell has a few tears quickly fall from his eyes. He flops forwards a bit and wraps his arms around Mel. "Thank you." Seconds pass as the pair share a deep hug. "I'm so sorry." Bell apologizes directly to Mel in a quiet voice.

"Don't be." Mel insists. She breaks the hug and stares at Bell firmly. "I love my daughter. I would never wish misfortune on her for any reason. I strive to protect her the best I can because of that love. But she is human. Humans can lose arms and they can be shot dead.

I've seen too much of the latter to not be glad I only have to address the former." She nods towards Bell. "You understand?"

Bell suffers a few weirdly rapid smirks then shuffles in place a couple of times. "*Still*, thank you."

Mel rolls her eyes. "Ylinia wants to see you, when you're ready."

"I'll go do that." Bell answers politely. He quickly sneaks past Mel in the hall and does his best to reach Ylinia's room without being detected by any of the others. Bell knocks on the door three times as quietly as he can without making it inaudible.

"Come in." Ylinia answers.

Bell quickly moves through the doorway and closes the door to a splinter behind him. "I'm glad you're okay, I can't begin to say how-"

"Shut up Bell." Ylinia cuts him off. "Don't you come in here presuming anything has changed." Ylinia sits up straight in her bed of white and red linens. Her room is small, longer then it is wide and very tidy. There is an ascending wall of shelves on one side of the wall that is covered with trinkets glued down strictly in display; little figures, castings of soldiers and the like. Ylinia is dressed in a long, thick, beige dress which has the right sleeve sewn over; bandaging presses against the seams of the stitching obviously.

"I, *uh*. That wasn't what I was saying?" Bell responds; unsure of the tone he should even adopt.

"But it would be, a few sentences later. That's what happens Bell. Something bad happens and people clamp down. But that won't help me. If he wants to take my other arm, and I can't do anything about it. *You might as well just cut the fucking thing off right now*." Ylinia states sternly without breaking eye-contact.

Bell takes a step back, smirks, then reclaims his lost ground. "You're right. We'll need to develop a very unique style for you. A style with Bumble that will prove unpredictable in the eyes of any foe." He nods. "We'll work on that as soon as you are ready."

Ylinia smiles dearly then closes her eyes and lets out a deep breath. "*Good.*" Her shoulders drop a bit and she relaxes. "I might just need a few days."

"Of course." Bell allows. "A few days, then straight to a routine. We've wasted enough time already." Bell takes a few steps closer and sits at the edge of Ylinia's bed. "Are you not the slightest bit upset?"

"It sucks Bell. I remember what it was like so clearly to have something in this place. It still feels like it is there when I am not looking." She admits then quickly takes a deep breath; releasing it aggressively. "Just that doesn't matter. I'm not interested in my misery. I'm interested in getting somewhere better." She smirks. "I don't imagine I'll get there sitting around thinking about how much it sucks."

Bell motions his shoulders in agreement. "I have to say I'm glad you think that way. But I have to admit, it's odd that you do."

"Why is that?" She asks honestly.

Bell shrugs. "Because almost no one does. All the logic in the world doesn't mean anyone is going to actually do what they believe. Most people just think what they believe."

Ylinia adopts a condescending expression. "Well that seems pretty useless to me."

"Useless to everyone, actually. But again, glad that you see it that way." Bell compliments.

A moment of silence passes.

"So I got to meet Izelle." Ylinia notes cheerfully.

"What'd you think?" Bell asks cautiously.

"She's a bit of a dork." Ylinia answers.

Bell breaks out in a loud laughter.

Ylinia smiles herself. "I just mean, she's *so* intense. It's almost a bit absurd. Like, she's gonna try to eat something and chew through her fork."

"The joke back in the day was that eventually she would go to the bathroom and find diamonds in the bowl from all the pressure in her gut." Bell explains with a silly laughter. He takes a few moments to catch his breath. "She's an important person though. Like a sister to me, if I had to be honest."

"Shes a target too, isn't she?" Ylinia asks solemnly.

Bell nods. "She is."

"Are you worried about her?" She questions.

"Mhmm." Bell ponders for a moment. "I never used too. I still think I don't. But she once said it to me herself. How realistic is it for someone to do something perfectly a thousand times in a row; and even if they can. What about the thousand and first time?" He shrugs. "I still trust her."

Ylinia nods. "Me too." She bundles up her lips and looks down to where her arm isn't. "She admitted she made a mistake. She explained to me every scenario that could of led to it. What could of been breached in her recon, what piece of intel must of been switched or corrupted. I think that was the only way she could have earned my trust. If she can say '*that sucked, now what*' instead of sorry fifteen times in a row; I know her head is in the right place."

"She is always looking forwards, for sure." Bell stares out the circular window. They are heading north-west. Towards the coastal mountains of Caelzun; the capital city featuring the Palacia Tranquil: an extravagant civic hall. "Will this be your first time to Caelzun?"

"I'm pretty sure." Ylinia answers. "Do you like it there?"

Bell shrugs his shoulders. "Its an alright place. Spent time there when I was *younger*. It was the first, *outside* settlement I ever visited. Though I admit it's a bit too crowded now a days for my taste."

"What do you mean by outside? Is Varyia all indoors?" Ylinia questions critically.

Bell sways his head. "Our homes, buildings and such. They were carved out inside mountains; *yes*. But we spent most of our days in the valleys. There are places so deep in the wilderness that they are beyond accidental discovery. They exist in a lost territory. Varyia resides in such a place. Everywhere else just feels like *outside*."

"Why leave at all Bell?" She asks.

Bell looks down. "Temple heard a rumour about the attacks your people were enduring. The first few skirmishes. Before the curtain of terror had completely been pulled over the country. When the news of a hundred people dying in some heinous massacre still properly surprised you. She felt that she could help." Bell smiles. "She did."

Ylinia smiles at Bell. "You both became heroes."

Bell nods a few times slowly. "Something like that." He smirks and closes his eyes as a few painful memories wash over him. "We did what we could. Because we felt like we could properly make a difference." He lets out a deep breath. "Because I didn't want her to have to do it alone."

"You would of just followed her anywhere, wouldn't you?" Ylinia asks with a warmed smile contained in her cheeks.

"You have no idea how hard it is *not too*. The type of love I felt for her. It is impossible to ignore. It is like holding a hundred pound bag of rocks. The entirety of all of it is just right there, heavy against your chest. You feel it in every step, consider it before you make a single move. Not a moment passes where it isn't in the forefront of your mind. The only difference with Temple was that the weight never bothered me." He laughs a bit. "I'd probably mind the bag of rocks."

"I don't think I can carry too many things now." Ylinia notes without really intending to say so; seeming caught off guard herself.

Bell stares at her shoulder then rolls his eyes around inquisitively. "Maybe not. I've seen some castings. For soldiers. They can't hold weight. But these artisans can put silk and steel together to cover what is left. I know I'd rather armour then a bit of dangling cloth."

"That could be pretty." Ylinia agrees with a suddenly appearing smile. "Maybe a bit of a cape as well. Like something that just goes over this side of my arm. Whatever that is called."

Bell shrugs. "No idea. But yea, we'll find you one. Not many better places to get a suit of armour from then Caelzun. Their smiths have such an overage of high quality ore that nearly everything they make comes out battle resistant. Even the door-knobs."

"I like that idea. I've never had armour before." Ylinia notes with a bit of disappointment.

A large smile grows across Bell's face. "That is a special moment, if I am honest." He stands properly and moves his shoulders into a formal orientation. "When you see every crisp line drawn in steel on your body. When you feel the weight perfectly balanced against your muscle. Every step, despite the constitution it requires, gives you the opportunity to feel powerful. To feel *proper,* put together. It is a sensation once felt you lament losing." He laughs. "It is why so many soldiers, even after their service. Still keep their uniform and blade at close hand. It is like a second skin, worn by the strongest version of who you are. A physical memory."

"Do they make armour in my size?" Ylinia questions naively.

Bell smiles and nods. "Armour doesn't sit on a rack. At least nothing for real use. Imagine the plates of steel in a suit of armour. If one of those plates was a bit too long and instead of covering your hip; it cut into it? You'd bleed to death during a light jog. *No.* Nothing you actually plan on using should be made for parameters other then exactly your own."

Ylinia nods. "Will we have time?"

"Maybe." Bell answers honestly. "We can get the process started as we arrive. The official address for the clash of the crown won't be until everyone has arrived. We don't know how long that will be."

"Who wouldn't come to the funeral of the King?" Ylinia questions curiously; void of patriotic rage.

Bell lets out a deep huff and puts his face in his hands. "Ehhh." He loudly vocalizes. "Have you ever heard of Dii?"

Ylinia sways her head side to side.

"Dii is, a brilliantly skilled knight. She fought under Izelle during the war as I did. While myself and Temple were benefited our abilities from our homeland. Dii gained her advantage via a pair of enigmatic tools known to us as *holy weapons*. She alone was able to endure the power of these tools and in doing so both her hair and eyes have become a complete bright white." He laughs a bit to himself. "Like you can see her glowing in a dark hallway bright."

"And she would not attend the funeral of The King because of this glowing?" Ylinia attempts to clarify.

Bell smirks. "In a way, *I guess?* Since she began wielding the holy weapons. Her focus changed. She saw the requirement for the war. She took part without contention. But she was always looking a million miles ahead of where we were. She believed that the Selemians were a threat best attended to quickly. So we could prepare for and fix *real* problems. When the end of the war neared. Her motivation burned brighter. Everyone else just started to want a break."

Ylinia raises her eyebrow inquisitively. "What does that mean; *real problems*?"

The train rattles a few times. Bell shrugs. "I can't say. Last I heard she was in a spiritual commune. Tending to soldiers who lost their way after surviving the war. Folks who didn't think they'd make it, and those not entirely pleased they did."

"She sounds like a good person then. If nothing else." Ylinia declares. "I don't think she would miss the funeral of a man exhausted by war."

Bell tightens his jaw. "I guess we'll see. Won't we?"

Ylinia nods. "We will. And we'll train soon too, right?"

"Of course." Bell confirms. "As soon as you're ready." He smirks. "Maybe a little bit before then." He jokes.

CHAPTER TEN

CLASH OF THE CROWN

Caelzun is a massive city and the host of The Citizenry's navy. The bulk of the city is built on top of and in-between two large ranges of round mountains; overlooking a long light blue salted ocean.

Due to its location along the western coast of The Citizenry; Caelzun was able to avoid the bulk of terror attacks during the war. While there were a handful of disastrous events which have transpired within the city; few are detested as much as the bombing of Semsori Tower. An elite unit of Selemian terrorists had infiltrated the city and planted a series of bombs around one side of the tower. As they caused it to fall down on its supports and crash into a nearby market; they opened up fire with stolen astaria firearms. The death toll was estimated around eight hundred; some of the corpses were too disfigured under the rubble to be properly identified. The bombing was executed by four men; their names have been intentionally hidden from history. As the city recovered it modelled its morale in the image of an ever resilient stone giant; enduring all suffering so that it may achieve an end to its day.

The Tristram is welcomed into the city. The train has been fitted with an inaccessible fourth train car; it contains the defence system invented by the casino. The war-train is led into a hanger then onto a large elevator. The train ascends a single floor below the surface of the mountain and is parked in place alongside a variety of other military transports within a well guarded garage. Bell huddles next to Izelle; both impatiently rush out of the vehicle and walk into the centre of the garage. Bell takes a deep whiff of the cold garage air into his lungs.

"That smell of cement. You can feel it on the tip of your nose how chilled the stone is. How, *still* this room is." Bell comments nostalgically.

Izelle closes her eyes and smiles slightly. "There wasn't an op that ever went bad when we set out from Caelzun. I remember being so scared one day we'd come across the one that breaks that record. That finally some day it would just be another place we were before something awful happened."

Howarth steps out into the garage himself; his focus fleeting between the crew and the collection of off road vehicles, armoured transport vessels and motorcycles spread across the garage. "What's with all of this?" He asks no one in particular.

"This is a military parkade. All these vehicles must be owned by people coming to attend the funeral." Izelle guesses.

"How many people have been notified of the funeral?" Mel asks as she joins the rest of the crew standing about.

Izelle shrugs softly. "Not many, *yet*. Various civic leaders, members of the military. I imagine a few guild heads as well; certainly the civic engineers. Word will travel through these people. They will be able to speak to the topic much more comfortably then we ever could through some mass bulletin."

The crew is approached by a young attractive man with long thin black hair and multiple layers of green trench-coat; underneath he wears a grey military officer's uniform. He extends his hand out formally towards Bell. "My name is William Lierre, pleased to meet you heir."

Bell raises his eyebrow. "How did you know?"

"How did I not?" William replies very factually. He quickly greets each member of the crew with a polite nod and a two-handed handshake. "Now, Bell. I will be your consul for your time in Caelzun. Any administration you require, messages sent, tasks achieved, training equipment prepared. Simply speak to me and I will be happy to assist you."

"They have taken an officer from his post to help me sharpen my blade?" Bell questions.

"The chief *requisitions* officer, sir. One who quite enjoys his position." William corrects without assuming offence.

Bell nods. "As it is then. Have we been provided housing?"

"Of course. A lovely hotel, our finest, known simply as *The Ivy Lodge* will gladly attend to each of you as cherished guests." William informs him with delight. "I admit, I am rather jealous. The lodge is legendary. Bookings are held months in advance. You and the other heirs have all been given a place in the *Royal Wing*. They keep it closed until just these sorts of circumstances arise."

Courtney lets out a loud excited noise and rushes up towards William. Ylinia follows close behind her excited friend. "What is the Ivy Lodge like? Does it have private chefs? *Can I get a massage!?*"

William smiles and nods politely. "I believe that some of the best chefs and masseuses have been trained at the Ivy Lodge. It is a place with impeccable standards. But for those that wish to truly challenge their skills; it is a platform unchallenged in prestige."

"I stayed at the lodge once myself." Alim speaks to the group. "A conference. I believe we were discussing the available options to reasonably accommodate those who had lost their careers to the automatic machines in our factories. Fascinating topic, I do recall the service as being beyond superb."

"The reputation of such a place *should always* precede it, don't you think?" William asks knowingly.

Alim smiles and nods. "Of course, what fun is there otherwise?"

"If you are all agreed to it, I have procured transport for us to the hotel. If you'll follow me please." William motions with his hands towards a smaller personnel elevator built into the wall of the stone parkade.

The crew all follow along and enter with William. He presses a button with a depiction of a circular sun upon it then takes a step back; relaxing his hands over top one another as a guard would.

The elevator raises at a steady pace that seems the slightest bit faster then it should be. No one speaks in the elevator. The glass walls of the elevator become windows as they breach the surface of the mountain and all around them surrounds the beauty of the land. On one side is an ocean of hundreds of shades of blue that stretches beyond sight; the other features a sprawling lively forest that leads to a breadth of continent covered in plains and mountain.

Squares of land have been carved out of the mountaintop so that the grass, trees and buildings that reside here now may stand. The summit of Caelzun displays a city of strong metal homes, various spiralling staircases carved across its terrain and powerful gusts of freezing wind.

A few steps from the exit of the elevator is a long windowless armoured vehicle. It features eight wheels and appears similar to the carapace of a lobster in design. A loud whir of electrical motors is heard as a side panel of the vehicle opens. William stands next to the opening and guides the crew inside.

The vehicle has been renovated from its original purpose as a military vehicle. The various bus style seats are now made of a polished leather instead of the metal they would have been previously. Each member of the crew cautiously takes a seat. Behind each seat is a shaded window made of one sided glass that mirrors metal from an outside perspective; it has been constructed to be resistant to both ballistic and explosive assaults.

William follows in after the crew and closes the door behind himself with rapid muscle memory. He knocks on the front facing steel plate wall and the vehicle begins driving.

Courtney raises her eyebrow and looks over to Howarth. "Do these things drive themselves?"

Howarth smiles but shakes his head. "As cool as that would be? Unfortunately not. There is an operator inside there. He enters from a hidden doorway that is automatically locked from within once he engages the vehicle. Once inside he is basically untouchable. He has an independent roll cage, high grade defences for any sort of resistance. All he has to do is focus on taking care of the people behind him." Howarth takes a deep breath and smiles. "As it should be, in all fairness."

William smiles. "The operator of this vessel is well trained. One of Teander's star pupils at the academy."

The roads built across the mountaintop range from wide and structurally sound to small wiry paths that instantly induce an active concern for ones well being. The operator is able to navigate through them without the slightest of concerns. Through the windows most of the crew are mesmerized by the beauty of the glimmering ocean. William smiles pleasantly in the silence as they travel to the Ivy Lodge.

They arrive at the bottom of a long winding road which leads into a fenced off property. The entrance is guarded by a military installation and closed off by a tall steel gate. The vehicle pulls up close to the guards and the top of the side panel door opens up. William pokes his head out of the vehicle and waves towards the guards then sits back down. A moment passes before the gate opens and they proceed to drive up the winding road.

"Welcome to the Ivy Lodge." William introduces as they reach the plateau of the winding road to gaze upon a beautiful forest of bright white birch and crooked sprawling yew. At the end of a very clean cobblestone road is a pink and white four storey palace cleanly displaying the title *Ivy Lodge* near its front entrance.

"It looks beautiful." Ylinia notes.

"It does." Mel agrees with an absolute smile.

Howarth leans towards his wife and places his hand around her back; moving it in a few soft circles. "Remember when we first met, and I promised I would take you here?"

Mel rolls her eyes sarcastically. "That was fifteen some years ago. I think this is called *ending up* here. Unless you planned this all along?"

Howarth laughs. "If only I were so maniacal." He pats her back before returning to his seat properly. "You seem a bit shocked over there Lance. You alright?" He asks courteously.

It takes a few seconds before Lance clues in that he is being spoken to. He shakes his head and looks over at Howarth. "Oh, I'm perfectly well. Thank you Howarth. I'm just, *very* pleased to be coming here. It has always been a dream. I spent three summers in Caelzun during my oil painting phase." He chuckles as he recalls that point in his life. "I found that the ocean can just take you away, if you let it. Just by staring and letting your mind become closer to the waves; you become one." He rolls his shoulders musically. "And you just *roll*."

Alim smirks widely and gives a devilish look to his husband. "We'll have to do so. I hope we can see the ocean from our suites?" He attempts to passively question William.

"Oh of course." William assures. "Each of you will have a balcony facing the ocean. A lucky few will have corner rooms that have both ocean and mountain views. But I must say there isn't a bad vantage point in the whole wing."

They stop right outside the front door of the Ivy Lodge and are met instantly by porters; they take whatever luggage is present and place it on a decorative iron cart. The crew are led through the hotel amidst an almost overwhelming supply of hellos, welcomes and general introductions.

Every one is given a key to their room. Howarth, Mel and Ylinia each share a suite. Alim, Lance and Courtney each share a suite and Bell is given a large corner studio apartment all to himself.

Bell walks out onto his balcony as the attendant who guided him to his room leaves. The ocean is so wide and so constant that it almost doesn't appear real. As if it is a very successful illusion cast out across a large empty plain. Yet as any real thing does; the ocean simply exists. An immeasurable amount of time passes before there is a knock at Bell's door. "Come in!" Bell shouts from the balcony.

William opens the door from the other side and enters swiftly. He shuts the door behind himself and walks out onto the balcony with Bell. "Are you enjoying the suite Bell?"

"Of course." Bell admits. "Anyone who wouldn't enjoy this is just lying to be an asshole." He chuckles a bit to himself as he answers.

"You would be surprised what some people will let themselves complain about." William states with an intense lack of patience in his eyes. "Do you mind if I smoke?"

Bell shakes his head and motions his hand permissively. "Give er."

"Would you like one?" William offers as he produces a small metal case and a well used bronze pocket lighter.

Bell shakes his head again. "No, *thanks*."

William opens up the metal case and removes from within a single long cigarette; which he places in his mouth. As a small switch is held on the lighter a steady crackle of electricity projects from the top of the device. William sucks the electricity into the tip of his cigarette and it ignites quickly. He takes a long drag and expediently exhales it. "I admit Bell. It is nice to properly meet you. It has felt to me like you are a character from a storybook for far too long."

Bell raises his eyebrow. "What do you mean by that?"

"I was responsible for organizing the paper trail of your military career. Before I made officer, I spent a lot of time as an archivist." William explains.

"I feel like I should apologize for my file. I didn't know the war was destined to last as long as it did." Bell states regretfully.

William smiles. "You have nothing to apologize for. Were it not for you and Temple leaving Varyia to aid our cause. The five hundred year war might have been the thousand."

Bell adopts a serious expression and stares at William. "You know of Varyia?"

"Only from what I have read. Were I not living in a world shaped by one of its people; I would not have believed it existed." William answers.

"Fair." Bell admits. "You said that if I needed anything you would be able to help me out?"

"Of course." William states.

"The young lady, Ylinia. You no doubt saw that she is missing an arm." Bell states bluntly. William doesn't react. "This was a recent loss. She has no clothing properly tailored to accommodate this."

"I'll have a tailor to her at once. I imagine she'll be attending the gala? I'll have a suitable wardrobe prepared for her." William notes.

Bell nods. "Good, then after that. An armourer. Send both here when Ylinia is done with the tailor."

"An armourer? For such a young lady?" William questions with concern.

"The best you can find." Bell affirms. "And don't refer to her as young. She is the least bit a fan of her age determining her presence."

William nods rigidly. "Noted." He looks out at the ocean briefly then back to Bell. "I'll be sure to have them both on their way as soon as possible." He lets out a deep exasperated noise.

"Is there something else?" Bell inquires.

"I have been informed that Dii still has not been heard from. She has a week before her absence disqualifies her status as an heir." William explains.

"Does she know that?" Bell asks casually.

William shrugs. "I'd imagine so. It has been the standard for generations."

Bell smirks. "Then we will see her in six days and roughly twenty three hours." Bell sways his head. "She prefers being somewhere exactly as she is required. Not immediately as she is requested."

"What if they are one in the same?" William asks with a concerned look on his face.

"She was always able to tell the difference." Bell admits. "*Somehow.*"

They both stare out at the ocean for a few moments; a large transparent whale leaps out of the waves in the distance, spins in the air then dives deep back down into the swaying blue. Both men smile as the sea swallows up the dispersed water and soon the waves appear no different then they had been before.

William steps back from the balcony and nods towards Bell. "Then I'll be away. I'll return with the lady Ylinia and an armourer of the highest quality." He snubs out the last bits of his cigarette with his fingers then stuffs the remaining filter into his coat pocket.

"Thank you William. I appreciate that." Bell states kindly; maintaining firm eye-contact as he speaks.

"Of course." William responds before taking his leave.

Bell gazes out at the ocean. He can hear Howarth and Mel on their own balcony raving pleasantly about the view. Bell smiles but doesn't announce his presence. Every reflection across the ocean flickers in varying hues of yellow and orange; the deep blue below sways through this palette. Salt is in the air. Birds flutter and squawk in the distance. The sum of all of this is that at the end of your deepest breath; there is no dire rush to let it out; you just let the next come as it may.

___JL___

Bell is curled up in a ball on the couch in his suite's living room. Both his mask and Ehre are on the coffee table; he has pulled the coffee table right up to the side of the couch so that it is no distance from him. Three solid knocks on the door cause him to wake in an instant and re-equip himself with the mask and blade. He strolls over to the door and opens it wholly.

Standing behind it is a tall man, notably lean and well dressed in a tailored suit of black silk. His hair is short, combed and gelled. He wears a long, thick black beard that stretches down to his hips with thick knotted braids. He extends his hand authoritatively; revealing deep dark runic tattoos across his hands and wrists. "*Silas Mendrivo*, Master Armourer." Bell shakes the man's hand. Standing behind Silas is Ylinia. She is thumbing through a thick book with illustrations of various styles of historical armour. "May we begin?"

"Of course." Bell allows; feigning a full and attentive consciousness. "Come on in." He nods towards Ylinia as she enters and she smiles back at him.

"I admit, I've never created armour for such a light frame. None the less with metal plate!" The armourer declares. He pulls the coffee table away from the sofa and into the middle of the room. "Go on, hop up." Silas gestures towards Ylinia.

Ylinia giggles, puts the book down on the edge of the table and jumps up on top of it. "*Here I am.*" She states while motioning her arm awkwardly around at the side of her hip.

"Did you see anything in the book you liked?" Silas questions.

"Eh?" Ylinia answers with a shrug. "It all looks kinda blocky."

Silas nods; considering her feedback genuinely. "Too often a man feels as if the shoulders of his armour are truly his own." He waves his hand in the air slightly then smirks to himself. "It is an inadequacy one cannot cease to see in themselves. An overcompensation of sorts." He smirks again. "That is not a concern I believe you will have. Instead, I believe for you, I must take notes from the dancer."

Ylinia smiles then tilts her head to pose a curious question. "The dancer? Is that another armourer?"

"Not in the typical sense." Silas answers; he speaks while collecting various measurements. "The dancer is an idol. A focus for the artisans of Rion. When a weaver puts a curve in a basket, or a plumber the flow in a fountain. These designs, the fluidity of motion, the connection and transfer of energy. These concepts are governed by the dancer."

"Have you met her?" Ylinia questions.

Silas laughs. "*Oh*, no. I apologize. The dancer can be seen throughout the world. But she is not *real*. She is a concept. A creation to be used as a starting point for thought. I can see through the perspective of the dancer how metal will protect you."

"Then what do you and the dancer see?" Bell asks.

Silas points to the side of Ylinia where she is missing her arm. "There is an inherent lack of balance here. This could be seen as disadvantageous. *However.* If I am now allowed to return an arm's worth of weight to this side of the body. I am able to integrate a shield of sorts. Ylinia noted she wanted something like a cape across her other side. I suppose that we make this cape of scales. We shall mould plates of steel across leather armour. With tidy rigging the weight of this armour shouldn't feel much different from a heavy winter coat."

"Don't go too light." Bell affirms. "She'll be training with a blade. And she should be quick. But I want her to be quick in armour that is going to do something, not something that *should*."

"Of course." Silas confirms. "Do you have a preference for colour my lady?" He asks Ylinia.

She considers audibly for a moment with a monotonous hum. "Black, grey...*annnd*, purple?"

"It will be done." Silas states with a subtle bow. "I will see you both in the future." He leaves quickly; excited by the prospect of a new project.

Bell smiles. "He seems like the positive sort."

Ylinia smiles. She is dressed in a well fitting pair of green canvas pants, black military boots, and an over sized off-white hoodie; the right arm of the hoodie has been professionally stitched closed. Her hair has been combed finely and braided down her back. "I like it honestly. It is like being around *light* energy. It brings you up."

"So how do you feel?" Bell asks as he makes his way over to the kitchen and begins preparing coffee with the provided resources.

Ylinia shrugs. "It is nice here. Caelzun is a beautiful city."

"It is." Bell responds impatiently.

"My shoulders are sore. I keep relaxing them, feeling what isn't there any more; then I tighten up again. Sleeping hasn't been as easy." Ylinia admits these things as if they are weightless.

"Mhmm." Bell vocalizes. "Coffee?" He quickly asks.

Ylinia raises her eyebrow. "Sure?"

Bell makes two cups of coffee and brings them over. He sits on the sofa across from Ylinia. "I knew a woman who lost her arm once. Same one as you actually. Granted she got off a bit luckier, just from half of the bicep down. *Still*, it is a lot to lose. She was a journalist. Brave as anything. She took a few years of training at the Neitheim military academy just so that she could go along with scouting groups and not be a hassle to their operation." He takes a sip from his coffee. "But a squad of boomies raided their camp one evening. Just two nights into a three day recon mission. I mean, you think the explosions are the worst, and sure, they are. But folks forget to mention how deadly the shrapnel can be. She got a few big ol chunks stuck in her and after the seven some hours of field surgery it took to keep her alive; she was glad all she had to lose was the arm."

"That sucks." Ylinia states without really knowing how to reply otherwise. "Did she have issues sleeping?"

"For months after. All she did was lament about the things she couldn't do. She had lost her writing arm and her journalism stopped dead. Her sleep went off, she lost any regimen or schedule to her life. She slipped through her own fingers." Bell admits sadly.

"So what happened?" Ylinia questions with a focused gaze.

Bell smiles widely and shrugs. "She figured she should learn to write with the other hand. As soon as she got back to that. Everything else started to make sense again."

Ylinia stands abruptly and smiles. "My shoulders won't feel better until I actually use them. That is what you're trying to say, isn't it?"

Bell finishes the entirety of his coffee in a deep gulp then stands with Ylinia. "Nothing will ever feel right unless you give it a reason too." He looks towards the door of the suite. "How about we go find William and get some training in today?"

"Absolutely!" Ylinia agrees.

The two leave the suite. They find William speaking to one of the front desk attendants. As William notices them he greets them both.

"Going for a stroll?" William questions.

"Looking for you, actually." Ylinia answers.

William smirks. "Oh, well. Glad to be here. Apologies I didn't accompany Silas. I've just been given word by our border scouts that two heirs are arriving together."

Bell raises his eyebrow curiously. "Who?"

"It appears that Saranias Nicholl has brought Dii with her. They travel together on a small caravan." William explains.

"That fits for Saranias. Though I admit I didn't expect Dii for much longer." Bell states. "Are they the only remaining heirs?"

"All others have arrived. Tonight we shall properly open up the clash of the crown." William notes with a stressed excitement. "The opening will be held in the Lord's Court Market Square at 7. It is imperative that each of the heirs is in attendance."

Bell nods in understanding. "Of course William. We're off to train for a few hours, but on our way back. We'll check in on Saranias and Dii. To insure they intend on going as well."

"Thank you Bell." William states genuinely. "I admit the other heirs are much easier to manage."

Ylinia's eyes open wide. "Who are the others?"

William looks up into his head for a moment before listing off the names. "Well there is Bell here, Izelle as well, Saranias, Dii,

Teander, Bristol, Wvendeiss and Leige. The eight heirs of this clash of the crown."

Bell thinks on the names. "I know a few of them. I suffer no surprise that Wvendeiss is amongst the heirs. Though I admit, maybe I have been on The Tristram for too long. I don't know Teander. I believe we heard his name earlier as well."

"Ah." William notes. "Teander is the Capital Commander of Caelzun. He leads each branch of the military in this district all while presiding over the curriculum of the naval academy. I admit as well that he is remarkably modest. There was no coronation when he gained his title. Despite the traditional celebration; he preferred to get straight to work."

"He gained his rank after the war?" Bell questions.

"A few weeks before the end if memory serves. Mind that he took a pilgrimage and has since been recognized as a master in a few disciplines. He was kept out of active service. Instead he was assigned to a forward looking division that would manage homeland security after the war." William explains.

"Thank you for the information William." Bell remarks kindly then smiles. "Now, I must ask. Do you think it would be possible for us to requisition a few training practice targets?"

"Of course." William takes a map from the front desk and opens it up. "If you just follow the grey stone path to here." He points to a large forest on the map. "You'll end up at a training site the military uses for winter camps. It should be empty and well supplied right now. You're more then welcome to it."

Bell smiles and nods. "*Perfect*, thank you."

"You're welcome. I'll see you both soon." William bids farewell before turning around and reconvening his previous conversation with the front desk reception person.

Bell and Ylinia leave the lodge and quickly find themselves on a grey stone pathway. It leads down a staircase cut from the face of the mountain, through a system of well lit coastal caverns and then into a dense and shadowed pine forest. Following the pathway through the forest ends the pair at a collection of log cabins all placed around a circular arena with a dirt floor. Bell retrieves three of the practice dummies from the shed and places them about two meters from one another in the arena. Each of these practice dummies is made from a canvas sack sewn into the shape of a person, stuffed densely with hay then installed onto a thick wooden rod.

Bell stands in front of one of the practice targets, quickly draws Ehre and stabs forwards with perfect form; piercing the centre of the target and knocking it flat onto its back. He motions to Ylinia and she takes her place in front of one of the standing dummies. She draws Bumble, prepares herself into an amateur's stance and stabs forward; making the first of many inevitable mistakes. Ylinia attempts another stab on the remaining practice target; dropping her arm half way through the piercing attack. Bell straightens each of the targets and they go again.

⎓⏚⎓

The evening grows dark quickly as winter nears. Bell and Ylinia continue their lessons in the centre of the dirt arena; which is now illuminated by a series of encircling braziers. Ylinia has tied her hair back and soaked through her outfit with sweat. She has repeatedly stabbed and wrecked each of the practice targets; one has been severed and lays broken on the ground.

A short distance from the arena a torch can be seen; moving in. It is too dark to determine the bearer; while the flickering flame further obscures the figure. Bell becomes instantly defensive and

173

points his blade out to the approaching torch. "Who goes there?" He questions in the direction of the flame.

"Well an enemy wouldn't have the torch." A soft female voice answers. "But, you know, believe whatever you want." The voice insists.

Bell relaxes and sheaths Ehre. "*Saranias.*" He states calmly. "Did you come looking for us?"

Saranias appears out of the shadows. She is a tall woman with an angular face and contrasting bubbly cheeks. Her hair is a dark brown, very straight and rather long; it is braided tightly down her back in a single strand. She is wearing a long jacket made from a collection of various tanned animal hides; it appears rather heavy. Underneath this jacket is an armoured military uniform patterned with a forest reminiscent camouflage. Saranias is visibly equipped with at least seven different knives across her body; each blade varies in length between four and nine inches. "We came to make camp. Heard the slashing and grunting in this direction." She shrugs. "Wanted to make sure everything was okay. Didn't expect to find you out here with an...*apprentice?*"

Ylinia sheathes her blade, wipes off her hand on her pant leg, smiles and steps forwards towards Saranias. She extends her hand to shake. "My name is Ylinia."

Saranias smiles widely; she shakes Ylinia's hand firmly. "It is nice to meet you Ylinia. How has Bell been as a teacher?"

Ylinia looks over towards Bell and then back to Saranias. "He is fantastic." She chuckles a bit then scratches her head. "Though I admit. I'm just getting used to swinging steel around." She laughs again then strains her back as if it is dreadfully sore. "Shit's heavy."

Saranias chuckles and walks over towards Bell. She throws her arms around him in a friendly hug. "It has been too long brother. I'm glad to see you."

"You as well Saranias." Bell admits; returning the hug.

"Are you from Varyia as well?" Ylinia questions.

Saranias shakes her head. "Our shared family was born through years of mutual experience, loss and triumph. Our blood however couldn't be more different."

"Then where are you from?" Ylinia continues her questioning.

"A community called Rea'liin. It is near the southern capital Antioch." Saranias explains.

"Her and her family are known as the *Jade Tigers*." Bell adds on.

Ylinia looks over at Bell with a fascinated expression. She then stares at Saranias. "I can't say she looks like a cat."

Saranias chuckles. "It is because of the martial art which we practice. Known to us as the *infinite cycle of edges*. This style of fighting uses stealth and a multitude of knives to entirely overwhelm any target. Those that lose to a practitioner of this style are left in a condition that seems very similar to the mauling of a tiger."

"A hundred tiny cuts and one decisive stab to the skull." Bell speaks as if reciting.

"Something like that." Saranias agrees with a sarcastic modesty.

"You said we, when you approached." Ylinia critiques. "Where is the we?"

Saranias smirks at Ylinia. "I did." She looks around inquisitively. "We isssss." She holds the '*s*' in her pronunciation while she peers through the darkness. "*There*." She suddenly points to a random direction deeper into the forest." About a half a kilometre through the forest there is a pale white glow. "You can spot Dii from a city away if it is dark enough."

"Why aren't you guys at the lodge? Surely you were given rooms?" Bell questions.

"Oh yea." Saranias acknowledges. "Really nice rooms, *actually*." She seems a bit disappointed.

"Dii wouldn't stay?" Bell asks with a knowing inflection.

"*Far too lavish for a soldier at work.*" Saranias does her best impression of Dii and her strict focus. "We're making up a camp in the bush for the time being." She looks up at the sky. "The opening is going to be in an hour or so. Should we all go together?"

Ylinia nods enthusiastically. "Absolutely we should!"

The trio pack up the training supplies and head over towards Dii. Dii is a broad shouldered and incredibly fit woman with long thick hair; there are a few intricate braids present throughout the lengths. Both her hair and her eyes glow a bright white. She is wearing complex plate armour that has been painted varying shades of grey and white. Her armour features oversized pauldrons each with three thick spikes. Her gauntlets are large, ornate and constructed out of pure gold. These gauntlets extend down to her elbows and appear to be fastened onto her body tighter then any equipment should be. Dii sits around a small fire-pit she has only recently finished digging out.

Dii looks up at Bell, smirks and then stares at Ylinia. "You've seen work today girl, haven't you?"

Ylinia nods with a heavy huff. "*Lots*, yes." She waves her arm around; emulating a crackling bolt of electricity. "I feel like I just got beat for a few hours." She admits with a chuckle.

"And will you do it again tomorrow?" Dii asks curiously.

Ylinia passionately nods her head and raises her voice. "Absolutely! Near the end of today I was actually kinda *getting it*. You know? I wanna see where I get after tomorrow!"

Dii smiles widely and seems to relax in posture. She stares up at Bell again and then down to her fire-pit. "We all have an event to attend. Do we not?" She stands and stretches her back for a few moments after doing so. "Lets go get it out of the way." She walks over to Bell, shakes his hand kindly and then leads the group in a hike back towards Caelzun.

CHAPTER ELEVEN

CAGES

The Lord's Court in Caelzun's rebuilt market is packed full of onlookers. Cooks and novelty merchants have taken heed and set up their stalls and carts alongside the roads leading the various people towards the grounds. Bell, Ylinia and Saranias follow behind Dii as she carves a path through the crowd with her sheer presence; whether people are moving out of the way because she is glowing or because her shoulder spikes are liable to accidentally take out an eye; it cannot be determined.

There is a wide and tall circular stage which has a stone plate postured upon it; stacks of wood pallets collect in a neat pile upon the plate. At the very top of the pile of wooden pallets is a blanket of red silk obviously concealing something underneath. There is a thin bronze microphone held in place on top of a wooden podium centred on the stage.

William stands on the stage in front of the stone plate alongside Izelle and Teander. Teander is a very tall, very handsome man with thin blond hair and broad well muscled shoulders. His aesthetic appeal is almost annoying in its absolute lack of fault. He is dressed in an entirely white military uniform with blackened plates of metal armour across his shoulders, ribs, hips and thighs.

Teander approaches the microphone and taps it softly; a bass-like sound echoes throughout the area. "It is impressive to see so many here." He compliments the crowd. "To bring this many of our people together, to have safety in our home. It is a truly beautiful thing to bare witness to. I commend you all for standing free." The crowd cheers in response to Teander. "Occasions such as these blur the lines between the world of the past and the one we live in now. While tradition holds that we reveal the purpose of this gathering only once it has began." Teander stares out at the crowd for a moment. "I suspect many of you have learned of its nature elsewhere." Teander takes a deep breath and releases the air forcefully. "The King has passed away." The crowd responds with a mature silence; one which Teander shares for a few moments. "He passed naturally, as naturally as the illness of age can be. At the age of one hundred and forty four, Richard Nio has passed on. He leaves his legacy as a general, soldier and sage of the civic sciences. However, he has not left us without anything. In lieu of his presence, he has recorded a message that has been left undisturbed until this moment."

The speakers built into the base of the stage crackle as they come to life. The voice of The King is heard throughout the festival grounds. "Hello all. I will be brief" Richard breaths heavily. "As my condition has not benefited me much stamina. *We do not live on a safe world*...I have likely only contributed to the harshness of its nature. The peace I have always dreamt of...*is possible*. But not with me. I will die before this goal can be achieved. Each of you here I have selected in my final days as heirs. Your achievements and abilities have all earned you equal right to be present. While I wish you all the best of luck; I want the sole victor to know. We do not live in a world where our monarch may sit on a throne. They must charge ahead with greater vigour then any of our armies; if they are to succeed."

William approaches the microphone; nodding towards Teander as they switch places. William waves his hand in a noble fashion towards the mighty crowd. "Richard Nio was a vigilant leader. He endured his position as monarch without complaint; despite the endless service such a role requires. He always fought for the betterment of the people even if it came at the steadfast disadvantage of himself. Now, he has gifted the title of *heir* to eight of our greatest. It is my pleasure to introduce the heirs of this clash of the crown." He takes a deep breath and smiles out professionally towards the crowd. "I will begin with those already on the stage. Capital Commander Teander; a man who has dedicated his personal and professional life to the benefit of our society and Spy Master Izelle; the tactical genius who orchestrated the end of the Five Hundred Year War. Both entirely deserving heirs." William announces their names pridefully and then looks out to the crowd. Izelle and Teander stand next to one another in a line. "For the remaining heirs, as you are introduced. Please take your place on the stage." A moment passes. "Saranias Nicholl of Rea'liin. An essential special operations member who worked towards the conclusion of the war." William speaks clearly. Saranias takes her place on the stage; momentarily acknowledging the audience. "Leige: Master of the Hunt. Leige is a teacher and warrior who has taught generations of hunters to protect us from the beasts of Rion." Leige takes the stage quickly and modestly. He is a very tall man with thick black hair braided down his back. He wears well maintained leather armour that has multiple latched pockets across it. At his hip he has a whip constructed of woven silver and on his back is a simple steel spear. William continues. "A holy knight and military hero, Dii." Dii joins the stage; intentionally avoiding the eye-contact of every single person in the audience. She stands in the centre of the stage; waves oddly then leaves the stage. William continues on without blinking. "Wvendeiss Silthers. A leading paladin in the southern provinces of the Citizenry. Wvendeiss has been fighting horrors on our behalf for fifteen years." Wvendeiss walks onto the stage and nods towards the audience; whom cheer back to him. Wvendeiss wears bright white full-plate armour with a few dull accents of yellow across the torso, shins and helmet. His long-sword is concealed within the tower shield he currently is wearing on his back. "Blade-Master Bell." Bell walks towards the stage slowly; not entirely excited about the upcoming spotlight which is to be thrown onto his face. "One of the great

warriors who allowed us to end the Five Hundred Year War." Bell
steps onto the stage, waves towards the other heirs lining up and then
raises his eyebrows attentively towards the crowd. William smiles and
looks back to the crowd. "Finally, we have Bristol. An advance scout
and master archer; she single-handedly held the Hou-Lao sea-fortress
against an army of Selemian invaders one thousand strong. Had she
failed, Caelzun its self would have been overrun in days." Bristol
walks in a way that is entirely seamless; she doesn't waste a moment
or motion. Her hair is short, her face angular. She wears a tight leather
suit of armour which has thickened steel plates across her shoulders,
hips and thighs. She takes her place amongst the other heirs without
hesitation and smiles towards the audience. William raises his hand
and motions it towards each of the heirs. "Soon one of these
exemplary citizens will become your monarch."

Izelle walks up behind William and touches him on the
shoulder. He smiles and allows her to take his place in front of the
microphone. Izelle waves in a small motion towards the audience.
"The clash of the crown has existed nearly as long as The Citizenry its
self. When we were just a hundred tribes of people scattered across
the plains of creation. It was this ceremony that decided which among
us is best suited to speak for the people, to fight for the people, to look
forwards for the people. There is no doctrine of noble blood." She
speaks solemnly and stares out towards the crowd. "Yet we are still a
noble people. We are a society that has forgotten what it is to properly
celebrate. We are a people that has forgotten what it looks like to wear
something regal without the bulge of armour underneath. It is because
of this I wish to revitalize an aspect of the clash of the crown that has
only been spoken to in previous years. *The Swan Gala!* A festival
celebrating all the fantastic things we can create. Both our culinary
and technological prowess will be on display. As well, we will feature
a ball." Izelle stares out into the audience again; attempting to pierce

through them. "If any of you have indeed remembered how to dance, that is."

A few members of the audience chuckle.

"In three nights time. We will rejoin here. To celebrate and formally open the first of the three tiers of conflict our heirs must champion. Thank you all for coming and we look forwards to seeing our capital city proudly in the midst of celebration!" Izelle channels her inner cheerleader momentarily before abruptly stepping away from the mic. With a swift switch in the inflection within her eyes she signals towards Bell and they both speed walk off the stage to a private area located in the back; they are followed by Saranias.

"Is something wrong?" Bell questions as he follows Izelle to the private room.

Izelle shakes her head. "Yes and no."

"That means yes unless we do something." Saranias translates with a sarcastic inflection.

Bell looks over at Saranias for a moment and restrains himself from smirking widely. "The Gala. You made a pretty big point of it in your speech. You even seemed a bit optimistic about the whole thing."

"Am I that transparent?" Izelle questions with a concern.

Bell shakes his head no. "I just know you."

"I want Caesar to target it." Izelle admits.

"Because that worked excellently last time." Bell critiques. "This isn't a person that can be trapped."

"Everything can be trapped. You just need the right equipment." Saranias notes authoritatively.

Izelle nods knowingly. "Saranias, I was going to ask for your assistance anyways. You have an understanding of these things."

Saranias smiles. "I do."

"This man, Caesar, he is likely to have many contingencies. I hope he does. As it increases the likelihood of him personally approaching us. However, he will be resistant to any typical tactic we utilize to gain information about these contingencies from him."

"*Ah*." Saranias states with a deep understanding. "I understand."

"You're wonderful at that Saranias." Izelle compliments. She looks back to Bell. "Are you willing to face him again?"

Bell adopts an intense energy. "I would prefer it to *only* be me."

"It will be, for a moment." Izelle admits.

"I'll be bait?" Bell questions.

Izelle chuckles. "Very briefly."

Bell laughs himself. "Good." He considers for a moment. "How could you possibly do that?"

"My intelligence network has been compromised. I don't know where, how, or for how long it has been this way." Izelle admits this with a frustrated shrug; attempting to let go of the stress it brings her. "I intend to send a very encrypted piece of information through my network detailing our preparations for the gala. When intercepted this intel will inform Caesar and his allies that you will be moving a large portion of explosives from the internal armoury out of the city to the Hou-Lao sea-fort. It is my hope that Caesar will attempt to commandeer the explosives to use them against the gala."

Saranias considers for a moment. "You would have to load real explosives for transit. His spies would know otherwise. He would never come if he already knew there was nothing there."

"Agreed. The transit will be moving at two in the morning and taking roads unknown to most merchants." Izelle adds.

"And what do we believe he will do to us?" Bell asks openly.

Izelle stares back at Bell without blinking. "Whatever he wants. If Saranias is there. It won't matter."

"I can be prepped for an extraction." Saranias quips with confidence; she stretches her hands out and cracks her knuckles loudly.

"Then it is our plan." Izelle confirms.

"What *is* a gala Courtney?" Ylinia asks as the pair lounge together in her family's suite.

Courtney shrugs. "When I read about it. It just seems like a bunch of people standing in a room, moving around in weird ways to music."

"Huh." Ylinia notes. She runs her fore-finger over the details of Bumble's handle; as she has likely done a thousand-and-some times by now. "So how do you tell if it is, *successful*?" She questions.

"The gala its self, or you at the gala?" Courtney attempts to clarify.

Ylinia shrugs. "Both, *I guess*?"

"Well, it looks like when people were still having galas. You had to dress the best you could to go stand in this room and a big room meant it was a higher quality event. There always appears to have been food, but unless the food is on a table with a variety of luxurious decorations; you want to be as far away from the food as possible while dancing. The further you have to walk from the table with food to the centre of the floor where people are dancing; the more successful your gala is. *It appears*." Courtney explains.

Ylinia nods. "I don't really understand the people from before the war. Standing around in a room, waving around, looking at decorations. It seems *so*."

"Wholesome?" Courtney offers.

"*Stupid*." Ylinia corrects. "That is what it looks like from the outside."

Courtney nods. "I kinda get what you mean. *Like*, back when I was still in school. Before we moved onto The Tristram. There were a few other kids in my class that came from non-combatant homes. Their parents were very beneficial to the community and as a result had access to homes built under the ground in protective caverns. Those kids never saw the war. They never feared the bombings. They were innocent and you could tell. Worse off, it was *annoying*. They seemed so far behind everyone else. Truth of it was we were all just dragged ahead by the trauma." She shrugs. "But that is the nature of life. We' re lucky to be the last generation that will have seen that."

"Are you excited for the clash of the crown?" Ylinia questions.

Courtney nods then wavers her shoulders. "I would be more so if I knew what I was going to see happen. Are they just going to bash each other to death?"

Ylinia shrugs. "I hope there is a bit more to it then that." She looks up for a moment then chuckles. "It would be funny for a little bit."

Courtney laughs herself. "Do you believe Bell will win?"

Ylinia nods the slightest bit. "I don't think that sort of confidence helps anything."

"But he is so powerful? Izelle seems pretty cool, but I think Bell would break her if they had to fight. Look at what he did to the Erkdwu!"

"True." Ylinia admits. "But there is more to it then that. Ego is just something between you and your reaction. The bigger you let it be, the more it slows you down."

"Do you think that is why he wears the mask?" Courtney questions.

Ylinia chuckles a little to herself. "I've never really thought of it." She looks up at the ceiling for a moment then hums for a few seconds. "I don't really know what the mask is for."

"He does have a face, right?" Courtney jokes with mild concern.

Ylinia considers for a moment. "Ninety nine percent sure, *yea*." She shrugs. "It looks like armour. It is probably armour."

"But I've never seen any other soldier wear something like that. None of the other heirs have something like that and they are all elite warriors."

Ylinia holds up Bumble as a gesture. "The blade-masters of the Neitheim basilica wore similar masks? Granted theirs covered their entire face." She shrugs. "Some things are just unique. Doesn't mean they can't be what they are."

"Yea." Courtney agrees. She stands and spins around in a swift twirl. "I don't think I'm going to be a very good dancer." She half-hardheartedly mimes a few movements that imitate a dance of some kind.

Ylinia nods with a polite smile. "I think you're doing pretty good."

Courtney stops and blushes. "You wouldn't know what to look for."

Ylinia stands alongside Courtney and draws Bumble safely. She points her blade towards the wall and swings it around her wrist delicately; causing the blade to leave a momentary swirl of yellow steel in the air. She follows through a few of the practice motions she has been taught thus far and fluidly connects different stances and stabs together. She stops, sheaths Bumble in a skilled motion and smiles at Courtney. "I think I can spot a pattern if there is one." Her eyes grow wide and she looks to the ground awkwardly. "I mean, I'd try."

"At least it looks like you know what you're trying to do." Courtney half-compliments. "I'm like a fish that suddenly remembered it can't breath out of water half-way into a hike."

"How did the fish get half way?" Ylinia asks with an unblinking stare.

Courtney returns this stare and they both share the eye-contact in silence. *"That's why it looks so bad?"* She offers a shaky justification.

Ylinia continues staring, closes her eyes, laughs and then nods. "Alright Courtney. Well, I think you need a dance-master."

"The gala is in a few days!" Courtney argues. "You may be a natural with that blade, but my feet can't learn to pounce around like that in front of hundreds of people with only a few days to learn!"

"Mhmm." Ylinia considers. "Well, if not a dance-master. Then a dance partner?"

Courtney smiles widely with a slight rebellion in her eyes. "I did read that many of the dances are traditionally done in pairs. Very close contact, foreheads pressed together, lips held just a short distance apart." Courtney explains with a dreamy inflection.

"So dance with someone." Ylinia states blatantly.

Courtney squeals slightly and giggles nervously. "Just *do* it?"

Ylinia nods. "That is the only way to have it happen."

Courtney pouts slightly and deflates. "Well, it is a shame I don't really know anyone." She exhales heavily. "Not here, anyways."

"Do you want to dance?" Ylinia questions.

Courtney takes a moment to think on it and answers with an almost embarrassed inflection. *"Yes."*

"Then when we're at the gala. Look for someone that also looks like they want to dance but isn't. Then dance with that person."

Courtney giggles nervously again as she considers the prospect. *"Okay."*

"Okay?" Ylinia confirms.

"Okay."

⊥⌐

Bell is walking alongside a convoy of wagons and caravans; each of which are covered in a heavy canvas. A stable's worth of steel steeds pull a few hundred pounds of explosives. Alongside Bell are well armed soldiers from the Royal Mounted Cavalry; each with a tower shield and a spear. They are all currently walking through an overgrown path of forest on the dark side of a stony mountain. A few small rocks trickle down the mountain side. Bell looks over with his eyes but doesn't allow himself to be concerned otherwise. The rocks settle in their new resting places and quiet again consumes all. Only the steps of the horses and the rolling of the vehicle wheels can be heard throughout the early morning.

"It has been too long since these roads have been serviced." The soldier with a goatee states. Bell was introduced to each of the soldiers but has since forgotten their names; in lieu of proper names he has identified them by their facial hair. "We might need to break out a felling axe if we need to make camp."

"Piss on that." The soldier with braided lengths argues. "This ere goddamn path is wide e'nuff for a horse drawn wagon. If that rickity old piece uve shit can make it. You can settle your bitching."

The soldier with a goatee laughs. "Old? B'y. You and that wagon are just about the same age."

Braided Lengths gets a bit aggravated. "My parents had electricity ya igna-*rent* prick. I didn't grow up huffing coal like some unlucky bastard from the start of the war."

"Whatever you say." Goatee retorts. "I just hope we don't have to scramble."

"Scramble all you like. It isn't my style to let the extras get away." The voice of Caesar interjects.

Bell raises his flattened palm into the air and the convoy stops instantly. "This is a cute trick. Talking like a ghost. You could be in any of these shadows, *I get it*."

Caesar appears suddenly a few metres down the path in front of Bell. He sways his entire body as he sarcastically rolls his eyes. "You're one of those people that can take the fun out of anything, aren't you?"

"I don't care to talk to you." Bell states impatiently as he draws Ehre.

Caesar draws his long knife and adopts a sharp smirk. "I forgive you. Who can truly fight their nature?"

Bell launches at Caesar with incredible speed; lunging with Ehre stabbing forwards. Caesar smacks his long knife against Ehre with enough force to disrupt Bell's attack; the knife shatters as a result. A few of the shattered pieces of steel cut across both Bell and Caesar's face. Before they fall to the ground Caesar snatches four of the shattered pieces of steel from the air and throws them at Bell as if they are darts. Bell smacks two of the steel darts out of the air but is unable to prevent the others from piercing the armour on his shoulder. Before Bell can remove the steel darts Caesar runs towards him and unleashes a flurry of kicks; fully realizing a few kicks every second. Bell steps backwards with all the attentiveness he can muster as he dodges each of the kicks but is unable to strike back at his opponent. As Caesar launches another triplet of kicks Bell dexterously steps towards him and grapples him from underneath his knee; quickly Bell lifts Caesar up off the ground and tosses him with brute strength into a tree a short distance away.

Mid-flight towards the tree at incredible speed Caesar centres himself, lands with both of his feet on the side of the tree then runs directly up it; disappearing into the foliage above.

"That is all you are, isn't it. *Tricks!?*" Bell screams out into the darkness of the forest.

"I am everything I need to be." Caesar replies. "I have no need for tricks."

"Maybe you should." Bell states as he hones his focus on Ehre. He swings the blade with incredible speed and force in the direction of the tops of the trees and a hundred explosive *CRACKS* all occur in an instantaneous chorus. The tops of all the trees ahead of Bell for a few rows cleanly disconnect from their bases and fall towards the ground; crashing downwards in an altogether messy combination of noise. Caesar is caught in the massive blast of energy and is flung from the tops of the trees down to the ground with the rest of the foliage. Caesar quickly collects himself and produces an astaria handgun from within his jacket. The handgun is entirely black with a fluid and heavy body design; a few panels alongside the slide showcase the ambient magical energy that crackles with life within. He briefly points the weapon out towards Bell then chuckles. "You are a natural disaster Bell. Do you know that?" He doesn't wait for an answer before he turns the weapon towards his own head. Caesar pulls the trigger as his hand is jerked upwards into the air by an invisible force. Caesar's arm contorts as if being pulled by cords and then he is quickly flipped and tossed onto the ground. Green light flickers behind Caesar as Saranias appears. Saranias holds Caesar tight as she attaches a series of restraints to his ankles and wrists. Caesar looks up at Saranias then looks back down at the ground; a defeated expression in his eyes. "This won't do you any good."

Saranias produces a syringe from a satchel on her hip and stabs it directly into Caesar's neck; injecting a small portion of liquid.

"I'll be honest with you. I haven't had to do the convincing in a long time."

Caesar rolls his eyes and coughs with a hack. "A truth serum? You've got to be kidding me. Nobody has ever found a way to make *one of those*."

"Maybe that would work as a product name." Saranias admits. "But I'm not really one for marketing."

"What are you talking about?" Caesar questions with sheer confusion.

"The Nai-Xi poison I just dosed you with. I suppose if I was to sell it, a decent product name would be *Truth Serum*. You know, it's kinda playful."

Caesar lets out a heavy huff of air through his nose. "You bitch."

"Get it out buddy." Saranias comforts. "You might as well before your jaw cramps up so tight you can't peep so much as speak."

Without contention Caesar relents in any attempt against the restraints. He twitches and holds his breath as his body is filled with pain. He seethes heavily before speaking. "Get on with it then. Before I fall face forwards into this dirt."

Bell watches over Caesar while Saranias ventures out into the woods to retrieve something. Bell looks down at Caesar as the poison throttles his ability to move; he suppresses his desire to smirk. "A dog eventually gets hit when it chases traffic. That is all this is."

Saranias returns on the back of a majestic bird; it walks proudly on two muscular legs which are covered in dark red and purple scales. Otherwise the bird has a rather round body which is covered in grey, white and black feathers; each of the feathers appears to be heavy like the blade of a sword. The bird has a long neck which leads to an angular falcon like head; the creature's beak is especially dangerous with a five inch dip that has been sharpened on either side.

Saranias leans down from her seat and picks up Caesar; tossing him onto the back of the creature and quickly strapping him to a saddle well concealed under the creature's heavy feathers. "I'll head back to Izelle. We'll reconvene soon?" Saranias questions Bell.

"Of course." Bell confirms. "Be safe, even as is. You can never be too careful."

"I'm always too careful." Saranias admits. She quickly focuses her gaze out towards her destination and is off at a break neck speed upon the running bird. After a mild trot the bird gains enough momentum to tear off the land and violently soar through the tree tops as it begins flying at immense speed; the absolute density of the bird smacks the air around it loudly in its flight.

Bell returns swiftly to the others. "Are you all well?" He questions.

"Yes sir." The general consensus replies.

One of the soldiers steps forwards. "Sir, I know, for the sake of professionalism. That we should just keep on going as if that wasn't an absolutely obscene display of power. But this is the real world. What the hell did you do just do?" His long braided beard sways as he speaks.

Bell looks behind himself, sheaths Ehre then looks back to the soldier. "Honestly I think that was me being a bit of an asshole cutting so many of those trees down. I feel a bit guilty about that."

"I mean, how did you do that. What was it that allowed you to perform such a feat?" The soldier narrows the terms of his inquiry.

"I know what you meant." Bell affirms, he rolls the tip of his finger alongside the handle of Ehre. "Have you ever felt passion?"

The soldier responds with a kinda stupid look and a blank stare. "*Sure I have.*"

"And what sort was it?"

The soldier chuckles a bit, looks to the ground, sighs very quietly then speaks. "My wife, I love my wife."

Bell smiles and nods. "Good, *good*. *Now*, without speaking to it. Think on every wonderful thing you have with your wife. The beauty it brings to your life, the purpose, the fulfillment. Think of the power that wells inside you. The rage that protects all of it desperately." Bell stares at the soldier intensely. "Do you feel what is inside you right now? The energy that surges even at the provocation of words?"

"I *do*." The soldier confirms. "What does this mean?"

"It means you can answer your own question." Bell states calmly. "If you can feel the power of that energy. If you can feel the power of passion its self. Then you understand the extent of what an individual can be."

The soldier smiles, looks down then back up at Bell. "I understand what you mean. And I'll respect your answer. But a part of you is lying."

Bell smirks widely under his mask. "Thank you for your respect." He addresses the rest of the group with his attention. "We'll hike a few clicks back before camp. Let us get some distance under us. I want to be home by tomorrow afternoon." Bell rushes.

_⏄_

"This may very well be the event of the century." Courtney states in half a panic. "Should I even be here? What if I mess up history?"

"I'm sure history can handle it darling." Lance attempts to comfort.

Lance and Courtney have arrived ahead of the others to the Swan Gala. Lance is dressed immaculately in slight gold heels with an entirely dull steel-grey suit; finished with a modest top-hat.

Courtney has had her hair professionally tended so that it is currently swirled in four bundles held in a tight bouquet above and behind her head. She has on a long mature gown cut from a luxurious purple silk.

"It better." Courtney affirms. Her face lights up with excitement as she spots the rest of the crew at the entrance to the market.

Alim has arrived in a lean mauve suit with a dark purple nearly black shirt underneath paired with a dark red tie. Mel has matched her dress with Howarth. Mel is wearing a white dress with a thin blue sash while Howarth is wearing a white suit with a blue tie and light blue collared shirt. Ylinia has been outfitted with a beautiful and well tailored green dress that features a sheen cape across her right side. Bell follows behind in formal military clothing. He has on a long black coat, a grey collared shirt underneath it and matching pants; he wears his mask regularly. Ylinia leads the crew in joining Courtney.

"You all look fabulous!" Courtney compliments.

"She's not wrong." Lance confirms.

Mel rolls her eyes with a wide smile. "Who among us has ever had this much help getting ready? I can't believe the treatment we got from the hotel. Everyone looks fantastic."

Alim kisses his husband and holds his hand closely. "It is amazing what a bit of fine cloth can do to elevate an evening."

Lance smiles sweetly and looks out as the first few stars fill into the night sky. "Are your fellow heirs coming with you Bell?" He asks with a friendly inflection.

Bell nods firmly. "Izelle will meet us there in a bit. I think Saranias is already there. No idea about Dii."

"Then lets get our party on eh? I've never thought I'd see a gala. None the less be at one." Howarth admits with a delighted yet bated excited. His eyes are focused down the cobblestone path to the centre of the market where dancing and music can be heard.

Bell smiles wide enough that it can be discerned underneath his mask. "Let's get this over with." He waves with the whole of his arm and everyone begins walking to the gala.

The market has been done up with orange, red and yellow lights. There are flowers across the floor and strings of ivy connecting from stall to ceiling; creating a web of decoration above your head. Music fills your chest as it plays from contemporary and much more consistent speakers installed on tall posts across the area. There is dancing, socializing, laughter, drinking and general happiness all around. Far at the end of the market on the stage is a full band playing pleasant classical music upon at least fifteen different instruments. Howarth takes Mel's hand to dance and they are off to the dance floor. Alim takes Lance's hand and they are off to dance. Courtney looks out to the crowd of people and then to the well supplied buffet table.

"Remember how to make something happen." Ylinia cheers.

Courtney closes her eyes and takes a deep breath. "By actually doing the thing." She speaks softly then marches out into the crowd. Ylinia smiles.

"You're the master now, *eh*?" Bell teases.

Ylinia blushes slightly then flicks her hair with pseudo-offence. "Of course." She chuckles.

Bell sways his head to discourage her sarcasm. "A good friend can be the greatest aid and a teacher with endless lessons. It is good to see."

"I just want to help her be happy." Ylinia admits without meeting Bell's eye-contact.

Izelle sneaks up from behind Bell, playfully spins around him and offers her his hand. "Hello my fellow heir. Would you care to dance?"

Ylinia sneaks off with a smirk and a skip.

Bell looks awkwardly at the wall. "*I can't Izelle. I'm married. It would feel weird.*"

"You *were* married." Izelle responds with a snap.

"I'll always be married Izelle. Thank you." Bell responds with a bit of a whimper and sulks off to go stand by the wall.

Izelle seems to feel bad for a moment, catches a flicker of a tear in her eye then lets out a deep breath. She continues on into the gala.

Like a bolt of lightning Dii makes a brief appearance next to the frame of the entrance into the market. She gazes at the various proceedings, the delightful food, the happy faces, the loud and passionate music. Without hesitation she turns to leave before her gauntlet is grabbed from behind. She turns to look down and spots Ylinia there holding her back. "What?" Dii questions without much consideration for her tone.

"Why are you leaving? This is your celebration too." Ylinia questions.

Dii scoffs. "This may be in my honour. But it is certainly not for me." She shirks Ylinia's grasp as she answers.

"You're being a child." Ylinia insults firmly.

"*Uhh.*" Dii doesn't know how to respond. She stares down at Ylinia for a few moments longer and she returns this gaze. "What do you mean?" She questions.

Ylinia rolls her eyes and motions her hand towards the darkness of every other direction. "Look where you're going compared to where you're supposed to be. I get it. The crowds, *and everything*. It is weird. I see that too. But there are also people here, people that you seem to care about, that want to see you. You're not just some anomaly that can pop in and out whenever you want. You need to be there for people just as they are there for you."

"It still feels silly." Dii admits.

"*Alright*." Ylinia accepts with a shrug. "Then it feels silly. Does that kill you? Are you not powerful enough to defeat a silly feeling?"

Dii rolls her eyes heavily then offers her hand out to Ylinia. "Fine. Then take me to this dance."

Ylinia accepts Dii's hand with excitement and walks her down to the dance floor gladly. There they join Mel and Howarth, Alim and Lance as well as Courtney and what appears to be a noble boy just about her age. They all dance to the music.

Bell finds himself eating a plateful of food at a table; watching the sky and lamenting the empty chair across from him. With a flicker of green light Saranias appears in the chair. She reaches over and snatches a dinner roll off of Bell's plate. Bell pretends to be annoyed then smiles. "Everything went well then?" He questions.

Saranias nods. "Everything went well. He's in a cell so isolated he can't even tell what time of day it is. Guards are being cycled with two on the door and two on personal over-watch. Nobody goes closer then 5 meters to him and he has not been cleared to be relieved of his personal restraints." She lets out a deep breath. "It should be okay for now. I'm letting him stew in the poison."

Bell makes a kinda concerned face. "*Eeesh*. Isn't that a bit too cruel?"

"Na-xi kinda plateaus after awhile. It is painful. Like a cramp in all your muscles. But if you relax. It will only keep you so uncomfortable you don't want to run away." Saranias explains without much remorse.

"*Alright*." Bell allows. "You should go dance with Izelle. I had to say no when she offered."

Sarania's eyes grow large with empathy. "Oh she did?" She pauses for a moment to think. "I'm sorry for you both. I'm sure she was only trying to be friendly."

"*I know.*"

"But you take stuff like that so seriously. So you must of shot her down pretty intensely. And it is so hard for her to break that professional persona."

"I mean."

"What a shame." Saranias concludes. "You love Temple Bell. No one can take that away from you." Saranias stands then scans the area for Izelle. "But you have to think about what she would want for you. I don't think this is how she would want you to treat your friends." Saranias rushes off towards Izelle.

"Well maybe if she was here I'd give a shit what she thought." Bell declares under his breath.

A few songs pass before William takes the stage and his voice is heard throughout the market. "What an evening this has already been. What an evening this shall become!" He declares. He stares out at the happy crowd and smiles. "I will be brief. Because I too wish to hear the band get on with it." The crowd laughs a bit alongside him. "In the upcoming clash of the crown. The match ups for the initial combat tournament are as follows. Bell will combat Wvendeiss. Izelle will combat Saranias. Dii will combat Teander. Leige will combat Bristol. The first of these matches featuring Bell against Wvendeiss will occur tomorrow evening an hour before the sun falls."

The night continues as William exits the stage. The band assumes control again of the mood and everyone starts to forget what it is they even heard. Aside from Bell that is. Bell sits by himself, watching everyone enjoy themselves. He doesn't drink and he can only barely finish his single plate of food. He stays for awhile but finds the desire to leave is too strong. He sneaks out before anyone can catch him and finds comfort underneath the heavy blankets of a nice bed.

Sleep, *however*, doesn't find him instantly; and demands a catalyst of sorts. Working as hard as he can to retain as much of his body in the bed as possible; Bell stretches out to drag a single leather luggage bag towards him. He quickly turns the small combination lock to the digits '*6-1-6*' and unzips the largest pocket upon the bag. From within he retrieves an old book; stained and torn through time and obvious extensive sessions of use.

The tome is a training manual for blade-masters. Each page is covered in illustrations depicting certain techniques, style studies or training exercises. Bell flips through every page of the book; passing out somewhere halfway into his second skim through the entire text.

CHAPTER TWELVE

BECOME SOMETHING

"And everyone just sang and danced for hours! I know it was only one glass of wine but I *think* it was a heavy one. I definitely felt it." Ylinia enthuses about the night before as her and Bell walk out into the forest a few moments before sunrise.

"Mhmm." Bell vocalizes. "I'm glad it was a good night." He carries with him a large clay jug on a shoulder sling.

"And you should of seen Saranias dance! Halfway down on the floor and she could still shake her whole body. She was a wonder to watch." She continues.

"I'm sure." Bell responds without much effort. They enter the training area and he quickly sets up the practice targets. "Warm up with these." He instructs.

Ylinia drops her bag on the ground and draws Bumble. She adopts a slim stance which poises her blade in front of her like an angled horn. She steps forwards and opens up her attack with a quick burst of stabs then dodges back to move to a more defensive position. She huffs then slashes diagonally in a cross towards the practice target; managing to cut two prominent marks across it.

"You're able to focus entirely Ylinia. I can see that. Your forehead tightens, your gaze becomes specific. I imagine that is why you've taken so quickly to our training." Bell speaks kindly then brandishes Ehre and carefully stabs it into the ground at his feet. "So I offer you a challenge."

"What sort of challenge?" Ylinia asks with an intrigued expression and raised eyebrow.

"Before I had become a master. While I was still learning the blade. I studied at the temple in Antioch. There they have deserts so large you would believe they could drink up the oceans. If you suffer the adventure through the valleys of desert; you can find a rare, red, oily sand." Bell explains as he uncorks the clay jug and begins pouring dense red sand out around Ehre in circles. "They used it in a ritual. Something I had never seen before. The slightest glimmer of *real magic*." As the jug empties he places it down behind him and produces from within his jacket pocket a bronze lighter. "Prepare yourself Ylinia. This fight will go on till the last breath." He lowers the lighter down to the sand and as soon as sparks fly; a massive ploom of fire explodes around Ehre. Bell steps back to a safe distance and watches. The flame dissipates and reveals a humanoid figure of swirling sand and flame; it wields Ehre as if the blade is its own.

"Are you serious?!" Ylinia shouts at Bell; he does not respond. The figure walks towards Ylinia confidently. She holds Bumble out and quickly stabs forward; the figure smashes her sword away and nearly knocks it from her grasp. The figure slashes down and Ylinia barely manages to dodge to the side. She slashes a few times at him and catches a bit of his wrist at the end. The figure steps towards her and checks her with his hip; knocking her down. As she lays on her back the figure stomps down with his boot only to have his foot be caught in tandem between Bumble's hilt and Ylinia's tightened wrist. Ylinia spins herself while holding up the figure's foot and kicks his knee in; knocking him backwards. As he falls Ylinia cuts at the hand which holds Ehre and slashes most of it off. The figure slips and falls. Ylinia quickly jumps onto the figure and stabs down into its chest just short of fourteen times. The figure melts away into dust; Ehre lays plainly on the ground. Ylinia collapses over and begins huffing intensely; char covers her pants.

Bell strolls over and picks up Ehre; sheathing it quickly. He offers Ylinia a free hand and she takes it to help stand up. "You did well." He compliments while gazing out into the forest.

Ylinia laughs cautiously. "Surviving was the only option. Was it not?"

"It was." Bell nods. "There may come a point in your life where your mind wants to separate from that fact. It can become about technique, prestige, *whatever*. But never forget that at a base level every battle is a defence of your life."

"Will yours be this evening?" Ylinia asks directly.

Bell laughs. "They will not be. These battles for the clash of the crown. They are fierce, and one will not win if they don't take it as serious as a lethal battle. But no. We're to fight to an *obvious victory*. Not a death."

"What constitutes an obvious victory?"

"It is basically what it sounds like. Once you've shown that you'll defeat your opponent regardless of what they do; the match is called in your favour. When Richard Nio won the crown he first battled against Riwena the Charmer. She fought with blades strapped to her wrists and swung her arms around as if they were striking cobras. His victory was called once he broke her arms with a definitive bash of his shield."

Ylinia cringes. "That still sounds awful."

"Undoubtedly." Bell agrees. "*Now*. With that challenge completed. I believe you'll be best suited by sparring for practice. Alongside study of more advanced texts. I'll have the books brought to your room this evening." He unsheathes Ehre and points it towards Ylinia. "*Otherwise*. I have until later this afternoon. Shall we train?"

Ylinia smiles with a spry confidence across her face. "*Of course*."

⌐Ⅱ⌐

Bell, Izelle, Saranias and Caesar all sit in a darkened room. There are two windows each with tightly shuttered blinds. Caesar sits in a cage in the centre of the room; chained by both his wrists and ankles. His clothes have been changed into a comfortable plain white prisoner's outfit; it is a single piece uniform with elbow length sleeves. The others in the room stand outside the cage peering in towards Caesar.

Saranias holds up a small bottle of light blue liquid in front of the cage. "Do you see this?" She speaks to Caesar.

Caesar nods. "Antidote I presume?" Speaking in a perfectly composed manner as to not prompt a cramp in his jaw.

"Then you know the offer on the table." Izelle progresses the conversation.

"You want to know my plan?" Caesar asks to none of the individuals present.

"Every detail." Izelle affirms.

Caesar chuckles madly, twitches in pain, then forces himself to speak. "There wasn't a plan. There was a surplus, a few good lines. I did my rebelling. That was what I was good at." He looks around the room then closes his eyes. "Have you began to wonder where the *Agents of the Cauldron are?*" He waits a moment. "Do you even know what I spent the past few days doing?" He makes brief eye-contact with everyone in the room then closes his eyes again. "I killed every single person who ever worked for me. Every agent, every sleeper, every fence, every informant. *You see,* I learned about something bigger then myself. I know that a few spies or a handful of heartless assassins can't help me. They can't help anyone."

Saranias unlocks the cell and feeds Caesar the antidote. "I'm sorry your life has been this way."

"Are you really?" Caesar questions skeptically. He looks down at the ground and stares.

"You'll be executed for your crimes Caesar. We will honour a last request. You may choose a meal and a leisure. These things will be provided prior to the end." Izelle informs him.

Caesar looks right up at Bell; who stares back at him unflinchingly. "You're loving this. Aren't you?"

Bell smiles and restrains an indulgent part of himself. "Cause and effect Caesar. Cause and effect."

Caesar smiles and becomes rather calm. "Isn't that the truth." He swallows. "I won't waste your time. You can scratch my requests. *Let us just get this over with.*"

Those standing share a simple look. Bell and Saranias leave the room; standing outside the door. They wait a moment and Izelle joins them; locking the door behind her. "It is done." She confirms.

"Good." Bell responds. "Our matches will begin soon. It is well that we can focus on them properly."

Izelle nods. "*Yes.* That is what is left after all of this isn't it."

Saranias smirks. "Only you could put the literal possibility to be a queen on the back burner Izelle."

"There is always more then one thing happening at a time Saranias. I once believed that I could see everything. But at most I get a fleeting glimpse of a few objects, and the trails which lead to the rest. I realize now that it is impossible to do something well; while trying to do everything else simultaneously." She responds.

Saranias smiles slightly, peers over towards Bell and then looks out in the distance. "We should prepare then." She tilts her head and grows a pleasant expression. "Best of luck *heirs*. I wish you both the best. I look forwards to our match Izelle."

Izelle nods. "To you as well." Saranias leaves and Izelle looks over towards Bell. "I'm sorry today didn't come quicker."

Bell shrugs. "You make things happen Izelle. The world is the world. Reality will always scheme. But you fight against that and accomplish things regardless. I am upset by all the losses as well. We all *should* be. But when it is put in its place and considered for what it is. You've made the best bouquet possible out of shit roses." He compliments.

"*Thank you* Bell." Izelle responds softly. Her eyes glaze over slightly and she loses herself in her head for just a moment. "If you don't mind, would you allow *me* to inform Ylinia of Caesar's death? I feel as if I owe her *that much*."

"Of course. She will appreciate that." He nods in understanding. "Best of luck to you with your fight."

"To you as well."

Drums and chimes can be heard throughout Caelzun to signify the first portion of the clash of the crown. The clash takes place within Nexubal Arena; renown for its giant scale and pristine curved designs. Rounds and rounds of seating encircle a concrete island *floating* in an artificial lake. There are five meters of water between the actual arena and the seats. There are two square holes positioned across from one another on the concrete island.

William stands from within the crowd with a microphone in his hands. He speaks clearly to the audience in whole. "Welcome all!" He declares proudly as the music begins to crescendo. "Such an event as this does not require much introduction. Those of you announcing the match for the radio; please begin your broadcasts."

Bell and Wvendeiss raise from the floor of the arena upon small lifts. The lifts become flush with the concrete floor.

"Our first match for this clash of the crown will be between Bell and Wvendeiss."

Bell unsheathes Ehre and holds the blade out formally. Wvendeiss retrieves his longsword from the hidden sheath within his shield then adopts a defensive stance with both; his armour shimmers in the light.

"This battle will be fought to an obvious victory in *three, two, one,*" William pauses for just a moment. The audience collectively takes a breath. "*Begin!*"

Bell launches at Wvendeiss with incredible speed and slashes at the paladin fiercely. The slashes are blocked but come at the cost of a few corners being cut *off* the shield. Wvendeiss smirks and smashes his shield forwards at Bell; as Bell dodges sideways Wvendeiss unleashes a sideways smack with the blunt side of his longsword; catching Bell in the ribs and throwing him to the ground. Bell quickly pushes himself up and acrobatically jumps to his feet; managing to kick Wvendeiss in the gut with dexterous swiftness. Wvendeiss takes a few steps back in recoil, readies himself behind his shield and advances towards Bell. Powerful solid stabs target Bell in a flurry; they extend too far and too precisely to be dodged. Bell deflects each of the stabs with Ehre. With both his hands on the blade Bell smacks Wvendeiss's sword out of his hand. Bell smiles and shakes unintentionally with a surge of adrenaline. Wvendeiss wields his shield with both of his hands and swipes it down towards Bell as if it is a great-hammer. Bell stabs Ehre through the centre of the shield, rips it from Wvendeiss's grasp and smashes him back a couple of metres with the conglomerate weapon.

"And that decides it everyone." William speaks over the microphone. "Bell is the victor of the first match." The audience screams out in celebration. Bell helps Wvendeiss up to his feet.

"Sorry about the shield." Bell apologizes with a dainty inflection.

Wvendeiss laughs deeply and heavily. "Do not apologize." He laughs again while stabilizing his foothold. "*That* was hilarious." He firmly shakes Bell's hand then walks back to the lift where he entered the arena. "Don't fret because you won. I would of done so just as gladly as you should."

Bell nods kindly then walks back to his lift. Both lifts descend and take the heirs to private rooms. Bell cleans himself up slightly then leaves to join William in the audience. There are a few cleaners tidying the arena of broken bits of shield and disturbance before the next fight. William looks over towards Bell briefly as he sits next to him. Wvendeiss joins them both.

"That was well fought. A very enjoyable match to watch." William compliments.

"Thank you." Wvendeiss responds.

"Mhmm." Bell agrees.

William stands as the cleaners finish preparing the arena. "Now if that wasn't enough for you. Our next match is ready to go ahead." Out of the arena floor rises Izelle and Saranias. Izelle has dressed for battle with well tailored armoured robes; she wields a mechanically augmented pole-arm with a long blade-head.

"We never sparred did we Izelle?" Saranias quips playfully.

Izelle smirks. "The only person I ever sparred with was *Temple*. Though I admit. I never did win those matches.

Saranias adopts a focused expression. "*Have fun babe*." She insists.

William's voice sounds throughout the arena. "The battle between Izelle and Saranias will commence in *three, two, one...begin!*"

Saranias disperses in a flash of bright green light. Izelle remains calm; adopting a defensive position with her pole-arm. She closes her eyes as if meditating. A few silent moments pass before

Izelle explodes into a spasm of motion and swipes wildly above her with the weapon. Izelle jumps a short distance then swings her weapon drastically into empty air; she smirks and looks around herself pridefully. "You're better at this then I remember." Green light explodes in front of Izelle and she swats her weapon into it. Saranias appears from a smaller flash of green light behind Izelle and picks her up. The moment Izelle is held entirely above Saranias's head; Saranias disperses with a flash of green light. Izelle flops onto her back and chuckles afterwords. *Much better.* Saranias appears again with a flash and drags Izelle a short distance by her legs; Izelle swipes at Saranias but connects with nothing as she flashes away. Izelle attempts to jump to her feet but has them kicked out from under her by a suddenly appearing and dispersing Saranias. "Alright I'm done with this." She smashes her polearm against the ground and launches herself a few metres into the air. While in the air she begins spinning her weapon around her with blinding speed. As she lands the intensity of her spinning starts kicking up dust violently around her; whirling up a storm. Izelle peers into the storm for a moment, launches herself into it and with a single swipe of her weapon she knocks Saranias to the ground with a decisive blow to the gut. Saranias becomes visible, attempts to sit up, chuckles a bit to herself in understanding then flops down onto her back in defeat. Izelle huffs, smirks for a moment then moves over to help Saranias up to her feet. The women share a friendly expression.

"And the victor of the second match is Izelle!" William declares.

Izelle and Saranias join William and the other heirs in the audience. Cleaners take the stage. William compliments both the women on the battle. A messenger rushes towards William and hands him a small rolled note, nods, then takes his leave. William opens the note with a confused expression and seems disappointed as he reads its contents. He stands to address the audience with microphone in hand. "People of The Citizenry, there has been a change in plans." The audience tenses as if they expect to all summarily be shot. "Dii the holy knight is nowhere to be found. In her quarters is a letter which refuses her involvement in the clash of the crown. As a result. Teander will be considered the victor of the third match." The audience is silent in response. "We will move forwards with our final match for the day. The combat of Leige and Bristol!" He announces as the pair raise from the floor of the arena. The pair nod towards one another. Bristol wields a massive long-bow strung with a steel cable while Leige wields his whip and spear simultaneously. "This battle shall commence in *three, two, one*...begin!"

The combatants simply stare at one another while walking slowly in a half circle. "Not going to charge?" Leige asks with a suave accent.

Bristol smiles wide; her complexion and large eyes make her appear much younger then she actually is. "Do you want to play it that way?" She questions, thinks on it for a moment, draws two arrows simultaneously then fires them at Leige as she continues to speak. "We can do that." The arrows cut through the air with such a speed that they are barely visible. Leige smacks one of the arrows out the air with his whip and dodges the other. Bristol fires three more arrows rapidly at him. Leige deflects the arrows as he sprints towards her with his spear primed forwards. As Leige closes in he stabs towards Bristol; she reacts by spinning her bow around in her grasp and smacking Leige's feet out from under him. As Leige falls Bristol casually takes his spear as he drops it. She quickly jumps backwards, draws the spear as an arrow in her bow and fires it at Leige. Leige moves his body back a few centimetres; allows the spear to fly right past his face then catches it with a full extension of his whip. Utilizing the pre-existing momentum Leige spins the spear around and aims it at Bristol; catching her in the side of the ribs with its blunt length and tossing her to the ground. She spins a few times and loses grip of her bow. Leige catches the spear then stabs it down at Bristol; she rolls to dodge it as it stabs into the ground precisely where her shin would of been. Leige cracks his whip towards her. Without hesitating Bristol quickly gets up onto her feet, tolerates the flaring pain throughout her chest and pulls a small dagger from her boot; using it to cut Leige's whip in half. Leige throws the whip's handle to the ground and walks towards Bristol. The two stare at one another for a moment, nod, then step closer to fight. Bristol slashes with the dagger, her arm is caught, she fights off the grapple, Leige lowers himself and picks her up by her knee, she tucks herself and rolls off his back, he attempts to spin to hit her and ends up catching a boot in the face as she launches herself off her hands into the air towards him. Leige falls down onto his back and Bristol flops her butt onto his chest; pinning him to the ground.

"Bristol is the victor!" William confirms with excitement as the crowd celebrates the battle.

Bristol gets off of Leige and helps him stand up. Leige smiles deeply. "I understand now, how it is that you protected this city." Leige compliments.

"Is that so? My technique makes sense to you?" She questions.

"Not at all." Leige notes with a chuckle. "You're a unique breed Bristol. An' whatever sort of unique that is, you got it running through your veins pure as anything."

The two step onto their respective lifts and disappear into the floor of the arena. William raises his hand high as if it is some sort of focus inducing symbol. "This concludes the first portion of the clash of the crown! Please join us this evening upon the Meire Estate where we shall be hosting a feast prior to the grand-battle between our remaining heirs!" He announces delightfully, returns to his seat and closes his eyes. "The enthusiasm being this loud requires is very, *taxing*." William speaks quietly to the heirs.

"Must you speak enthusiastically?" Wvendeiss inquires.

William nods. "It has been noted that any speech delivered via microphone with less then an obscene amount of positivity is *heart-wrenching and entirely awful*. As per a study we performed prior to the clash."

"It couldn't change that much?" Saranias questions.

Izelle chuckles. "I'd believe it."

William smiles. "It makes a huge difference. People start to feel guilty if you don't seem like you're enjoying yourself."

The audience begins leaving; the heirs and William remain. Leige and Bristol join the heirs to compliments regarding their battle. Their adrenaline keeps a rather shallow conversation going for a bit; each reciting what they had just watched happen; or confirming what did and didn't. There isn't a comparison between the victors and the losers; they are each simply heirs.

Meire Estate is a five acre property preserved for the Monarch of The Citizenry. There are various buildings and structures across the property; connected by a simple dirt path through a dense pine forest. It is nearly always shady throughout the estate with small rays of sunlight providing most of the illumination. It is quiet and delightfully chilly due to a slight wind.

A massive feast is being hosted within the guest house known as *Shore*. Shore is located very near the entrance to Meire Estate next to a barn garage sizable enough for eight vehicles. The guest-house its self is reminiscent of what would happen if a manor was built in the style of a log cabin. Bell arrives late to the already ongoing event. He approaches the guest house but moments before he steps up onto the front porch his attention is called into the bordering bush.

"Hey, Bell, *a moment?*" Leige shouts just loudly enough for Bell to hear him.

Bell looks over at Leige, nods with acknowledgement then walks over towards him. "*Leige*. How can I help?"

"Nothing to help with, unfortunately. Just wanted to ask someone who knew er. What gave with Dii not showing at all? Can't see her glowy face around *ere* either." Leige states rather curiously.

"Dii operates very...*essentially*. These constant parties, excuses for events. It is a fad she doesn't intend to tolerate. While most people are reasonably excited to just relax. Dii isn't built that way." Bell explains; finishing his remarks with an apathetic shrug.

Leige nods with a slight smile. "Shame." He admits, looks out into the woods then sighs. "Hopefully she's onto something worthwhile then."

"It tends to be." Bell responds honestly. He motions his hand briefly towards the guest house. "Do you want to join me?"

"*Nah.*" Leige declines the offer. "I already snagged a bottle of rye. I'll have'a better time with it by myself in a hammock down on the water then with all that *noise* and *bother* about."

Bell spends a moment focusing on the noise and finds himself thinking about how dreadful such an event is to someone with great hearing. The music, glasses clinking, shoes scuffing, varying conversations at varying pitches, food being eaten, tables being moved, plates getting scrapped, speeches being made, dances being fumbled and apologies being offered. Bell shakes his head with disdain and takes a deep breath. "They require great patience *for sure.*"

Leige chuckles. "I can see it in your eyes. You're only going to this cause you feel like you gotta." He chuckles again.

Bell smirks as if he has been caught cheating on a test. "And *yet*." He turns to leave. "I wish you the best Leige, enjoy your bottle."

"No other way b'y. No other way." Leige advises kindly then takes his leave.

Without much hesitation or distraction Bell opens the front door of the guest house and is overwhelmed by the atmosphere almost instantly. Loud music played on varying styles of guitar, drum and trumpet fill the building with bouncing energy. People are eating, drinking, smoking and dancing. Guards are posted at every door, throughout the party and near the borders of the guest house; each appears like a stoic statue among a herd of lucid entities. Bell strolls through the party. He finds Courtney and Ylinia sharing a small portion of wine with other younger folks while all playing a game of billiards. Mel, Izelle, Saranias and Teander alongside a few nobles sit outside around a large fire happily drinking and laughing. Wvendeiss is in the midst of a very intense ale drinking competition against Bristol; they appear to be evenly matched. Alim and Lance dance with their foreheads pressed together lovingly. Bell observes all of this with a smile then takes a seat at the long fifteen stool bar in the house's lounge. One of the few bartenders on staff walk right up to him and greet him with a smile.

"Anything to drink for you sir?" The bartender asks.

"A single mead." Bell orders with a compromising tone. "Something to eat as well if that is an option. Bread, roast, with something dark green and covered in salt."

The bartender nods. "Of course sir. And if I may add. What a wonderful battle! It was a spectacle to watch."

Bell smiles modestly. "Thank you. Wvendeiss is known as a goliath. His prowess with defence is almost so great it supplants his need for offence. I just figured if I could bust that defence, I would have a chance at putting him off his game."

"Fascinating strategy." The bartender acknowledges before quickly darting off to attend to the order.

"And what have we here!?" Howarth declares loudly from behind Bell.

The bartender arrives with Bell's drink and serves it with a smile and polite nod of disengagement.

"I thought you didn't drink!" Howarth questions as he takes a seat next to Bell. He looks over towards the bartender as he gets comfortable on his stool. "I'll have whatever you think is fun." He orders.

"I don't really drink." Bell admits. "But I imagine even the water at an event like this would have an alcohol content. So I made peace with a single drink."

"There's water around here?" Howarth remarks with genuine surprise. "I guess they're just like curtains. You'd be crazy to notice they're there if you weren't looking in the first place."

"*Uh.*" Bell responds humorously. "*Yea*, I guess so." He pauses for a moment to take a sip from his mead. "Are you enjoying yourself Howarth?"

Howarth chuckles a bit then leans in towards Bell. "*Honestly?*" He asks under his breath.

Bell nods. "*Exclusively.*"

"I'm having a great time." Howarth admits shamefully. He leans back, accepts a tall glass of rosé from the bartender then smiles widely. "Bit worried admitting that is gonna screw something up though. Do you know how long it has been since I've been okay with my wife being in another room from me? I mean, don't get me wrong. It isn't like I've been afraid she's gonna go take a crap and then she's gonna flush herself accidentally." Howarth begins slightly slurring a few of his words as he continues speaking with fewer and fewer breaths. "But there wasn't a way I was gonna have her anywhere far when the war was going on. Neither Ylinia. That was the point of *The Tristram*. Load up an advanced train, get my family. It wasn't until we were assigned you that I even saw the title of the whole operation: *Blade of Rails*. Poetic name for the safe-keeping of a war hero. But now here we are, envoys of an heir, sitting at a feast, *enjoying it*." He laughs profoundly. "Who coulda guessed the world wasn't a big bag of shit floating in the middle of nowhere."

Bell sips his mead. "It'd take a pretty devoted maniac."

"So are you worried?" Howarth inquires.

"About?"

"The clash. Big ol battle. Not only will you have to battle Izelle, but you'll have to do it while dodging two others as well." Howarth states.

Bell laughs slightly to himself. "Is that how you see it?"

Howarth shrugs. "There wasn't an unworthy fighter in that tournament. But Bell, from every story I've ever heard. The only person who's ever matched your abilities was Temple. I don't know if anyone can beat that, or if you'd even let them."

"I don't think I'll ever let them." Bell admits.

"Ever?" Howarth seeks to confirm.

Bell nods solemnly. "It must get annoying, hearing me explain how much I love my wife. But that is how powerful it is. Even if something has the slightest bit of her in it. Even if it isn't even something real, like her being my best match in a fair fight. I am not ready to lose that connection as well. *I can't*. Not even the small things."

Howarth smiles, takes a drink, then looks up at the ceiling. "Well I don't think you'll have to lose anything. *You're protagonist kinda guy*. I'm sure everything will be alright."

"I don't know. Nothing ever really plays out like we expect it to in our heads." Bell considers.

"Wouldn't that be the worst?" Howarth jokes; his eyes wide. "I mean if everything played out like I expected it too! The world would be over in twelve minutes. I'd open the door to go to the bathroom and *BOOM*." He shouts loudly enough to startle the bartender. "The toilet would blow up; killing me. Quickly afterwords Selemian death squads from hidden chapters within our own population would rise up and slay my family and everyone else with semi-automatic firearms." He stares at Bell; at the entrance into the event then back at Bell; he takes a drink.

Bell nods; then begins to stare at the wall behind Howarth. "It is funny how that impulse sneaks into your life." He sways his head as he considers the concept humorously. "I mean, I've had cupboards close quicker then I expected, slam a bit, and scare me so deeply that I can't sleep for thirty some hours." He chuckles, takes a drink of his mead then extends his free hand out into a confused gesture. "I mean, what is my brain even thinking? That there is someone hiding in the cupboard? That that little innocuous sound is suddenly going to summon a platoon over my head?" He shrugs. "Yet still, it seems only time tapers off those reactions."

Howarth nods; the focus in his eyes flickering. "I want it to be okay though." He admits; a bit more emotionally then he probably intends. "I think it will be."

There is laughter all around. Music plays loudly. Every other member of the crew is enjoying themselves. Bell and Howarth are the only two people *staying* at the bar; everyone else simply steps up and leaves with their drink.

"I think it will be too." Bell agrees; then finishes his mead in a long single pull. "I just know we'll be the ones who have to make it that way."

CHAPTER THIRTEEN

WHAT WILL ACTUALLY HAPPEN

It requires a four hour hike along the mountain side trails from Caelzun to reach the ancestral forest where the second conflict of the clash of the crown takes place. The forest has been walled in to create a large natural arena. It is about a five square kilometre area densely packed with pine, spruce, birch and poplar trees; each interconnecting frankly with thick bushes and spindly vines. Bell, Bristol, Izelle and Teander each stand at an entrance into the walled off arena. A flare is shot off from the centre and each heir is able to pass through a gate inwards.

Bell walks forwards into the forest. The sun splays through the tree-tops in beautiful rays. There are small puddles of rainwater collected about and bright resilient mountain flowers at the base of most trees. Bell's ears flicker and he hears from half a kilometre away the unmistakable crackling of a burning log. He makes haste towards it and stealthily approaches. There he finds Teander sat up on a simple log bench a short distance in front of a campfire; both his sword and shield are laid on the ground behind him. Bell approaches with his hands held up mercifully. "Just enjoying a bit of flame?" He questions.

Teander smiles warmly. "I hoped it would make someone stop for a moment, and chat."

"Your trap has sprung successfully." Bell offers. He removes Ehre in its sheath from his belt and leans it against a tree. He sits next to Teander and stares down at the fire. "You got that going quick."

"I hate wet boots. You know? You can hike for hours and forget. But the second you sit down. You remember how awful your feet feel. *So*, a quick fire gets dry feet faster." Teander explains.

Bell smiles. "Makes sense." He warms his hands on the small but focused flame. "So what is it that you wanted to talk about?"

"*Well*, I worry some could see it in the wrong way. Given the path I've taken to receive the rank I hold. But this massive, predatory battle. There is no civility here. It is primitive; from the time of the tribal warriors who installed the practice." Teander sighs. "I hope that I can convince my fellow heirs to battle simultaneously. All together. As this competition should be." He looks out into the woods with a roll of his eyes. "Or maybe we'll end up playing cat and mouse."

"I see what you're getting at." Bell admits. He chuckles a bit to himself. "It figures old dumb hunters would reckon the best fighter was the best leader." He peers out into the woods, notices something, smiles, then continues speaking. "I can't help but feel as if we should be grateful for it. Considering what ended up happening after those tribes founded The Citizenry."

Teander sighs with frustration. "*Of course*. But would it not be better to have our history framed with golden nostalgia? We cannot live in the past forever, and attempting to do so is the only thing which may tarnish it."

Bell smiles. "I wish we could of spent more time together, during the war. I feel as if you would of been a much appreciated level head."

Teander prepares to speak but is stopped by Bell.

"Don't think that I don't see the value of what you have done. Mind, I doubt very much if you would of helped the war end any quicker; a few days, perhaps? No more then any other skilled individual. *But,* what you accomplished in Caelzun? The framework you created for the other Great Cities? I honestly admire your contribution to The Citizenry."

"*Thank you*." Teander accepts the compliment. He looks around the dense woods and then back at the fire. "I feel as if we're being watched."

"We are." Bell notes casually. There is silence and then the disturbance of twigs and bush a short distance away. Izelle emerges from the forest with a stupid smirk on her face.

"I honestly thought that would work better." She admits.

"Planned to wait for us to take each other out and then jump on the weakened remainder?" Teander questions.

Izelle stands next to the fire and smiles. With a single motion she stabs her polearm into the ground and takes a seat; crossing her legs over one another. "So what's the plan, emerge from the forest with our hands held tight and a resilient optimism?"

"We're to abide the ordained rules." Teander notes. "But without the harshness of such deceitful combat."

"I've never seen this *honest combat* you are inferring. Have you perfected a manner in which to *cleanly* kill someone?" Izelle critiques. "Fighting for your life. Hunting a worthy opponent. That is the closest to honest you'll find when it comes to mortal combat."

Bell laughs. "I once met this Selemian; during the war. Not that I ever got his name. We duelled in the ruins of a market. His squad had fallen before him but he had escaped; only to run right past me just out of view. I could of taken him out right then and there. But instead, I gave him the chance. We shared a glance, a nod." Flame flickers against Bell's glossy eyes. "I counted out only seven seconds for our duel. A thrust, a parry, two quick steps of recovery and a final blow. *Yet*, he was a different person by the end of it all. I could see it in his eyes. Had I let convenience murder him, there would be just that little bit less peace in our world." Bell pauses for a moment. "I don't think that is a sacrifice worth making."

The trio sit around the flame for a few moments. Bristol emerges from the woods with an armful of stacked wood. She drops it near the fire, takes a seat next to Teander then smiles widely. "Sorry it took a bit, lots to look at in here. Got a bit distracted." She admits.

Teander smirks. "No concerns at all Bristol. *Welcome.* Have you by chance overheard our plans?"

Bristol shakes her head '*no*'.

"He wants us to all battle simultaneously." Izelle informs her.

Bristol stares at Izelle and then Teander. She closes her eyes, takes a deep breath then exhales pure excitement. "*Absolutely!* That sounds super cool!"

Bell chuckles. "That settles it then." He stands up definitively. "Where shall we battle?"

Teander stands as well. "The trees are rather annoying obstacles. Not that I believe that should discredit them entirely."

"There is one option." Bristol suggests. "There is a pond. Not far from here. It is the depth of your ankles. But it is a clearing large enough for the four of us."

Teander sighs deeply and looks down to his recently dried boots. "It makes more sense then fighting through shrubbery."

After putting out the fire. The heirs follow Bristol to a calm green pond. They wad through it and each pick a relative *corner* to begin in. Silence draws. There are no birds, no insects and the wind has been muffled entirely by the dense forest. The heirs all stare out at each other; clenching their weapons and preparing their muscles for a sudden burst of action. The entirety of the moment stands on the precipice of explosion; culminating in an experience that is relatively awkward and quiet. They all stare out at each other, share some sort of inflection and then begin sprinting towards each other in an instant. The water splashes around and disperses with chaos.

Teander swings his sword wide and spins himself around to break up the collecting group. Bristol fires off two arrows at him quickly and he ducks to dodge. Water whips across as feet raise and sprint and the edges of weapons smack the tips of the pond. Blades clash as Bell and Teander duel; each slash by either of them being expertly deflected or dodged. Bristol fires a few arrows off at Izelle then quickly dodges into Teander; knocking him off his stance. Bristol fires an arrow point blank into Bell's foot but it is swiftly dodged and followed up by a powerful boot kick that sends Bristol a few metres back and out of the pond. Izelle flings herself towards Teander and is blocked with his shield; she lands onto it and pounces up high in the air; landing a short distance away with a loud splash. Teander swings to slash at Izelle while dodging a simple strike from Bell. Izelle jumps back and Teander follows. Bell prepares himself and slashes out at the air with intense focus and speed; a moment passes and then a large portion of the water in the pond flies towards Teander and Izelle; the wave forcefully smacks into them. Bell walks forwards as what remains of the pond sloshes into place. With acrobatic flair Bell begins swinging Ehre around his wrist; creating a sort of swirl of steel. Izelle tosses away her polearm as she allows herself to lay in a puddle a short distance outside of the pond. Teander pushes himself up to his feet using the point of his blade, takes a deep breath then calmly begins approaching Bell. The two men smirk before stepping towards one another. Bell slashes, Teander blocks with his shield then drops his posture to stab up at Bell. Bell jumps back and parries the stab; poking Ehre through the hilt of Teander's sword. With a quick flick of his wrist Bell rips the sword out of his hand and tosses *both* blades out of the pond onto a tuft of grass. Teander is caught in his surprise with a forceful combo of punches to his stomach and jaw. Teander steps back then throws his shield out of the water. He spits a bit of blood from his mouth and readies his unarmed stance. Teander steps forwards and expertly feigns a series of predictable jabs; earning him a straight on strike aimed right at Bell's nose. As the strike connects Bell screams out with frustration and charges at Teander. Teander braces himself against Bell but cannot stop him from picking him up and throwing him to the other side of the pond. Before Teander even splashes into the water Bell rushes over towards him; climbs on top of him and begins to restrain him in the shallow pond with consistent punches to the sternum. Before each punch Bell stops, looks down at Teander and provides him a moment to stop resisting; it isn't until the seventh strike that Teander finally gives in to defeat. As soon as the moment passes, Bell normalizes himself and helps Teander up.

"*Sorry*." Bell responds casually as he makes his way over towards Ehre; quickly attaching the blade to his hip again.

Teander appears tired and relatively swollen. "*Congratulations*." He mumbles. "I should have believed what I read."

"Which was?" Bell questions in response as he hands Teander his weapon.

"Of all of our living champions. You are the strongest Bell. If anyone is to complete the final conflict of this clash. It will be you." Teander affirms.

Bell seems off put by the compliment. "Do you know what the final conflict is?"

Teander shakes his head. "How could I? Do I look like a wizard to you?"

"As if I would know one if I saw one." Bell retorts.

"*Oh you would*." Teander ensures him. He peers around the forest and seems disappointed by what he discovers. "Have the women left?"

Bell shrugs and begins making his way to the exit. "Izelle isn't a fan of wasting seconds and Bristol certainly seems the sort to fancy company."

Teander rolls his shoulders as he considers the concept and becomes calm as he accepts it. "Then we'll be off ourselves." A moment passes. "My mother studied magic users you know. She always said they tended towards the absurd for their fashion. So, *you would* be able to see one. If you did."

"That's the problem though, isn't it?" Bell critiques. "It isn't like you run a small chance of passing by one on the street. What have there been, three magic users in all of recorded history?"

"My mother believed there used to be more. *Not many*. But a small village with a population of maybe a hundred or so? She was never able to discern what happened to them or why it is that the magic users of our era are so infrequent."

"Well it isn't like it is easy, to just, toss a ball of fire from the palm of your hand." Bell interjects.

"Of course not! Even for the magic users we know of, all of them are elderly; their abilities only having truly began to manifest in the final years of their lives." Teander explains.

Bell perches his lips for a moment. "Is that because they're closer to magic when closer to their deaths?"

"That was the running theory for a *number of years*." Teander admits. "*However,* the contemporary opinion was changed upon examining an actual spell book. It was found during a ruin expedition; seeking magical relics to convert for essence engines. The sheer *volume* of content contained within that text. There was a disambiguation for every single phrase and symbol throughout the book. There would be seven hundred character long instructions for the pronunciation of the first syllable of a magical incantation and even then its specific intent was up to interpretation."

Bell laughs. "That's ridiculous."

"*Precisely!*" Teander exclaims. "For a magic user to appear in our generation. Not only must they be born with an aptitude for the arcane arts but it must be accompanied by an absolute dedication and work ethic."

"Is there a way to discern whether one has magical potential? Surely the only test cannot be wasting your whole life trying?" Bell inquires.

"Nothing definitive." Teander notes. "Well, at least there is nothing you could see or touch. But there is a belief that an individual with magical potential will find themselves drawn to it. They will feel the life in a magical relic or dream of a place that could never exist in our world."

The pair reach the edge of the arena. They nod towards one another as they exit to be greeted by a massive crowd; each member cheering. They are approached by William.

"*And here comes our victor now!*" William shouts out to the excited audience. He rushes up to Bell and takes him by the wrist; holding his hand up high. "Bell is the victor of the second conflict!" William announces again; the crowd cheers. Teander stands in place beside the men with a stoic look on his face. "Soon Bell will face the secrets and danger of the third conflict! Not even I know what befalls him. It is for that exact reason, that for the very first time in history. The third conflict of the crown will be broadcast on radio so that all may partake!"

Bell seems confused by the announcement; but smiles professionally as the audience seems to be rather riveted by the concept. Bell nods and murmurs something too quiet to discern under his breath.

"Tune in tomorrow at ten in the morning to catch the broadcast!" William informs them.

Bell leans in behind William. "Not even you know what will happen?" He whispers.

William shakes his head. "I do not. Past this point. You will be guided by The Citizenry's historian; Aizenel." William speaks the name without much ease; seemingly unused to uttering it. "There is a meeting scheduled tomorrow, you'll share breakfast prior to the conflict. I will, *however*, escort you from your suite to the meeting."

"I appreciate that." Bell admits. He nods towards Teander and begins his trek back towards Caelzun.

⎯⏚⎯

Following a shared wagon ride with Izelle and Bristol. Bell arrives back in Caelzun. They are immediately flagged down by a messenger in a great panic. *"Heirs!"* The messenger shouts as she rushes up towards them.

Izelle becomes very serious. "Yes, *speak*." She orders.

"The body of your convict. *It has been stolen*." The messenger speaks with a grave inflection.

Izelle immediately looks over towards Bell; both share a very intense expression. They both leap out of the wagon in a rush. Bristol stands and jumps out with them.

"Can I help?" Bristol offers; attempting to not seemed pleased with the opportunity to assist.

"*Yes,* come with me. We must secure the grounds. I can use your eyes and bow." Izelle responds swiftly. "Bell, you know what to do. Full sweep, start from the cells."

Bell nods and rushes off in an instant. His focus is only on what is in front of him, and where his foot must land next in his dash. He quickly rushes through the castle and into the cells. There is nothing. He wastes no time and rushes through the halls only to be stopped in a large garden courtyard by the sound of a dry laugh.

Caesar is sitting on a bench in the centre of the courtyard; his neck bares the deep wound of a slash. He makes eye contact with Bell, stands, and then points at the revolting wound. "You have *no idea* how hard that is to fake."

Bell chuckles himself. "I'm not gonna pretend that isn't pretty impressive."

Caesar smiles warmly. "*Man*, see. In another life. We could of been friends. I'm sorry we have landed on opposite sides of, *all of this*."

"What even is all of this Caesar? This doesn't have to be something." Bell argues. "We *can* be friends."

Caesar sways his head with deep emotion. "You *know we can't!* You killed my family Bell! My people! Just because I like you does not mean I can forgive you. I can *never* forgive you."

"Wait, *what do you mean*?" Bell asks apprehensively.

"You know, deep down. You feel it. You feel your repulsion for me. You crave the death of a Selemian. *Admit it!*"

Bell stares at Caesar. "No?" He stares for longer. "*No way.* Every record was checked. No stone left un-turned. There was to be no one left to form any rebellion."

"I changed the records. Dropped myself into the paper trail of another blood-line." Caesar explains. "I hid right behind the curtain of terror. Just so I could be sure *you people* don't forget. You may break down our cities and return them to nature. Make mulch of the books of our history." He attempts to shake his head; seemingly unable. "There is not the slightest of Selemian influence throughout *your citizenry* that has not been rewritten or reclaimed." He stares down at Bell. "I didn't want everything I had the misfortune of being born into to be *erased*. As if it truly did mean nothing. Like it was failed from the start." Caesar explains then drops to his knees; quickly slashing a blade up both his wrists. "We were never going to fight Bell. The fighting has already been done. One of us won, the other, *fades*." He drops from his knees; his face smacking hard against the ground.

Bell walks over and sits apprehensively next to the corpse. He sits there for a couple of minutes before Izelle, Bristol and a detachment of about ten guards find him.

"Are you hurt Bell?!" Izelle screams with concern as she rushes over to him.

Bell shakes his head. "*No*, I am fine. He never touched me."

"How did he get back here? Was he *alive?* " Izelle asks; her rushing heart ruffling her pronunciation.

"He faked his death." Bell states plainly. "He faked steel cutting his throat, he faked his ancestry." A short silence passes. "He was *the last Selemian* Izelle. Or, at least, I have to believe he was."

"There is no way Bell." Izelle states strictly.

Bell stands and stares down at Caesar. "He seemed to believe so."

"Well of course, what sort of poisons would one have to take to prevent death from such a wound? He could have been rife with insanity. Did he slash his own wrists?" She critiques.

"Without so much as a wince." Bell confirms. "You should have the body cremated." He looks up at the surrounding guards. "Preferably with many witnesses." He looks back down at the corpse. "Then bury the ashes and seal them with concrete."

"Are you sure?" Izelle questions with a bit of a smirk.

Bell stares right down at Izelle. "*Yes*." He assures her without any delight.

"*Alright*." She allows; adopting his seriousness.

Bell sways his head and takes a deep breath. "Are we rid of calamity now?"

"If Caesar is dead, and this isn't the start of some bigger ploy." Izelle states with a blank expression then takes a moment to look up at the sky. "Then we should be fine for now, *yes*. You should go rest Bell. All accounts note that the final conflict is gruelling." She smiles as warmly as she possibly can. "Thank you for your help, we will take it from here.

"*Mhmm.*" Bell vocalizes; intending to say more; he finds himself unable too; he continues back to his suite without further delay. He locks the door behind him as he arrives and walks straight out onto the balcony. He leans against it and stares out at the ocean. When his feet begin to hurt he sits down and leans against the railing, maintaining his gaze out at the water. His mind is racing with thought, cycles of the same considerations repeat endlessly. His frustration tires him and soon he falls asleep with his head cradled against his arms; all of him puddled up on the balcony floor.

___⊥L___

"Ylinia?" Izelle asks; appearing suddenly behind her in the hall of the Ivy Lodge.

Ylinia smiles; turning on her heels to smile up at Izelle. "*Yes?*"

"I just wanted to let you know, even if it doesn't really change anything." She takes a deep breath. "The man who took your arm, *Caesar.* We found him. We made sure he couldn't hurt anyone anymore."

"So he is dead?" She requests bluntly.

Izelle nods. "He is. Turned to ash by now."

Ylinia stares at Izelle for a moment, closes her eyes then nods in confirmation. "Thank you for telling me." She steps forwards and wraps her arm around Izelle; who holds her in return.

CHAPTER FOURTEEN

THE THINGS THAT LIVE

A few quick knocks on the door awaken Bell. He pulls himself together and wades over towards the noise; opening the door with an absolutely astounding lack of interest. Standing there diligently with well laundered clothing and a sharp expression is William.

"Good morning Bell." William greets him kindly.

Bell stares at William, looks over his shoulder towards the light outside and then back at William. "What time is it?"

"Six *something*." William answers shamelessly. "I received a notice from Aizenel. He has prepared quite a feast apparently; and has scheduled you enough time to properly rest prior to the conflict."

"Alright, I want a coffee before we go." Bell informs him.

William stands with his hands together and a warm smile. "Of course, of course. We can collect one along the way?"

"It is, six *something* in the morning. Where can we just go get coffee?" Bell questions as if the premise is entirely ludicrous.

"At least, seven places, within a fifteen minute walk of us, right now." William answers honestly; doing his best not to sound condescending.

Bell just stares at him.

"Please, follow me. We will refuel your attention span."

"It appreciates that." Bell responds.

The men leave the Ivy Lodge and enter their escort vehicle. Their ride is not far to a nearby cafe which roasts its own beans and prepares every aspect of its beverages on sight and within view of the customer; including the very paper cups they offer their products in. They return to the vehicle with their beverages to continue the escort.

It takes half of his coffee and a few dedicated eye stretches for Bell to feel in any sort of mood for conversation. "This is tasty." He notes as pleasantly as he possibly can at this point in time.

"Of course." William notes as if it is obvious. "Caelzun requires all workers to receive a great deal of recompense in return for their efforts. If a business is not successful enough to complete their contribution to the community; there is no way to cheat a half-victory. Either you are good enough to make it, or you will not exist." He explains this rather pridefully.

Bell nods in understanding. "*Well, good.*" He looks around the vehicle briefly. The upkeep is phenomenal for what was once a military vehicle; it is likely no one has even died in here recently. "Have you ever met this Aizenel?"

William shrugs. "A few times. Quiet fellow. Seems rather, *obedient* for a historian."

"Should you expect something else from a royal historian?" Bell questions.

"Well, *no*. But his published work could fill entire rooms with only a single copy of every title. The man has authored a book detailing every grizzled bit of violence, every victory, every sparkle of value throughout the ages. You would imagine at least a portion of that flavour would transfer over."

"I had always hoped for the same thing myself. But I have observed that people of great action may be rather simple dorks when their blade isn't at hand." Bell admits with a smirk.

William smiles. He closes his eyes, listens to the area around him then looks contently at Bell. "We are near."

A few moments pass. The vehicle stops. Both men get out. Ahead of them is a large stone tower with half of its body contained within the peak of a mountain. There is a long and formidable road leading from central Caelzun to here. William motions his hand to the front door of the tower; which is rusted in some places. They both enter the tower into an incredibly welcoming lobby. The floors are a bright oak hardwood, the walls a polished stone. There is a fireplace against the northern wall which trails up throughout all the floors. An elderly man wearing a fine brown robe greets them. He is starting to bald and walks with a mild hunch. He seems pleasant and capable otherwise.

"Greetings Aizenel." William speaks warmly.

The elderly man smiles. "Welcome to you both." He peers at Bell. "Are you the heir who has been victorious so far?"

Bell nods. "I am."

"*Congratulations*. I remember meeting Richard during his clash. It is a challenge which demands everything from even the most skilled of individuals." Aizenel commends him.

"Mhmm." Bell responds. "It has been. *An experience*."

Aizenel turns to look at William. "William, thank you greatly for escorting the heir here. From here, we will share a private breakfast. If you do not mind."

William smiles and shakes his head kindly. "Not a concern at all. I wish you both the best." He bids farewell and returns to the escort vehicle. Aizenel watches the vehicle with a focused gaze and doesn't speak until he is assured it has gone. "Please follow me Bell. You may call me Mr.Len."

Bell raises his eyebrow with a confused expression. "Do you not prefer your first name."

"*It is not mine to claim*. I am Mr.Len. Aizenel, *prefers* to not be known by his face."

"You do not share that information with many, do you?" Bell questions with a bit of a whisper.

"None but the highest of royalty. However, I can see your place amongst them already. So it is not a secret I feel will be misplaced." Mr.Len responds kindly. He leads Bell up through the tower to the very top level. The door entering the penthouse room is locked in three separate locations; each of which require a different key. With rather obvious muscle memory Mr.Len swirls around a ring of keys; unlocking each part of the door as swiftly as is likely possible. He opens the door for Bell and stands in place outside; motioning his hand inwards.

Bell nods in passing as he enters a massive golden library. In the centre of the room is a humanoid statue of a middle aged man; dressed beautifully in decadent robes. He wears a long beard upon a slim mature face; with three separate pony tails running down his back. The statue faces a wall full of books which are being peered upon by a series of complicated magnifying glasses. There are ten different books hanging page by page in exact order across the room; for each of the hundreds of pages is a magnifying glass angled perfectly so that it may be read from the statue's point of view. A loud whirring sound begins and all of the magnifying glasses rescind into place. A bronze mechanical hand stretches out from the wall and takes down each page of one of the books. Another hand emerges and places a new book onto a table; then begins taking each page out from the book and hanging the pages in place where the previous ones had just been. As the new book is hung in place the magnifying glasses return and adjust themselves to provide an optimal view of each page. These hands appear skeletal in their form with the exception of their palms; as they are accented with a smooth piece of formed copper. Bell walks up behind the statue and stares in amazement at the machinations.

The statue cracks in some places then suddenly bursts. From the dust emerges a living rendition of the man the statue previously depicted. The man turns to look at Bell. "You understand now, *yes?*"

Bell looks between the man and the books and shrugs a bit. "It is so you can read, as a statue."

"My eyes are open, and they see all that is in front of me. My studies, they are laborious. They require you to mine through endless patterns of nonsense to find a single flicker of use. Then once you have found that flicker; you must maintain it. You must cultivate it. It cannot be extinguished. Yet we are plagued with distractions, as you no doubt know. The pangs of hunger, or lust. A requirement for rest, and social interaction. We are at a loss for dedication when we wear our flesh."

"Is that truly the reason you do it?"

Aizenel smiles and shakes his head. "They are but tertiary benefits."

"*Then?*" Bell questions.

"Then there is a reason you are met by my attendant as opposed to myself. I have been the historian here for nearly three hundred and fifty years. I have been known by many names, and I have *died* as is fashionable every hundred years or so. While history is a vessel which I shall never tire of travelling upon. It is my position as *Chief Arcanist* which I take most seriously."

Bell stares in disbelief. "You are truly a wizard?"

Aizenel nods. "I have more then but a single trick up my sleeve. *Yes.*" He motions his hand towards a large doorway. "But please, go ahead. I have had a wonderful meal prepared."

Together the men walk into a large dining hall. It is simpler then the overt elegance of the library previously. However there is immense charm. Hand carved wooden pieces cover the walls and accent the ceiling. A circular table sits near a window which overlooks a beautiful snippet of the mountains. Stacked on the table upon various levels of serving apparatus is: a few dozen strips of bacon, a few links of sausages, buttermilk pancakes, potato pancakes, devilled eggs, grilled ham sandwiches, hash-browns, roast beef with gravy, pepper and bacon quiche & scrambled eggs with spinach and tomato.

"It is just the two of us, yes?" Bell questions as his entire body quakes with excitement at the unveiling of so much delicious looking food.

"It is, but don't feel as if you must contain yourself. We can have more if need be."

Bell chuckles and takes his seat quickly. He nods towards Aizenel. "Thank you for this meal."

"*Please*." He insists. "I'll send your thanks to the chefs. I stood still while all of this was being made, reading something about the canonical determination of personal duplication; *most likely*."

"Sounds...*interesting*." Bell admits as he begins plucking items from each serving tray to create a dense collection on his plate.

"It is." Aizenel admits with a smirk. "But not as interesting as how someone from Varyia came to Rion. Especially looking-" Aizenel lingers his gaze upon Bell's legs and hands. "*Well,* as you do."

Bell is struck with a sudden surprise. "Can you see my origin so easily?"

Aizenel nods modestly as he takes a few small pieces of roast beef for his plate. "Some things are more obvious then others."

A few moments of soft chewing pass; Bell attempts to eat as much as is reasonable before responding. "*Mhmm*." He vocalizes as he chews and swallows. The first bite satisfies his excitement and he feels a bit of patience return to him. "I chose to leave. I understood *the-*" Bell holds his hands out in front of him and stares at them distantly. "*-the* sacrifices that would be required to make the passage."

"I see, but how was it that you performed this passage. Was it as simple as walking here?" Aizenel inquires; for the most part ignoring the food on his plate.

"Well it is not like I could fly."

Aizenel chuckles. "I guess not."

"The passage is something of a secret. Known only to a certain few; each sworn to the protection of this very realm." Bell states stoically. He stares down at his still very full plate of food. "What sort of secret would you offer against it in trade?"

"Would it not be treason for you to share?"

"This secret in your hands would be futile in combination with everything but academic intrigue. The passage can be used from but one direction, and only by a *Varyian*." Bell admits.

Aizenel huffs. "You do well to tarnish your own goods." He jests. "Then, I believe the only reasonable chip in my possession to barter with, would be the origin of the clash of the crown."

Bell chuckles. "The hundred tribes of origin formed together to create *The Citizenry*. They sought someone to become the leader of the society and the clash was created to facilitate this process." He shrugs. "It is not a secret."

"*Ah*, you know the edited version which is but a children's *tale*." Aizenel responds confidently.

Bell prepares himself to feast upon his meal. "Then please, *go on*."

"When the hundred tribes of the first generation emerged upon the plains of creation, they did not find themselves upon a land which happily had them. The world as we know it today was carved up in ownership between six of what humanity deemed *Vile Beast-Lords*. These lords were immensely powerful and each commanded an army of lesser beings. The wars of our ancestors were brutal and constant. They fought back against the lords and through their conquest discovered *Our Heart*. How it is that such an item came to exist so deep in our planet; not even I can say. *Our Heart* is a massive relic which allowed the engineers of The Citizenry to construct a great prison; known as *The Hearth*. This prison was designed to be the home of five of the six beast-lords." Aizenel takes a sip of his tea which he has let sit to cool. "The sixth, launched a desperate attack upon The Citizenry. Our first king: Felix Kanthe; slew the final beast-lord in single combat. It was as a result of his victory that the clash was considered at all. As it was the faith in his people and the might of his blade which made him such a successful leader; the people of the first ages idolized such traits. The clash was designed thereafter; the nature of its final conflict kept a secret from all but prospective heirs."

Bell gulps down the last few bites of scrambled eggs, bacon and sausage dipped into gravy left on his plate. "So many secrets." Bell states with a bit of amusement. "Why is it that nobody ever references these beast-lords? Are they an *official* secret"?

Aizenel shakes his head. "Nothing of the sort. A few of my publications go over the exact instances. Though I admit the detail utilized in such texts may be considered, rather, *dry*."

"Typical." Bell admits with a smirk. "Alright, then, you wish to know of my passage from Varyia?"

Aizenel nods.

"It is a pond. Entirely silver, like mercury. While it may sound beautiful, even on approach you can feel that there is something amiss. The pond consists entirely of acid. *Magical* as it may be; each step which plunges you deeper burns away another portion of your flesh. It isn't until you have been fully submerged for a few moments and the drastic burning has flooded your lungs that you finally emerge on the other side." Bell reminisces without much joy. "The air is colder then anything you could possibly believe it to be. But in survival, there is potential."

"It does not sound like a pleasant journey." Aizenel attempts to empathize. "Why make it all?"

"We could hear screams through the passage. They did not end, nor did they discriminate speaker. We heard children scream out for their mothers as they were crushed under the metal shoes of stampeding steeds. Bombs suddenly turn afternoons into disasters. The horrors that were *broadcast* to our home. My wife; Temple. She pleaded to our order to let her leave her post; to allow her sacrifice and permit her to pass through to Rion." Bell exhales. "They granted her wishes." He closes his eyes and makes attempts to not tear up. "And helping her achieve her dreams was my favourite thing to do."

Aizenel smiles sweetly; brushing away a small tear from his own eye. "Thank you for sharing this with me." He motions his hand towards the feast upon the table. "Did you get your fill?"

Bell shuffles his posture and smiles. "Unless you want to leave the room and let me pig out shamelessly. I'll be good."

"*I can*?" Aizenel half stands from his chair and looks towards the exit.

Bell laughs. "No, sit, it is okay."

He returns to his seat.

"The final conflict. What can you tell me about it?"

"You'll be facing the last of the beast-lords. This one is known only as *The Blue Phantasm*."

Bell raises his eyebrow. "Where would I possibly combat such a being?"

"In its prison cell, of course."

"I'm not exactly a fan of murdering a fish in a barrel." Bell objects.

"This being is no fish, and this prison no barrel. The Blue Phantasm would burn down every home in every city, as it did before, were it given the chance. I promise you that if you are capable of performing its execution, it will be done in good faith."

Bell nods a few times then stands with a grunt. "Then let us be off to this prison. I at least wish to see this *hearth*."

"Of course, *but*." Aizenel notes with a formal inflection. "There is but a bit more tradition which we must pay attention too, prior to this final conflict."

Bell silently sighs so aggressively it may as well shrug the room around him. "*What?*"

"There is a small farewell. Do not worry." He raises his hands to perform air quotations. "*I*" He chuckles. "As in Mr.Len; have organized it with the members of your escort. There is a room near the entrance of the prison designed for this very purpose. You will have a few moments with them before moving forwards into the final conflict."

"*Ah*." Bell softens. He looks around the room and swallows a bit of guilt. "That sounds fine then." A quick breath escapes him as he straightens his postures. "But we can leave for that now, *right?*"

Aizenel nods. "You can, of course. Mr.Len will accompany you. *We* shall see one another soon. Best of luck heir. This will be a challenge unlike any that have come before you."

Bell nods with unconvincing modesty. "I will see you soon Aizenel. It was nice to properly meet a wizard." He smiles then speaks softly to himself. "Totally would of recognized that though."

___JL___

"Calling it a farewell doesn't come off very hopeful." Howarth notes with a large warm smirk. "You'll do fine I figure, eh?"

Bell smirks in return and shrugs. "I imagine so. If I die today it'll be the first time it has ever happened." He jests.

Together the crew all sit together in a beautiful pine cabin. There are windows along only the southern wall which peer out towards the mountains and a patch of forest. Courtney and Ylinia have shared a couch. Howarth stands next to Mel who is seated upon a single reclining chair with a foot-rest. Alim and Lance stand beside one another smiling softly towards everyone. There are a few pitchers of juice, wine and water on the table in between bits of dried meat, crackers and cheese.

"Do you know if anyone has died on this part of the clash?" Courtney asks aloud.

"*Oh certainly.*" Alim speaks up. "Roggard the Black. He bested the first two conflicts with a nearly peerless display of combat prowess. He was struck upon the top of the head and killed within the first few moments of initiating the third conflict. Following him was Frost-Drinker Stell. Just as fearless as any leader must be. Following the final conflict, all that was ever discovered of her was a hand clutching her own hair so tightly it required mechanical assistance to remove."

A brief silence follows the uncomfortable explanation.

"What a bode of confidence dad." Courtney chirps at him.

"Ahh." Alim vocalizes loudly. "Bell is a strong fighter with a keen mind. Plus he has that mask, *thing*." Alim looks over at Bell. "Does it have a name? Half mask? Mouth cover?" He shakes his head awkwardly then looks back at Courtney. "He'll be fine."

Bell laughs. "I once tried to wear a full mask. It was incredibly comfy by my standards. But too many people started to get a creepy vibe off the guy in a full face mask. *So.*" He mimes cutting a line in the middle of his face with the flat of his hand. "*Less mask.*"

"Eyes make the difference." Mel chimes in. "When your eyes get shadowed off by a full mask. They look intense; like you're peering in through a window at people who don't want you there."

With wide eyes Bell stares at Mel. "Maybe that is half the fun."

She chuckles a bit. "You don't really want imposing. I just think you don't like feeling people stare at you."

"That could be a part of it too." Bell admits.

"How is it that we'll be listening on the radio?" Ylinia questions.

Howarth raises his eyebrow. "That is a good question. It isn't like William could just stand nearby and annotate the whole thing?"

"There is a lot of trickery in the arts Howarth. No doubts they've figured some backward manner to watch with three perfectly aligned mirrors and a safety box." Lance explains confidently.

"I'm sure it is something like that." Bell agrees. He leans backwards to stretch and lets out a bit of a yawn.

"You should take this more seriously." Ylinia states very intensely; devastating the pleasant energy of the room.

Bell stares down at Ylinia and she stares back up at him; she is unflinching. Bell nods and corrects his posture a bit. "You're right."

Mr.Len enters the room quietly and greets the group with a smile. "*Heir*." He states as pleasantly as he can. "It is time for the conflict to begin."

"Of course." Bell complies. He walks over towards Mr.Len then turns to face the crew. "I won't make you bid farewell. I shall fight, and return."

They quickly exit out into the cabin hallway. Mr.Len turns on his heels to lock the crew into the visitation room. Bell raises his eyebrow with obvious concern.

"*Why?*" He questions strictly.

"No harm will come to them. This part of the prison is public, it is however, but an entrance. The dangers contained below must never be tampered with by the likes of mere men." Mr.Len explains.

Bell stands tense for a second then releases his breath and continues to follow along. They walk into the main chamber of the cabin where a massive stone fireplace installation stands in the centre of the northern wall. Mr.Len approaches the fireplace; roaring with a blaze within; and clicks a series of keys into hidden locks across the stone mantle. As the final key is turned the flame is instantly extinguished by a torrent of air. The entire installation moves back into the wall a few meters, splits in half vertically and then descends straight down; revealing a staircase entirely sealed behind it.

The men quickly rush down the stairs and open up a large steel door; the moment the steel door is opened the fireplace installation returns to its original placement and darkens the small secret hallway. Behind the door is a small room with a panel full of buttons on the wall. They both enter the room and close the steel door behind them. Mr.Len presses the lowest of the many buttons and the entire room *shakes*. They descend into the planet for a few minutes at a brisk speed before stopping rather suddenly. The steel door opens again and ahead of the men is a degree of elite architecture unseen anywhere across Rion. The walls, floors, doors, and all accents are a near glimmering white. Standing at the end of the hall is Aizenel.

"Welcome Bell." Aizenel greets warmly. "What do you think of *The Hearth* upon your first impression?"

"It is unlike any prison I have ever seen previously." He waves his arms around. "Also the only one that is a hallway with two dudes in it."

Aizenel chuckles. "There is no *spectacle* made of imprisonment here. No one-sided windows, no slotted doors. There aren't even guards here to become ever crueller towards the imprisoned."

"Then what separates this *prison* from an *inn* with unique accommodations?" Bell questions.

"Everything the beast-lords require the hearth provides for them. They may never taste food but they will never feel hunger.

Sleep is impossible but one will never feel tired; so on and so forth. They are free to their fantasies, to make their own schedules." Aizenel explains as he walks down the hall to stand beside one of the tall white doors; it has no apparent knob to open it. "All because they are unable to pass through this door."

Bell squints and stares at the door. "Is there something special about this door?"

Aizenel chuckles. "*Obviously.*" He stares. "Do you think it is cool paint and wishful thinking that keep such creatures at bay?"

"It would be convenient is all." Bell responds with a plain expression.

"Every *cell* is tailored specifically to the entity it contains. It is not specific to primitive monster kings. Were it set to contain you its parameters would be set *just* above your insurmountable amount of strength."

"Huh." Bell vocalizes. "Then inside, is, *what?*"

Aizenel shrugs. "We don't *really* know." He focuses on a spot on the bare wall and waves his hand. "*Eye of Guile; reveal your view.*" As he speaks the command a *mirror* appears upon the wall; its reflection shows a young boy sitting alone inside an expansive white cube. "I can see inside this way. I'll watch whatever happens. But the phantasm is very capable. *And we know* that he isn't actually a young boy."

"What a mix up that would be eh?" Bell notes.

"He has been here since the first age, so, *yes*. It would be quite a mix up."

"And you would of discovered an immortal kid. So that is just a combo of unlikely happen-stances." Bell jokes.

"Mhmm." Aizenel agrees. "Before you go ahead. Could I show you something?"

"I don't see why not." Bell allows.

Mr.Len nods towards the men and brings out a pocket sized book from his back pocket; leaning comfortably against a wall as he rediscovers his most previous page.

Aizenel leads Bell down the hallway where they pass through one of the doors on the right side of the hall. They trail down a small set of stairs then around a corner. The room before them is mostly white with four solid lines of black tile running throughout like a centred cross. Levitating in the centre of the room is a mostly circular object which shifts in form, colour, shape & size at regular intervals as if it were a beating heart. One moment the object looks like mushed corn sparkling with bits of purple or red then a moment later it is a thousand perfectly formed cubes each leaping out from one another amidst a detailed gradient of silver and blue. There is an impossible to ignore pleasantness which is brought upon all your senses simply as a result of being near the odd object.

"This is *Our Heart*. As Felix Kanthe and the other members of the first generation deemed it. They found it mining for additional iron. The excavations they made into this whole site formed the basis of *The Hearth's* entire layout."

Bell is fixated upon *Our Heart*. "It is, beautiful. I almost don't believe what I'm looking at is real. Despite it being right there, in front of my face." He shakes his head slightly then focuses again on *Our Heart*.

"It emits magical energy a thousandfold what an astaria engine can produce; and it does it without even the slightest of qualms." Aizenel explains. *Our Heart* beats and the room moves in motion with it; as if reality is distorted around it. "I am confident it is being under-utilized."

"Does it only power *The Hearth*?" Bell questions.

Aizenel nods. "The beast-lords, like any worthy captives, cannot be afforded escape. It would spell far too much disaster."

"Of course." Bell responds. He walks in place a little bit then flickers his hands against the side of his leg.

"Thank you for letting me show you this Bell." Aizenel compliments. "Are you ready for the final conflict?"

Bell nods. "Is there any other real choice but yes?"

The men begin walking back. Aizenel sways his head. "Not really no. Even the ones who are scared shitless lie." They return to the hall. Mr.Len nods towards them both and packs away his book. He folds his arms and stares down at the door ahead of them. Aizenel presses his hand *into* the mirror upon the wall; then turns his fist. The door opens into a small hallway where an even further re-enforced door has been installed. With the implication clear Bell steps into the hall and stares back at Aizenel and Mr.Len as the door descends behind him. He looks ahead. The hallway is completely dark. A column of light breaks through as the other side of the hallway opens up into the innards of a massive white cube. The walls appear to be constructed with metal of some sort and there is a *humming* everywhere that never ceases. Sitting on the floor in the middle of the cube is a young boy. His clothes are well tailored; his hair fashionably cut. He is without eyeballs; the small empty sockets are pink with mush. He crooks his neck, locks it in place and stares at Bell without taking a breath.

Bell takes a few steps into the room. The moment he passes the threshold the door behind him closes; sealing so perfectly that it can't be distinguished from the rest of the wall. Bell smiles at the odd child; turning his head a bit to the side. "*Hello.*"

CHAPTER FIFTEEN

ODD CHILD

The young boy stands without breaking his gaze. "You're not one of them. Why are you here on their behalf?" He states with a distorted voice that crackles as if it were artificial.

"There are many reasons, I think." Bell answers.

"They don't know you shed your skin, *beast*." The boy speaks without making any sort of eye-contact.

Bell rolls his eyes. "*Some seem* too. But it doesn't matter."

"They will hunt you, put you in a cage just like this one. Make you spend every second you own on a damnation you can't end."

"I see what you're trying to do." Bell states while looking around the area. "It might work, on someone that cares more. But I'll save you the time. I'm rougher on myself then you ever could be."

"So be it." The boy responds; dispersing in an instant the moment he finishes speaking. Snow begins to fall from the ceiling. A tall deep shadow grows in the distance across from Bell. A new deeper voice can be heard everywhere. "I never feared your kind."

Bell unsheathes Ehre with a swish and flick. "You should."

The shadowed child laughs and sways his hand; knocking Ehre away from Bell. A blue storm of electricity forms around the room and all visibility is lost.

Each footstep is drudgery as Bell ventures towards where he saw his blade land. He can just barely begin to spot it before the storm dissipates violently and he is thrown far from it. He lands on his back, loses a few seconds in the fall then finds himself having tumbled onto his chest. As he pushes himself up he stops to kneel and look around. All around him is a great plain; a wide open blue sky above. An army of humans riding tepid and muscular horses rush through the tall yellowed grass. Each of the men wears a bronze armour that Bell recognizes only from museums; it is short in all places, square, and covered in runes. The horses rush straight towards Bell and pass through him as if he is a ghost.

"*Hello?*" Bell shouts at them to no avail. He shrugs, takes a deep breath then launches into a sprint after the horses. Quickly he is only a few paces behind and follows as the men descend upon a massive hole in the ground. Each gets off their horse and orders it to rush away from the opening. They brandish heavy slashing weapons, share a quick look between one another and begin marching down into the opening. Bell follows along; but he already knows what he is going to become witness to. He can see it in the body language of every individual; taste it in the air. There is going to be death; and those obliged to cause it will spend every night following this one trying to forget about it.

The men file down into the hole with torches lit. They barely speak. They pass through burrowed out tunnels and slay every beast which comes their way. Some are young, some old; the soldiers do not posit an inspection prior to fulfilling their orders. There are screams of horror and small skirmishes against the unprepared and terrified. It is a slaughter; as any successful raid aims to be.

Bell lets out a deep and incredibly tired sigh. The images all around him sweep into a storm. The young boy emerges from the storm. "Do you share a blindness in your heart as those soldiers did? Those who slaughtered my kind; having never provided us an option to be anything other then villains."

"And I'm sure there is a memory just as brutal from a farm boy watching monsters rip away his family. The suffering of your people was heinous, *obviously*. But it was not unique. You killed and were killed like every other group of *idiots* on this planet. Not one of us has ever sought to end violence with anything but more *successful* violence. Unless you plan to do anything other then that. You're just repeating the cycle. I can see how absolute that is now."

"*Then I guess.*" The boy ponders. He disperses like dust in a breeze and from the dense storm of snow behind him emerges a massive monstrous being. It has a shifting face of a thousand monstrosities and a broad humanoid torso placed tortuously into a levitating brazier flush with blue flame. The creature has arms which end at raptor like claws covered entirely in a thick blue fur. The creature screams, slashes out at Bell halfheartedly then just drops its arms like dead weight. "Even if I win." It picks its arms up and stares down at the floor. "I don't want to wait in a room until another mortal comes to try and kill me." It drops to its *knees*. Ehre flies from the storm of snow at incredible speed straight into Bell's hand. "Be done with it, before I-"

Bell plunges Ehre directly into the beast-lord's heart and as he pulls the blade back out; alongside a splendid portion of thick black blood; is an explosion of ecstatic blue flame. Ehre burns brightly with the blue flame and refuses to be extinguished no matter how dramatically Bell swashes it around in the air. He stares at Ehre with confusion; the blade hasn't been harmed in the slightest by the flame nor has the heat morphed the metal. The storm dissipates around Bell; as do the remains of the child. Bell lowers the tip of the blade to the floor and the licks of flame burn a spot on the ground. He raises his eyebrow and cautiously moves his free hand toward the flame; it is so ineffective against him that he can place his fingers right against the steel of the blade and feel it to be cold. With a hopeful enthusiasm Bell places Ehre into the sheath; he is pleased to discover the flames are extinguished. He waits a few moments then draws the blade again; it is completely barren of flame. He pleasantly swings it around his wrist as he has a million times before and halfway through the motion the blade erupts entirely into blue flame again. Bell sheathes the blade, smiles, then walks towards the exit door which has once again become discernible.

Aizenel bows towards Bell as he returns. "Congratulations Bell. I admit I was unable to see through the storm as to what happened. But it is obvious you have emerged victorious."

Bell looks up with an empty expression for just a second before remembering himself and smiling. "Of course, thank you. It was, a trial, *certainly*."

"*So*." Aizenel states a bit awkwardly. "Now comes the legislature part."

"Ah, *yes*, about that. I've been having some thoughts about it, and-"

"Hold them for a moment." Aizenel notes. "Mr.Len told me where it was he saw you in the royal family. I admit, it is not a position I would of expected."

"*Um*." Bell responds.

"To be the champion of the clash of the crown does not beget you with *the crown* as simply as that. It has placed but one more obstacle in your path."

Bell nods patiently. "And that is?"

"*A decision*. Your reward as champion is to appoint the individual whom you believe should be the leader of The Citizenry. In the past; every victor has opted to elect themselves. While it has not been seen why. Destiny has already written that this will not be your path."

Bell chuckles a bit. He looks around the room and smiles; allowing the true weight of the moment to occur to him. "I'm just doing what I can to keep distracted now a days. Maybe you understand?" He sways his shoulders. "Though you're so focused I doubt it. I figured that even if this competition ripped my entrails out. Even if it was endlessly awful from start to end; at least it is *something to do.* Of all the options, of all the distractions. A bit of obligation. A bit of competition. Something to put my head into. I figured it would be good for me." He shakes his head. "The issue is with taking care of yourself. You start to become blind to where you're headed; what will come of all your self medication; you know?" He holds his hands out in front of himself then drops them down into his legs. "But the truth of it is. I don't *want* to be a king. I'm a soldier and no matter how fancy you make that title. If you ask me to look out at a sunset. I'll tell you that just over the horizon is a battle; because that is what I know to expect." Bell lets out a deep breath. "And we don't need another king who can see only war in his future."

"Then do you have someone in mind? It is a tremendous thing to bestow upon someone. It cannot just be any one randomly decided upon."

Bell shakes his head. "No, it wouldn't be." He smiles slightly and nods a few times to himself. "There is a woman in my envoy; *Ylinia.* Quite capable. She has a mind that so far seems unharmed by the temptation of extremism. There is a balance within her; a potential for wisdom, strength and genuine leadership that I believe would be entirely betrayed if it were not given an opportunity like this."

"It is more then an opportunity."

"It is only pride that makes you think that. Everything is but an opportunity, a passage way; regardless of how prestigious it seems." Bell motions his hands around in the air around him. "This is all just *stuff.* None of it inherently means anything. No single piece of it has an existential value above another piece. We've sorted it all and organized it into a fashion that we fancy; *sure.* But no matter how *big* a role may seem. That is all it is. A role."

Aizenel smirks and nods. "I can see your logic Bell." He pauses for a moment as he visibly considers something. "So this Ylinia. She is the one you wish to offer the monarchy?"

Bell nods solemnly. "She is."

"As you wish. If she accepts the position. We shall unveil her as the Monarch of The Citizenry." Aizenel states blankly. "Though I doubt she will reject the opportunity. You *would* be the first to do so." He nods a few times to himself. "I'll have her summoned for a private meeting. Please follow me to a more suited room." Aizenel leads Bell to the main hall, all the way to the end, through a locked doorway and down a half-flight of stairs. They enter into an entirely white room with furniture and details distinguished only by bold black outlines; making it appear as if every object in the room has simply been drawn into place. Aizenel walks into the centre of the room with great enthusiasm. "I hope this will serve as both a distraction and an acceptable lounge."

"You say that as if I could not be impressed." Bell states pleasantly as he looks around. He kneels down to stare at a chair which can be denoted only by a series of straight lines with bright white space between them no different then the walls, ceiling or floor. Bell cautiously pokes the object and discovers it is both *real* and *rather soft*. "Who decided to create a room like this?"

Aizenel laughs. "*Right?*" He chuckles a bit more. "I asked myself the same thing. I guess the story goes that when the team putting this prison together had their first meeting. The lead architect and the lead designer just *really jived*. They inexplicably got what one another was shooting for. Only issue was; for some folks anyways; was that their *vision* was pretty *niche*. Some sort of speculative series of designs? I guess?" Aizenel shrugs. "They never get dirty either. It freaks me out. I've taught myself spells that can bend the fabric of reality. But get this. I spill juice on one of these seats. I touch the spill.

It is there. I turn around then turn back and look at the spot and *the spill is gone!*" He shrugs dramatically with a stupefied look on his face. "It is goddamn *black magic*."

Mr.Len appears in the entryway; beside him is a simultaneously confused and super pumped Ylinia. She spots Bell and instantly calms down. "Did you win?" She shouts at him.

Bell nods. "I found victory, *yes*."

Ylinia smiles widely. "I knew you would."

"I hoped the same."

Aizenel stands and walks over to Ylinia. "It is nice to meet you my dear. I am Chief Arcanist Aizenel."

Ylinia nods. "Yea *Mr.Len* gave me the scoop on the walk down here." She admits with a bit of guilt in her expression.

"Of course." Aizenel notes with a pleasant smile. He looks towards Bell. "We'll be back before too long. Don't feel rushed with your conversation. *Alright?*"

Bell nods. "Of course. Thank you."

Aizenel and Mr.Len leave together.

Ylinia stares up at Bell with an incredibly suspicious look on her face. She raises her eyebrow. "How did the final conflict go*? Were you harmed?"

Bell sways his head. "No, nothing of the sort. Barely broke a sweat if I'm being honest."

Ylinia laughs loudly; pretending to be guffawed by the seemingly confident remark. "And what *was* it that happened? They kept the broadcast as interesting as they could; but it was pretty obvious that they could only make out so much. They saw a big monster burning alive for sure. Was that in there?"

"For a bit there, yea I guess so." Bell admits with a shrug. He takes a deep breath and prepares for an awkward transition. "*Ylinia.*"

He states as directly as he can. "What is it that you believe *the monarch* is responsible for?"

"*Well?*" She responds skeptically. "Dad said the monarch was someone who fulfilled their contribution to *The Citizenry* by working as a sort of civil servant. Kind of like a face of progress and insight across our own society. A personification of all our people that speaks to and through The Citizenry."

Bell nods. "Sort of. Though it has always been that slightest bit more. The monarch is not our god, he is not our father, she is not our commander. He is a mortal trying to do good. She is transparent and resilient to corruption. He is all attempts at the ideal. She must strive to be the best of us; and never be prideful of the accomplishment. It is a task with unrivalled difficulty."

"The last king, he chose the path of extinction. It was the verdict of his glimpse into the people." Ylinia states plainly. "I can't imagine the leagues of considerations which preceded such a choice. To be the one responsible for such a decision?" Ylinia thinks on it for a moment. "I imagine it feels very heavy."

"Unimaginably so; and yet. *Ylinia*; I ask that you bare the weight of that burden." Bell requests suddenly.

Ylinia laughs then stares at Bell with a deadpan expression. "Me? The monarch? Bell, *you* won the clash. It is not my right, I am no heir."

Bell shakes his head. "I won, yes. But what I won was a decision, not a verdict. I believe that you should be the monarch." He waits a few moments. "I would act as the head of your guard, if you would allow it."

She stares. "You can't possibly be serious. That is such a massive decision to linger on but a response."

Bell shrugs. "How different is it really? Any change that has ever happened, starts with the simple decision to begin. There is no *grander* way to take on responsibility." He chuckles. "It just starts. It is terrifying. Then suddenly you've been doing it for a few weeks and it is your new normal."

"I can't say I ever dreamed of this happening." She remarks in a sort of shock.

"I would of figured it a common dream to wish yourself the queen." Bell notes.

Ylinia shrugs. "When I dream. I remember where I put things down. I often garden, lay down a spade and return a few nights later to find it in the same spot. A queen picks up and places back again so many pieces." She smirks. "My dreams could never keep up."

Bell widens his eyes. "So, Ylinia, will you accept the offer?"

Just short of three seconds pass; and nearly a thousand half prepared considerations. "*Yes. I will.* So long as you keep your promise as head of my guard."

"From here on out until I cannot." The oath is sworn immediately with stern language.

Ylinia smiles, swallows down what must be a few different emotions; then closes her eyes. "Then lets *begin*."

Chapter Sixteen

Our Future Defined By Fine Print

"So you are saying our daughter is now a queen?" Howarth and Mel question in near unison.

Bell, Mr.Len & William each nod in response to the inquiry. "*Yes.*" They answer confidently.

Howarth leans forwards to focus and Mel leans backwards to take it all in. "And you're sure about that?" Howarth questions.

"Without a doubt." Bell responds with great confidence. "She will be a leader among a council of amazing mentors and thinkers."

"She is young for a monarch, is she not?" Mel asks with a concerned inflection.

Bell considers the comment for a moment then sways his head side to side. "I think it might be the opposite. Some may be *too old* to lead. They may be wise and well informed. But they have adapted their entire life surviving underneath leadership. Their success is found within society; not above it. To go from such a pinnacle of understanding to something that is in so many respects foreign? You'd be no more an amateur then a child. At least starting young; you may experience the mistakes required of you in a time and place where you're still *looking to learn*. Instead of figuring you already have."

Mel sighs then nods a few times. "Then it is well that Richard's might was enough to end the war." She notes with exceptional gratitude. "I wouldn't want to watch Ylinia struggle with such an affair."

"If she had too though." Howarth remarks. "I think, she would actually come out alright."

"Of course she would." Mel retorts. "It isn't whether or not she will survive that I am worried about. It is the condition she'll persist on with afterwords that raises my concern." Mel pockets her lips into the corner of her expression. "She would suffer a thousand times over so someone else didn't have to once. If the world needed to push her that far; she would let it."

Nobody speaks for a few moments; it is apparent on Bell's face the *sort of comment* he initially intends to make. "I think she has seen suffering, and likely will again. And the fact that it shakes her, the fact that she cannot look away from the vile implications of every memory from the past. It means there is a part of her that is undying. Something that will burn on long past the time of her flesh. And no matter how hard she tries; it is something which so passionately illuminates what is wrong with the world around her that it will become impossible to ignore." Bell pauses for a few moments and smiles. "It is a good thing. For all its faults."

Lance pokes into the conversation and smiles as widely as he can to deflect the intrusion. "So *where is* Ylinia?"

William clears his throat very astutely. "Our Queen is undergoing a briefing of sorts prior to being ordained into the position. Her unveiling will arrive to the general public in short of an hour."

Mel's eyes well up with tears as her cheeks and chest flush with emotion. "*Oh*, so I won't get to see her, until she is up there?"

"She knows she goes everywhere with your love, *love*." Howarth comforts his wife with a strong arm around her back.

"She's probably excited, is all." Mel notes with a teary eyed smirk. "She's so cute when she is excited."

Bell motions towards Lance. "We'll accompany her together." He looks down at Mr.Len. "I guess that is how it works?"

Mr.Len nods. "The royal family has never consisted of blood lines; but those of a bond far greater. The alignment of stranger souls to depict a family is a truer structure then a base simply born and put into place." He motions his hand towards Alim, Lance and Courtney.

"None of your bloodlines intersect with the Covestoffs, and yet. By our definition, you are all members of her royal family. Her parents, most naturally; and the head of her guard as well." Mr.Len speaks with the comfortably paced tone of a tenured professor.

A unique sensation of wholesomeness spreads throughout the room. Smiles occur instantly when eyes accidentally meet and there is an unspoken sense of pride among the members of the royal family; for no singular or specific reason.

Alim steps forward with a tray of prepared drinks. "Then I wish to extend a small congratulations. To you Bell, for your victory. And too Ylinia, for her selection as monarch." Everyone grabs one of the drinks then raises it in unison. "To a rein of peace!" He declares.

"To peace!" The glasses clink together like little optimistic chimes.

_JL_

The evening has opted to darken early; and a chill has set in before it even seems right. All of Caelzun and many of the citizens from each of the *Great Cities* have gathered in the markets to behold their new monarch. Torches are lit, many are covered in thick blankets. They all stand in place without complaint; silently raising and dashing hope for this second to be the one where something happens.

William steps out onto a wide balcony and greets the people. "Greetings to you all!" He shouts out pridefully. "Thank you all again for adventuring out into the world to join us here today." He compliments sweetly. "In just a few moments; you will be met for the first time by your new monarch. There must of course, come an explanation first."

The crowd gasps almost in unison as if they have already predicted the worst.

"The rulings which govern the *clash of the crown* have been honoured to the word since their implementation into our country." William continues. "It is these very rulings which have allowed our monarch to gain the title they now hold. While some of you may know, I understand even myself that what I am about to say is semantic at best." He takes a deep breath to prepare himself. "Victory within the clash does not make one a monarch. They are instead given the ability to select whom they believe is best fitted in their opinion to take on the role of monarch. In the past, all have chosen themselves. This evening, for the first time, I present to you the *elected monarch: Ylinia Covestoff.*"

Ylinia steps out onto the balcony adorned in a perfectly tailored set of leather and armour; an embroidered cape of shimmering red scales curtains her left side to just below her hip. She approaches the railing of the balcony and stares out at the people; they stare back up at her. There is shock from both perspectives and for a few moments it seems neither is sure who will be the true audience. Bell steps out onto the balcony alongside Howarth and Mel; each of whom stand politely in the back with a wide smile. Ylinia looks back towards them swiftly then smiles confidently out towards the audience. "I can't imagine how it makes each of you feel. To see a young woman like myself receive a position like this." She takes a few short breaths and places her hands out onto the railing. "I imagine that you're worried I could be a hundred different things, awful things, unprepared things, disastrous things. You're not wrong to have those thoughts." She leans forwards towards the audience. "Truth be told I've had them too. But what I have found myself thinking. Is that I am not supposed to know everything yet. It is not my responsibility to presume knowledge regarding every aspect of our world; to carelessly profess insight I do not have. My responsibility lies with our collective heart. It has given me patience not so I can endure endless suffering, but so that I may infinitely learn all that will ever be asked of me." She smiles shortly. "So that is all I will ask of any of you, as families, or individuals. Tell me what I can learn, where I can look to see what I must see. Please show me exactly what it is you see in your dreams; so that we may bring it here together." She stares out at the people for a few moments then partially bows towards them all. She looks back for William; who quickly assumes his place. He stands and prepares to continue on with a rather administrative bit of speech and is interrupted by an out pour of excitement and cheering from the audience.

⌐⌐

A calm breeze flutters through the woods throughout Meire Estate. Ylinia is standing outside the estate; staring up at the building as if she cannot believe it is really there. Bell walks out through the front door; in the midst of bidding a short farewell. He smiles down at Ylinia as he walks up towards her.

"You wanted to see me Ylinia?" Bell questions simply.

Ylinia nods. "We've haven't moved for what feels like a long time." She states without shifting her gaze from the building. "I forgot what it was like. When we moved onto The Tristram, I had the same bed for so long; it started to feel like mine." She waves her hand towards the building. "*Now,* this is beautiful. All of it is. As was the suite we came from." She huffs. "I feel like I am a plant constantly being shifted from window sill to window sill."

Bell smirks. "I would like to think you're done for awhile." He stares up at the building himself. "It is a beautiful home." The front entrance of the building is accented with two carved pillars and leads into a multi-level manor of immaculate quality and modest styling. It is as clean and pristine as one would presume of any royal household.

Ylinia nods. "It is, *tremendous*. We have two families here and you would be hard pressed to encounter another person if you didn't want too."

"That sounds a bit like a treat." Bell jokes.

"I know you're not really joking when you say that." Ylinia states with a blank stare. "You did pretty good. But I can tell you're not exactly fond of sharing space with so many people."

Bell chuckles, he stares up at the sky and smiles. "It isn't as easy as I wish it was. That is for sure."

"Do you really think that?" She questions with an innocent inflection.

"Sure?" Bell answers with a casual shrug. "I think I'm a bit difficult. I know that I can be particular and at times pedantic. The truth of it is? I find peace in those things. When I can set my world in an order I find pleasant; it is exactly that. However I realize that it can be misinterpreted by others. The pretense of conflict is draining though. Constantly having to hold your tongue, cover your ears or quietly leave a room. Respect can at times be boundless, but it can be exhausting as well."

"Then the end result is the same." Ylinia rounds out the sum of Bell's explanation. "There was, of course; a spot for you in the manor. However, I figured a permanent home with so many shared walls wouldn't be the best choice." She denotes pleasantly then points out into the woods. "I had *The Tristram* brought in and put up on a bit of a foundation. Even Dad agreed. It is your home now if you will accept it."

Bell just stares down at Ylinia with a dumbfounded smirk on his face for a few moments. He shakes his jowls loosely then wipes a bit of distress from his eyes. "*Thank you*." He states genuinely. "I'll be sure to keep a look out while I'm there."

"Of course." Ylinia responds permissively.

A woman approaches; dressed in tight athletic clothing with a large fortified bag upon her hip. She nods towards Ylinia; slightly jogging in place. "Message for you my queen."

"*Ylinia, please.*" She insists.

"*Ylinia.*" The mail-woman affirms. She produces a blue envelope from her bag and hands it to Ylinia. "This has arrived for you. Unknown sender. But be at rest, it has been inspected nearly twelve different ways for safety." She smiles dryly. "The boys in the lab are *entirely sure* it is *just* paper folded around another smaller piece of paper." She bows slightly before rushing off to deliver other bits of mail across the estate.

Ylinia turns to face Bell while opening the letter; she shoots a curious expression and raised eyebrow his way as she unfolds the page contained within. The page is large, off-white and wasted almost entirely to share a single small printed message.

I saw something within you.
I'm curious what it means.
Find me upon the winter training grounds; show me
how it is your blade sings.

"Is it awful that I just want to go?" Ylinia asks outright.

Bell chuckles. "What, you mean cause it seems like a trap?"

"Exactly that!" She agrees with her words and the dramatic raising of her hands. "*Like,* I understand that falling for these sorts of things is really bad tactically. But, I dunno. It seems kinda poetic. It makes any threat seem slightly more mild."

Bell nods his head rather genuinely. "No I totally understand that." He points down at the letter. "I mean I'd be tempted to go just to see who it is."

Ylinia pushes her lips into the corner of her mouth then sneers at the page. "That is the mystery isn't it. There is no name, no signature. Not even the first letter of their name like they do in the spy novellas."

Bell pauses for a second, looks down at the ground with a bit of an absurd expression then laughs to himself. "Alright, *so*. Long shot here. *But*, what if the reason they didn't do that. Is because if they did; it would instantly give them away?"

Ylinia stares blankly.

Bell chuckles again. "I think it is Dii. But, if she put her name. It would just be the letter 'D'. Which is how you say her name anyways...*so*." He admits as confidently as he can.

Ylinia continues to stare. She looks at the page, the sky, then back to the page. "I actually think that is it."

⌐⌐

Bell and Ylinia alongside Dii all stand together in the centre of the winter training grounds. Dii seems a bit disappointed.

"You *knew* it was going to be me waiting for you?" Dii asks with a deflated tone.

Ylinia smiles as kindly as she can. "We had a feeling!"

"Were you *told?*" She inquires rather seriously.

Ylinia wags her head. "Just a hunch." She smiles sweetly towards Dii. "I'm glad you didn't really leave. I was worried we wouldn't get to meet again."

Dii resists a deep smile. She looks away to prevent herself from breaking a wider grin then she already has begun too. "History has changed." She notes pridefully. "If things can truly change; I will not run from the cause."

Ylinia smiles widely. "*Good.*" She affirms, glances up towards Bell then focuses again on Dii. "You wanted to, see my blade sing?"

"*Yes.*" She notes. "You visited the Basilica of Neitheim, did you not?"

Ylinia nods; her hand sub-consciously rests on the handle of her blade Bumble.

Bell takes a step back; finding a spot to lean against a bit of wall without being too far away.

"Draw your blade. I see the passion you hold for it even in the tips of your fingers." Dii requests.

Without hesitation Ylinia draws Bumble and adopts a confident defensive position; poised to snap or dodge at a moments notice. "I accept your duel."

"That is not the request." Dii states formally. She clacks her gauntlets together and in an instant the entire forest is filled inescapably with blinding white light. As the world comes back to order Dii remains in place; her entire body now covered in rapidly changing bright white runes. Her hair flows as if caught in a warm breeze. "I wish to see if you can hit me." She speaks as if her voice is coming from three different locations all at once. "Try if you please."

Ylinia continues to stare. She looks back at Bell; who kinda shrugs in a 'what did you expect?' sorta way. She looks back at Dii, stares down at Bumble and with an energetic shrug; takes a few dashing steps towards Dii. She stabs out at Dii only to fall through her body entirely; as if she was never there.

Dii's image dissipates as another rendition of her walks up from behind Ylinia. "You can't just trust what you see." Ylinia slashes around with Bumble; swiping uselessly through Dii as she ploofs away into coloured fog. Dii kneels down in front of Ylinia. "What makes you think I am really standing anywhere you see me?" Ylinia thrusts her blade through Dii's face only to dispel another cloud. Four renditions of Dii all begin walking in a circle around Ylinia. "What use are your eyes if they're being lied too?"

In a calculated panic Ylinia throws Bumble past the encircling group of women and into a blank space in the field. Each of the renditions of Dii stop and an inexplicably more present one appears next to Ylinia. She kneels down next to her. "I admit, that wasn't even close." She creases her brow. "But it was tremendously creative. *And I can work with that.*"

"What would you do with it?" Ylinia questions naively.

"Improve it! Show you how you can become the best version of yourself; using all of your advantages. You're a queen! There isn't an excuse for you *not* to become more of a badass bitch." Dii enthuses; showcasing the top layer of her perfectly protected passion." She stares over towards Bell with a teasing smile. "Besides, I heard your old trainer got a promotion. Or, is it a demotion? How does an heir end up as the help?"

Bell rolls his eyes. "A wise man always accepts the higher ground. A practical one first measures his tallest tower." He stares back at Dii humanely. "I know where I am most effective."

"As do I." Dii agrees. She stares down towards Ylinia. "So what do you say?"

"*Uh.*" Ylinia remarks; then stalls for a few seconds simply staring around the space. She points over towards Bumble and casually walks over to pick it up; walking back still in the midst of consideration. "You know I can't glow, and make a bunch of different versions of myself right? Because I don't want to be in a position where you're trying to get that too happen; and I just have to believe in myself enough for it too happen, *and it isn't.*" She shakes her arm beside herself slightly like a squid. "And I kinda already know I'm not filled with some secret glowing light."

Dii shakes her head. She closes her eyes, exhales and in an instant the glowing aura around her diminishes to its regular brightness. Her hair agrees to obey gravity once again; settling around her shoulders. "I have no expectation of you other then that you will consistently be yourself." She focuses her gaze upon Ylinia's wide eyes. "Can you do that?"

"I believe, *at times*, it is all I can do." Ylinia admits.

A short, pleasant, silent moment passes.

"Where is it that you went, when you left?" Bell asks after visibly with-holding the question as long as he possibly can.

Dii sighs. "I hoped that we just weren't going to ask." She admits. She takes a deep breath, holds it at her upmost then releases it in a long steady stream. "It used to be that when I felt far from the world. I would climb the nearest mountain, scout across its expanse to find the coldest of streams then lie naked in the depths of that frozen water until I was deprived of every sense but my most inherent connection to this planet." She closes her eyes. "Yet now, I find greater solace in an inn with a locked door and a broad enough selection of tea; that I may simply steep in silence."

Bell smiles and chuckles a bit. "You gave up naked river baths?" He notes as if actually surprised. "I never thought I would hear of the day."

"And yet it has come. Like so many things before it which we presumed equally as permanent." Dii responds solemnly.

"Do you have any other pressing responsibilities Dii?" Ylinia questions rather abruptly.

Dii appears embarrassed for a moment; without even really understanding why herself. "I am available to you during all of my waking hours; if you require them."

She nods her head. "Then I will accept you as my personal trainer." She looks around; then nods again affirmatively. "I hope that isn't a diminutive title."

"Not at all." Dii admits. "However, I offer my training as a trade. I will require no great reward, or extravagant lifestyle."

"And yet there is still something left to seek?" Ylinia teases.

"There is a piece of knowledge that I seek. I do not know what it is, even what it regards." Dii explains.

Bell raises his eyebrow. "You're still stuck on what Richard said? *Dii*, he was drunk."

"*Precisely*. He was drunk. Not captive, nor high, nor near death. The King was made privy to something. Something which guided his leadership and informed every motion of his hand. We had argued for years, battled through debate after debate. It was only in the few months prior to his death that I thought he might finally crumble and reveal to me what it truly is that he was made responsible for." Dii explains.

Ylinia squints slightly as her brow creases with consideration. "Did it have to do with the war?"

Dii shakes her head. "No, it never did. Not directly. His patience was strong almost every day. But sometimes, you could sense that all he really wanted was to have everything finally end. It was like he was waiting for something, and couldn't let himself relax until it arrived." She exhales heavily and stares down towards Ylinia. "Whatever that is. I want to know."

Ylinia stares back at Dii and nods affirmatively. "Then let us train."

CHAPTER SEVENTEEN

TRULY OUTSIDE

Ylinia sits in the back of a horse drawn wagon alongside Bell. Two mismatched horses pull the wagon which is made primarily of pine and oak; then stained to a slightly darker shade. With each thump of the road Ylinia breaks into an impossible to restrain smirk of joy.

A particularly rough spot in the road jostles Bell around in his seat; prompting him to reach out with both of his arms to secure himself in place. "This really is your *preferred* method of transportation?"

"It is classic." Ylinia affirms.

Bell jostles around a bit more; becoming less and less enthused by the moment. "It is primitive."

"*Timeless.*" Ylinia counters. She looks over towards the horses and admires the creatures. Their coachman is dressed in armour with plates of blackened steel formed and folded to resemble a fine dress suit; the joints of his armour patched with thick leather. He stares out at the road ahead of them without much concern for the conversation behind him.

Bell lets out a huff and smiles. "I just feel so *slow*."

"And?" Ylinia asks; resting her feet up a bit on the side of the carriage to stretch out in place.

"And?" Bell repeats the word. He looks around himself. They are surrounded by mountains, deep ravines of forest, animals and all sorts of natural beauty. Even the contrast of near red dirt against cobbled grey road dashing down the greenery of a hill is lacking just a title to be considered traditional art. "I guess slow means the same thing as bad in my mind." The carriage reaches the top of a small hill to reveal in the short distance Aizenel's tower.

Ylinia nods with a large smirk; still half distracted by the horses. "Do you feel that there is a proper pace?" She waves her hand around a little bit. "*Like*, for everything."

"I guess I must?" Bell admits with a curious twist of his inflection. "It takes a very long time to adjust to getting up and going at any moment. To never truly settle. To always, *always* have the back of your mind focused on the fact your safety and prosperity are not guaranteed." He lets out a deep breath. "Even when things are not as dire as I've seen them be. It is hard to tell the difference."

"So it is just another casualty of the war?" She turns to peer at Bell; squinting her eyes as she moves closer towards him. "I dunno." She teases then returns to her seat. "I think that has been there for a lot longer then that."

Bell laughs then closes his eyes. He puts his hands in his lap and leans into his seat; removing his mask. "I've spent most of my life not being able to catch my breath. Even when I was at my mightiest. I would have a steady chest while I work then become a collection of shambles moments after I'm done. I thought eventually it would leave me. When I became strong enough, smart enough. When I had seen enough of the world, or acquired enough of *something*. That rest never came as a status, but a temporary infliction. Calm to me was like a vaccine my wife was the sole producer of. Like a man sick his whole life; I did not truly know health until I met her." He lets out an exhausted breath. "And I did not know the weight of my suffering until such an awareness was mine to bear."

"I do not understand how you see your suffering as anything other then an opponent to be conquered." Ylinia admits coldly.

"*Huh?*" Bell responds; instantly snapping a bit out of his emotional limbo.

"You just said yourself that you have the awareness of it. You can see what troubles you. Yet you've decided only to be beaten by it."

"It isn't a wound I can simply dismiss Ylinia."

"*Alright,* nor do I think you should! If it is gone. I am sorry to say, it is gone. But you cannot keep on putting weight on a limb that isn't there. You will fall; every time. No matter how skilled you used to be at using it." She fights back her own welling tears as she speaks. "It does you no good."

Bell just sits. He stares ahead; rotating his shoulders as if simply reminding himself he has arms. Tears slowly build in the corners of his eyes and spill down in steady streams. "I just don't want to forget her."

"You never will." Ylinia comforts. "I know you never will. I don't think anyone who has ever met her has!" She notes with peculiar excitement.

Bell smiles ugly through his tears and attempts to wipe half his face off with his sleeve before he accidentally swallows too much of himself. "Thank you Ylinia." He remarks softly then turns to peer out towards the forest; he returns his mask to its usual placement.

The carriage sputters over a bit of a wooden bridge to the entrance of Aizenel's tower. From here Bell and Ylinia get out, thank their coachman and meet Mr.Len in the lobby of the tower. Mr.Len simply nods as they pass and continues on with himself down a hallway; a clipboard at least a textbook thick held out in front of his face at all times. Bell leads Ylinia into Aizenel's study where he stands as a statue. The statue quickly crumbles away and Aizenel steps down from his small podium to smile towards his guests.

"It is well to see you." Aizenel greets them with a gruff yet warm inflection.

Bell nods. "And you." He gestures out with the tip of his finger towards the various pages of books held in place across the room. "New books?"

"Old books read recently. So yes, *new books*." Aizenel responds swiftly.

Ylinia peers out at the books but suffers the same fate of all those who attempt to read arcane works without the required education. The words upon the page will always appear *similar* to the language you understand; yet indescribably inaccurate. There could be an entire paragraph of similar looking letters and grammatical structures yet upon inspection they don't make even the slightest sense. It bequeaths a series of progression to all whom peer upon it: intrigue, curiosity, confusion and finally frustration. Ylinia sneers as she looks away from the hundreds of book pages mounted throughout the study. "What is it that you were studying?"

Aizenel laughs. "I had worried you would ask me such a thing."

Ylinia becomes rather severe. "*Why?* What is it?"

"Don't worry young monarch." Aizenel comforts her. "It is simply that I wish I were reading something more significant. There are likely a hundred more relevant tomes then this one; and yet it has still called out to me louder then any other on this day."

"What is it about?" Ylinia questions further.

"I can only be so sure, and I admit bits and pieces seem to change every time. But what I am sure of, is that this is a story discussing a great hero. He wields a blade nearly twice his own height and battles against an army of evil men. Only, in the story, it seems he hasn't a friend across his entire world. The people he fights to defend loathe him; even if he is their only hope." He pauses for a moment; rolling his eyes around in the top of his head as if remembering a few hidden details of the story. "So he decides, that despite the many years he has fought against the men of evil. To approach his long time opponents, with his blade sheathed at his feet; requesting a place alongside them." Aizenel smirks and rolls his eyes slightly. "And he gains it. He uses his skills to advance the borders of his new family and quickly rises through their ranks to become rather noble."

Ylinia waits about half a minute into silence before appearing a bit confused and frustrated. "That's what happens to him? He joins the killers, becomes one, and that is what the moral is?"

"*Maybe.*" Aizenel allows. "These arcane texts. They were not crafted on a whim, or by the sudden spur of someone's pen; nor would their creation have been assigned to the common thinker. They were thought exercises, taboo considerations, acts of desensitization towards a bevy of variant and nonsense concepts." He waves his hand towards the pages behind him. "The question becomes now not what you believe is right; because it can never truly be proven. Instead, you must determine what it is that you can do with what is actually in front of you." He takes a breath, closes his eyes and exhales into a wide smile.

"Interesting." Ylinia does her best to respond sweetly. "Though, I must admit I don't see the connection."

Aizenel smirks subtly. "I see it as a reminder of what it is to be human." He lingers on the consideration for a moment. "We can never shirk our requirement for happiness; for in the moments that we do. We can betray ourselves in the most severe manner."

Ylinia nods shortly a few times. "You believe it is a lesson on, *focus*, ultimately?"

Aizenel smiles and wavers his shoulders. "I believe that whether we require focus, attention, love or deference. We're going to do so in a human way. It doesn't matter if we must empty the planet or reach the clouds; we will simply raze the forests and build stairs up past the stars." He chuckles a bit to himself. "And I can't explain why it is that I find that so comforting."

The doors into the room open energetically and Dii follows quickly afterwords. She smiles confidently towards the ground as she approaches and extends her hand out respectfully towards Aizenel. "I'm Dii. I'm here to see the secret stuff."

Aizenel chuckles. "Of course. It is well to meet you, I am-"

"Aizenel." Dii cuts him off. "Royal Arcanist. I know, I know. I've actually read your books. So this is much more my honour then yours." She admits.

"*Ah.*" Aizenel responds with mild surprise. "Very well then." He looks around the room then lets out a deep breath. "This tower has not always been my home. It has been passed down through the generations from royal arcanist to royal arcanist. Yet, it is just as much a responsibility of the position as it is a perk." He walks over to a corner of his room and presses in one of the bricks; causing a secret staircase to emerge underneath the flooring. He waves his hands towards the stairwell and waits as the others join him. The stairs are cold and barely worn from use; despite their ancient age they appear functionally brand new. "We're headed into what was once known as *The Pythia*; a natural spring of noxious gas. *Initially*, the experiments that took place here were relatively meaningless. The efforts amounted to slightly more then *experimentation. And yet.* After enough time, they began to gain a degree of competence in regards to the hallucinogenic gasses they were allowing themselves to inhale. They were able to predict the absolutely accurate outcome of a few small events. They continued their *studies* and tuned their exposure right up to the point where they thought it was perfect, and then; they broke Mr.Poet. Despite the accuracy of the predictions its use could muster; The Pythia fell out of usage afterwords."

"Mr.Poet?" Dii responds with great surprise. "I remember reading his books when I was a kid." She thinks for a moment. "*The pages don't pay you enough time to put anything on em prettier then words*." She quotes. "Half of his work was talking about why the other popular half wasn't as good as we thought it was."

"Splendid soul, delightful writer as well." Aizenel admits. "He was a dedicated researcher in his leisure time; maybe you knew this. He was always searching for secrets beyond our world." Aizenel exhales with disappointment. "It is a great shame that he never knew it himself, but through him; we were shown something far beyond us."

The group reaches the bottom of the stairs to discover a large steel door; secured in each of its corners with an odd plastic fixture. Aizenel twists and pulls out each of the fixtures which allows the door to be opened inwards; immediately as he does a thick green gas begins spilling out; crawling across the floor as if it is heavier then air. Beyond the door is a bright white cave filled with crystals gleaming brightly in shades of pink, green, purple and blue.

Aizenel holds out his palm towards the cave, closes his eyes and begins to speak an indecipherable language under his breath. As he does the gas throughout the entire cavern begins to collect and condense in his palm. In just under a minute all the fog has been gathered and now remains in the form of a solid green marble; which Aizenel tucks away into his robe. "We should be safe for the next few moments if you wish to enter now."

Dii rushes into the cavern, reaches the middle of it, turns to her side and stands in complete shock. As the group catches up with her they share her awe and stare out towards a massive sheet wall of stone; completely covered in thousands of rough papyrus scrolls. The wall stands at the end of a hundred metre long stretch of beautiful crystal canopied cavern. Each scroll has been placed perfectly in place next to one another. At this distance the collection of scrolls have the text upon their pages arranged in such a way that it appears like a giant monstrous skull has been painted unintentionally across the wall. "Mr.Poet did this?"

"In part." Aizenel responds with a wavering tone. "Each of those scrolls is a poem authored by Mr.Poet in the midst of a transcendent episode. He was frantic for nearly a week straight, not eating, sleeping, taking care of himself in any way. All he did was slave away upon the creation of over *five thousand* scrolls of poetry." He flicks his hand in the air dismissively. "And not a word of it makes common sense."

"That seems right in your area of expertise *Aizenel*." Ylinia remarks.

"Of course, and were it actual arcane script. It may be. But it is all *common language*. Just speaking about things which make no sense. Every sentence is drawn out, or references a single line amidst the thousands present. To understand any of it, you must examine *all of it*."

"And what does it say?" Ylinia questions; peering out at the scrolls with a steadfast determination.

"We're unsure, entirely. Each poem was numbered, and they have been set in proper order to create that *image*. But Mr.Poet collapsed dead the moment he finished the final scroll; and we have only pieced together snippets of what any of it means."

Dii points out towards the scrolls. "This is what Richard worried about, the *shadow* he felt peering down over him."

Aizenel nods. "Richard had the scrolls studied following their creation. His team of researchers believed the scrolls to be a *prediction*. That a storm of darkness will descend from the sky and drain all life from our planet. This is an event supposedly occurring in *seventy some years*." He explains.

"And this research, how thorough was it?" Ylinia questions without breaking her focus upon the skull.

"*Mhmm.*" Aizenel hums as he considers. "I do not know." He admits. "Resources for these sorts of projects have never been guaranteed. In the midst of a total war, a war right to the end. If something could either be used here, or *there; there* always won."

Ylinia turns towards Bell and tightens her gaze slightly. "Izelle is technically under my command, is she not?"

Bell nods. "She is the chief intelligence officer for the *RMC*, your *spy-master* if you would. While she is primarily self sufficient; she does abide your outlines and institutions."

"*Good.*" Ylinia remarks confidently. She turns back to Aizenel. "I would like you to work together with Izelle. She is to be caught up with all matters related to this *prediction* and reevaluate its purpose and message as comprehensively as she possibly can."

Aizenel smiles widely; revealing the slightest bit of his round white teeth. "I have heard of this *Izelle*. If these rumours are correct; I will need to re-stock my papyrus in order to accommodate the length with which she will *comprehensively* produce an evaluation."

"Whatever need be." Ylinia allows. She continues to stare at the skull upon the wall; peering into its eyes as if she will somehow prompt them to blink.

Dii creases her brow. "*Ylinia*, I would appreciate the opportunity to work on this project as well."

Ylinia nods. "Of course. *And you will.* By preparing me for whatever may come."

Dii smiles widely. "Of course my queen."

The edges of the cavern begin to fill in with a light green gas; increasing the warmth of the room. Aizenel peers out towards the lingering skull one last time before raising his hand to motion towards the exit. "We should begin making our way out."

Ylinia leads first; Bell is never more then a few paces away. Dii slows her pace to walk beside Aizenel as they leave the cavern. She whispers quietly just for him to hear. "What is it, *exactly*, that this gas does?"

Aizenel sways his head with an empathetic smirk. "I understand your interest. But I must admit. Outside of the episode with *Mr.Poet*. The findings of the *sages* who came to this place were nothing but a few *very lucky* guesses. The vast majority of their time, if their published journals are any indication; was spent on a pretentious and frivolous series of discussions. They would debate the semantics of semantics then settle into comfortable disassociation as if they had done themselves some sort of favour."

"*What a shame.*" Dii notes with avid disappointment.

"You're looking to find the voices, *aren't you*?" Aizenel guesses.

Dii just stares in response.

"I'm not judging. I've always been interested in the relics of our world. How they appeared across Rion, *why.*" He pauses for a moment to insure that he has closed the door to The Pythia securely behind him. "Every individual who has ever bonded with one of these *holy* relics has reported *a voice* distant in their thoughts."

"Like it is always there, but millions of life times away. An echo of existence." Dii speaks mostly to herself, peering at the floor as she speaks.

"*Exactly.*" Aizenel remarks. "Whoever owns that voice, their name is not to be found within the fumes of The Pythia." They begin to follow behind Bell and Ylinia who have taken quite a lead away. "However if you ever feel the need to prove me wrong; you won't be forbidden."

Dii smiles wide with a bit of rebellious passion. "I'll be sure to let you know, if I ever need to *indulge* in such a curiosity."

Aizenel and Dii rejoin Bell and Ylinia who are waiting across from one another in slightly oversized lounge chairs. They peer over towards the pair as they return, share a knowing smile between themselves then share it with the others.

"*Dii*, we'll be returning to Meire Manor for dinner. Would you like to join us?"

Dii peers around the room and takes a few deep breaths. "Are you sure?"

"Why wouldn't I be?" Ylinia questions; honestly confused. "Please, I would like to discuss this *Mr.Poet* a bit more if you wouldn't mind."

Dii nods kindly. "Of course. I'll meet you there in half an hours time? There is something I would like to collect on my way."

"*Of course*." Ylinia allows with a simple smirk. She stands up with an instant leap and begins towards the door. "Thank you for showing us The Pythia." She thinks on her words for a moment. "Are you going to join the other researchers in person Aizenel?"

Aizenel freezes a bit; locking his gaze upon the young queen. His robe flickers around his frame as if caught by a breeze. "*I-*" He speaks with a shortness in his breath. "I don't spend much time off of my pedestal."

"I don't find you *that* cocky." Bell jokes.

"I meant literally. The pedestal where I study and stand as a statue. More of my life has been spent there then anywhere else. Had it not been, death would of found me generations ago and stolen tomes of discovery from the libraries of Rion with it." Aizenel speaks while unintentionally refusing to make eye-contact the whole time.

Ylinia smiles and nods. "You'll always be welcome to join; if you ever find the time. There will be no pressure, but I am sure such talent will benefit the analysis regardless."

"Ah." Aizenel remarks. "Thank you for understanding. *I'll,* see how things feel."

"Of course." Ylinia remarks sweetly; she fully turns to leave. "See you both later!" She chimes as she rushes off.

Bell nods towards Aizenel and Dii; following behind Ylinia with long steady strides. They collect themselves onto the back of their horse drawn wagon and are off as quickly as such a transport can be. Their path has them pleasantly trot off on winding mountain roads back towards central Caelzun.

⎓⏚⎓

Amidst the many sections of Meire Manor there are numerous apartments divided up for the various members of the royal family. Privacy is a virtue in the home that is carried throughout the designs of all residences within The Citizenry. There is never a child that shares a bedroom, nor a lobby left unfurnished, or a living room with only a single large piece of furniture to sit upon. Kitchens are almost always divided from living rooms. At the highest level of concern; is the noise proofing. There isn't a wall, a floor, or a bit of architecture anywhere near where people are expected to live that would let loose even the slightest of creeks. Silence is the privacy of the mind; and it is to be left just as undisturbed as the cleanliness or energy of any dwelling space.

One of these apartments has been provided to Mel and Howarth. It is at the very end of the manor where their new home resides. It is a relatively new addition to the manor; transitioning from a darker grey stone to an amber brick. The wood details across the entire building are bright white and stained in such a way that they almost glimmer. A large garage is attached to the back; its wide doors slide down into the floor.

Howarth stands in the middle of the garage beside Bell. The men are surrounded by a multitude of motorcycles in varying degrees of function or total disrepair; sorted relatively into square piles and rows.

"That is, a lot of bikes." Bell states with blunted shock.

Howarth nods slowly a few times. "That was my reaction too."

The men stare around themselves for a bit longer; losing their focus into details that lead into further details.

"And they just, dropped them off?" Bell inquires further.

Howarth nods. "Big ol transport and a crew of about twelve folks. It took them nearly three full loads to get everything over here." He chuckles. "I've spent the past couple of days just organizing it."

Bell smiles and chuckles a bit to himself. "What a way to spend a few days."

"Right?" Howarth responds with honest surprise. "What do you do with a day that isn't spent preparing for tragedy?" He laughs. "I mean, I could wake up tomorrow, any time of the day and that would be alright. There aren't lives on the line, there isn't some horror that is sucking the joy out of every hour I spend looking away from it. There is just *being here*."

"How is that?"

"It feels more then I thought it would."

Bell raises his eyebrow. "Does it *feel like* anything?"

Howarth shakes his head. "It just feels. It all kinda just does. I mean, you know what a dream feels like because you remember it as a dream. This feels like walking into a painting and seeing the depth of something beautiful only to discover it looks better on the other side."

Bell shrugs. "That doesn't sound bad."

"I don't think it is." He remarks honestly. "But it is the scariest thing I have ever felt."

Bell nods in understanding. "All that much more to lose."

"Mhmm." He agrees with a dull rumble.

Mel pokes her head into the garage. "Have we lost you both to the machines?"

Howarth turns in an instant and smiles over towards his wife. "*Almost.*" He admits; then takes a few short steps towards her. "We'll come along now."

"Lovely. Courtney just got in. Apparently she has a bit of news she wants to share with *everyone.*" Mel explains.

Both the men raise their eyebrows; forging an emotion somewhere between concern and elation.

"I recognize the packing. She's brought with her a uniform."

From the garage is a simple hallway; entirely floored with a bright pine; that leads down towards an open living room. Alim and Lance have taken a seat in front of a coffee table; there is a spot cleared for Courtney to sit but she is obviously too excited to stay in one place. She has in her arms a relatively large rectangular box that is wrapped in simple cardboard coloured paper. Ylinia is seated beside Dii; focused intently on some sort of story. Courtney instantly smiles over towards Bell, Howarth and Mel as they rejoin everyone.

"Hello, are you guys ready, and good to go?" Courtney blabbers out towards them instantly. She takes a deep breath, closes her eyes then chuckles nervously. "Sorry, I'm just." She motions towards one of the empty seats. "Would you take a seat?"

They do.

"It is wonderful that everyone is here, and honestly, I love seeing it." Courtney speaks as smoothly as she can muster. "*Ylinia!* You're my sister, you always will be. To see you now as the monarch, as our queen. I realize that it is a position which has long awaited you; as it doesn't seem the slightest bit misplaced."

Ylinia smiles up towards Courtney.

"And yet despite this joy. I have found myself looking inward. Considering what is it, in this *new world*, that I want to do? Where do I want to fit!" Courtney continues right up to a beaming smile. "*I decided I do not know*...but more then that. I have come to peace with the fact that I may never know. That I may forever be pursuing different versions of happiness; all of which have destinations spread out across our world." She smiles sweetly; there is an intelligent depth to her eyes that warms your heart. "So it seems that the best thing I can do, is gain as many skills as I can, learn everything presented to me, and see all there is to see." She tears off the wrapping paper of her box to reveal a well upholstered chest in a dark brown canvas fabric. She opens the box and places it on the table for all to peer into. Within the box is a crisply folded *Caelzun Naval Academy* uniform. It is primarily dark blue with accents of grey, black and white. The overcoat is a solid blue with black elbow patches and a white lining. This is worn alongside a soft blue denim vest with military adornments and a pleated pair of armoured canvas pants; in dark grey. Mechanical boots are interlocked on top of the uniform; they are a thick brown leather with polished steel limbs of fortification running across the top like the *veins* of a leaf. "I was accepted into naval academy." She proudly declares.

Alim and Lance shoot off the couch and cover their daughter in broad hugs. "Oh darling!" Alim shouts.

"That is so tremendous!" Lance adds on.

Courtney smiles as wide as she can; causing strain in the height of her sharp cheeks. "You're sure you're alright with it?"

"Courtney! Of course. Sweetness! To pursue passion, to provide yourself a powerful education. It is one of the best things you can be doing!" Lance assures her.

Alim smiles wide. "And with the war past. The resources you'll have at your finger tips. The analysis of every victory, and loss. It will be invaluable to a military university!"

"Thank you so much." Courtney speaks; half through suddenly summoned tears.

Howarth and Mel walk up towards Courtney and share hugs with her as well. "We're so proud of you Courtney." They both share the compliment.

Ylinia smiles and wraps her arm around her sister shamelessly. "You're going to blow them away!" Ylinia assures her.

Courtney does her best to handle the attention; smiling just because she's pretty sure that, *socially*, she should be; whilst looking outward towards the windows for a few quick moments as is required. She shares a brief smile with Bell; but he doesn't dare break the small crowd forming around her.

Quickly the scent of a catered dinner begins wafting through the house; and celebrations are inspired to move around a table; where glasses can more easily be filled with wine. A massive dinner is prepared and laid out for the family to indulge upon. A large platter of roasted turkey is accented with baked beets, potatoes and leeks. Loaves of warm onion bread. Green apple and spinach salad with brie and sea salt. All paired with a rose scented red wine; sweet with traces of garnacha. Celebration swells with dinner; and conversations run on in cycles; congratulating Courtney throughout most of the evening.

CHAPTER EIGHTEEN

END UP WHERE IT IS PRETTY

The training ground has taken on a bit of frost; as the fall comes to an end and winter claims its first few mornings with chill. Amidst the light white bellowing of early winter snow is the trio of Bell, Dii & Ylinia. The royal training grounds are hidden expertly in the middle of Meire Estate with camouflage and well placed mirrors. Within is an open courtyard that transitions up to a square platform of marble; surrounded by four tall columns. The area is large enough to store racks of weapons, droves of training decoys, stands and tools alongside targets and athletic furniture. Bell is set up right against a wall with the chair underneath him turned around so that his chest is pressed up against the back rest. He has a very tall steel mug of coffee resting just near the foot of the chair; with the lid unscrewed and tilted at an angle to allow steam out.

The women; embroiled in a combative training session; both have dressed in thick white karategi; snugly tailored to fit each of them.

Dii dives down at Ylinia but misses as she lunges out with a snapping strike. Ylinia twists herself around; swinging Bumble forcefully at the edge of her grasp to manipulate her momentum. Dii kicks high. Ylinia ducks and stabs out at Dii; missing almost all of her. Dii dodges just enough to have the side of her thigh slashed with the very edge of Bumble's thin blade. A few trickles of blood splay from the wound and splash against the white tile floor; dramatically contrasting against the white.

"*Oh shit*, I'm sorry Dii!" Ylinia apologizes the moment she notices.

Dii stops in her place and looks down at her leg; a clean slash has cut right through and opened up a half inch deep gash just above her knee. "It is alright." Dii admits with a soft smile. "I'm more impressed then anything."

"Should we call for medical attention?" Ylinia questions; her voice wavering slightly with distress.

"I think we'll be alright." Dii notes calmly. She drops down to one knee so she can inspect the wound closer; squinting her eyes to peer into the cut as much as she can. "Excellent blade retention my dear. *Honestly.* You'd laugh if you knew how hard it was for some people to keep a blade edge straight."

"I'm glad that you're proud of me Dii, But unless pride is going to stitch you up?"

"*Relax.*" Dii comforts her. She raises two of her fingers; and the entirety of her gauntlet begins to glow white. There is a blur of motion surrounding her hand like invisible steam. She passes the two raised fingers above the wound; and it zippers its self back up as if compelled. The bleeding stops in an instant and as she wipes the remaining bits away with some of her outfit; there isn't the slightest sign of any scar at all.

Ylinia raises her eyebrow. "Were you speaking? Just now?"

Dii shakes her head. "Not at all. But you heard it, did you not?"

Ylinia nods quickly in triplicate. "Faintly. But it was there."

"What did you hear it say?" Dii inquires.

Ylinia shrugs. "It was not words I heard, but, it felt, *peaceful.* There was love."

"*Mhmm.*" Dii agrees with a smile. "The light that flows through these gauntlets. The warmth that I feel within them. Love is the most accurate comparison."

Ylinia points towards what is now only a bit of torn fabric with a stain upon Dii's leg. "Is that all that the light can heal? If pressed?"

"Similar wounds." She shrugs. "I've never found a definitive limit. But the rule of thumb has been that if field surgery could mend the wound; I'll probably be able to help. Serious ailments, excess blood loss, *decapitation?* There are some things even wondrous light cannot fix." Dii admits.

"That seems to be what it is. *Wondrous*." Ylinia notes. "If only it could touch more. Make safe every road from beasts, remove vile possibilities from our world."

Dii smirks. "Wouldn't that just be a gift? Even better, a button to press; and fix all in an instant?"

"That is the dream." She admits with a chuckle.

Dii nods; her tone the slightest bit distraught. "It is, isn't it?" She asks; not seeming entirely convinced.

"Do you disagree?"

"Not at all!" Dii quickly responds. "I know what I want. *To be safe, to end up somewhere that is pretty*. It is just that until I'm convinced that there isn't strife remaining; that evil won't appear in the blind spots I create. Thoughts of paradise simply remind me how far from achieving my goals I am."

Ylinia nods softly. "If it were anyone else, I'd say you are too hard on yourself Dii." She takes a deep breath and releases it calmly. "*Yet*, I imagine that if you weren't so motivated to push yourself. We might all be at a disadvantage."

Dii rolls her eyes. "I only hope that you are right."

Bell stands up in an instant. He turns to look out towards the entrance into the courtyard.

William appears as if from nowhere; one of the many illusions of the series of mirrors. He smiles and waves as he approaches. "I'm glad I found you here! I've been poking around behind random trees for the past half an hour." He has slung over his shoulder a beautiful purple book bag; featuring thick supportive stitching.

Bell laughs abruptly. "Well you have finally made it. How goes it?"

"Well, *of course*." William responds with a charismatic smirk. "I have brought with me something that I believe will aid our young queen greatly."

Ylinia instantly has her attention perk up. "*Oh?*" She inquires with obvious excitement.

William smiles sweetly. He brandishes from the book bag a large tome covered in a thick brown leather and holds it out towards Ylinia. "I found myself considering that you may not have had the opportunity to study every law and tradition in the detail your position requires. I also realize that to swallow all of that stale information would require such a substantial amount of digestif; the ruinous state of your liver would undermine the knowledge gained." He chuckles slightly to himself. "Thus, within this tome, are all of the important things you must know as Monarch of The Citizenry."

Ylinia takes the book, holds it in her hands and then moves it around; as if trying to determine what sort of present is inside. The book is about the thickness of a human skull with just the bulk of the pages. "And it all fits in here?"

"Is that sarcastic?" William seeks to clarify.

Ylinia sways her head very genuinely. "Not at all, I just, *worry I would miss something*."

William motions his hand towards her permissively. "Not a concern at all, on each page. All rules, standards & traditions have the source material of their stipulations noted. If you ever wish to pursue a particular notion to its furthest reaches."

"Thank you William." Ylinia speaks kindly. "Is there anything I have missed so far?"

William nods kindly. "There is of course a second reason I have sought your audience today. It is rather standard for a new monarch to engage in a *tour* between the Great Cities. To speak to those whom are now under your care; for them to learn the look of your face, hear your voice." He explains. "If you would have it, we could begin the planning of such an event."

"As is tradition?" Ylinia questions.

"One of the few near all monarchs abide."

"Then it is a simple matter to address. We shall prepare for a tour at once." Ylinia declares. She turns to Dii. "Will you be alright to train me on the road?"

Dii smiles widely. "Of course. Training in all sorts of locales can only be a benefit."

"I'll begin to prepare at once." William speaks proudly. "Bell, so long as you won't mind, your assistance in planning the security protocols for the tour would be greatly appreciated!"

"Of course." Bell agrees. "However, would you be able to send out a request?"

William turns his head to an angle and raises his eyebrow high. "What is it that you seek?"

"Cavalry Master Nuinez. She serves with the *RMC*. I would love to have her and her cavalry on as the security detail for this tour." Bell explains.

"And more prestige finds our young Cavalry Master! I must admit there doesn't seem to be a week where I don't receive a briefing with her praise being sung within it." William admits proudly.

"I hope then that she isn't busy."

William sways his head; entirely convinced of something. "She wouldn't say no to this opportunity."

Dii sneaks up behind Ylinia. "And neither should we."

Ylinia turns to look at Dii and rolls her eyes sarcastically. "We'll prepare to leave after the hour William." She shouts out to him while maintaining her gaze upon Dii.

William smiles as if watching a kitten figure out a mirror. "If only we could just up and leave within the hour!" He chuckles a bit. "I'll prepare the planning, and if all goes well. We'll have Cavalry Master Nuinez off from Neitheim in the morning; and we'll be able to begin planning for the coming weeks once we have received them."

Ylinia lets out a confused sigh. "*Ah.*" She remarks. "*Well alright then.*" She turns back to Dii. "Shall we?"

Dii smiles and readies her stance. "Until we cannot my dear."

The evening has come on quicker then expected; but despite that it is still not surprising. Streaks of bright orange decorate the sky with a foreground of dark blue clouds; all swept together with an increasingly cold and harsh breeze. Ylinia has ripped through and torn the knees, elbow and portions of the torso of her training outfit. Dii herself has had large portions of hers slashed away from repeated wounds. Ylinia sheaths Bumble and lets out a deep huff.

"My arms no longer feel like arms." She declares, pauses for a moment then sighs as she corrects herself. "*Arm.*"

Dii chortles; almost awkwardly. "And what is it that your arm feels like now?"

Ylinia rolls her shoulders around; flapping her arm and cape with equal lucidity at her sides. "*Just*, like a sock filled with pudding." She laughs to herself. "That just got the crap kicked out of it."

"That does make me question the pudding." Dii jokes with a stale inflection.

Ylinia makes an odd smirk. "Do you not feel sore at all Dii? I *literally* stabbed you a few times."

Dii stretches her back in a comfortable fashion and lets out a deep satisfying groan. "I almost forgot the feeling." She admits blankly, shakes her head then focuses on Ylinia. "I think it is possible I've become so sore in this lifetime that I can no longer distinguish the very sensation from simply being alive."

Bell laughs. "Do you think it that bad?"

Dii shrugs. "I couldn't tell. Truth be told. I can barely feel pain anymore." She quickly shoots a glance down at her gauntlets. "Such sensations have been *dulled*."

"Goes a bit both ways when it comes to advantage then, eh?" Bell ventures the guess.

"About that, *yes*." Dii confirms. She turns to Ylinia. "Shall we call it a night?"

Ylinia nods with her whole body, spirit and essence multiple times. "*Yes please*." She takes a deep breath and lets it out while a passionate pleasantness spreads across her face. "I need enough rest if we are too begin again tomorrow."

Bell and Dii share a laugh. The trio leave the training grounds within Meire Estate; appearing on the other side as if suddenly manifesting in the middle of the wood. Bell leads with eyes fixed upon every detail ahead of them; Dii focuses on the trail behind. Ylinia watches the grass and dirt below her feet; doing her earnest to keep up with the pace despite each step inviting her to flop and nap wherever she may land.

The walk requires of them only twenty or so minutes. The night is warm when still and brisk while the wind wisps throughout; the strong scent of sea salt brightens up the senses at each encounter. They walk up towards the manor; Bell stops just at the threshold of the property.

"Dii, you're staying in a guest room in the manor, *right*?" Bell questions.

She nods. "I argued against it, but I just got a room with a slightly *smaller* balcony in compromise."

"That does seem like compromise with a queen."

"I'd rather we stop with the whole *calling me by my job* thing." Ylinia groans out slowly. "It would be like me calling you *Sword-Guard* and you *Trainer*. Do you define yourself enough by those recently earned definitions that you'd like to be entirely referenced by them?"

"*Apologies*." Bell remarks with a subtle nod. "Will you two be alright from here?"

Ylinia glances over towards the front door of the manor which is maybe ten or so metres away. She raises her eyebrow as if attempting to detect a punchline. "*I'm pretty sure yes*."

Bell recoils slightly with guilt. "*Good*." He stares away for a moment. "I'll see you both in the morning."

"*Night*." Ylinia murmurs before quickly ushering herself off towards the door.

Dii stands for a moment and maintains eye contact with Bell; then follows off behind Ylinia.

A star studded blackness has entirely canvassed the sky. Bell stares out at each glimmering white light; a few shine brighter then others. Black endlessness stretches on forever; *approaching* from every direction. With half his focus still up in the stars Bell begins to walk towards The Tristram. Without the handicap of company he walks comfortably at the pace of a partial sprint.

The Tristram has been parked in a semi-circle; hoisted up onto a bright pine foundation. Outside the train is a blazing fire-pit; which Izelle and Saranias have each taken a seat around upon a log stump. Saranias glances up as Bell approaches and smiles brightly towards him. "How is our young monarch fairing with her combat training?"

Bell picks up a stump, drops it nearby the fire and takes a wide comfortable seat upon it. He stares into the flame; burning away a few halved logs. "She's a hard worker for sure. Runs herself right up till she can't."

"Admirable." Izelle compliments.

"A bit sad if you ask me." Saranias admits.

Bell raises his eyebrow. "Insight from your own youth?"

Saranias rolls her eyes. "*Yes, actually*. The routine is nice, but you're never taught how to function without it because there is an unspoken expectation that it will always be present." She turns to stare at the fire; throwing on one of a few logs from beside her seat. "I imagine her time will not just be drills and suffering however; so I hope the experience is different."

"Of course." Bell agrees. "*Now*, I have to ask. What brings you two out tonight?"

Izelle and Saranias share a knowing look then smile towards Bell. "We both missed camp."

"*Ah*." Bell responds with absolute comprehension. His focus tightens and his breathing becomes deep and intentional. He smiles a bit and an instant welling of tears forms just in the corner of his eye. "Do you remember that first series of *stealth* tents they sent out to us in special ops?"

Izelle chuckles. "You mean the ones that basically suctioned onto your whole body once you got in them?"

"Oh shit!" Saranias remarks as she has a sudden reminder of her own past. "*I remember those!* You felt like you'd been swallowed by a thousand foot snake and just got finished being crapped out through the tightest series of sphincters possible as you woke up."

Bell nods a few times. "Those were the ones." He chuckles a bit. "Myself and Temple once shared one. Completely intentionally; which is almost worse." He looks up at the sky in a jolt, out into the woods then back at the fire. "We both woke up with the imprints of body hair across our entire bodies; we'd been *smooshed* so finely together. We ended up looking like some weird species of people with soggy rice for skin."

Izelle laughs; Saranias joins on with a bit of a cackle. "Why would you ever share something like that? Could you even breath?" Izelle asks while straightening her posture.

"*Slowly*" Bell admits sarcastically. "We wanted to try out the new tech. So we both requisitioned one. When the first night came where we had an opportunity to use them; after setting up our individual tents; staking them out properly on the ground; adjusting the camouflage armour. We looked over at one another and realized we didn't want to spend one of the few nights we were lucky enough to share; sleeping apart on different splotches of dirt." He shrugs. "I admit our love was always *a bit silly*. We consistently preferred to suffer any inconvenience together as opposed to finding peace alone."

The trio watch the fire crackle. Saranias impatiently tosses on another log; encouraging the flames higher then need be. "I miss her too Bell." Saranias states while staring at the ground. "It was the cutest thing to watch how excited she would get once she realized you two were going to be together again." She smiles brightly. "It didn't matter what we had come back from; or whatever new vision of horror we'd witnessed just the previous night. Once she knew you two would be together again; she counted down the seconds. She would pace any room she was in; have run on conversations just to pass the time; sleep as much and as long as she could just to *skip ahead*." A few small tears roll down her cheek. "You could see how much she loved you, just in the way she stood up on the tips of her toes to say your name."

Bell nods his head slowly a few times. "I'm glad you got to see her light up. It was always delightful."

"Have you spoken to her much, even, unintentionally?" Izelle questions sharply.

"*Uh.*" Bell remarks; confused how to even begin his response.

"*Sorry*, I just mean." Izelle stops to think quickly; tightening her lips together and staring up into the top of her head. "I've heard that is normal. And, I guess, I mean. *I have.*"

"*Oh.*" Bell notes. He moves his seat over towards Izelle and puts one of his arms around her.

Saranias butt scuttles her log over to join and wraps her arms around both Bell and Izelle.

Bell lets out a few tempered tears. "I don't know why, *but*, I haven't really thought much about the fact that you lost her too."

Izelle begins crying. "She was my sister Bell. To all of us *she was family.*" She sniffles loudly. "I haven't had a day where I'm not upset she had to be one of the ones who didn't make it."

"But you didn't lose all of your family Bell." Saranias adds on. "You don't have to suffer her loss alone."

Bell doesn't react too much. A distance grows in his eyes. The tips of his fingers become cold; and his muscles refuse to carry their own weight. Steady streams of tears pour from the corners of his eyes and he lets himself fall truly into the embrace of his friends. They hold him tight; despite what must seem like an earnest attempt to eat the dirt.

With a deep commanding breath Izelle speaks as softly as she can. "You know you still need to live though, don't you Bell?"

Bell breaks away from the embrace and shoots up onto his feet like a cat caught by a cold splash of the sea. He stares at Izelle like she has wounded him. "*Obviously.*"

"But what you're doing to yourself Bell. It is similar to living; yet doused too heavily in constant strife to truly be the same. There is variety in allowing yourself to be alive, not the same consistent drag. I fear you've set yourself into a trench which will only ever dredge further down until you're suffocating under the earth you've moved."

She speaks articulately; without breaking eye-contact for any reason other then to blink.

Flickering between Bell and Izelle with her eyes; Saranias lowers her head to look at the reflection of the flame against the dirt.

The flame is nearly extinguished as Bell exhales with incredible force. He looks straight up into the night sky and closes his eyes purposefully; as if preparing himself to endure something. "I don't know how to let this go."

"We are here to help you with that Bell." Izelle affirms.

Bell shakes his head. "*No.*" He states firmly. "This isn't like that. It isn't that I don't think I'm capable of the effort to move on; it is that I *do not believe I will survive the transformation.* I am like a thousand yards of vines growing up a crumbling cobblestone wall. Were it not for the framing of the wall; as frail as it may be; I would collapse like cord into bundles of myself."

Izelle smiles warmly. "I believe that it may *feel that way.*"

"*It is not a feeling!*" Bell lashes out at Izelle. "Temple was not just some woman I met at the bar and fell in love with, nor were we just a single story of beautiful romance. Where we came from, *Varyia.* Had we not come here to fight in the war; we would have lived together *eternally*. Not years, not just moments. *Eternity.* There would have been no sickness, no violence, no form of death which could touch us. And yet, with the same decision to come here; we left behind our destiny." He begins weeping nearly uncontrollably. "We left and now she is gone *forever. I was never supposed to be without her.*" He raises his hands up to his temples; the creases across his forehead tighten and his mask struggles to stay in place. "You must see that I am not a man standing without his partner, I am an entity torn asunder from its self. A tower without a ground floor somehow standing upright. So I ask that you suffer my sorrow. Whether or not it is healthy, whether or not that I will be better for it. It is the slightest remainder I have of what was once the defined path of my soul; and I cannot be the person who I am while also deciding to throw it away. *I simply cannot.*"

"Varyia truly exists doesn't it?" Saranias asks behind a thin veil of intrigue.

Bell nods. "It does."

"All these years. In a way, I didn't know if you were being serious. As if it were a cover for the *mysterious history* of the man who found a way to fight in nearly each of the years of the *Five Hundred Year War*." Saranias jokes; mostly to herself. "But I see now that you've never misled us about it once." She stares at Bell with a critical expression. "That means, if the legends I've read are true. You come from *the land of dragons*."

"Is Varyia not the *fabled home* of the second age gods?" Izelle questions; her eyebrow raised a full inch above her brow. "I think that was the case; in the tales my grandmother would share with me."

Bell looks out into the blackness of the wood. His brain paints humanoid figures in the darkness; while his mind works just as hard to convince him that they aren't there. "There was a mistake made, initially in *our* history. Were there such static laws to break at the time; three Varyian's; undeserving of their names; would have been known as criminals." He takes a deep breath, exhales and looks out towards the women. "*Sorry*, is this something you even want to hear?"

Both women nod.

"Yes, please. Come back and take a seat." Saranias encourages.

Without too much difficulty Bell walks over and returns to his seat upon one of the log stumps. He looks between both Izelle and Saranias; then focuses on the flame. He reaches over and grabs a log to toss into the fire. "*So*." He begins. "These *criminals*. They were banished from Varyia; in such a way that they could never return." He closes his eyes with a bit of resignation. "Our decision to send them here was made prior to the knowledge that anything *was here*...as you must understand. We believed that the loss of their wings, and the adoption of soft flesh would mellow their hearts." He shakes his head. "We were like children; despite sitting atop thousands of years of experience."

"These criminals. What became of them?" Izelle seeks a faster answer.

"They took advantage of the strength remaining from their previous forms. Sought to become more then mortal once again; as the curators of faith." Bell explains stoically. "I have only ever known it as history, as even *I* am not old enough to recall. But once the faithful sought war; with blades, politics and all in between. Varyian warriors were sent, from a band of willing volunteers. To come here and *end* them."

Izelle nods. "I have never heard of these criminals, despite how ancient their involvement must be. So are we left to presume these warriors were successful?"

"*Mhmm.*" Bell confirms. "They performed thorough kill-checks upon each following their capture. Their corpses were burnt, the remains entombed in rubber, bound in leather and set inside a vault."

Izelle chuckles. "That seems like an obnoxious amount of overkill."

Bell shrugs. "That was a bit of the point I guess? To show what will happen if you find yourself believing the delusion that you alone should decide how all things are designed."

"You'll be made into some odd sort of art project?" Saranias quips.

Bell chuckles and nods towards Saranias. "*Precisely.*"

"Is there truly no way to return to Varyia?" Izelle inquires; her kind eyes resting in a gaze.

Bell holds out his hands and peers down at his fingers; curling them in reflex to his inspection. "There is no passage you could step through. We know that to be impossible. *Yet,* the soul is not as limited."

"Then it isn't *entirely impossible.*"

"It isn't." Bell snips, then sighs.

"So, what then. What must you do?" She presses on.

Bell shrugs. "With practice, it is possible to bring yourself into an expansive trance; wherein your perception is not limited just to the body of your origin. You channel yourself to the frequency of a passage hidden behind the flow of our reality; directing your energy through an invisible and nearly incomprehensible maze. This passage is easily detected by those who call Varyia home; but your appearance there is harmless for better or worse. As you can not be touched, nor are you capable of anything more then walking freely about the ground."

Izelle shuffles her shoulders in consideration. "I believe you should return then. Allow yourself to find this trance. See your home, even if it is just for its own sake."

The night sky is clear and crisp; causing each star cast across the sky to appear twice its size. Bell watches as a few of the little white dots appear suddenly and others are gone just as quick. "I wouldn't know what to do there."

Saranias giggles. "That's a misconception my friend! This belief that we have to do anything when we get somewhere. Sometimes the value is simply in finding yourself there. The rest of what is supposed to happen, *if anything actually is meant to,* will find its way to you regardless." She throws her hands up in the air carelessly. "It isn't as if you can control destiny. Even if you did? It would only be your destiny to screw up your destiny."

Bell smirks. "*Alright.*" He concedes. "What is it you two believe best?" He asks with a bit of a sarcastic taunt; growing his smirk alongside his pronunciation.

"Take Ylinia." Izelle states plainly.

Bell stares back at Izelle, looks up at the sky, looks back at Izelle, looks over at Saranias, the fire and finally back to Izelle again. "*That is actually a pretty good idea.*"

"Right?" Izelle commends him for agreeing. "She is to be the youngest monarch The Citizenry has ever seen. With the time she has in the position, a lifetime to grow into the role. Every lesson she can find; she should take heed from. There is no way to predict what the future will require of you; especially if you are responsible for the world."

The fire crackles loudly; spitting embers out across the dirt.

"We'll prepare for this prior to her tour. I feel as if it will be a more authentic start to an otherwise intangible role to fill." Bell responds softly.

"I believe she is going to have tremendous fun." Izelle remarks pleasantly.

"Who wouldn't." Saranias jokes. She stares deep at Bell. "I still don't see where the scales would have been."

Bell chuckles. He peers around the area; then at the back of his hand. "And yet I still find myself forgetting they aren't there."

The group chats for a bit longer; not about much. Then spends the rest of their time in comfortable silence; watching each of the logs they have prepared ignite then fully burn away. They sit around the fire soaking in the smell of smoke nearly until the morning; watching it until even the final few embers lose their colour; then share brief hugs before they disperse to find sleep.

Bell stares up at The Tristram; the foundation has been installed in such a way that the whole train could quickly leave if it needed to. A few steps lead up to a small wooden deck and the entrance into the third car of the train. Bell quickly finds himself inside; flopping onto his spot on the couch to crash.

CHAPTER NINETEEN

DECIDE IT MATTERS

An incredibly early morning crawls across the Meire Estate. Pink streams of sun shoot through the quills and leaves of the various trees densely rooted across the grounds. Ylinia creeps down the stairs from her room into the kitchen of the manor.

The kitchen floor is a smooth grey tile; and rather cold to the touch. The counters are accented with stained oak wood and granite tops. The most modern of appliances have been installed; including a stainless steel icebox, an electric coffee grinder, a coffee machine and a sink with near instant varying water temperatures.

As Ylinia pokes into the room she is instantly met by Courtney; who is sitting in the central island of the kitchen at a stool. She is dressed entirely in her academy uniform; with at least three books splayed out open in front of her. Her hair has been pinned back into a tight ponytail; which in combination with her sharp shoulders and firm collar gives her an incredibly formal appearance.

"Hey Court, have you even slept?" Ylinia asks sweetly.

Courtney violently shakes herself awake; nearly falling off of her stool. She takes a moment to collect her breathing then peers over towards Ylinia with a subdued smirk. "Sorry, *what?*"

Ylinia chuckles. "Is the coffee still warm?"

"*Erm*" Courtney voices her confidence then shrugs dramatically.

"I'll freshen the pot."

Courtney takes a slow drink from her cold mug of coffee; swallowing it down as swiftly and strategically as she can; as if it were a helpful poison. "Since when do you drink coffee?" Her eyes open wide as she begins to speak more clearly.

"Just recently, *I guess*." She admits as she pours out the cold coffee into the sink and begins preparing to make a new pot. "But I figured if I'm going to be the type of person who is up this early with any kind of regularity." She shrugs. "I should start becoming a coffee person too."

Courtney laughs a bit. "Makes sense." She attempts to peer over towards whatever Ylinia is doing but can't make out anything from her perspective on the island. "Have you ever made coffee before?"

The electric coffee grinder begins whirring loudly; shockingly not instantly distressing everyone in the local area. "*I think I got it!*" Ylinia shouts over the mechanical disturbance.

"*Alright.*" Courtney bids farewell to her concern over the matter then turns her attention back to the books in front of her. "I can't even remember what I was reading last."

"Didn't you *just* get into the academy? How do you have that much reading already!" Ylinia questions with earnest confusion; and a bit of an empathetic panic.

Courtney shakes her head. "I'm actually still a bit away from the start of classes. But I contacted some local book stores to track down the entire curriculum for the first few years. I finished all of the first years reading last night, then flew through the second." She yawns deeply; nearly unhinging her jaw. "And the third has thrown a bit of a wrench in my gears; but I think it has all found its place in my head now."

The coffee machine begins hissing as it quickly steams water to drip down over the grounds. Ylinia walks over to the ice box and retrieves from it a four litre jug of milk. She fills a mug half full with milk before putting it back; then swirls about three and a half table spoons of sugar into the milk. She stares down into the granular concoction she has created with a moderate amount of pride. "And do you remember all of it...what you read I mean?"

Courtney nods. "Once I can repeat it to myself. Not exactly, like, *the precise words*, but the idea. Once I comprehend the essential things to understand; I never forget." She slowly peers up towards the ceiling.

"I wish I had that." Ylinia admits. "I can read a page, say the words to myself out loud or write them down on as many different note pads as need be. But if I can't interact with something; if I can't *see it*. I can never learn about it." She shrugs. "My mind just draws a blank otherwise."

"Your mind is in more places then your head Ylinia." Courtney states with a blank expression.

Ylinia crooks her eyebrow up at a wicked angle. "Have you forgotten you're awake Courtney?"

She shakes her head. "You think that just because you don't have words in your head that your mind is empty. But it couldn't be further from the truth."

Ylinia nods politely. "Well, thank you."

"I mean it. Do you think that when you swing around your blade it is your arm doing the thinking? What is it you think you teach when you practice a strike? Because while you may certainly use a muscle, I don't believe that is the whole purpose of the exercise."

"So my arm has a brain in it?" Ylinia critiques as pleasantly as she can.

Courtney rolls her eyes. "Of the many types of intelligence we possess. The few which dictate your spatial awareness, your expression of physicality, your basic hand eye co-ordination. Each of those parts of yourself have proven better then standard. They may not speak in sentences; but listening to them will still leave you the wiser."

Ylinia smiles. "I'll trust that then." She takes in a deep breath, stretches the slightest bit then stares towards Courtney. "Thank you for not treating me any differently Court. Everything has been so sudden, and with some people. It is almost like a wall has emerged between us; that requires a constant vaulting over-top for even the slightest of communications."

"*Mhmm.*" Courtney agrees with a firm nod. "It isn't very much like a proper citizen to covet the role of another. I wish you success in your objectives as much as you wish me in mine. So long as we're capable of success; why languish on anything other then the positive outcome? I can't see the benefit in pretending I see a division if our whole society is set up to never have any."

Alim walks down into the room; dressed in a dark blue silk set of pajamas with a thick burgundy house coat over-top. "Good morning to you both." He announces himself as he enters the kitchen. "I must say I had the oddest dream that I would find you both here this morning."

"Oh?" Courtney responds.

"Well, *sort of.* You were reading squid instead of books. And Ylinia had a very handsome beard." He smirks oddly then rolls his eyes; as if confused even by himself. "I believe my hands were chairs as well, just on occasion, but they would switch depending on who I was talking too. Recliners one moment, stools another." He chuckles. "I am glad to see you haven't grown hateful of the early morning sun regardless."

"The world is prettiest in the morning. Just as it has woken up; and yet to be disturbed by the day." Ylinia remarks softly. She fills her mug with coffee, tightens on the lid and begins walking out towards the lobby. "I'll see you both later for dinner!"

"Training again? I thought you and Dii did that together?" Courtney questions; catching Ylinia in the transition between rooms.

She turns around and nods. "Of course, I'm sure Dii is outside right now, alongside Bell as my escort."

Alim pokes his head out of the kitchen and then down towards the lobby; where there are no signs of passage. "Has Dii left?"

Ylinia laughs. "I imagine she leap off her balcony." She shrugs a bit. "I guess she isn't big on small talk? *So,* she avoids the door when possible."

Courtney nods very seriously; as if noting something down for later. *"Makes enough sense."* She admits. "See you later Ylinia, *be safe."*

"Always." Ylinia promises. She nods towards Alim then quickly spins around to rush out into the lobby. Just on the other side of the manor's front door is Bell; alongside Dii; standing across from one another silently drinking from their own travel mugs.

Bell looks over towards Ylinia and nods. *"Morning."*

"Morning." Ylinia replies. She walks up beside Dii; smiles with excess enthusiasm then begins onward towards the mirrored training grounds.

On the third floor of the Meire Manor is the bedroom of Howarth and Mel. They sleep right up until the sun shoots through their window and beams them in the face with warmth. As he wakes Howarth lazily rolls over closer to his wife and wraps his arms around her; pulling her like a loose bundle of warmth against his bare chest. Mel swoons and makes pleasant sleepy sounds; herself in lavender coloured silk sleeping attire.

"Morning darling." Mel responds; speaking mostly into her pillow. She opens her eyes to a squint.

"Morning love." Howarth responds. He kisses the top of her head and takes a deep relaxing breath; letting it out at a peaceful pace. "How was your sleep?"

Mel rolls her shoulders and yawns loudly with a possessed dedication. "*Wonderful.* Honestly wonderful." She closes her eyes again. "I truly had myself convinced that the beds we had in our cabin on The Tristram were the pinnacle of luxury."

Howarth shoots air from his nostrils. "They were for a time." He smiles widely. "But looking back, they were just thicker then a strip of bacon weren't they?"

"And small." Mel complains; opening her eyes again with a force of will. "I love sleeping next to you. But it is beyond nice to be able to stretch out and also not risk sucker punching my husband."

"I'm a fan of that too." He admits with a chuckle. "Do you want to leave this bed?"

Mel rolls over to look up at Howarth. They share an instinctual kiss; lingering their foreheads together for just a few moments of connection. "I want the bed to come with me. You're the engineer! Put wheels on it *please*." She requests with the demeanour of a young innocent lady.

"Maybe some day." Howarth jokes. He sits up on the bed and places one of his legs beside Mel; so that he is kneeling over top of her. He leans down to kiss her forehead then wraps his arms all around her; pushing his hands between her and the bed to wrap around her back on both sides. He holds her tight; kissing her again a few times. "But today you'll have to come with me." He whispers into her ear with a calm deep voice. He slowly motions to a straight posture; the full muscled breadth of his chest expanded from Mel's point of view. Howarth smiles modestly, steps off the bed and offers his hand to his wife. "Come with me love. I've been putting together a little date. And I think we have the perfect day for it."

With delight Mel reaches out to take his hand; pulling herself out of bed with his assistance. They dress in casual attire; simple denim trousers paired with single tone, fitted collared shirts. Howarth throws on a well worn brown leather jacket; which fits his shoulders profoundly well. Mel pairs her outfit with a knee length dark grey military coat; an elaborate black tree is stitched across the back of the jacket. They walk hand-in-hand into the kitchen where Alim, Courtney and Lance are all sat around the central island; roughly fourteen or so thick tomes are open and stacked about across the table-top.

"Coffee is fresh." Courtney shouts out the instant Howarth and Mel enter the kitchen.

"*Oh perfect.*" Howarth declares; instantly setting off to prepare himself some.

"You people are all addicts I swear." Mel jokes. "I've never seen this much coffee get slurped down outside of a bunker on the border." She rolls her eyes and takes a seat; scanning across the various bodies of text on the table. She looks up at Alim. "New research project?"

Alim shakes his head. "Courtney is reading in advance. *We're helping.*"

Mel laughs then smiles over towards Courtney. "You're getting excited then?"

"Very much so, yes." Courtney admits with a few energetic nods. "But I'm not very good at just sitting still and being excited, *so*, I figured I'd do something about it."

Howarth places a full mug of coffee in front of Mel then takes a seat next to her with one of his own. Mel rolls her eyes with a smirk then takes a short sip from the mug. "Well, if you want something to do. My old surgical instructor is still giving lectures at the academy here in Caelzun. I can put together a writ of passage so you can attend if you'd like?" She shrugs. "I know it isn't exactly *military* training. But even just getting a feel for that level of class might be beneficial."

"Could you do that? Actually?"

"*Sure.*" Mel states with a subtle smile. "Professor Baelynn loves teaching. More then anyone I have ever met before. She would pack her classroom full of every person on the streets if she could!" She enthuses. "I'll put together the pass before we go."

"Thank you Mel!" Courtney nearly shouts. "Are you sure you don't want to come yourself and see the professor again?"

Mel smiles and sways her head. "She's a lovely women, and brighter then anything. But not exactly what I would call *sentimental.* She's happier with me being off in the world; using what I was taught. Not limiting both our usefulness by repeating a conversation between ourselves."

Courtney nods firmly. "A pragmatist then. I will strictly study her teachings then. No funny business."

"She'll like that." Mel admits.

"Besides, we're going to go on a bit of an adventure today." Howarth speaks proudly; placing his arm around Mel without even realizing he is doing it. "And I'm not letting anything steal her away today."

"Aww." Lance admires. "I'm glad you two still date each other! When you're together you just look so young; like you're still newly wed."

Mel laughs with a bit of a cackle. "Well thank you for saying so Lance." She leans to look over at Howarth. "What has it been...seventeen years? Nineteen?"

"I thought twenty." Howarth admits with a shrug. "Or maybe I was just born next to you? I can't really remember what the hell I got up too before."

"I'd believe you were born beside me." Mel teases. She stands; placing a single hand on her husband's shoulder. "Would you come with me Courtney? We'll do up your pass."

Courtney stands and joins Mel.

"I'll meet you in the garage, okay love?" Mel asks while staring at Howarth.

He nods. "Of course, see you in just a bit." He smiles then turns to look out at Alim and Lance; then takes a sip of his coffee.

Courtney and Mel walk off together into the manor.

"So how is helping going?" Howarth asks no one in particular.

Lance looks over towards Alim and they share a smirk. "Given the kind of help it really is, it is going splendid." Lance responds whimsically.

"Oh yea, *good*. Have you two studied much of the academy?"

Lance shakes his head diligently while Alim loosely shrugs. "Courtney doesn't really need help with the books." Alim admits.

"But we miss feeling useful all the same." Lance notes; faking a smile. "The academy will provide her with so many amazing opportunities; it would be pure selfishness to be opposed. *Yet still*. I know how much she will have to travel, how far she will go in that world. We'll very quickly go from always living together, to hopefully visiting for the holidays."

Howarth stares down into his mug of coffee. "You'll always share your connection. Because I've come to realize that the bond we believe we have with our children *isn't really there*. Not in the sense we all think it is. There is love, and a connection so deep, so inherent that it may never need to be spoken for to feel its impact throughout. But there is falsehood in the belief that that connection is only beneficial when standing together in the same room. For every lesson you have taught her, every bit of understanding and love you have shared. You've given her that many more tools upon her belt. So when she is busy living her life away from you; as she was always destined. She'll succeed that much more because of your connection; I promise."

Lance nods. "Of course." He smiles and looks over towards Alim.

"And where are you two off too?" Alim questions.

Howarth smirks knowingly. "I don't want to ruin the surprise, so I won't even risk saying it out loud. But we'll only be gone for a few hours. And we'll return this evening."

"Of course." Alim responds calmly. "Enjoy yourselves."

Howarth leaves just as Courtney is returning to the kitchen; her writ of passage clenched securely in her right hand. She takes a seat between her parents; unable to stop smiling.

"Excited sweetheart?" Lance asks with a curious expression.

"Very much so." Courtney admits. She looks between both her parents. "Are you guys gonna get ready?"

Alim and Lance look between themselves confused. "The writ is just for you, isn't it?"

"*Sure*." Courtney agrees. "But I still think we could go on the walk together! You two can go out for lunch while I'm attending the lecture." She stands up and tugs Lance to his feet a little. "Come on you two, don't just sit around all day reading books." She jokes.

Howarth opens up the door into the garage; Mel stands next to a canvas tarp draped over something about waist height to create an ugly looking tent. She points towards it as Howarth enters the garage. "What have we here mister?" She questions with a sweet inflection.

"Go ahead and look." Howarth instructs; walking slowly towards her.

Without hesitation Mel whips the canvas cover off to reveal a pristine motorcycle with all bronze mechanical components. The seat is a pitch black leather which sits down near the back wheel; leaving the front end wide and free. The tires are about six inches wide and large enough to fit a truck. Every aspect of the vehicle appears heavy and industrial. Mel smiles as she admires the machine. "It looks pretty."

"*Pretty* is the word you use?" Howarth feigns damage to his masculinity. He smacks the taunt leather seat in a silly and seductive manner. "Is that what you would call this sweet piece of ass?"

Mel rolls her eyes; unable to withhold her growing smile. "It looks amazing Howarth. I imagine you put it together? You did a beautiful job." She steps up onto the bike and bounces on the hydraulics a bit. "Now lets get it on the road, eh?"

Howarth joins his wife on the bike; she wraps her arms around his chest. He puts an odd square shaped key into the ignition; located on the handle bar central console. The machine instantly kicks out a hateful ball of fire from the four rear exhaust pipes then begins to purr like a blues inclined bear wrecked twice over with rough rye. Howarth pulls back on the throttle a little and a crackle of electrical energy stirs within the machine; causing a cascading mechanical chorus. He quickly peels out of the garage and speeds off down the pathway towards the ocean coast.

⊥

"How do your muscles feel this morning?" Dii asks as her, Bell and Ylinia all walk through the woods towards the mirrored training grounds.

"Better, actually." Ylinia notes. "I thought I would have to sleep for a week to feel halfway alright, but, even just getting into bed helped a lot."

"That will happen." Dii remarks. "The better you get, the more you train. The less uncommon it is for your body to push its self that much. Soon you'll be able to shrug off a marathon I'm sure!"

"If only." Ylinia responds skeptically. "I don't want to rush right up to my threshold."

Bell slows down slightly. "Do you actually believe you have one?"

Ylinia nods. "Of course. I won't lie to myself and say I am some *super woman*. I can learn pretty quickly, but that doesn't mean I can learn *everything*. There are limits in the world. There just are."

"Should we take your remaining arm then? If you are to be bound by limitations?"

"*Holy shit Bell.*" Dii defends. "That is a bit intense isn't it?"

Ylinia sighs. "No he is right." She huffs a bit. "It is just, *I dunno*. I have all these responsibilities now. I am *The Monarch*. Yet I do not feel like it. I feel like a girl, I feel like a student, and a daughter. I may see closed gates as limits but even if that is the case; I haven't a clue how to pass through them. How to properly get where it is that I am trying to go."

Bell takes a deep breath; encountering a realization in the process. "Dii, would you mind if today was spent training in another environment?"

"I don't see why not. Variety is a multiplier of experience." She responds then stares at Bell with a single squinting eye. "What is it that you have in mind?"

"I would like to take Ylinia to Varyia." He states plainly.

Ylinia instantly lights up with excitement. "Are you being serious? I don't even know where Varyia is? How do we get there?"

Bell laughs. "We walk first. If you are willing to do so?"

"*Of course!*" Ylinia agrees as if any other option is preposterous.

Drawing a solid line with his arm; Bell points out towards the vast range of mountains to the north of them. There is one specific rectangular peak which stands out from all the others as being slightly wider and slightly shorter. It is despite this; twice as magnificent and absolutely dense with greenery and colour. "Then we must make it there before midday." He points towards the sun; now gaining a bit of an advantage over the sky. "I imagine we have four or so hours."

Ylinia rushes off down the path whilst screaming. "Then let us waste no time!"

Bell and Dii follow after her; jogging just a pace or two behind. "I've hiked these mountains. Even the ones you pointed out. *That is a dormant volcano.* You do know that, right?"

"I do." Bell affirms.

"Then how is it that it is also Varyia?" She questions.

"It isn't." Bell admits. "But that is because you cannot *walk* to Varyia no matter your skill, speed or even if you have been there before. There is no tunnel you can pass through to find yourself there once on the other side. It is not that sort of place."

"Then why the volcano? Can you see Varyia from there? Jump for it somehow?"

Bell chuckles slightly. *"In a sense?* The volcano is dormant, but not dead. That massive amount of natural energy that is swirling underneath emits an aura of enhancement. Now in a traditional sense there isn't much we could do with that. Under a more abstract lens, this energy is a catalyst for any spiritual practice. It can be used to enhance the capabilities of focus; or the extent one may feel the world around them."

"*Huh.*" Dii responds.

"We'll require you to watch over us while we meditate. Our minds will find Varyia, but our bodies will remain here. We would be unable to protects ourselves were something to go wrong." Bell explains.

"*Ah*." Dii remarks with understanding. "I'll keep you safe, of course."

"We know you will Dii." Ylinia chimes in. "You're more then a fighter. You're a sweetheart as well."

Dii laughs softly. The trio hike onward towards the dormant volcano.

The academy is located alongside the largest of the various harbours built across Caelzun's coast. There is a central cobblestone path which leads directly to its front gates; which themselves are ten or so meters high and tipped with electrically charged spikes. Outside the front gates of the academy are two posted officers; each dressed in long armoured coats; with short-swords at their waist.

Lance leads Alim and Courtney down towards the academy. The streets are sparsely filled; with most activity located around a cafe named *Delicante*. Many of the members of the crowd are dressed in formal academy uniforms; Courtney has changed out of her own to avoid the confusion. "How much time do we have before your lecture begins Court?"

She stops in place and looks around; spotting a large traditional clock built into the face of the tallest of the academy towers. She squints for a moment; taking her time to translate the analog. "*Just over an hour,* actually." She responds; a bit surprised even herself.

Lance snatches Courtney's hand and begins to walk her towards the cafe. "Then we have time for a bit of a snack."

Courtney chuckles; resisting the urge to roll her eyes. Alim double checks the time himself against his own pocket watch then quickly takes a few double steps to catch up with his family.

The cafe is set in an old brick building; which has obviously had a *split* repaired at least five or six times in the past decade. The wooden floor begins from a centred tear wherein new product has been cut and filled to accommodate the spreading foundation. The second and third floors of the cafe have been mended just as well so that in design the building resembles a sideways layered cake more then any real structure. Despite this there is no active *wobble* and the effect is charming once it stops seeming odd and overwhelming. On each floor is a different style of seating with the very ground floor being set up very communally; with large circular tables and benches. The second floor; which has access to a balcony is set more for small parties or couples; with dimmer lighting, soft music and comfortable chairs. Prior to entering the third floor one passes by a large wall with a written warning; decorated with small filigree in the corners. The warning simply reads.

> *There is to be nothing but silence past this point.*
> *Please respect the books.*

Following this wall is a beautiful library designed in such a way that there are roughly forty or so individual tables; with single chairs tucked neatly into every single one. Each table is walled off on three sides with the back of a bookshelf so that the entire floor is like a maze with multiple hallways; and none of them predestined to connect. It is very much a place you can be lost, or pleasantly difficult to find.

Lance orders an assortment of desserts alongside three steamed fruit lattes; made in over-sized mugs that are then capped past the brim with a thick eggshell-white whipped cream. He takes a wooden block with his order number burned into it then meets Alim and Courtney out on the balcony of the second floor. "*Soon*, we shall have deliciousness." He declares as he takes his seat among the others; sharing a small round table with a tall umbrella sprouting out from the centre.

"Thanks Dad." Courtney remarks sweetly. She peers over her shoulder at the academy; which is only a five or so minutes walk away. "I imagine I could come here pretty frequently."

Alim looks around at a few of the other patrons sitting at their tables; many of them obviously from the academy. "I imagine it is a popular spot for that reason, yes."

Lance sighs dramatically. "It almost makes me miss my time spent working in a cafe. Very similar to this one, though I admit I'm jealous of all the room they have here."

Courtney raises her eyebrow with a smirk. "Why do you miss it?"

"Life was but a breeze then! I was so sheltered in my youth. Hidden away from much of the war. I had but to find a way to effectively contribute to The Citizenry four hours a day five days a week to earn my token; and the rest of the time remaining was mine to be spent as I wished. My friends at the cafe were sweet, and similarly naive. The worst of our troubles a broken machine or ill tempered customer. To have your home, your food, your lifestyle given to you for such a simple contribution. It is very peaceful, blank, *easy*. But I loved it all the same." Lance peers over towards Alim. "It is because of that job that I met your father. He was a regular *and much more flirtatious* in his youth." He teases.

Alim laughs and rolls his eyes. "I guess I was, was I not?" He admits as modestly as he can. "At first I just liked the way we could talk. I would give him an order, then all of a sudden we'd be halfway into a semantic debate about something completely pointless. We just liked talking. We started talking after his shifts, then in more of our own time." He smiles lovingly towards Lance. "We fell very naturally in love. And I think that was the only reason I was so *flirtatious*." He teases his husband with his pronunciation.

A server brings over a large platter of different pastries; bidding a short farewell before leaving. On the platter are bars of chocolate styled to look like realistic pebbles, rocks and gems, as well as croissants entirely drenched in layers of chocolate and caramel. The trio each take one of the croissants and quickly find themselves inhaling them. They share a blank stare between each other in absolute silence; finalizing a few rough swallowing endeavours.

"I'm going to get so fat." Courtney declares very abruptly.

"You'll just have to run here." Lance argues.

"I'm going to be running here no doubt." She admits.

"Run between each pastry then. For each one run between here and the academy."

"I'll end up spending all day running that way." Courtney notes with concern.

"We can find you better shoes then?" Lance offers.

"Not if I eat so much pastry that I keep needing new pairs." She counters.

"Well your feet don't typically gain weight Court." Alim advises honestly.

"No, but my feet will tear through my shoes if my ass keeps growing up on top of them." She jests with a serious inflection.

Lance bursts out laughing. "I think you'll be fine my dear. I think most people can survive a primarily pastry and coffee based diet for at least four years? I mean, that's the scientific make up of any proper adult student."

Courtney breaths out a sigh of relief. *"Alright."* She picks up another croissant and points it at Lance threateningly. *"But I'm trusting you."* She remarks before stuffing half of it into her face; practically melting just as the chocolate does against her tongue.

Each of the chocolate pebbles has a core of something sweet; either loose caramel, toffee, candied fruit, peanut-butter or jam. They are devoured casually alongside drinks; often eaten whole but left to melt before swallowing.

The trio clean up their table a bit; and bring over the tray to a disposal station. They bid a softly spoken farewell to the staff of the cafe then squeeze out past the crowds of the first level to return to the main street. Alim and Lance hold hands as they walk just behind Courtney right up to the front gates of the academy. They are immediately met by the guards. Each of the guards wear form fitting helmets alongside thick steel armour with a formal grey military trench-coat over-top; trailing down to their knees with obviously dense fabric.

"Writ of passage please." One of the guards states clearly towards the trio; a minor technological distortion in his voice.

Courtney produces the writ and hands it over to the guard. While the guard inspects it; she turns to her fathers and hugs them both. "Thank you for coming out with me."

"Of course." Alim assures her. "We'll wander back before you're done so we can head home together."

"Sounds lovely." Courtney confirms. "See you soon!"

"Enjoy yourself love!" Lance speaks just loudly enough for her to hear; squeezing Alim's hand as he does. "We'll be here waiting for you."

The guard takes a step back and produces a portable radio; wired to a battery system concealed within the armour of his belt. He speaks into it quietly; but not in an indecipherable manner. "Passage

has been granted by a *Melissa Covestoff*. Please confirm." He holds
the radio against his head; waving his hips side to side slightly with
impatience. The radio murmurs something out to him and he returns it
to his belt. He nods towards Courtney. *"Alright, go along. We have an
escort for you."* He nods to the guard opposite of him and the gate
into the academy opens right up. On the opposite side is a well
dressed female officer; dawning a blue coat with the accolades of a
ten year career stitched across her chest. Her blond hair is done up
tightly in a bun and her extremely aesthetic features have been
downplayed in every instance; her makeup is subtle and ages her
slightly, her uniform fits perfectly onto her shoulders but is looser
across her bust and hips; benefiting her with a more rectangular
appearance. She smiles politely at Courtney as she approaches.

Ylinia pushes herself up over the ledge of the final portion of her
ascent; utilizing most of her chest, her arm, her shoulders and both her
legs in precise placement to achieve this success. She quickly
scrambles forwards towards the crater of the volcano; overwhelmed
with gratitude for secure footing. Dii follows behind closely; pulling
herself up over the edge without concern. Bell appears suddenly from
below as if he simply *jumped* up the remaining fifty meter incline.
Bell wipes off dust from his pant leg then turns around on his heels to
peer out at the forest and mountains; alongside the entirety of the city
of Caelzun; all painted perfectly in place in the distance. The sun has
only just found its place in the centre of the sky; barren of even a
single cloud to disrupt it.

"We made good time." Bell compliments.

Ylinia finishes huffing; catching her breath within a few short
attempts. "Does the time of day really matter?"

Bell shakes his head. "Not really. I just don't want to be up here till the middle of the night." He shares as honestly as one can.

Dii laughs. "Of course that is the reason you'd impose a rush."

"Well then." Ylinia states impatiently then jumps right up to her feet. "Let's get right to it! What are we to do?"

Bell walks over towards the crater and peers down into it. The volcano has been settled for years on top of years and as such is now nothing but a deep bowl of stone lightly dusted over with dirt. Beautiful flowers have grown all around the crater and across the sides where once destruction reigned. Bell motions his head towards the centre of the crater. "We'll need to set up there."

The moment the statement is made Ylinia carefully begins surfing down into the crater; balancing herself with her arm tucked against her chest and her hips countering any undo momentum. Bell smirks, shrugs and does the same. While Dii stands at the top of the crater. "I'll watch out for you from up here. I don't want all three of us to be blind to an ambush!" She shouts down towards them.

As she finds herself right in the centre of the crater; Ylinia stares straight up at the sky. Bell joins her quickly. "It looks, odd, from here. Like it is so far away." She states with a lucidity in her tone.

Bell nods then takes a seat. He straightens his back and then looks up himself. "I think it is the shadow all around us. It darkens the sky a bit." He closes his eyes then returns his head to a more natural posture. "Would you take a seat Ylinia?"

Ylinia stares down at Bell, shrugs then takes a seat in front of him. "Okay."

"Tell me what you feel." He requests.

She takes a moment. "The ground, a bit of a breeze. My back is a little itchy and I can feel my hair is curling around my ear."

Bell chuckles. "Good, *now*. Remove those sensations from your awareness. Don't try *not* to feel them as that is impossible. Instead allow yourself to be at peace with their placement; and remove yourself of the responsibility to bother with their concern."

Ylinia has her breathing begin to hone; and the form of her entire body begins to relax. She closes her eyes and becomes more and more lost in the simple repetition of her breath. "I feel, *a tingly feeling now*." She states softly; almost too quietly to be heard. "*All across my fingers, in my chest, behind my eyes.*"

"Follow that then." He remarks confidently. His breathing focuses as well, and quickly his mind is suspended upon nothing but the base flow of reality; feeling out for only the most essential of vibrations.

Dii watches over the two like a hawk. She crooks her head with fascination as both Bumble and Ehre begin to glow like rainbows are mounting an escape from within; with every known colour represented. The weapons illuminate a sphere almost half the size of the crater, shoot up a beam of light into the sky and conjure up a notable breeze. Both Ylinia and Bell shake for a moment; then lock into position with their backs straight, legs crossed and fists held tightly together.

⊥⊏

"It is beautiful Howarth!" Mel shouts out as she steps off the bike onto a little secluded beach; fenced off on all sides by tall pieces of red and orange coastal shale; appearing as if the coast is covered in crystallized fire. Howarth parks the bike and walks up behind his wife; taking her in his arms then kissing the back of her head. The ocean is five or six shades of blue and green; each hurdling over one another with the tide.

"It is just ours for the evening." He states confidently then points out to the sea. "Apparently, *right in that spot there*, the sun will set." He moves his finger from the horizon down a straight line to a spot on the beach. "And there is this beautiful *beam of light* that settles right there. We can just watch the day end, give it an opportunity to do so in a way we might not mind as much."

Mel lets out a deep breath of relief; then pushes her back against Howarth to be even closer to him. "Thank you for this my love."

Howarth laughs. "Of course Mel. There wouldn't have been much of a point in marrying you if that wasn't my plan." He kisses her again. "That is my job! And I'm going to have a lot more time to do it now." He smirks proudly. "I want to show you that all that time I spent wishing I could just love you all day wasn't a lie. I'm not going to miss out on the opportunity to love you every second I can."

"I love you too." Mel swoons. She turns around to lean up and give Howarth a quick kiss. She then rushes off onto the beach, takes off her shoes and walks right down towards the water. The ocean is chilled even in the afternoon; but feels refreshing in an instant. The chill of the water is a better tool for abrupt consciousness then any coffee or morning beverage could hope to be. "Is is weird to be here?" She asks without any prompt.

Howarth simply smiles as he joins his wife out in the water. "No, the water is nice. I like it too."

"That isn't what I mean. I mean, *here*. This place, this planet." She picks up her arms and motions around her. Towards the bright colours of the shale, the dull yellows of the sand, the sun filled sky painted in all places with endless blue and the invisible air around them. "Sometimes it just feels so *odd. Just, how odd it is that we live here at all.*"

"Isn't it?" Howarth agrees. He takes his wife's hand as they take a step deeper out into the water. "I think I've settled on us just being lucky."

Mel giggles. "Is that so?"

Howarth nods with absolute confidence. "Of course. Of all the things we could be, or not be. Of all the odd forms this life could have taken. We are people on a planet full of people, we can keep ourselves alive, build and create, learn and lose. We get lives, we have reality at our fingertips and in our heads." He takes Mel by the waist and pulls her close; peering down into her eyes with every seductive instinct he has. In that moment a rainbow of light shoots up from the mountains; stretching across each range of snow and peak of forest to trail off towards their coast; reflecting off each piece of shale with radiant beauty. Their smiles grow brighter and Howarth moves in closer to linger just apart from Mel's lips. "And there is such beauty in this world, beauty I know I'm lucky to behold. Beauty I am lucky to have found in my wife, and to feel for real every time I hold her." They kiss passionately, as every shade of coloured light washes over their skin; diluting in the ocean water below. The kiss breaks but the connection lingers. "Thank you for everything my love."

CHAPTER TWENTY

BEHEST OF BURDEN

"Where are we?" Ylinia shouts out into an endless void.

"There may not be an answer to that question." Bell responds.

Their bodies remain safe and perfectly still in the crater of a dormant volcano while their minds have drifted somewhere else entirely. Time, space, sound, sight, light and all other senses; each renewing themselves as they are removed from the filter of flesh. There is tumbling, falling, climbing and endless crawling. In a few mortal seconds the mind has perceived weeks; and mourned their loss as sincere.

There is light, then warmth, sound and feeling all at once. Bell and Ylinia appear in a field; dense with a lush grass as thick as carpet. There is no sky in this place. In every direction there are wild peaks of mountains and endless forests; varied with trees of a thousand different species. In all directions as the terrain continues onward it continues upwards; craning over like the inside of a perfect sphere so that the *sky* is only the ground far *above you*. There are nearly five thousand kilometres between the *ceiling* of mountains and the endless ranges surrounding the pair. Static shapes of bright glowing clouds fill the air in between; pouring rain or snow in any of three hundred and sixty possible directions. The air is cool; just warmer then freezing. Wind sweeps down from the mountains; carrying with it a fierce screech.

Bell opens his eyes slightly, peers around then quickly pushes himself up to his feet. He smiles wildly; spinning in place at great speed to peer around the area. He stops to kneel beside Ylinia and shakes her shoulder to wake her. She groans in frustration as she slowly sits up; crossing her legs and adopting a tired expression. "Welcome to Varyia."

Ylinia raises her eyebrow, blinks heavily then stares *behind* Bell to investigate the mountains where the sky should be. "Are we in danger?" She asks; skeptical of whether or not she should be skeptical.

"Not even slightly." Bell declares. He offers his hand down to Ylinia and she takes it; popping up quickly to her feet. "Have you ever wondered what is inside our planet?" He asks while motioning his hand around them. "Now you know."

"Trees and mountains?" Ylinia critiques. "I'm confused *why* they are here?"

Bell shrugs. "Varyia has always been. When I was young we considered it a possibility that this was the planet as it first appeared; and as life evolved; so did the world." He shrugs again. "But no one truly knows why. What we do know is that *all around* Varyia; is a fierce barrier. Nothing can travel inwards to reach these mountains, nothing can tunnel through. This barrier is as hot as a star; and has never ceased once."

"Ah." Ylinia responds. "So that is why there is no way to physically walk here."

Bell nods.

"Then, are we truly here? Or?" Ylinia debates.

Bell extends his hand; it appears no different then it ever has. "I counted twelve weeks spent on our passage here. As if they passed both in an instant and an eternity." He swallows slowly while staring out at the mountains. "But I am still sure that we remain in the crater. With Dii only a moment away."

Ylinia turns her head in inquiry. "Then we are, what? Projections? Memories of ourselves?"

"*I would imagine something like that, yes.*" Bell agrees.

A great blast of wind presses over the mountains behind the pair. The wind crashes into them; scattering their foothold. A massive shadow trails overhead. Both peer up to spot a silhouette of impossible dimensions; with two sets of wings stretching out nearly a kilometre in length on either side of the being. The being flies straight up then dramatically tail spins around; engaging at a barrelling speed towards Bell and Ylinia. Ylinia reaches for Bumble and prepares to draw the blade; but is stopped as Bell catches her hand and guides Bumble back into its sheath.

"There is no danger here." Bell assures her. He takes a step forwards and smiles towards the entity flying down towards them. He opens his arms wide. As the being gets closer details can be made out revealing it to be a dragon with purple and green scales throughout. The dragon continues to fly down and stops against all laws of physics in an instant; the sheer force throwing Bell and Ylinia back onto their asses with a burst of wind. The dragon roars out with such volume that the very contents of your stomach would become unsettled. Upon each of the dragon's four wings is a bright blue webbing that radiates in colour like the rolling light of an astral anomaly. It has four legs; and a long muscular body. The very frame of the dragon is just over three kilometres long; with a tail nearly half that trailing out in a few coils. Its head is predatory like a bear; with bright kind eyes. The dragon lowers its head towards Bell and he wraps his arms around its nose as much as he can. "It is good to see you *Meredia*. It has been too long."

Ylinia squints in disbelief. "You, *uh,* know each other?" She questions.

Bell smiles proudly then turns towards Ylinia. "*Of course.* Ylinia, I would like you to meet my *sister*. Meredia, this is Ylinia Covestoff; the Monarch of The Citizenry." He states formally.

Meredia bows her head slightly; tucking each of her wings closer to her body as she does. She coos out like a pigeon; the chime resounding throughout the valley. "*It is well to meet you.*" The words appear in the minds of Ylinia and Bell; spoken with a soft and kind voice.

"You are a beautiful...*person...dragon?*" Ylinia stumbles in her attempt to be polite.

"And your soul is just as well Ms.Covestoff." Meredia responds with a pleasant expression in her eyes. She opens up her wings out to their full extensions as she stretches out entirely. "Please let me take you to my home. We are not required to stand in a field."

Bell laughs. "Onto your back then?"

Meredia nods. As she does both Bell and Ylinia appear right upon her shoulder blades; where there are scales small enough to be easily grasped with human hands. "How long has it been since you have been up in the air Bell?" She asks the moment her wings begin to flap in a synchronous harmony; propelling the entirety of her form up into the air at quite a speed.

"Quite a while!" Bell shouts out as the wind becomes torrential; loudly censoring all but the most determined noises.

"*WHOOOOOO!!!!*" Ylinia shouts out without restraint as they gain real height above the ground. The mountainous peaks in Varyia are extreme; craning and crooking over one another; leading up into impossible heights, angles, or even curls. There are valleys just as deep as any peak is high and across the entirety of Varyia; there are dragons. Every colour, varying sizes, some with legs and some without, some like serpents and others like great fish that swim through the air. Far in the distance is *a city*; beginning within a massive range of mountains and spreading out through the forests.

In an instant Meredia swoops down into a long ravine; following it nearly all the way to the bottom only to swoop up in the last moment into a beautiful cavern; carved out to adopt an ornamental style. There are tall columns, polished walls, murals of art and nature, tile flooring, massive over-sized pieces of furniture adopted in shape for draconic bodies and varying potted plants; each growing a fruit or vegetable of some kind. Bell and Ylinia are roughly 1/16th the size of all the objects throughout the cavern. As Meredia swirls herself up comfortably into one of the recliners; Bell and Ylinia appear suddenly on the arm of her chair.

Ylinia looks around; obviously deeply confused. "How does that keep happening?" She questions; a bit concerned.

Bell peers up towards Meredia with a smile. "We are within her domain. *Her territory* so to speak. All across this part of Varyia; she is the ultimate authority. She can go wherever she wishes, build what she wants, and has certain capabilities that benefit her in doing so. So long as she remains within her borders."

"Is there war on the borders?" Ylinia questions genuinely.

Bell nods with understanding then sways his head. "Nothing of the sort." He attempts to smile but fails. "There has never truly been such a conflict here."

"Not that we have not seen it, or heard of its atrocities." Meredia adds. "There is no violence attached to our borders. Only an understanding that when you cross them; you are entering the world as another being wishes to see it. It is not yours to judge, critique or change; but simply enjoy for what it is."

Ylinia tightens her forehead; popping out a few forced crinkles. "And that works?"

"Most days, *yes*. Though nothing is perfect. Sometimes something must come to be understood, or taught. Empathy has to be grown, patience found. There is no eternity without dedication and progress; those are the only vehicles moving forwards." Meredia admits with a deeply compassionate inflection.

"Ever the idealist." Bell compliments.

"There is no other way to happily live." She quickly counters.

Bell raises his hands to jokingly request mercy; smirking without relent. "Of course not."

"It is amazing to see you well Bell." Meredia states sweetly. "Though I am surprised I can recognize you at all. I thought if we ever met again, it would take convincing. *Yet*, despite your appearance. Even though your form isn't familiar to me in the slightest; I haven't even a single doubt that it is you."

"*Flesh, scales*." Bell shrugs. "They are but receptacles for the soul. A means to go out into the world. I am sure even bare of both we would be able to recognize one another."

"As am I." Meredia shares the sentiment. "So please, do not misplace my curiosity for a lack of joy. But I must ask, why is it that you have come?"

Bell smiles and looks down towards Ylinia. "There are some challenges so esoteric; so abstract in their required approach; that they appear impossible. Ylinia has accepted the role of monarch for The Citizenry. It is now the purpose of her contribution to listen to the people; and lead them into the future." He looks up towards Meredia. "I thought that if we could come here just to see another world. To compare the differences. Maybe it would help re-imagine our *new one*."

"So it is a quest for inspiration?" Meredia questions; on the verge of critique.

"As if I would quest for something so temporary." Ylinia interjects.

Meredia turns her head and peers down at the lively little human. "Oh?"

"Inspiration lasts right up until something actually is a challenge! Inspiration is the call to duty." She shouts, shakes her head then huffs loudly. "I think I just wanted to know that there was more then what is in front of me." She takes a deep breath and quickly exhales it. "I wanted to know that if I chose to believe in there being something better; that I had a chance of being right."

"Oh you can always find something better." Meredia implores. "Never think that there is something as *perfect enough*. Nothing that settles lasts forever. You must look for the cycles. Spot what will come before what; where it all leads. Improve what will happen anyways; prevent the evil you can; secure things to do better next time. If you find a place that is comfortable enough for your mind to linger forever; it just might. And I have never seen something remain still for a generation and become stronger for the dedication."

"It is better to sail out towards the horizon then it is to sit and watch it then?" Ylinia asks.

"You can sit, or sail, or do nothing at all. Such simple actions don't weigh as heavily as you might believe. They condense down to styling; and personal touch. What is important, is the effect you have with the path you take. If you are to go forwards; then move towards something new, something beneficial, *something radical*." Meredia appears to smile slightly; a thin line of white fangs visible behind her scaled lips.

Ylinia smiles in tandem. "I can make that work." She admits with a giggle.

Meredia pulls her lips further back into a full smirk then widens her eyes with intrigue. "May I ask, what is it that happened to your arm?"

Ylinia looks down at it; her stump is still covered by the cape. She fluffs the cape out with her free hand then looks back up at Meredia. "A knife, *technically*."

"Wielded by someone desperate to make, *some kind of point?*" Bell adds on.

Meredia investigates further; moving closer to inspect. "It is just interesting, as your appearance in your current form is based on how you see yourself. You see yourself without the arm. Even though you could just as easily of had it."

"Could I?" Ylinia asks calmly? "*Huh.*" She vocalizes with a subtle realization then shrugs. "I accept things as they are. Not as I wish them to be." She peers down at the cape. "It may be cute to consider that underneath this cape my arm remains in perfect condition; but if I think that long enough. I'll get to lose it again every time I remember it isn't."

Meredia peers over towards Bell. "I enjoy this one." She states pleasantly.

Ylinia beams up at the dragon.

"She is a positive being." Bell agrees. He motions down to sit on the edge of the chair's arm then takes a deep breath. "How have things been here?"

"Bittersweet." Meredia answers simply. "We watched as Temple fought against a horde of soldiers. We watched as thousands were turned to ruin at the edge of her blade." She closes her eyes with regret. "We postponed the funeral for seventeen days; unsure of whether or not you would return for it."

Bell looks down at his feet. "*I'm sorry.*"

"Don't be." She assures him. "There wasn't a soul here who judged you for not making an appearance. After a loss like that, there isn't always comfort in company."

"How is everyone here? Has Tylo been alright?"

"As well as can be expected." Meredia admits.

Ylinia sighs loudly. "If I'm going to listen to the conversation, can I at least be made a part of it?" She requests.

Bell looks over with a slight guilt. "Of course, *apologies.* Tylo is Temple's brother. He and I, were very good friends once."

"What happened?" Ylinia questions with a softened posture.

Bell lets out a heavy breath; briefly flashing a glance towards Meredia. "Before we left Varyia. Temple and I often debated getting involved in your war, *the war*. She was adamant from the first moment; but I *resisted*." He looks away a bit shamefully.

Ylinia smiles up towards Bell. "There is nothing wrong with that. It is honest. It is real."

"It was an opinion that Tylo shared with me. Neither of us wanted Temple to go. He often *fought* alongside me to convince her that your people would be able to solve things themselves." He shakes his head. "When Temple made it clear that she was compelled to help by something stronger then herself; I told her I wouldn't let her leave alone. I promised her I would abandon our home alongside her." He takes a quick breath. "We bid farewell to everyone the morning after. Tylo arrived full of hate; directing it at me. He said that Temple would never truly leave without me; and that in going; I was killing her." Bell sighs. "I don't imagine his sentiments have changed."

"What a prick." Ylinia declares.

Bell shoots a surprised look over towards her; his eyes wide like plates. "Is that how you see it?"

Ylinia nods firmly. "She is your treasure! He should know better then to think you could abandon her." Her eyes begin to water. "It is just so *mean*."

Meredia lowers her head towards Ylinia and nuzzles her back slightly with the tip of her nose. "You have seen far too much harshness, haven't you my dear?"

A few silent moments pass before Ylinia allows herself to come to the realization. She looks up with surprise, her eyes welling with tears, she waves her head side to side. "*I guess so yea.*" She admits.

Meredia smiles beautifully; extruding positive energy. "Would you like to see something tremendous Ylinia?"

Her tears stop in an instant; and are wiped away into the soft bit of leather between the plates of armour on her sleeve. "*Yes please.*"

In an instant all three of them appear in a valley accented on either side with endless waterfalls. They stand upon a long expanse of light blue grass which trails all the way down to a large stone monolith. It stands about twenty five meters high and is entirely smooth and grey. All around it grow wild flowers, beautiful herbs, grasses and vines. Animals of all species from the surrounding wilderness have come to rest around the monolith; intermingling in absolute harmony. Large grizzly bears lounge beside foxes and deer; while moose play pillow for wolves and eagles alike. "This is the marker we've placed for Temple. It stands as a monument to her and even though it is only stone; it has become much more. Creatures come here under a truce, plants of all sorts grow nearby. *And* once you get near enough."

Ylinia and Bell take a few steps closer to the monolith; and then both stop in place. They look around, share a glance between themselves and then relax entirely. They let out deep, exhausted sighs of relief. "What is that?"

Meredia shrugs. "*We don't know!*" She announces with tremendous elation. "How cool is that?"

Bell holds his hands out in front of himself and concentrates. "It, *almost feels like her.*"

"Doesn't it?" Meredia confirms.

All three of them move towards the monolith. Meredia shrinks herself in size to about twice the size of a human so that she may coil up around the monolith alongside the animals. Bell leans his back directly against the monolith; laying his head back and closing his eyes. Ylinia sits between three deer who each move themselves over to cuddle up to her; which she accepts with absolute excitement. They drift into a pleasant trance; where time passes indifferently and the flow of perception and the flow of conversation are two separate yet parallel processes each being fully experienced.

"Hey, you two?" Ylinia asks out loud.

"Mhmm?" Bell and Meredia answer in tandem.

"Where are your parents?"

"They don't exist." Bell answers casually.

"*Oh,* I'm sorry to ask." Ylinia apologizes.

"*No.*" Meredia corrects. "They literally don't exist. We don't have parents as far as we can tell."

Ylinia scrunches up her forehead. "So, *uh,* how does that work?" She inquires.

"Every, maybe, fifty years or so? We discover an egg somewhere across Varyia. Set in the middle of a river, deep in the earth, up in the clouds. They appear from nowhere, even right in front of your eyes if you're in the right place at the right time. Yet each is a unique soul; born to claim a portion of Varyia themselves and grow in whichever shape they so please. If you are found; it is those who find you whom become your family; your brothers and sisters."

"That sounds nice." Ylinia states; her tone a bit far off as if she is between half way asleep and recently woke. "So who found who?"

"I found Bell." Meredia explains. "I was born in a lake by myself. I had no family to begin; but I did not know that was something to find sorrow in. I was far in the wilderness; and hidden away from all others. There was but a river for me to follow; and I did. It spanned on for half a year; yet I followed along it regardless. Finding my meals beside it, and sleeping every night near its stream. At the end of the river; where it collected into a large pond. I found Bell; settled pleasantly on a log floating out in the water."

Ylinia laughs. "*Of course* that is the sort of place you would find Bell. It is so *him.*"

Meredia laughs loudly. *"Isn't it just?"* She agrees.

One of the eagles spreads it wings; shouts out loudly then shoots off into the air; disappearing in a blur.

"How long have you been studying your blade Ylinia?" Meredia asks kindly.

"A couple of weeks now." She states as formally as she can. "I've become quite attached to Bumble. Though I must of, if I can see it here with me." She admits.

"Actually, that isn't as unrelated as you may think. That blade you carry, it was forged by one known as *Titus*. Correct?"

"It was actually."

"Then it was smith-ed by a dragon; born in such a way that it is inherently connected to this place. It is likely what allowed you to gain passage here as quickly as you did."

"Did Titus leave for the war?" Ylinia questions innocently.

"No. He left long ago, as a volunteer to fix another tragedy. His presence upon Rion now is more a testament to the longevity of dragon blood; then it is his will to stay."

Bell stands up in an instant; instantly disrupted of his peace. *"Something is wrong."* He notes suddenly.

Ylinia jumps to her feet and states towards Bell. "What is it? What is happening?"

"I can't tell." He replies in a confused haze. He shakes his head. "I think we're being woken up. Dii must need us."

The projections of Bell and Ylinia begin to waver; flickering and distorting like smoke.

"I have missed you Meredia. I promise I'll return to see you all again." Bell states with a smile.

"I will see you soon." Meredia unintentionally bids farewell as Ylinia and Bell disperse entirely at the end of her sentence.

⊐⊏

Dii stands in the middle of the crater; shaking Bell as aggressively as she can without harming him. His eyes open as if they had just been glued shut; revealing the entirety of his eyes to be black. He shakes his head and the blackness shrinks to become strictly pupil. He shoots up to his feet in an instant; nearly screwing up his landing as his body acclimatizes to someone being in it again. He groans out oddly, cracks his neck and knuckles then stares at Dii. "How long were we there?"

"Just short of an hour." Dii answers in a hurry. She stares at Ylinia who still hasn't come out of her trance. "Was she coming with you?"

Bell nods. "It might be a little longer for her. She's on the way." He stares up at the sky; it is still bright with barely a cloud in sight. "What has happened?"

Ylinia shakes and begins to come back to formal consciousness.

"I don't know yet. There was a flare shot out from the Palacia Tranquil. Bright purple. That is a signal for the monarch to attend an assembly." Dii explains.

"What's going on?" Ylinia murmurs as she flops over onto her side. Her eyes half closed as if still sleeping.

"We need to go now. They need you back in Caelzun; in an official capacity." Bell speaks softly while offering her assistance to her feet.

Wind whips down through the crater; carrying with it a chill.

Executed on the whim of sheer will; Ylinia picks herself up and takes a few steps forwards; each more proficient then the last. She takes a deep breath and pushes through the pins and needles present within every muscle across her entire body. "Then lets go."

The trio quickly collect themselves and begin back towards Caelzun at a pace twice that of their trek here. They rush down the mountain side; leaping and hopping as best they can to improve the speed of their descent. After a few moments both Bell and Ylinia have fully relieved themselves of any lingering physical dissonance. Dii is capable of jumping down the mountain at dramatic and dangerous angles; landing even unsure leaps with absolute ease. Ylinia appears the slightest bit like a curtain as her cape whips vicariously beside her in her haste. The trio pushes from the mountains out of the woods and onto a more formal roadway; so that they may jog alongside it. Dii leads the trio as they run alongside the road with Ylinia in the middle and Bell behind.

An incredibly disruptive series of explosions move down towards the trio as Howarth and Mel approach; aboard a motorcycle. They stop in an instant; kicking up dust and debris. "What is happening?" Howarth shouts out. Ylinia rushes over towards her parents with delight.

Bell walks towards Howarth and Mel as he responds. "We don't know yet. We were out for a training exercise."

"No chance you brought a radio?" Mel inquires.

Bell sways his head. "I didn't even think to bring one." He peers out towards Caelzun far in the distance.

"*Alright,* then, *Ylinia?*" Howarth asks.

Ylinia tilts her head to the side. "*Yes?*"

"*Get on.*" He requests. Mel gets off the bike; gives Ylinia a big hug then moves over to let her get on. Ylinia wraps her arm tight around her father's ribs. "A little lighter." He requests. She giggles and eases off. Howarth shares brief eye contact with Bell then focuses on the road ahead. "Follow behind me Bell. We'll go a lot faster this way."

"Of course. Go on, I'll do my best to catch up." Bell responds. Without a moments delay Howarth rips off on the motorcycle; shooting off into a blur down the paved pathway. Bell turns to face Mel and Dii. "Will you two be alright to get back? I'm going to give chase."

Dii nods formally. "Of course. We'll take care of each other. Go!"

In an instant Bell breaks into a sprint; following behind Howarth with all his capability.

—⊥—

Every other step in Bell's sprint disrupts the ground under him; either chipping a piece of the cobblestone roadway or leaving a small crater in barren dirt. As he passes into Caelzun; he is only a few minutes behind Howarth on his bike. Without delay Bell rushes towards the central Palacia Tranquil. He bursts in through the front door; guards instantly point their spears towards the disturbance before realizing what has caused it.

"*Sir,* The Monarch has found her way to the central chamber. You'll find her there." One of the guards informs Bell.

"Thank you." Bell speaks as quickly as he can; his rush infusing an aspect of frustration into his tone. He scouts out the halls then hops off down them; moving about as fast as he can despite the overly prestigious surroundings of the palace. He finds himself in the central chamber where Ylinia, Howarth, Izelle and Saranias are all seated. Izelle peers up as Bell approaches then seems to let out a relaxed breath. The chamber has a false ceiling made of a one way glass; the sun diffuses through gold filters that colour the room luxuriously. There is a long table of bright white wood that runs twenty meters long; just short of the length of the entire room. At the very end of the table the others have found their seats.

"Good, you're here now." Izelle states strictly.

Bell nods as he moves closer to take a seat upon one of the many high backed chairs. "I didn't realize that *I* was being waited on, apologies."

"It is by my request." Ylinia states soundly. "This matter requires more then just my perspective."

Bell's momentum shifts to become heavier. "Then what is it? What is the cause for alarm?"

"The prophecy foretold in Mr.Poet's poems? It had previously been mistranslated; pages misconstrued to arrive at an incorrect conclusion." Saranias explains.

"And this means?" Bell presses further.

Izelle takes a deep breath; smiling professionally. "It means that whatever calamity has been predicted is not set to occur seventy years in the future. It is set to occur in *seven months*." She states calmly. "All these years Richard was sitting on the pages. All those years he wrote them off as insignificant; he spent so much of the time we could have had to prepare."

Bell firms himself up; his brow tightens; his eyebrows adopt a sharp curvature. "What will this calamity bring Izelle?"

"*Darkness swarms, drawing in membership from every generation of the dirt. The tide of souls will collapse over all; to defeat the maddening cycle.*" Izelle quotes. "It is the only phrase in the entire poem that refers to the event as anything more then *calamity.*"

Bell closes his eyes; motion flickers under his closed lids. Saranias stares over towards him; stifling a tear with a saddened expression. "Then," He peers up towards Izelle. "*We must prepare for war?*"

Izelle turns to Ylinia; widening her eyes as if to deflect the question towards her. Ylinia looks up at Izelle then meets eye contact with Bell. "We will prepare for the worst." She confirms.

Silence grips the chamber. Nobody speaks. Nobody is content. There is sickness, dread, anxiety, loathing, exhaustion and panic ambient in the air; increased with every subtle motion or missed glance. An invisible switch irrevocably flicked.

"Who was it that performed the translation?" Bell questions.

"Aizenel actually. He has spent sleepless nights studying the pages. He created some sort of *cipher* that allows him to reference the various abstract patterns present throughout each of the poems." Saranias answers. She smiles. "He has sought to confirm his findings three times over; each time assuring himself that he has the correct translation."

"We still have seven months to prepare." Ylinia states optimistically. "We could have used every possible portion of time, *certainly*. Maybe we could of even considered a seventy year warning with more dread and have been so prepared it wouldn't matter! But we are here, not in some hypothetical circumstance. So we must deal with things as they are." She stands and walks up to the front of the room; staring out at everyone in the chamber. "I believe we must begin to put together an organization that will focus on our defence against this upcoming calamity."

"Cavalry Master Nuinez is already on her way here to report as your security adviser. She and the Royal Mounted Cavalry will certainly join the ranks." Izelle explains.

Ylinia shakes her head. "This isn't to be a *military operation*." She states strictly. "I don't want to just transfer in a few platoons to fill the space. I want informed volunteers only. Those who bring with them a beneficial skill against an unknown threat. I want people who want to be there, not just those who will promise to show up every day."

"That is what the army is *for* Ylinia. They are defenders of the realm; sworn in their dedication."

"*They are.*" Ylinia acknowledges. "But they are also tired. They are only weeks from the end of atrocity. Each of them has finally left behind a nightmare. I don't want to force them against another." She speaks confidently. "During my tour. I will speak to the people. I will explain what we have discovered, and that the possible threat is unknown. I will then ask for volunteers; veteran or civilian alike. As it is the right of all of us to step forwards against this *calamity.*"

"You will have me at your side, till whatever end we may find." Howarth declares.

Ylinia peers over towards her father with a tear in her eye. "*Dad.*"

"Don't bother saying anything other then thank you *love*. There isn't a way in this world I'm going to abandon you and our people." He replies sternly.

"Thank you." Ylinia speaks softy as she wraps her arms around Howarth; hugging him tightly. She spins in place then faces everyone else again. "How many of the heirs still remain in Caelzun?"

Izelle looks up into her head for a moment; numbers count out silently across her lips. "I believe everyone but Wvendeiss opted to spend time in the city. The paladin, however, was required by his order; and left rather promptly afterwords."

"Please, have William summon them when Nuinez arrives. They are to be the first I will brief about what lies beyond the horizon." Ylinia requests subtly. She closes her eyes, takes a quick breath then smirks.

⌐⊥¬

The evening is cold. Clouds have abandoned the sky leaving only an endless grey; pierced in a horrific manner by rays of moonlight. A slight breeze never falters to keep a bit of a whistle in the air. Bell sits outside the Meier Manor; just on the edge of the stairs leading up towards the entrance. The lower portion of his back is flat against the stair behind him; while he is otherwise leaning over with his elbows on his knees; cradling his head in his hands. He stares up at the moon; the creases in his brow lessening as each strand of wind blows across him and returning as the air grows still. He raises his eyebrow suddenly then lets out a huff. "Is everything alright?" He asks blindly.

Izelle takes her time to walk up and sit next to Bell before responding. She smiles up at the grey sky. "All is well."

"You would not be here if all was well." Bell responds presumptuously.

"Or everyone has opted to go to bed so we may return to the matter at hand in the morning." Izelle informs him; disregarding his tone.

"*Ah.*" Bell responds. He peers over towards Izelle and showcases mild guilt upon his expression. "*Sorry.*"

Izelle shrugs. "It is fine." She huffs; running her fingers through her hair with stress. "It is not a seamless transition; for anyone."

"Did anybody mind that I stepped out?" Bell inquires.

Izelle shakes her head. "On this property alone we have more then a hundred guards; each capable of multiple martial skills. The central chamber is guarded by no less then sixteen of those individuals. Not to mention that myself and Saranias can handle most of the scarier-then-average threats around." She shrugs. "You're allowed to step out, and be a person, to need a breath. You're not my operative anymore. Your life isn't in service *to service*."

"And yet, it will be, again, will it not? Will you not assemble another special operations force to address the less then common concerns of this calamity?" Bell questions skeptically.

"*I will not*." She affirms; changing her posture to properly get comfy on the short stair. "I see what your idea was, *with Ylinia*. I understand why it is you would pass off such an influential position to such a young soul. While I admit, many parts of me see it as *utter insanity*." She waves her hand out apathetically in front of her. "Who among us knows how to be a monarch? I can play spy, you soldier. Saranias could teach her to appear wherever she so wishes with great practice. But each of us have spent our lives building skills in a world that presumes we won't be the leader. Even me, for all my conjecture; *should never hold that title*. For I have diluted it in my perception so greatly; it is no different then a resource or bridge; that must be utilized simply to reach where you wish to be." She stares at Bell for a moment; smiling slightly. "I want to see what will happen. I want to see that your optimism hasn't betrayed you. Because if I can find myself in a world that never needs me, or my skills, or the atrocities I am capable of." A small tear slides down her cheek. "I will be a properly happy person."

Bell stands up; quickly adjusting his outfit to sit properly across his torso. Izelle stands alongside him. He walks up to the front entrance of the manor. "Does it feel different to you?"

Izelle shakes her head. "It always feels the same to me. A tightness in my chest, electricity in my finger-tips. Every now and then something will cramp; and I won't know why." She chuckles masochistically.

"I don't feel that way this time." Bell speaks confidently. "I thought I was going to be scared, *angry*. I thought I was going to be frightened of seeing a new page in what has become a history book of horrors. Yet, none of that rests inside me. There was shock, but now that it has passed."

"You feel alright with it?" Izelle interjects.

Bell smirks. "I feel like I'm the sort of person that can help. I know what might come, I know how I will react to it. And that knowledge is *mighty* in the face of chaos." He lets out a deep breath; his entire body posture relaxing. "Yet, better then that. I have no fear regarding what may come next. I cannot say what we will face in the coming months, but I do know that whatever it is; I am ready for it."

⊣ TO BE CONTINUED ⊢